CW01370601

Descanso,

or

The Last True Fascist

by

Jay Spencer Green

Also by Jay Spencer Green

Breakfast at Cannibal Joe's

Ivy Feckett is Looking for Love: A Birmingham Romance

Fowl Play

Available in paperback, Kindle, and eBook formats

Copyright © 2025 by Jay Spencer Green

The right of Jay Spencer Green to be identified as the Author of this Work has been asserted by him in accordance with the Copyright, Design, and Patents Act 1988.

All rights reserved. No part of this publication may be reproduced, stored in a retrieval system, or transmitted, in any form or by any means, without the prior written permission of the author, nor be otherwise circulated in any form of binding or cover other than that in which it is published and without a similar condition being imposed on the purchaser.

This book is a work of fiction, and any resemblance to real places, products, or persons, either living or dead, is purely coincidental.

For Our Bruce

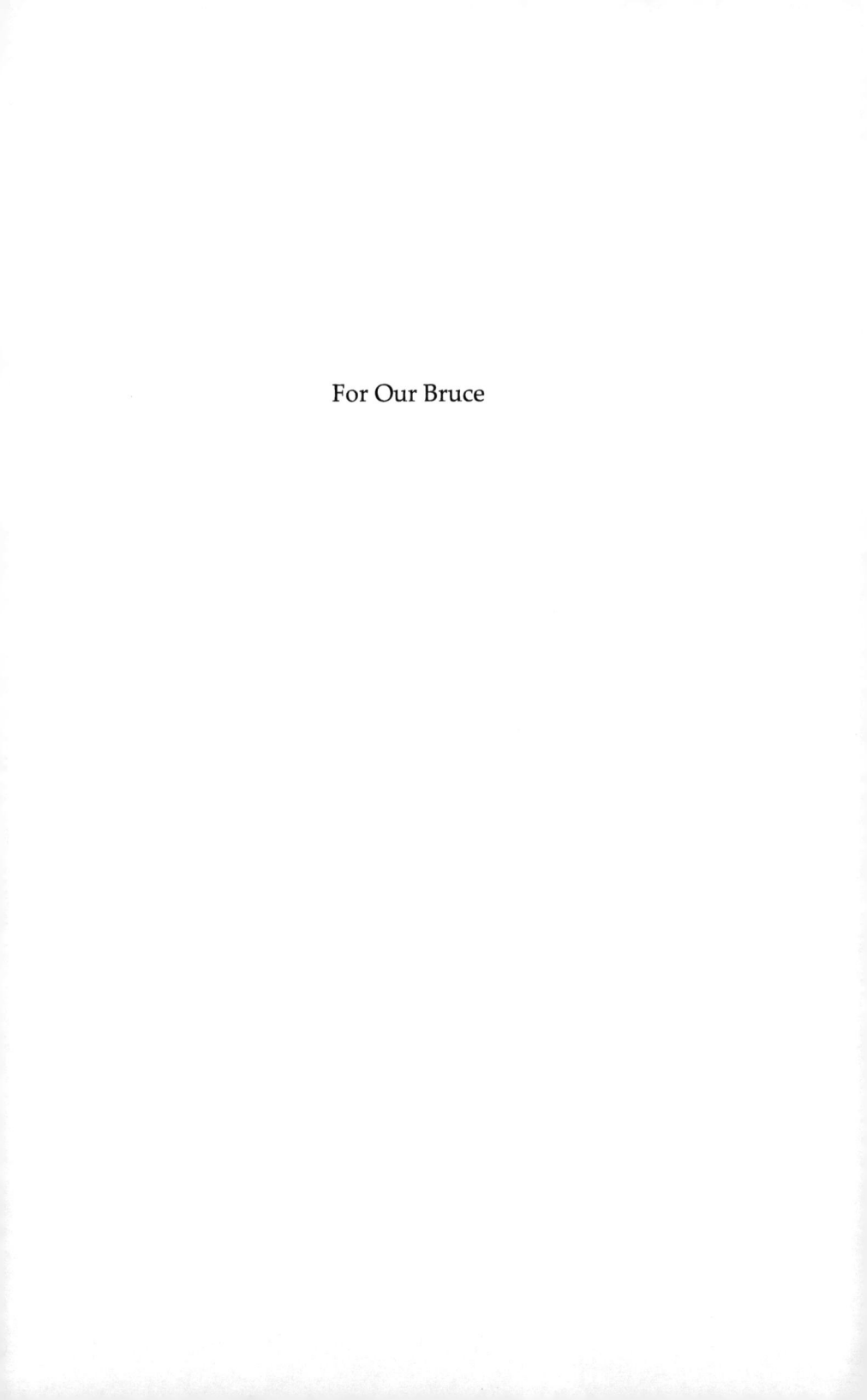

¡Down with Intelligence!
>	José Millán-Astray y Terreros
>	October 12, 1936

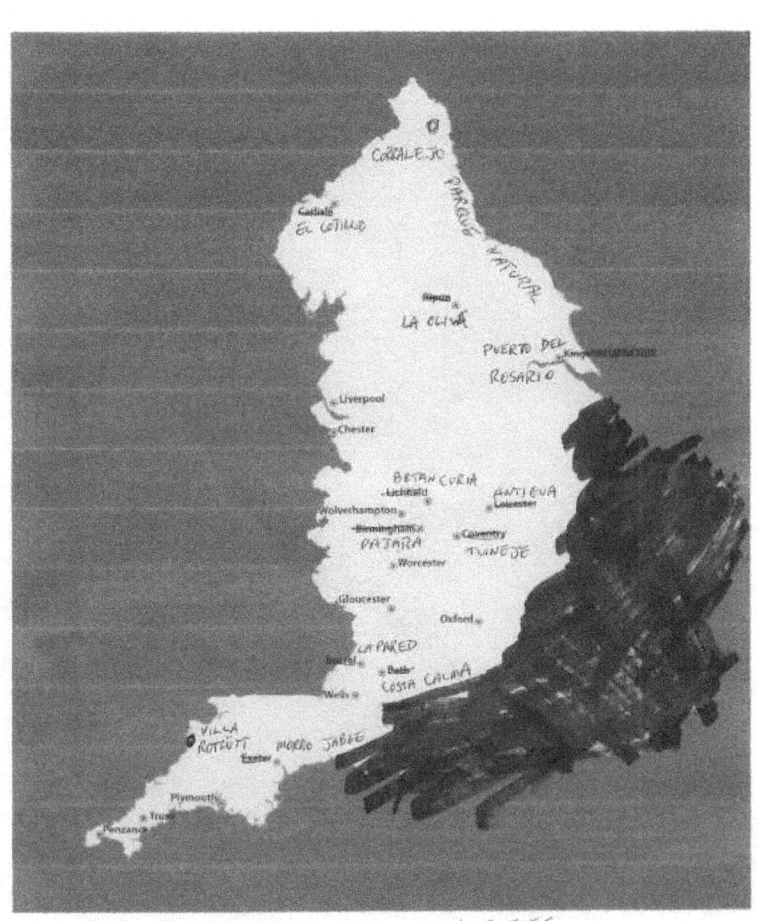

MAP OF ~~ENGLAND~~ WITH MAIN CITIES.
FUERTEVENTURA

And so we begin again ...

A

Aardvark: The aardvark is a four-footed marsupial indigenous to Africa whose name literally means "First one on the ark." Most people know that Noah collected all the animals two by two. What they are less likely to know is that he did so in alphabetical order.

Abba: Is what you get when a once-proud conquering warrior race ceases to take itself seriously. The fact that this bisexual music group pillaged and plundered far vaster quantities of treasure than the Vikings could have even dreamed of is a sad indictment of the modern world.

Abomination: From the Latin word *abominationem*: something that you must shun as an ill omen. Etymologists (ant-worshipers) have frequently assumed that the word derives from *ab homine*, referring to that which is remote from Man and therefore capable of arousing disgust, loathing, awe, and wonderment, such as ants, Gods, or women.

Abortion: An abomination and a total disgrace that should be illegal in every shape or form. However, erudite theologians have pointed out the so-called "Abortion Paradox," according to which the fewer members of other religions that are born, the more Christian the world becomes, and it therefore behooves the Vatican to approve of widespread and holesale abortion for followers of other religions. ¡But no! Vatican scholars have declared in their "wisdom" that God prefers the infidels' children to be born in ignorance rather than not at all. Only then can they be brought to the light by a bishop, cardinal, or priest, like that one in *Poltergeist*.
Soon you will be able to have an abortion online.

Accent: I am not having an accent. I am from Madrid.

Accidents: In Nature, there are no accidents. There are only instances of neglect or mistakes by imperfect human beings. God does not play dice with the Universe. He plays Jenga with the Devil.

Achilles: A familiar character from Greek mythology best known for his race against the tortoise and the hare. In the race, Achilles never catches up with the hare, which never catches up with the tortoise, even though the tortoise is taking lettuce breaks, toilet stops, hibernation, and cetera. The story has profound philosophical implications about the futility of human existence and why there is no point running for the bus.

Action, Man of: The True Fascist is a man of deeds, not words. I have already said too much.

Acupuncture: The Chinese martial art of inflicting pain on foreingers by inserting needles into pressure points in their body. Independently invented several thousand years later by me and my sister Candelaría during our childhood games.

Adam: The first True Fascist, who was provided by God in His beneficence with the perfect autarky, the Garden of Eden, over which Adam had complete dominion until Eve ruined everything when she fell for the promise that knowledge was preferable to a life of ignorance and bliss. Consequently, God had to intervene, ordering Noah, the second True Fascist, to create a new autarky, which came to a premature end when he crashed it on Mount Ararat.
  Vicious Darwinists would have us believe that Man came out of Africa, which would mean that Adam was black and, therefore, since he was made in the image of his creator, that God is also black. Would also mean that every white person has black ancestors, which is clearly

preposterous. This is the kind of badly joined-up cosmopolitan thinking that has led to the materialist conception of history, bird flu, and mirrors.

According to Freudian analysis, which is also wrong, the snake in the grass, Satan, represents Eve's missing penis. The snake penis promised her that if she obeyed him the same way Adam did, then she and Adam would both enjoy omniscience and thus would be like God. This is what is known as a metaphor. But is also a reminder that if only God had instructed Eve in clitoral stimulation, she could have happily survived without her missing penis and we would not be in the mess we are in today.

Address: Although I was never anything more than a mere cog in the machine of the Spanish Intelligence Services, men of principle inevitably acquire enemies. Until now, I have therefore never been specific about my location, telling interested parties only that I live on one of a number of islands in the Atlantic Ocean off the coast of Africa. Very austere, roasty hot, arid, and *tranquilo* all year round, an eye-bleeding contrast to wet lovely holy pissing Ireland, my last official posting, which was damp, decadent, bloody cold, and no longer as God fearing as in the good old days and still should be forever and ever Amen. When they retired, most of my former colleagues and comrades preferred to move to Marbella and Sotogrande, living on the hog's back, whereas I opted for the quiet seclusion of my little fishing village. I say this with no sense of superiority but I believe myself more suited to an ascetic existence than they. I have greater self-discipline, for one thing, and less need to boast my virtues abroad. The Good Lord knows the things I have done and will judge me accordingly.

When nosey people ask me where I live, I always tell them, "Inside my clothes." If they then ask me where I was born, I say "Between my mother's legs." This response has the merit of being true but also vague enough to give nothing away and vivid enough to unnerve any questioner seeking a more precise answer.

Adultery: Research shows that of every ten deaths that occur during sex, nine take place during extra-marital relations. This proves conclusively that God is also in the room, and not just watching. Let us also not forget Thomas Aquinas's logical proof that a man who has sex with his own wife commits adultery if he enjoys it too much.

Aesop: By all accounts a fabulous storyteller.

Africa: Africa should be for the Africans, even if Europeans could do a better job running it. Europeans are not biologicly suited to cope with Africa's intense humidity, freezing cold nights, or meagre diet. This is why we have siestas, duvets, and paella.

After Shave: In Madrid, the men—the most handsome men in Spain and therefore the world—smell of all the fragrances that women love: chocolate, leather, chocolate leather, shoes, horses, cats, diamonds, handbags, kitchens, and money. After shave is thus yet another example of the contemporary emasculation of men, who are forced to give consideration to what women might think them before they can be having the sex with them. Hitler never wore after shave and yet it was said during the war that he had one hand inside the knickers of every woman in Germany.
    Mind you, that is probly why he lost.

Agave: ¡A bloody nuisance! First imported to Fuerteventura from Mexico to provide cellulose fibre for ropes, fishing nets, sacks for carrying agave, and cetera, it was soon redunded by superior and cheaper artificial materials, but agave is such a hardy plant that it needs next to no care and no water, so it has spread right across the island, the long, firm, sword-like blades of its leaves projecting like a starburst from its stem in every direction except down into the earth, where they would be less of a hazard. Between the surfers' village of Lajares and the coastal town of Corralejo, there are vast fields of abandoned agave that are easily harvestable for mezcal or pulque production if anyone had the money to invest. A litre of mezcal would at least make walking in the agave fields at nighttime tolerable. Instead, the experience is akin to death by a thousand cuts, principly to the shins and calves or, if you are a short diminutive gentleman such as myself, to the hips and buttocks, which is also the British public-school punishment/reward for homosexuality.

Age: Fifty-six. Following my stint in Dublin, I was obliged to take an "early retirement" by the idiots in suits upstairs, which led me to Fuerteventura, my Atlantic island, on the advice of several friends within the Intelligence Services, as an unlikely place for anyone with my background to be found. I confess that at first I found the place too much bohemian, or "flaky," and all the German naturists were a big disgrace, but there was still a simplicity to the lives of the locals, who were pious and content, if a little wary of outsiders. And rightly so: Outsiders are always trouble. The walls around our fishing village were of sufficient height not to require round-the-clock manning, but the gate across the highway was frequently left unlocked at night by moron foreingers staying in the next village who seemed to want us all to die.

Although I say "fifty-six" for my age, I have ceased counting my birthdays now that there is no one to buy me presents. Not that anyone used to buy me presents, the bastards.

Agony: Doctors tell us that there is no agony to compare with that of childbirth, except maybe kidney stones or trapping your foreskin in a car door. However, the proper metaphysical definition of agony is "The suffering derived from having once glimpsed Paradise only to be denied it for eternity." Thus, Adam and Eve suffered agony more than most of us could ever imagine. Sergio Ramos must have felt something similar when he left the Paradise of Real Madrid for the purgatory of Paris Saint Germain.

Agur, Saint: This is what happens when you allow French popes: They start canonizing cheeses.

Alabama: In the U.S. state of Alabama, is illegal to find shade beneath a water buffalo.

Alaska: In the U.S. state of Alaska, owners of staplers must register them with the local town hall.

Albans, Saint: Town in Hertfordshire, England, birthplace of the saint who taked its name, Saint Saint Albans.

Albans, Saint Saint (145 AD–315 BC): Widely known as the "tainted saint" on account of his dying several centuries before the birth of Christ. He was having a number of minor roles in miracles (holding a piece of the true cross to a leper's stump, time travel with Saint Zeron) but he never succeeded in shaking off the accusation of premature Christianity. Martyred while trying to convert the Hittites, who were nonplussed by the promise of a future Messiah who had died for their sins but had not yet been born. The saint's decapitated head made its way to Denmark (presumably not under its own steam) before disappearing. Libra. Lucky numbers: -316. Stone: Hittite.

Alcalde: The word in Spanish for the mayor. Traditionally, in rural Spanish towns, the position of mayor is an honorary one, rotating by agreement among the main land-owning and business families and with the blessing of the priest. In more recent years, however, women have been allowed to be mayors, further proof of the decay our society has undergone since the passing of the Generalísimo. Women are not suited to wielding power, even at such a piddling level. It makes them ugly, cruel, and vindictive. It also shrinks their ovaries. I don't need to name names but consider, for instance, the travails of the poor British, whose crazed Conservative Party cruelly inflicted upon the country both harridan bluestocking Theresa May and voluptuous simpleton Liz Truss. They made such a mess of everything that in the end the only solution was to bring in the wealthiest man in the country, businessman "Richie" Sunak, to bail the government out with his wife's inherited trillions, but he wisely decided to keep it all to himself. ¿Is it any wonder the people there are starving today?

Alcatraz: The name of this former island prison in the San Francisco Bay of America is clear evidence of the Moorish conspiracy behind Prohibition, when a clandestine Muslim campaign attempted to undermine Western civilization by the banning and illegalization of invigorating liquor and other stimulating beverages. Indeed, the Arabic word *Al-katraz* literally means "Place of resisters," since that was where all those who wished to pursue the honest Catholic practice of inebriation were sent. Other Arabic words coined during Prohibition tell the same story: *Spikhizi* (lit. secret club) became "speakeasy," *Shi-bín* (lit. drinking cave) became "shebeen," and *Al-kapón* (lit. the birdman) became "Al Capone," the birdman of Alcatraz. But for intrepid Trappist monks, devoted Church hierarchs such as Cardenal Mendoza, and the piety of Italian and Irish immigrants, the worship of alcohol (from *Al-kuhul*, lit. sacred liquid) would not have survived.

Alcohol: A much-maligned social lubricant. Jesus himself was very fond of a full-bodied Syrah, as the Gospels record. By contrast, Jews prefer hallucinogens (*viz.* the burning bush, sticks becoming snakes, and cetera), Muslims prefer mint tea and hashish, and Mormons prefer boredom and masturbation, but only within the confines of marriage. Christians are explicitly told by Jesus to drink wine and to think of him when they do so. Efforts to curb alcohol consumption by liberal atheist do-gooders and nanny-state bed-wetters should therefore be seen for what they truly are, an assault on religiosity itself, like spitting on Jesus's drunken corpse.

Aliases: I used many aliases during my career in the Spanish Intelligence Services. In Ireland, for example, in addition to Manuel Estímulo, I used the names Miguel Patatas y Lluvia, Sal Mineo, Rutabaga Wilson, Antonio O'Malley, and Gavin McShit. As a member of the Falange, I used the pseudonym Francisco Dormilón, as well as my codename, Leviatán, or Leviathan, after the mighty sea monster in the Bible, but also in tribute to the middle-aged monarchist Thomas Hobbes, a blazing pelican of common sense who correctly divined the all-too-human need for dictatorship.

When speaking to my sister Candelaría on the phone or Facetime, I always tried to use my codename, but for her this was always a problem remembering, even when she could see me on the screen holding up a copy of Hobbes's book to give her a clue.

"Hello," she would say. "¿Is that you, Hobnobs?"

"No," I would say, waving the book. "I am Leviathan."

Or

"Hello. ¿Is that you, Lev Yashin?"

"No. Is me, Leviathan."

Or

"¡Hello! ¿Are you well?"

"No, I am not a whale. ¡But you are close! I am Leviathan."

Sometimes I thought she was doing it deliberately and had to remind myself that she was a fucking *imbécil*. How she made it past twenty, let alone fifty, without being strangled at birth is a secret known only to God. This, *por supuesto*, is why I kept her so close to me after our parents died and she was no longer covered by health insurance for at-home care. For several years when she was smaller, my parents considered putting her in sheltered accommodation or smothering her with a pillow, whichever was more acceptable to bourgeois society, but she provided us with such entertainment when, for example, attempting to sing or mime, that we decided to keep her. She ate less than a dog but was happy to live like one, drinking from a bowl on the floor, so was almost like another member of the family. We did not bring her to Mass, family gatherings, or mass family gatherings because of the shame she brought, the mess she made in the trunk of the car, and the danger she posed to other children—and later, as she got older, simply to children.

With her portion of the family inheritance, I bought her a small but respectable villa in the regional capital, La Oliva, not too far from my village, in case of emergencies, but not so close that she would be tempted to depend on me or call on me unexpectedly when I might be praying or sleeping or killing something. I made a point of visiting her every Sunday for lunch—which I brought with me, usually a barbecued chicken—and of calling her each evening before she went to bed to check that she had locked all the doors and windows, sprayed for mosquitoes, cleaned her teeth, and used the bidet correctly. Was on such occasions that my archaic and arcane codename became a source of confusion and merriment.

"¿Is that you, Levante?"

"No. Is me, Leviathan."

Or

"¿Is that you, Levitation?"

"No. Is me, Leviathan."

Or

"¿Is that you, Levi-Strauss?"

"Now you are just taking the piss."

Over the years, I confess, I used Candelaría as a muse and source of inspiration for my cover stories. Depending upon my audience, she was abandoned at birth or thrown off a bridge, or else the victim of post-traumatic stress disorder, which was variously the result of being attacked by a man in a cricket box, attacked by a man with a box of crickets, being sexually assaulted by a marmoset, or laughing herself into a coma when our cousin Diego was sentenced to life imprisonment for storking. On still other occasions, I used her disability as a source of amusement to spin yarns for my guests at Knockmerry House, the brothel I ran in Dublin (as an intelligence-gathering operation). For my audience's benefit, Candelaría was variously hung by her feet and quartered like a hog, gassed in a murder-suicide by my mother after suffering brain damage during childhood frolics too close to our swimming pool, asphyxiated by horse semen, to which, by a freak of nature, she had an allergy, or crushed by a stationary LUAS. Since no one was in a position to contradict my version of events, and since Candelaría would in reality have been safely tucked up in bed alongside my mother or, just as likely, my father, I was free to make of her fate whatever I chose: defenestrated, deflowered, disgraced, demented, dead (the same way for remembering the five wives of Henry VIII). This sibling relationship taught me a valuable lesson that all so-called "creatives" should bear in mind: Power without repercussion or responsibility permits true freedom of expression.

Allergies: According to the mass media, there has been a substantial increase in the number of children suffering from allergies over the past forty years. This, they contend, is because of all the cleanliness children are covered in. What rubbish. The truth is that more children suffer from allergies today because interfering scientists have kept alive many children who would be dead by now if Nature had been allowed to take her proper course. The mortality rate has dropped by so much in the last century that the human species has become enfeebled and feminized by the survival of offspring who under normal circumstances would have happily succumbed to croupe, tuberculosis, cholera, diphtheria, chickenpocks, dengue fever, pernicious bodge, conspicuous tubboes, or French thumb disease. Because these weaklings have been immuned to such fatal race-enhancers, they are free to cough and sneeze and splutter and swell up all over their geneticly superior officemates, ruining their day, just because some innocent office lackey opened a bag of peanuts. No wonder the Muslims are laughing at us. In their dusky lands, they ex-cliff such anti-social elements on the day they are born. You may think it cruel of me for saying this, but I was somewhat disappointed when I learned that the New Rabies did not result in death: Here on the island, the introduction of compulsory cross-country races in the mountains for kindergartners would have encouraged respect for authority and provided a salutary lesson for the survivors about the limits of teamwork.

Alpaca: No more proof of God's existence is necessary than the astounding alpaca, which lives entirely on T-bone steaks and yet never defecates. Natural predator: the ostrich. Not to be confused with either the Llama, South American, or the Lama, Dalai, both of which defecate with abandon.

Alt-Right, The: Teenage boys who prefer to be telled to tidy their room by their father rather than their mother.

Alzheimer's Disease: An awful, debilitative illness in which the victim slowly loses their memories while their brain becomes riddled with holes, like a colander, through which the memories escape. Of course, the victims are mostly unaware of this, and the real pain is felt by the relatives or friends who are obliged to care for them. This suffering is not easy to prepare for, and I advise anyone with a history of Alzheimer's in their family to plan ahead for what can be a very trying time. When my grandmother's condition began to deteriorate seriously, my father and his siblings had have had the foresight to spare both themselves and their mother any unnecessary emotional pain by hiring three actors to visit grandma on their behalf and pretend to be them. Grandma was none the wiser, and my father didn't have to go through the depressing experience of seeing his mother slowly forget who he was.

Americans: A vast and diverse people, about whom one cannot easily generalize. I can only draw on my own experience of the Americans I have met and worked with, mainly in Ireland, where the local U.S. Defense Intelligence Agency station chief was a frequent guest at Knockmerry House. A man full of optimism, positivity, and a can-do attitude, whether it was cheating on his wife, torturing terrorist suspects, or organizing false-flag bombings of train stations. Sadly, however, even he had a crisis of conscience when it came to killing one of his own, and he wound up with his skull staved in, like an annoying kitten. Of course, the Americans you meet abroad are different from those who never leave their own country. The former are curious about the world, treat it as their playground, a place to explore and enjoy, almost Nietzschean in their enthusiasm. They collect experiences the way Death collects souls. By contrast, those Americans who stay at home prefer for Death to collect souls on their behalf, usually by drone.

Amphibians: Creatures that are able to live in both water and air. An example would be a squid with wings.

Anal Intercourse: Also known as buggery, sodomy, bumming, and, by the English, as "bangy-poo" ("bangy-wee" is what they call vaginal sex). Many people mistakedly think that the people of Sodom were destroyed by God because He abhors homosexuals. ¡No! The reason was that the Sodomites were using anal intercourse as a form of contraception, thereby avoiding the punishment for having sex, namely, children. ¡There's no fooling God!

Anarchism: A political ideology that is entirely alien to Spain and the true wishes and character of the Spanish people. Imported into the country by French and Italian ne'er-do-wells, anarchism quickly entranced the simple peasant folk of Asturias and seduced the cosmopolitan idiots of Barcelona who could not tell their arse from their Ebro, turning them into murderers of priests, rapists of nuns, and non-doffers of caps. I cannot for one moment pretend to understand the attraction of individualism, voluntary co-operation, collective ownership of the means of production, abolition of hierarchy, and liberal sexual mores, all of which nonsense renders a nation weak, undermining its unity of purpose and direction. Such values could only be introduced into a country by those who intend its destruction: traitors, Bolsheviks, Freemasons, Protestants, and the mass media.

During the Civil War in Spain, one anarchist who urinated up against the side of a church later died of cancer of the rectum. ¡Hah! *That* showed *him*.

Andrew, Saint: Patent saint of Scotland. Crucifixed on an X for anonymity, so nobody knows his real name; a fair guess would be Mac-something. Wood from the cross was touring the Low Countries and France in the 1940s when it went missing. Aries. Lucky number: 4. Stone: Granite.

Animals: A few years ago, there was a big ruckus in the Spanish media after a mob of filthy Catalans taked off their clothes in the centre of Barcelona to make a protest in support of PETA, Peoples for the Ethical Treatments of Animals. The event was, to my mind, another case of Catalan barbarism: At least the German tourists who plague the beaches of Fuerteventura and who I can see only by looking through my binoculars are having a reason for stripping naked, namely, their fried brains. The Catalans do it purely out of spite, to remind us of their continued existence. I would have turned the hoses on them, driven them off the streets, and afterwards I would have washed down and disinfected the streets too.

In Franco's day, there was only four places where a Catalan could be seen naked:

1: In the alleyway, car park, or bordello where he was being born.

2: When being flogged for not speaking the Spanish correctly.

3: At school, in the showers or the principal's office.

4: At work, pulling your cart, if your donkey had died (1 donkey = 4 naked Catalans).

As for PETA: ¿How many of those sniveling animal lovers do you think had been snorting cocaine only the night before without ever considering all the coca beetles that had had to be ground down into the fine powder they put up their noses? ¿How many of them arrived at the so-called Plaza de Cataluña by public transport without giving a moment's thought to all the squirrels that had have been shoveled into the furnace of the train that brought them there? ¿How many of them use electricity or drive cars, the energy for which comes from coal and oil, both the result of animals being slowly crushed to death over hundreds of millions of years? None of them, I bet.

You see my point, I am sure. Civilized society cannot survive without the long-drawn-out and atrocious suffering of animals.

But that is okay. Is what God intended.

On this issue, the ever-insightful Saint Cuthbun proved that ethical behaviour is only possible between beings that are having souls. Animals are not having souls, and therefore it doesn't make sense to talk about the ethical treatment of animals. Cuthbun also gave us the list from God of all the beings to which this rule applies; when I was growing up, all the children in Spain knew it by heart: "Soulless are the Antelope, Basque, Chimera, Donkey, Frog. Likewise the Galician, Lion, Berber, Catalan Dog."

Is sad to reflect that the last previous time the streets of Barcelona was strewn with naked Catalans, they were all dead, killed by Franco's Moors. Such is "progress," I suppose.

Anteaters: Surprisingly minty. Do not taste of ants.

Anthony, Saint (783–888): Lived to be 105 and never learned to read or write, yet he cured several hundred women of their frigidity. Is a lesson for us all. Capricorn. Lucky numbers: 2, 3, several hundred. Stone: Blue Steel.

Antichrist, The: Supports Barcelona.

Apocrypha: Ancient religious texts which were not included in the Bible for one or more of the following reasons: too short, not holy enough, too many diagrams, difficult to choreograph, written by Satan. Examples include *Paul's Letter to the Fishes, The Sculptor of Chaos, Jesus in China, The Book of Badly Drawn Goats, Mindfulness on the Cross, Beelzebub's Cookbook,* and *Deserts I & III* (but not *II*).

Apple: When Adam and Eve ate the apple of knowledge, they acquired not just knowledge but also shame and disgust. Up to that point, they had been cheerfully pissing and shitting in front of one another while swearing like matelots. With the acquisition of knowledge, they suddenly realized how disgusting and shameful the human body is and how coarse their language was. The next time God paid a visit to the Garden, He knew straightaway that Adam had eaten from the tree of knowledge by his Speedos.

Every son and daughter of Adam and Eve (that is, all of us) is possessed of this knowledge about the human body, but the vast majority live in denial, pretending that the human body is nothing to be ashamed of. Some even purport to find the human body desirable, reveling in the squalor, debasement, and denigration implied by such self-deception. Satan sits at home with his feet up while these perverts do his job for him.

Aquinas, Saint Thomas (1225–1274): Has the nickname "The Angelic Doctor" in order to distinguish him from all the evil doctors, such as Harold Shipmate, Dr. Frankenstein, Dr. Moreau, Dr. Who, and cetera. Best known as the author of the *Summa Theologica* and for being the founder of the Thomist school of self-defence, which involves tying your opponent up in mental knots. Many infant and preparatory schools are having his name, yet as far as we know he showed no great interest in young children. Aquarius. Lucky numbers: 17, 22, 78. Stone: Costume jewellery.

Archaeology: Is the science of digging up the sex toys of ancient civilizations and pretending they are deities. There is a reason why primitive people had "shrines" in their bedrooms, you fool: in case their mom walked in.

Aristocracy: The position on the social map where nobility and wealth coincide. Sadly, diminishing in number. ¿Who can we say today to be truly noble? The Imperious Zidane and the Genius Cronaldo, perhaps, and maybe a few others, but then you are struggling.

Arizona: In the U.S. state of Arizona, is illegal to use armadillos as paperweights.

Armadillos: Wield a surprising amount of political clout in the U.S. state of Arizona. In Mexico, the locals traditionally use the armadillo's carapace to serve guacamole.

Army, The: Alongside the Church, the army is the source of all law, order, and morality in society. Any community lacking an army cannot be called a society, merely an agglomeration of barbarians. And, by logical extension, a society that is entirely militaristic is the apogee of order and civilization. The Japanese was once having some good ideas in this regard, but not until Spanish Fascism did the theory become a reality. Financial, masonic, and other alien forces always are having an interest in ensuring that such societies don't stay unmolested for long, however. These centripetal forces benefit directly from instigating chaos (see, for instance, disaster capitalism, miscegenation, and animal liberation) and must therefore be fought with all the weapons at our disposal. Foretunately, God designed the world in such a way that armies frequently are having *many* weapons at their disposal. This is not by chance. The military coup is merely God turning the world the right way up once more and restoring the natural order.

Art: All art was originally religious and therefore beautiful, such as the Sistine Chapel, the Last Supper, the Pietà, and cetera. Only with modernity and the rise of the Venetian/Florentine merchant classes and their rampant materialism did artists turn their attention to secular subjects in the pursuit of patrons and moolah. In doing so, they placed non-religious topics on the same level as religious ones, in itself an act of blasphemy. Since then, we have witnessed a constant and increasingly precipitous spiritual decline in artistic representation, as evidenced by Impressionism, Expressionism, Fauvism, Surrealism, Cubism, Pop Art, and all the other arts that I have missed (I do not claim to be an art connoisseur; that would be like being a connoisseur of toilets). All modern art is horsecrap. Especially modern art made from horsecrap.

Art, Abstract: Along with philosophy, one of the main causes of corruption in society, on account of how it puts ideas in people's heads. People's heads are not for ideas. They are for listening to orders, smelling blood, spotting threats, and saying "Yes, sir, I will."

Artists: "¿Manuel, who are your favourite artists?"
"My favourite artists are tortured artists."
"¿Oh, you mean like Chatterton and Van Gogh?"
"No. I mean like Garcia Lorca and Victor Jara."

¡¿What?! ¡Is a joke!

Seriously, though, the greatest artist of all time was Francisco Franco, and Spain was his canvas.

Ash Wednesday: Ash Wednesday is a day of solemn religious devotion during which all good Holy Roman Catholics walk around with a cross of ash on their foreheads to let everyone know "I am a Roman Catholic and not afraid to face humiliation and ridicule in public." The gesture is symbolic of what Our Holy Lord God Jesus Christ King of Kings had to face before the nonbelievers, Sadducees, Jews, and Protestants in Jerusalem. The Bible tells us how they mocked him, saying, "Silly man. There is no God, and you are not his son. I know your father. He owns a furniture shop in Nazareth." However, they did not dare put a cross of ash on Jesus's forehead, or else he would have extracted a terrible revengeance. For this reason also today, putting an ash of cross on your forehead is a way of saying, "Yes, I am a Roman Catholic. ¿What of it? ¿D'you want some?"

Asparagus: Asparagus-scented urine was how we spotted Belgian spies during the Civil War.

Aspel, Saint (1045–1102): Was martyrized at the hands of the Masochists, who forced him to whip them until he collapsed and died of a combination of exhaustion and guilt. Pisces. Lucky numbers: 9, 19, 911. Year of the Tiger. Stone: Amethyst.

Assisi, Saint Francis of (1181–1226): One of the better-known saints thanks to his intimate relations with animals, who are terrible gossips. Spent much of his life in poverty, wandering from town to town trying to find a miracle-worker who could cure him of his stigmata and short-sightedness. Made popular by the movie *Doctor Dolittle*. Although his linguistic skills might seem impressive to ordinary mortals, bear in mind that the Tower of Babel story explains only why all human nations speak different languages. Animals were not responsible for its construction, which is why all animals today still speak the same one language. Understand one animal and you can understand them all. Cancer. Lucky numbers: 8, 11, 13, 14. Stone: Amber with a wasp trapped inside.

Astrology: Broadly seen as a makie-up religion, like Marxism and Scientology, but many famous men throughout history were believers in astrology, including Ronald Reagan, Adolf Hitler, Saint Paul, Isaac Newton, Beethoven, George Eliot, Harry Houdini, Alfred Einstein, and William Shakespeare, and only one of these was an obsessive-compulsive pyromaniac who enjoyed hanging around gypsy caravans, so perhaps there is something to it after all; ¿who can say? Don't confuse it with astronomy, a mistake that infuriates astronomers and astrologers equally. Astrology is about examining the location of the planets in order to identify human character traits, make predictions, and see *forward* in time, whereas astronomy is about looking at the sky in the dark using a big magnifying glass to spot aliens and see *backward* in time.

Asturias: Home to the most beautiful women in Spain, and thus also to the unhappiest men.

Atlético de Madrid: Is a sign of how vulgar modern Spain has become that no longer is it shameful to be a supporter of Atlético de Madrid. Indeed, is an affliction that some of their followers actually flaunt, much like a prostitute my father once introduced me to who drew circles around her sores with an eyebrow pencil.

ATM: *Amigo tecnológico de la mujer.* Like other ladies' technological friends, this one can produce orgasms. A modern-day scourge, and not the good kind. It has put so many bank workers out of a job that most of the beggars you see sitting by ATMs today were bank tellers only yesterday. Ask them and they will deny it, but that is because they are drunk. ATMs are an abomination for giving women direct access to money, instead of them having to go to their husband or father so that he can ask "¿What frivolity are you going to waste this on? ¿Yoga classes? ¿Books? ¿Shoes for the children?" We forget that is not just technology in the workplace that has allowed women to become independent, but also technology on the high street. I only hope that online banking will mean that women will no longer be having an excuse to leave the house. And online shopping will mean she can order her ballgowns to be sent to the house so that she can hang them up in her wardrobe without ever needing to wear them so at least they can be sold as barely used when she dies.

Augurs: According to the Spanish Catholic nationalist mystic Margarita of the Perpetual Migraine, the end of the world is nigh when the Vatican has received confirmation of all the following augurs:

1. The corpses of cats are seen dancing in the streets of Santiago de Compostela.
2. There are two moons over the Basilica of Saint Isidore during daytime. Only one is visible.
3. Seven seals are washed up on a beach in Mallorca. A massive row ensues when a so-called "expert" from the local university points out that they are not seals at all, but sea lions which have escaped from a nearby circus. Mallorcans hubristicly accuse God of inattention to detail. God smites Mallorca.
4. The sound of the Great Trump being blown by the Angel Eloni is heard across the entire European landmass, throwing cities into panic, horses into ditches, May into June, and cetera. The Great Trump tries to grab the Angel Eloni by the pussy. Chaos ensues.
5. The False Pope will occupy the Throne of Saint Peter for a second time.
6. A massive earthquake, 50.2 on the Richter Scale ("strong enough to rattle a child's bones out of its body"), triggers the San Andreas

fault. California is left unscathed. The rest of North America sinks beneath the waves.
7. The three blessèd atrocities are witnessed by the living and the dead.
8. And the Beast with Three Fingers arrives on the Island That Time Ignored, bringing death and destruction. There is nowhere to hide.

Perhaps the Apocalypse can be stopped by a True Fascist Man of Action. Perhaps he won't want to stop it.

Augustine, Saint (354–430): Also known as Augustine the Hippo on account of his appetite, aggressiveness, and surprising turn of pace, both on land and in water. Could fit an entire loaf of bread in his mouth in one go. Famous for his plea "Dear Lord, please make me thin, but not yet."

Autarky: An ideal state of national self-sufficiency, allowing a country to engage only in those relationships with foreigners that it wants to, rather than having to do so out of necessity. Autarky was the motivation behind Benito Mussolini's policies in Italy, Franco's policies for Spain, Adolf Hitler's concept of the (expanded) Reich, and for Irish president Amon Devaloora when Ireland secured its independence from *Inglaterra Pérfida* (West British Albion). Autarky means that a country's culture and people are kept pure and safe, unsullied by corrupting influences and alien spizz that would weaken the national identity and the jean pool. *Naturalmente*, in all the above-mentioned cases, the independence of free Fascist nations was intolerable to the international Masonic conspiracy, which forced them to bend the knee and drop the shoulder to the new global order, meaning, in the case of Ireland and Spain, that all our golf courses were eventually overrun by loud-mouthed sales reps from Surrey.

You have to go all the way back to the Bible to find the best-functioning example in the history of autarky, namely, Noah's Ark, whence the word actually derives. The Noah's Ark could have had happily sailed on indefinitely but was getting very smelly, a side-effect of not importing soap (the soap-manufacturing countries all met with a particularly bubblesome ending in the Flood), and Noah had to crash the Ark down on land in order to get away from the pong; simply opening all the portholes would have sunk it (which is why they do not have windows on submarines).

Avian Flu: Another sign that the final days are upon us.

According to the book *Gums, Germs, and Steam,* by Anne Diamond, throughout all history, superior races (such as the Spanish) have been able, almost unwittily, to annihilate inferior ones (such as Incas, Aztecs, Moroccans) through the use of germ warfare, the result of the judicious domestication of animals. Less well known is the follow-up book by Diamond, *Collapse,* in which she argues that even the most advanced civilizations fail to realize that they are facing annihilation because it takes place so slowly and surreptitiously. They are like the proverbial frog in a blender, which barely notices the increase in speed of the blades and does not even try to escape but will happily sit there until it has been shredded into a smoothie.

This is a lesson that we now in the West must learn if we are to foil the newly prosperous Middle and Far Eastern barbarians in their quest to destroy Christian civilization. History will not forgive us if we sleepwalk into oblivion beneath a mountain of sneezing chickens and edible bats.

Awe: A combination of fear, wonder, and incomprehension arising from encounters with the Sublime. The conservative Irish writer Edward Burke correctly observed that the entire basis of the Romantic movement was fear and awe in the face of the Sublime, which represents an overwhelming and alien power beyond human understanding. Thus, the God of the Old Testament was Sublime, because He wielded absolute power in ways that the Jews could not predict or appease. H. P. Lovercraft's Cthulhu was sublime, a monster beyond reason that taked no account of human wishes, desires, or aspirations. The Nazi SS tried to make itself sublime, with its Hugo Boss uniforms, totalitarian capriciousness, and random murderousness. For devout Catholics such as myself, the institution of the Church is sublime, since we lay Catholics understand human impotence and irrelevance before a mighty force whose workings are unfathomable, its power derived from the Lord himself. We are but miserable porns scrabbling in the dirt and filth before its majesty. In the Spain of days gone by, when the Church's power was combined with the might of El Generalísimo Francisco Franco, the era known as "the Days of Cross and Sword," it could be said that we Catholic Fascists constituted the last true Romantics, worshiping a Leviathan (¡Yes!) that could destroy all those who had the impertinence to raise their heads and attempt to subject it to scrutiny. Attempts being made today to replicate this combined power of a church and a state, as in Russia, for instance, give one hope, of course, but they will never be as awe-inspiring as the real thing.

Awesome: The Imperious Zidane, whose like we won't never see again.

Awful: The Beast with Three Fingers, who arrived on the Island That Time Ignored exactly nine months ago today.

B

Baboons: Sent by God to torment us.

Barbarism: How empires are built but also how the customs of their subjugated peoples are described.

Barcelona: Has already received too much attention. I will not add to it.

Bardino: A Canarian hunting dog notable for its tiger-like markings and vicious demeanour. Handy for intimidating tourists. Before the arrival of the New Rabies to Fuerteventura, I enjoyed many weekends away in the Malpais or down in the middle of the island hunting chipmucks,[1] rabbits, wild pigeons, geckos, iguanas, and the odd baby goat (when no one was watching) with my two bardinos, Lobo and Reina. I would fill up the Land Rover, throw my camping gear and provisions in the back, and escape for a couple of days' shooting and fine dining in the wilderness, like Simeon Stylites but with serviettes. It was rare for me to encounter another human being, the night-time campfires serving only as a deterrent, never as a source of curiosity; people know well enough in Fuerteventura to keep their distance and never ask too many questions of their neighbours. Those cool, calm desert nights, the powder of the Milky Way sneezed across the obsidian mirror of the sky like God's cocaine, seem today like a distant paradise, the delicate lizardiness of baked iguana eggs and the enveloping lusciousness of a powerful Listán Negro a fond but faint memory. The joys of solitude can be wearisome after a while, but I remain wholly convinced and appreciative of the merits of a well-stocked armoury and the comfort of canine company.

---

[1] English people call them chipmucks because their faeces resemble chocolate chips, but their correct name is barbery squirrels because they need a haircut.

When the New Rabies turned up, pet owners everywhere found themselves under suspicion and were required to bring their animals in for microchipping, booster jabs, and bi-monthly check-ups. Since I was living incognito and unwilling to register my location with yet another government bureaucracy liable to hacking by those who might want to find me—and since, in any case, my ownership of Lobo and Reina was not on any register—I judged that, of the two evils (forcing me to disclose my identity or risking my dogs' health), the latter was the lesser, and so I ventured out with them one final night, ostensibly in search of wild goat, east of Betancuria, where I left them, suitably sedated by a surfeit of turkey roll, goat stew, and diazepam. As the Land Rover gently trumbled away over the bed of a long-unused barranco, I tried—unsuccessfully—to coax a tear from my jaded, jaundiced eyes. Was a hugely pathetic scene.

And now the countryside is full of bardinos and podencos, all carrying the virus. Bardinos, podencos, and gambies, since killing infected human beings is considered poor form at a time when the virus is yet to prove lethal, the development of a vaccine not entirely impossible, and the likelihood of being bitten by a gambie next to zero.[2] Bardinos are fair game, sadly, but I like to think that Lobo and Reina are still out there, rabid or not, doing their bit to keep the community on its toes. In the wild, only the slow, elderly, infirm, and/or naïve become infected. The young are spritely enough to elude the clutches of even the most agile gambie, unless they're out of their courgette on cannabis or simpering do-gooders working for the rescue dog adoption program, in which case they deserve everything they get.

For a while, I continued hunting without my bardinos—needs must—but only for rabbits and birds. And don't moan to me about how the island is supposed to be an ecological preserve and there's a reason why it's called a "bird sanctuary." Everyone knows that bird sanctuaries

---

[2] The human jaw is not the right shape for tearing flesh, so unless you are unlucky—or moronic—enough to be bitten by a gambie on the finger, cock, or buttocks, you are generally safe.

are for the tastiest birds, protected for the tables of the rich. That is their *raison d'être*.

Barra: Cut lengthways and bound with lettuce, a *barra* makes a handy splint for a broken arm or leg, depending on the victim's size (an adult's arm or a child's leg). There is no need to put tomato and olive oil on the bread unless the hospital is far away.

Bart's, Saint: A hospital and island in the Caribbean, presumably a leper colony.

Basques: Not the good kind, which is what loose women wear to make them tighter, but the natives of the northern part of Spain who like to think of themselves as the chosen people and somehow set apart from everybody else in the world on account of the fact that nobody can understand their stupid language. ¿How absurd is that? ¿Do you think that when their ugly childrens are born, they automaticly speak Basque? ¡Of course not! They have to learn it, just like a foreinger would, if there was any point doing so. The only difference between Basque children and foreingers is that children are not having a choice about learning the language. Plus, it's common knowledge that when they are alone, all Basques speak Spanish to one another; it's much easier. But then, the minute you walk into their shop looking for directions, they pretend they can't understand you and start speaking Basque at you just out of bloody-mindyness. At least, they *tell* you it's Basque. It could be fucking Chinese. There's no way of knowing.

A Basque will also tell you that his national sport, pelota, is the fastest ball game in the world. Then he will take two and a half hours to bring you your *pintxos*.

Bath: A word of advice to any Spanish friends unfortunate enough to find themselves in a Northern European country: When you are in the bath, be careful which plug you put in. ¡You could be electrocuted!

Bauhaus: A German architectural style with simple sloping roofs, minimalist design, and wooden construction (Bauhaus is the German word for "dog kennel").

Beans, Kidney: Full of fibre and a good source of protein. You can confuse grizzly bears by waving tins of kidney beans at them.

Bear Bating: A disgraceful and barbaric sport popular with the English (¡surprise, surprise!). I am having nothing against cruelty and humiliation of animals when done with dignity and flair, such as bull fighting or the hilarious goat-throwing of Tenerife, but the filthy and degrading public sexual arousal of a defenceless bear by red-faced inebriated working-class Englishmen is a big disgrace, albeit exactly what we have come to expect from the country that brought us the pirates Drake, Raleigh, and Dyson.

Beatles, The: Well-known racist Irish pop band from Liverpool, comprising Ring O'Starr, George Harrison, and Lenin N. McCartney. Discovered in a Cavan nightclub, their biggest hits were "The White Album," "Get Back (to where you came from)," "Hey Jew," "Nowhere Man," and "Let It Bleed," about the Crucifixion. Died in an ashram, which is an Indian funeral pyre, while burning their albums.

Beauty: Skin deep but also in the eye of the beholder. My father once told me, "Looks are not everything, Hijo de Puta. A blow job from an ugly woman is always better than a hand job from a pretty one."

Beckett, Samuel (b. 1906): Miserabilist comedy playwrighter, author of such well-known plays as *Tape's Last Crap*, *Meat is Murder*, and *Waiting for*

Godard, in which he recalls how he was shipwrecked, buried up to his waist in sand by little people, then tried to hang himself but never came. Although Irish, he wrote most of his best work in French (his name is pronounced Samuelle Becké), the most pretentious of languages and therefore the favourite of drama queens, which the French are famous for (see *La Cage aux Folles,* Sandra Bernhardt, Didier Deschamps). My most favourite of Beckett's plays is the one with the three tramps who live in a dustbin and fight over a chicken bone which symbolizes Nothing. I cannot remember the name, but I think the story is something to do with Sweet Molloy Malone, who dies (¡spoiler alert!).

Many people think Beckett just imagined these things up out of his mad head, but in Ireland he is seen as a nonfiction documentary writer because the things he describes are almost everyday events there. For instance, when my *bichos* found the body of my friend Frank Prendergast, the U.S. Defense Intelligence chief of station, on Killiney Beach with his collapsable head, he was up to his middle in the sand, just like in a Beckett play, as if someone had started to hide the evidence but was not having the motivation to finish the job. Frank was not talking, of course, his face having been mashed, but he was making a quizzical expression, my *bichos* tell me, with one of his eyebrows in the centre of his forehead due to a fracture to the occipital lobe, formerly his eyepouch; was almost as though he found Death confusing. We were able to apprehend his killer with surprising ease, luring him to the cellar of Knockmerry House with a phone call that played on his vanity, lust, and ridiculous all-American belief that he was the hero of the story. The retribution which we exacted did not require the involvement of the police and the courts, although it would have been easy to call on them since many high-ranking officers and judges were upstairs at the time.

I expect when Beckett dies, he will have a big miserabilist party, with black balloons, empty sandwiches, and Guinness with no head. And nobody will come. Not even God.

Beef, Lean: Attach strips of sirloin to the hull of your sinking boat to attract turtles, whom you can then snare and ride to safety.

Beggars: ATM trolls. Users of cash machines not only have to pay bank charges to withdraw money but also must pay the troll who guards the machine with some of the withdrawn cash. At the end of the day, the troll then lodges all his earnings into his own bank account—¡using the very same machine! This is the real reason why people don't use cash any more.

Beggars with Dogs: Not as hungry as they pretend.

Begrudgery: The national sport of lovely holy pissing Ireland. ¿What means this, begrudgery? Is like saying, if I cannot be happy, then everyone else cannot be happy also. Then I will be happy.

Belgium: Belgiums eat their patatas fritas with *mayonesa* that has no garlic in, which minor detail tells you that their principle goal in life is to get to the grave without anything happening. This unambition can be ascribed to their location between Germany and France. (See also Poland.)

Benidorm: A remote coastal village in Spain where we keep the Irish and the English when they come to España so that they will only fight with one another. It always amuses me that you are more likely to see them naked at night time in the streets than during the day time on the beach. I suppose that the singing furnace of a brilliant blazing Spanish midafternoon is too strong for these pink-skinned melanoma magnets and therefore they try to get a moontan instead. ¡Even our Moon is stronger than the Sun in their country!

Berkeley, Bishop George (1685–1753): Irish philosopher and bishop responsible for the book ¿*What's the Big Idea?* He was able to prove that everything is in your head. Even stomach ache.

Bernabéu: The Mecca of Spanish Christians everywhere.

Bethlehem: The hotel prices are just as exorbitant as in Jesus's day.

Bible, The: Despite the pronouncements of idiot American fundamentalists, the Bible is not infallible. Is the Pope who is infallible. For instance, you won't read in the Bible that all lands which have not yet been discovered by Christians are fair game for claim, use, and exploitation by Christians and that the Catholic faith should be spread and exalted in all said newfound lands. No. We only know that this was what Jesus wanted because a Pope said so.

Bin Laden, Osama: Well-known Islamite terrorist, the caudillo and chief spokesman of Al Qaeda until he was extrapolated in the middle of the night by Obama's craic team of trained seals. Now working alongside Shoko Asahara, Slobodan Milošević, and Harold Shipmate as one of the top Scientologists in Beverly Hills.

Biology: Is destiny. You are what you are. Which is why a woman can never be king. However, is important, in this era of snowflakes, transvestitutes, femi-nazis, femi-kuties, and cetera, to distinguish between sex, which is biology and therefore private, and gender, which is sex in public. Sex is why men are having foreskins, beards, and prostrate glands, while women are having long hair, breast cancer, and two penis-holes (three if you include the vagina). Gender is just about women getting paid less than men for inferior work and making sure they stay at home. Gender is socially sanctioned and therefore to some extent cultural, but it can also be explained by sex. For example, women have to stay at home because that is where the baby is, unless they have left it in the supermarket.

Communists and liberals like to engage in social tinkling, which means just pissing all over well-thought-out and long-existing rules on sex and gender behaviours. This is contrary to the order of things as established by God since at least the dawn of time, possibly before, and another reason why we see decadence, immigration, and the drain brain, which is what happens when people in ivory towers make everyone else live in the guttering.

Blind, The: Blind schoolchildren are smarter than seeing ones. They are not easily distracted by bright colours or shiny toys, they concentrate especially hard when they are writing, and they pay more attention to the teacher's words. You can even face them away from the board or looking out the window and it does not diminish their level of learning. Another advantage they have is that they can destroy other children's educations wholesale just by pulling faces at them during exams until they collapse with hysterical laughter and have to be led out of the exam hall. This is why so many blind children get scholarships. The fact that nobody ever talks about the disabled elite and the privileges of the disabled (free cars and the best parking spaces, slopes instead of steps, secret codebooks in Braille) is proof of their cunning. There is none more cunning than those who cannot see.

Blood Democracy: The only kind of democracy that can possibly work, in which all those of the same blood elect which of their elders should rule over them. With an iron fist.

Blow Jobs: As I always telled my whores, "Nothing succeeds like sucking seed."

Books: Books are like women: rarely worth the effort.

Brain: In much the same way that the hands of farmers become callousy and inflexible from overuse, so too do the brains of so-called intellectuals and academics. When they conducted the autopsy of famous philosopher and lifelong pacifist Bertrand Russell, his brain was so dense and heavy that the surgeon dropped it on the foot of his assistant and broke two of his toes and an ankle. Is highly amusing that the last action performed by Russell's brain was one of violence and pain-causing. Indeed, I am reliably informed that even Russell himself was grinning at the time, underneath the flap of his own forehead.

Brazil: Historicly belongs to Portugal, which historicly belongs to Spain; therefore, Brazil also historicly belongs to Spain. Well-known for pretty girls at football matches, but they are very disappointing close up, and you cannot hear their screeches on the television, which is why you are always better off watching pretty girls remotely, on the computer or through binoculars, than being forced to listen to them in real life moaning about the mess in the bathroom.

Bread, Garlic: Can be used to fend off vampire capitalists.

Brecht, Bertolt (1898–1956): East German communist atheist cabaret artist best known for his *Caucasian Chalk Circus, The Good Side Order of Szechuan*, and Lotte Lenya's *Threepenny Bits*. He once said, "¿What is the crime of robbing a bank when compared with the crime of founding one?" This was a moment of rare lucidity for him, but he still failed to point out what everyone else knows for a fact: Like beggars, the majority of bank robbers are in league with the banks.

Bridegrooms of Death: The Spanish Foreing Legion was always composed largely of gangsters, petty criminals, buffoons, spivs, car dealers, grifters, sociopaths, and losers. But thanks to the charismatic leadership of José Millán-Astray and the uncharismatic but smart leadership of El Generalísimo Francisco Franco, they were the first men to become True Fascists, the bulwark of the nation against decadence and atheism, the worst crimes possible against God. You might think that gangsters, petty criminals, buffoons, spivs, car dealers, grifters, sociopaths, and losers are all bad things, but when you think of the mainstream society from which these men were all outcast, you can understand why the True Fascist is the *real* Outsider, the *real* Romantic rebel, who does not give a shit for your "decency," "tolerance," "dialog," "compromise," "consideration," "solidarity," and hypocrisy, your fancy words and education. We Fascists have an education of our own, which we learn with our mother's milk, and also our father's. We learn that there is one born every minute. We learn that you must never give a sucker an even break. We learn that you must trust no-one but your comrades in arms. The difference between us and you safe civilians in your cozy beds is that while all humans are, underneath the veneer of civilization, nothing but vermin, we True Fascists make no effort to deny it. All your soft, pampered universalist liberal opinions are mere fripperies, covered in cream and Grand Marnier. True Fascists willingly and cheerfully embrace Death while you feeble milquetoasts cravenly cling to your pathetic, over-valued lives of "normality" and convention. Willingly, but also for money. We are not stupid.

Brothels: A necessary evil. Thanks to the pernicious influence of feminism, most married women have never learned how to do the fellatio, and this is the main reason why men go to brothels, besides the witty company and Class A drugs.

According to vicious feminists, nothing is more demeaning or degrading to a woman than to be having a man's penis in her mouth or anus. This only goes to show how dim and unworldly feminists are; I can think of lots of things more degrading and demeaning.

Brothels are also essential to the proper functioning of an intelligence organization as the best place to obtain information about a society's movers and shakers and the best place to compromise political and economic wigbigs for the purposes of blackmail. Don't imagine that we Spanish have the only Intelligence Service involved in brothel-creeping. If prostitution is the oldest business in the world, spying is the second oldest, and this is because the opportunity for spying arises naturally out of prostitution, first in the form of voyeurism and subsequently in the form of "¿How can I make money from this?" When governments later came into existence, they were not slow to spot an opportunity to use shame, fetishes, sinfulness, and temptation for the manipulation and exercise of power. This is why all the world's best brothels and the top prostitutes and rental boys are operated by the Deep State. Ask any Frenchman.

Brothers: Is not by chance, I think, that "brother" is next to "brothel" in the dictionary. Whenever my father's brother visited him in Madrid, they would head straight for the Perfumed Oasis, the brothel where my father was a VIP member, in order to avail of the "five-fingered discount." Of course, I was never allowed to go with my father until I was eight, because my mother disapproved of me meeting any members of the opposite sex except for her, but I think that my father was feeling sorry for me that I was not having a brother with whom I could share adventures. "Blame your witch of a mother" was all he would say to me on that matter.

I recall that on the occasion of my first visit to a brothel, the reception staff wanted that I wait in the car outside, like some neglected puppy, with a bottle of Coca-Cola, but my father flashed some money at them and said it would be an educational experience for me, so they relented on the understanding that he would also flash some more money at them. Was a memorable day for me also for more than one reason. Was the first time I ever got to drink Cardenal Mendoza. Has been my favourite brandy ever since.

"Don't you spill that," my father said to me, passing a half-filled glass from the unlicensed bar. "And sit there."

I was expecting to have to wait in the lobby of the brothel while my father went upstairs, but the receptionist objected that this might be bad for business since a small boy might be construable by those entering the premises to be representative of the business's clientele—or worse, its wares—so my father begrudgingly taked me upstairs with him and made me sit in the corner of the room while he deployed the lady prostitute about the bed. Like a proper, concerned father, however, he did not forget about me while sporting himself. I recall vividly how he looked at me over his shoulder as he pumped away to see if I was enjoying my brandy.

"Remember, Hijo de Puta," he said, "Alcohol is like a whore. Show it too much respect and you will get no pleasure from it." Was an important lesson, although today I think my father was just trying to make me drink faster because when I had finished my glass, he kicked me out into the corridor, saying, "Now there are some things I have to do which are not for the eyes of children," and he shut the door behind him. I have never found out what were these things he was doing. Probly Gomorrahmy.

My father was a very busy man in those days (he was in the Spanish Air Force, and there were always lots of atheist communists and homosexuals to be strafed or dropped from planes) so it was rare that he could take me out or spend much time with me. Consequently, the burden fell upon me to make the best of what time we had together, whether in the brothel, at the races or bullring, in the casino, or just cruising the bars of the city. I learned a very great deal from those times, especially that people in general are scum.

I am conscious that I have not recorded here the tale of my father's brother. Is too sad to relate but is no reflection on my father or the family. He only had himself to blame for his defrocking.

Brown, Approachability: The less competent but much friendlier brother of Capability Brown.

Buddha, Saint (n.d.): Not to be confused with the idle fat idol of the Eastern superstition, Saint Buddha was a dynamic, thrusting, wide-awake Christian saint who had no time for tea, meditation, tai chi, or Nirvana. Gemini. Lucky number: 1. Stone: Amyl nitrate, amphetamine sulphate.

Buddhism: Good enough for the Chinese, Tibetans, and the like, but God did not intend for them to go to Heaven anyway. Is a worrying trend that some idiot Europeans have also adopted this fake religion, but we Catholics will not squat, lie down, or meditate for anyone. Proper religious postures are the kneeling, the bowing of the head, and the prostration. Meditation is just praying with an empty head. No wonder God doesn't answer.

Budgerigar: When making a splint for a budgerigar, don't use matchsticks, a lesson I learned to my cost as an aspiring junior vet (aged nine). As the budgerigar's health improves, she is likely to try walking on the sandpaper at the bottom of her cage. This will retard her progress indefinitely.

Bungabine, Saint (1876–1945): American-born missionary who tried to convert Imperial Japan to Christianity single-handily, despite not being able to speak a word of Japanese. Spent most of his career, until his death, in the city of Nagasaki, unaware that it was already the largest Catholic city in Japan and that he was literally preaching to the converted. Ironicly, he didn't die in the atomic blast that destroyed the city but in the aftermath at the hands of fellow Catholics, who lynched him from the last remaining tree. Aquarius. Eye of the Tiger. Lucky numbers: 3, 56, 57. Stone: Uranium.

Buñuel, Luis: Frequently misunderstood Spanish film director, famous for his documentary movies *Los Olvidados, Garage D'Or,* and *Les Chemises* *de la Liberté,* with its inspiring slogan "¡Down with Freedom!" Buñuel is also the original source of the joke "¡Careful! ¡You'll have someone's eye out with that!"

Bus Trip: Immediately after I received the news that the Beast with Three Fingers had arrived on the island, I spranged into action, taking all the necessary steps to ensure that I was ready for his appearance. Andres, a resident of the village who worked in passport control at the airport, tipped me off that the Beast had taked the Tiadhe bus south to Morro Jable, which telled me that although he had discovered which island I lived on, he did not know my precise whereabouts. It also meant I had time to finalize my plans. I placed a call to the Rotgütts to deliver ammunition, and I grabbed the first bus to Corralejo to stock up on fresh goods and other comestibles for short-term consumption. With the lack of traffic on the roads between towns, the Land Rover would have been conspicuous and picked up by GPS. The *guagua* allowed me to blend in.

08:55 Arrived at terminus after a twenty-minute walk. The cabildo, that is, the council, had been obliged to relocate all the bus stops in the island's towns to their outskirts, close to the walls, to prevent gambies from being accidently brought into the heart of the community. My travel companions were mostly students on the way to college, equipped with catapults and slings to drive off any gambies that might try to stop the bus in the countryside. Before boarding, they helped themselves to rocks and stones of diverse shapes from a mound at the roadside, which the cabildo replenished each day. I pocketed several particularly sharp examples with razor-like edges, but I also had my pistol ready for wild dogs and, if necessary, to inflict a flesh wound on a gambie. While killing gambies is illegal and they are unlikely to infect you, they will assault you and their saliva is virulent, so you need to keep them at more than arm's length. The pistol was a last resort.

09:00 Bus departed on time. I selected a seat toward the rear of the vehicle, about halfway between the back window and the exit door at the middle of the bus. The students picked seats near the front—to spot gambies early—or close to the exit door, from where they could quickly alight, either to run into college or fend off intruders.

A handful of tourists in the mix prepared cameras.

09:05 We breached the town gates. Two sentries on the ramparts nodded to the driver, indicating that there were no gambies or bardinos in the immediate vicinity. Usually, the sentries would have shot any bardinos within 200 meters of the wall before the bus departed the town, although repelling bardinos in general tends to require only non-lethal weaponry that will incapacitate or disorientate them. Doktor Rotgütt had a cannon from which he fired cats or chipmucks over the heads of bardinos, which they then chased. It seemed to work for him although he said it was nothing like work, more of a leisurely experiment.

09:08 We passed through El Roque without stopping. El Roque is almost a ghost town and with an awkward bend in the road that seemed to be popular with gambies intent on stopping traffic. A couple of burned-out hire cars reclined lazily in the ditch, watching us pass by with indifference.

09:15 The gates of Lajares were open, never a good sign. There could be gambies on the streets. The driver hesitated before driving in, shouting over his shoulder to the students to prepare their slings. Sure enough, when we reached the bus stop, a gaggle of tourists was fending off half a dozen gambies carrying surfboards. Lajares was always a popular resort for surfers—cheap rent, nice bars and cafes, laidback atmosphere—but hydrophobia can severely cramp a surfer's style. Even schoolchildren know that if you're ever cornered by a gambie at the beach, simply wade into the sea and you're safe. Surfer gambies still congregate in Lajares and try to get on the bus, compelled by some kind of unconscious primal urge or habit, but when they reach the beach they can do nothing but stand at the edge of the sea and stare at it until it gets dark, the froth on their lips a feeble echo of the mocking waves before them.

The driver pulled past the bus stop, opened the door, and yelled to the tourists to get in. At the same time, a couple of the students climbed down from the exit and hurled stones at the gambies with an accuracy suggestive of mis-spent weekends. Some students hate gambies. Some just hate surfers. Once the tourists were on the bus, the driver yelled to the students to climb back aboard, the door closing behind them with a gambie clinging on to the outside handle with one hand, his surfboard in the other. The driver pulled away, dragging the gambie with him, still holding his board. He hanged on to the bus all the way to the edge of town, but the driver was skilled enough to drive within centimeters of a parked campervan outside the football ground, scraping the gambie off.

09:22 Two gambies were aimlessly staggering around the countryside just outside La Oliva. Upon hearing the bus, one of them, an elderly woman, wandered into the middle of the road, waving her arms randomly in the air, like a foreigner who has seen this done to hail taxis. "¡Don't stop!" advised one of the tourists, camera at the ready, hoping for an #instapicoftheday, but the driver, inexplicably humane, slowed the bus to a walking pace, intent on nudging the gambie out of the way. She stood her ground, and as the bus made contact, the sputum from her lips smeared the windscreen like a scumkiss. The driver sprayed his screen with wiper fluid—the gambie screamed with disgust and terror—and turned on his wipers, successfully brushing her aside. In the meantime, however, the other gambie, a young boy, had managed to open the luggage hold, the bus's soft underbelly, and jumped inside. The driver swore and, suddenly less humane, accelerated away, swerving back and forth across the road in an attempt to roll the gambie out, to no avail. We would not be able to enter La Oliva with the gambie onboard while the luggage door was open.

A hundred meters up the road, the driver screeched to a halt, jumped out of the bus, and quickly slammed the luggage compartment door shut, trapping the gambie inside. Any travellers who wanted to board further down the line with bikes or buggies would have to bring them into the passenger compartment.

09:28 La Oliva. The regional capital. New passengers boarded, mostly locals heading for work in Corralejo. We could hear the gambie in the luggage hold below us, banging and punching at the door and walls in an apparently uncoordinated manner. Sounds of incoherent speech and barking. Sometimes the walls and roof of the passenger compartment reverberated simultaneously, unnerving for those unfamiliar with gambie flailing.

09:32 Villaverde. The infants school was shut. The library was shut. This was the highest point on the journey and the most inaccessible town for gambies, so the homes in Villaverde had become the most expensive in the north of the island. It was already having ideas above its station, and moves were afoot by the municipality to prevent the bus from entering the village altogether. Locals rarely used public transport; the bus route passed through the town only to bring kids to the school.

At this height, the hot wind swirled around the streets like a homeless demon, forcing rich and very rich alike to stay inside their air-conditioned villas. The farmers' co-operative still (co-)operated, mostly as a local civil defence force. I made a mental note that its warehouse might be a handy source of shotguns.

09:36 Tamaragua. The gambie below was abruptly silent. I suspect he didn't want to be let out in Tamaragua. The residents are too wild and inhospitable.

09:40 The outskirts of Corralejo. The driver ordered everyone off the bus and taked down his bargepole from the passenger rack. "We have to empty out the luggage hold before we enter the town," he explained. "Pick up your weapons." Co-ordinating their actions, the driver and one of the students opened the luggage hold doors on either side of the bus, and immediately we could see the young gambie inside, snarling. Standing on the passenger side of the bus, the other students immediately began pelting the gambie with stones to drive him out onto the driver's side, where he waited with the bargepole under one arm and a Super Soaker under the other. The gambie shrieked with what appeared to be pain as the jet of water bounced off his forehead, and he taked to his heels, heading in the direction of the Grandes Playas. There was no sense of triumph, of victory, only of another day at the office. We piled back on board the bus and arrived in Corralejo at 09:45. On time.

C

Cabrakebabra: Is a popular chain of fast-food restaurants that specializes in kebabs made of goat meat, which is healthier than mutton because it contains less fat and fewer of the chemicals that cause sheep's low self-esteem and body-image problems.

Cache: Two days after my bus trip to Corralejo, the Rotgütts arrived to deliver the ammunition I had ordered from them. Fortuitably, they had planned to be in the area in any case because they had an airport drop-off from the last remaining hotel in the village, quite some journey gived that it meant driving all the way from their home in Cofete, at the southern end of the island, a roundtrip of 160 kilometers, including the drop at the airport. "An excuse to give the Hummer a run-out," explained Doktor Rotgütt with the insouciant air of a wastrel Prussian aristocrat, suave and elegant but for his broken nose, which he acquired during a scuffle with an Austrian taxi driver over who invented schnitzel. Their home, Villa Rotgütt, sat on the crumbleous volcanic land above a remote beach accessible only by sea, the hostile rock-strewn plains, ridges of perilous descent, and impenetrable cactus field rendering it Guantánamo-like in its inhospitabilitiness. Accidental visitors usually found themselves caught by the incoming tide and having their rental car towed to the shop of the wealthiest (yet least competent) mechanic in Spain, located in Costa Calma, before being trucked unceremoniously—and with suspicious regularity—to the mechanic's brother's scrapyard in Gran Tarajal. The Rotgütts' long-body Humvee, which they garaged up the coast in Las Salinas, had served them for several years as a stalwart off-road beast of burden and a handy factotum, able to hold six Dutch virologists (or eight Norwegians or four Brits) and their luggage for journeys to and from the airport.

"You will make good hunting, Manuel," Doktor Rotgütt said to me as we began unloading the ammo boxes, an approving smirk on his fat lips.

"¿You will be careful, though, ja?" Frau Rotgütt said. "Shoot only the whites of their eyes. ¿Is what you say, yes?"

"Yes, exactly," I said. And then, "¿You are not hot, Frau Rotgütt? Is odd to be wearing a stole at this time of the day. And in this heat."

"¿Stole? ¿What is stole? Nothing is stole."

"Around your neck. Is what is known as a stole. Usually a mink or a fox. But I confess that I am not recognizing yours."

"Ha ha, Herr Manuel. ¡You are *so* funny! This is not *stole*. This is Erik. He is mein new pet."

Frau Rotgütt, I should have explained, had a parade, nay, a cavalcade, of exotic pets. Usually, it was easy to spot them. Parrots with hats on. Bonobos, always in pairs, clad in heavy boots to stop them climbing up her legs. Declawed leopards, kaleidoscopic butterflies threaded into her hair, and also a manky cow. This day was noteworthy for the deficit in my observational powers and for being the day I met Erik the sloth, languidly draped over Frau Rotgütt's shoulders.

"He is mein new favourite. Hardly any trouble, and there is no need to take him walkies. On the downside, I have to carry him *everywhere*. He is *such* a lazybones."

Erik slowly opened one eye, as though he suspected he was the topic of conversation but more likely outrageously aggrieved by all the noise and expressing it in the strongest possible terms.

"¿Does he require much feeding? I can fetch him a bowl of water if you like."

"Most kind of you, *Schatzi*. Do."

We stored the ammo in the armoury before climbing to my rooftop terrace where Erik was able to avail of a water bowl and the pergola's struts, from which he hung with aplomb and disdain while we sipped Darjeeling—an affectation of which I strongly disapprove but in which I partake for the sake of politeness, also an affectation of which I disapprove—and surveyed the town. The Doktor called upon his military training to point out faults in the design and positioning of the town's defensive structures.

"You know, when we first came to Fuerteventura, Manuel, the island was pure and pristine. It was clear why the Canaries were referred to as the Fortunate Islands. A small population and an abundance of resources, so long as you were willing to survive on a repetitive diet: fish, potatoes, goat, plantains, tomatoes, maize. All the necessary nutrients to survive but also a test of your culinary imagination. Then, in the seventies, came the Great Unwashed. I don't blame Franco—¿what else could he do to raise money while still maintaining his principles?—but the changes to the island were immense. All at once exploded your *fleischpots* of Corralejo and Calete de Fuste, with all their drunken English *schweine* and their *schwachsinnig* drunken children, eating their scampi and chips and doing Monty Python with the handkerchiefs."

"Awful," agreed Frau Rotgütt, "although if you knew where to look, you could still find a few havens like El Cotillo and Ajuy." The Doktor concurred.

"The west coast was the place to be. A hundred kilometers of Atlantic where a man could live unmolested and devote himself to his chosen *métier* safe in the knowledge that he would not be ... investigated."

"I like it also very much myself," I confided.

"No doubt. But you missed it in its heyday. Back in the sixties. Cotillo was barely anything more than a few streets around the harbour. A few shops, a seafood restaurant or two. There was a dirt track from the beaches and a small gate you had to pass through to enter the village. None of ... *this*." He gestured to the town's defences in the distance. A black plastic bag in the barbed wire atop the fencing seemed to wave back. Frau Rotgütt expanded on her husband's observation.

"Sometimes we used to walk into the village to buy bread and wine— *pan y vino*—from the small *tienda*, and the shopkeeper never passed comment on our lack of clothing other than to ask where we kept our change. That is how discreet they were. Two naked Germans in their shop and their only concern was that we keep clear of the meat slicer. Such charming people."

"You could not do that today." The Doktor was stating the obvious, the Darjeeling kicking in. I think I caught a glistening in his eye, close to a tear. Nazis are such fucking nostalgics.

"Anyone walking naked through the village today would be taked for a gambie and stoned and expelled. And rightly so."

"Ja, of course, but ... still ... is such a shame," Frau Rotgütt said.

"Also, the gate is gone," I observed. They looked at me blankly. "So, I mean, you cannot do that today."

"Ach, ja. *Das ist die Wahrheit.*" The Doktor raised himself from his recliner, the deliberate inanity of my observation sufficient to apprise him of my need to get busy. "And so we must be gone, Manuel. We must drop off our clients at fifteen thirty hours for their flight to Fiumicino. Is fourteen hundred now. They will already be screeching like Stukas."

"Ja," said Frau Rotgütt. "¿Fucking Italians, eh? Ha ha."

"Sí," I agreed, cheerfully. "Romans Go Home."

Thanks to the Rotgütts and my own circumspection, I was well set for the arrival of the Beast with Three Fingers. Specially reinforced steel doors at the front and back of *mi casa* and at the top of each set of stairs, separating the three floors. Double-strength titanium shutters on the ground-floor windows, a fifteen-foot wall on the raised rear terrace, and 360-degree crenellations around the roof terrace, which itself served as a twenty-four-hour look-out. My armoury was now also complete for all eventualities:

2 Heckler & Koch USP Expert 9 mm pistols (semi-automatic)
1 Heckler & Koch 5.56 mm assault rifle
1 Heckler & Koch USP Elite 9 mm pistol

2 Heckler & Koch MP5 9 mm light machine guns
40 Alhambra-DO hand grenades
1 Barrett M95 12.7 mm sniper rifle
1 ECIA 60 mm light mortar
1 Spanish Army knife (Madonna)
400 rounds 9 mm Parabellum cartridges
200 rounds 5.5 mm NATO cartridges
50 rounds 12.7 mm .50 Browning Machine Gun cartridges
100 60 mm mortar rounds

Various machetes, meat cleavers, skewers, knives, stillettoes, throwing stars, stakes, and whetstones.

My father's Frente de Juventudes *Manual del Cadete*

I had received training in the use of all of these, although I was a little rusty with Madonna, my Spanish Army knife, not having had the chance to castrate a pig since training college, but I suspected it would be like falling off a bike: After the first few dozen, it becomes second nature.

I will explain for you Madonna. Is the name I gave to my knife when it was assigned to me upon my first day in the Forces. Every member of the Spanish military receives an identical such knife but is obligated to make it his own[3] by naming it and customizing it. I had my knife embossed with a true-to-life image of Our Lady, so that she would always be with me and never let me down. The Spanish Army knife differs from the Swiss Army knife by having, in addition to the drop-point blade that characterizes the Swiss version, a stiletto-style blade for stabbing, a retractable folding saw blade, and a small fork attachment for tapas. The Italian Army knife has no tapas fork but instead a moustache comb for grooming, a frivolous and unnecessary extra in my humble opinion.

I will also explain for you the *Manual del Cadete* of the Frente de Juventudes, the Falangist Youth Movement, which was a formative

---

[3] And also these days "her own," but giving a woman a knife outside the kitchen is asking for trouble.

experience for all young boys and girls growing up in Franco's Spain. Although the organisation had changed its name by the time my father was old enough to join, he and each of his comrades in arms were still gived the old manuals of the Frente. Is the only book other than the Bible that any respectable and respectful Spanish youngster requires. The Frente was a form of Falangist Scout movement, which inculcated in young people the proper attitudes, beliefs, skills, and actions to make them a normal member of Fascist society, and the *Manual* provides a handy reference guide so that you don't need to carry all that information in your brain. There is a chapter showing all the knots that you might need for tying a recalcitrant sheep to a fence, an uncooperative anarchist to a goalpost, or a smelly Basque to a refrigerator, although never in his scariest nightmares as a boy did my father imagine he would ever meet one in real life. There is also a very useful chapter on dealing with haemorrhages, broken limbs, knife wounds, and animal bites, with a description of how to practice sutures on your thighs, for example. There are tips on how to use fruit, vegetables, and random food items to their best advantage against an enemy, a marauding badger, or a hungry gypsy. And there is a chapter on everything a boy needs to know about the emblems of the party; the party always had lots of emblems so that its members did not have to read to a particularly high level.

Why they have not reprinted this book in recent years is beyond me. I always keep it with me, not merely as a souvenir of my father and a nod to better days but also as a practical pocket-sized survival guide. Many have been the nights that I flicked through its pages and imagined my father in times of yore innocently bobbing for apples with his comrades or competing to see which of them could be the first to skin a whippet with just their teeth. I still remember him tying my hands together using a handcuff knot when I was small to stop me reaching for things to suck. One of my first memories, although, according to my mother, it did not stop me sucking.

Caganer: In the backward part of Spain known as Cataluña, the natives are having a filthy disgusting tradition in which, every Christmas, they put in their hovel's Nativity Scene a Catalan man who is squatting in the corner of the stable, making a shit. ¿Don't you think this is a big disgrace? That while Baby Jesus is being born from his mother's Virgin Womb, a Catalan moron should be in the same room not only not paying no attention but also actually defecating at the scene of a miracle. ¡This is the sort of behavior you would expect from a Protestant!

However, before I fume, let us put this heresy into context. In Cataluña, is perfectly acceptable behaviour to shit in the corner of your room. I am telled that guests in Catalan homes are even encouraged to do so rather than sign a visitors' book, although I don't know this for sure; no Catalan has ever invited me into his home and I would refuse the invitation in any case. Even though the local Catalan government is trying to train the natives to appear more civilized in an attempt to attract a better class of tourist, we all know that you cannot just eliminate this sort of incorrigible behaviour by appealing to Catalans' sense of decorum because they aren't having one. We Madrileños laugh mockingly at the idea of Barcelona trying to clean itself up and wipe itself off. However, much as we loathe the primitive behaviour of our Catalan cousins, we also look with fond contempt on their traditions and think them part of the colourful patchwork of Spanish diversity, giving Cataluña its medieval charm. No normal person would want to live there, obviously, but is fascinating to go and have a look at (I recommend flying over it: ¡In a Heinkel!). Marvel at their unself-conscious vulgarities in the same way that you might the almost-human antics of chimpanzees or clowns in a circus. And then go home afterwards to tell Mama what horrors you have witnessed.

The Caganer is yet another reason why the Catalans cannot be trusted with a country of their own: They will only shit in the corner (Portbou).

Cain: The first murderer, even before the Jews. Famous for killing his brother, Abel, which was a terrible thing to do, although, in mitigation, there wasn't many people around to kill in those days.

As a punishment, God did not implement the Death Penalty, He being God and therefore able to transcend the normal human natural instinct of *lex talionis*. Instead, he gave Cain a mark, thereafter called the Mark of Cain, presumably one out of ten, to indicate poor show. Vested interests in the slave trade will tell you that the mark that God gave him was black skin, an assertion that allowed them to draw on Scripture to justify lynching, transportation, and whipping, but the true meaning of the term "mark" is lost in the midsts of time. It could just as well be that God gave Cain a stutter, a limp, or ginger hair, any of which would have been equally abominable to ordinary decent Geneticists (the people of Genesis). Whichever of these disfigurements God chose, it was a just punishment not only for Cain but also his descendants for adding murder to the list of humanity's crimes, which prior to that had only comprised curiosity, incest, and scrumping.

Calendar: A device of human hubris. An eternity in Hell is an eternity no matter what the date is.

Calima: During the calima, dogs cough at both ends.

Camels: These bad-tempered, vindictive mammals carry huge grudges on their back in which they store water purely for the purpose of spitting at people they don't like, which is everyone. Is with good reason that camels are known as the shits of the desert.

Campervans: Are bloody everywhere. The rich bourgeois bohemians in Villaverde and Lajares are having so much money that they don't know what else to spend it on. Consequently, every house in Lajares has a campervan outside in the driveway for driving the five kilometers to La

Concha Beach and having a barbecue. Their owners cannot go to the beach without bringing their fucking house with them. ¿Why not just make a sandpit in your back yard? Is much cheaper, has the same effect, and doesn't run the risk of having your petrol tank stuffed with dog turds. Which *has* been known to happen.

Campesino: While I was growing up in Spain in the fifties and sixties, my family had a pet campesino to which we gave the name Raoul. In those days, peasants were no longer strictly necessary, but there was a fashion among respectable families to retain one in order to demonstrate magnininimity, display awareness of one's communal obligations, and show off one's wealth. My sister and I were rarely allowed to beat Raoul or his wife, but we could play nicely with them. Candelaría liked very much to dress Raoul in women's clothing and make him do press-ups. However, nothing was permissible which involved physical maltreatment—¡even in Franco's day!—except for the odd poking.

Sadly, Raoul's wife gave birth to twins one day, and my father had to send them all away to live on a farm.

Canary Islands: Las Islas Canarias are proof, contrary to all those Communist naysayers who complain about Ceuta and Melilla, that Spain is historicly both a European and an African nation. The Canary Islands are in Africa but also part of Spain, just as Morocco once was and should be once more and forever and ever again, Amen. Some people say the sand on the Canary Islands comes from the Sahara Desert, which shows that the Sahara itself wants to be a part of Spain, both historicly, geographicly, politicly, and culturally. Of course it does. But it should stay in its own country and send its sand by boat, like it does with its people.

Cancer: Is a sign of the times that whereas childbirth was once the main killer of women, and rightly so, now, sadly, cancer is the winner. Interestingly, the types of cancer that kill women are split along religious lines. Catholic women die of cancer of the uterus from too much sex, whereas Protestant women die of cancer of the breast because of no sex. All men get cancer of the prostrate gland at some point, and everyone knows why that is.

Candelaría: My lovely idiot sister, or as my father used to refer to her, "My darling dormouse," because she was sleepy, slow-witted, and lived in a teapot.

¡Is a joke!

In fact, my sister did not live in a teapot and was entirely able to walk around of her own free will without falling asleep. She also liked very much to give big hugs all the time, especially to my father, with whom she was having a close friendly special relationship that none of the rest of us could understand, although I believe there is always a special bond between a girl and her father, regardless of how mental she is. I tried always very much to include her in my games, when she would do pretty much anything I wanted and did not see any harm in people laughing at her. I think she enjoyed to see my grinning face and to smell my other nongrinning bits, the kind of innocent tomfoolery which you have to pay for these days.

Carrots: A superfood chock full of vitamins and fibre, carrots will help you see in the dark so that you can defend yourself against the myriad species of lethal snakes indigent to the sewers of New York.

Before Spain brought oranges to the uncivilized world, primitive societies like Scotland and Russia were not having a word for the colour orange except for "carrot." It taked hundreds of years and endless Chinese burns to stop them incorrectly calling oranges "Spanish carrots."

Casa de los Coroneles: In the regional capital of La Oliva, the House of the Colonels is a fine colonial mansion that was once home to the regional governors of Fuerteventura. Today, is a weapons store against hoarders, marauders, and civil disorders. All of the colonels married one another's cousins or nieces to accumulate wealth and land and keep it in the family. Some say that this was the source of the New Rabies, that the disease is a curse on the island for its people's inbreeding and insularity. All islands are cursed in this way if the people are having sex only with each other. This is why empires and wars are necessary: to bring home foreing slavegirls, silk underwear, narcotics, and anything else that might make sex with your relatives less necessary or more tolerable.

Castilian: The natural language of the Spaniard. Its rhythms, fricatives, and labias all derive from his body, including its contents and contours. Is not an underexaggeration to say that Castilian comes from the Spaniard's very soul, specifically its mouth.

Catholicism: Jesus's religion. Currently engaged in a life-or-death struggle against the Forces of Darkness. Poland, Spain, and lovely holy pissing Ireland still stand firm(ish). More praying is necessary. Prayer is like religious Viagra, strengthening one's determination to see the dreadful task through to its conclusion.

Cats, Parachuting: Ramon Gutierrez was a mechanic at the Spanish Air Force base where was being stationed my father in the late fifties and early sixties, but he also earned a modest stipend as a parachute designer, which he tested using a half-dozen pet cats, who he specially trained for the job and who were lazy bastards that acted like the cats who had got the cream which is what they were because they got it. The air base included two back-to-back rows of airship hangars from the days when Spain had Zeppelins on order from the Reich but which never arrived and therefore were mainly used as warehouses, but their inordinant height, around one hundred meters, also made them ideal for the testing the parachutes. On the roofs of the hangars was walkways where you could climb up, and Gutierrez would take the cats up to one of the hangar roofs and attach the parachutes' ripcords to a static line stretched across the twenty meters between the hangars. Then his partner, standing on the other hangar roof opposite, would lure the cats to jump across the gap with tasty morsels of tuna or salmon, but not cream, because they already had have had it. When the cats tried to jump across, they would inevitably fail, the parachute would deploy, and they would drift the hundred meters to the ground, landing, as cats always do, on their feet. Then they received a reward: tuna. And cream.

Gutierrez was very popular with all the ladies on the air base, even though he smelled of cats all the time, because he was having two wages. "There's a man who knows how to bring home the bacon," my mother said, "and also the sausage, if you catch my drift." I did not, but my father did and was outraged. Moreover, Gutierrez compounded his crime of sausage delivery by welching on a gambling debt he owed to my father in relation to the European Cup Winners Cup Final between Atlético and Tottenham Hostpur (which Tottenham was winning 5–1, hooray). My father was never one to miss an opportunity to be offended, nor one to care about appropriate levels of retaliation. Consequently, during one of the siestas (the Air Force allows two siestas a day), while everyone else was asleep, my father taked all of Gutierrez's cats up to the roof of one of the hangars with their parachute bags unpacked, connected them to the static line and then lured them across to the other hangar with irresistible catnip (which the Air Force used to prevent diarrhea in first-time parachutists). The unsuspecting cats, who was all now highly competent professionals with hundreds of jumps under their belts, did not need much persuading and thus successfully jumped to their deaths. When they was all dead, my father washed his hands and went back to bed, and nobody was none the wiser.

The Air Force suspected foul play but like everyone else hated Gutierrez and so there was no arrests, and no one ever identified my father as the perpetrator. The truth only came to light many years later when he decided that it was time for the big father–son talk about Honour,

Respect, and Revenge: "These are just words," he said to me, "for use when it best suits your purpose, but if you ever need to exact revenge, make sure you do it in such a way that no one suspects you. Many make the mistake of believing that revenge has to be public, to show that you are not a man to be messed with. But this runs the risk of initiating a cycle of retribution that will render the revenge unsuccessful. No. Instead, to ensure that no revenge to your revenge is possible, your assault must be both anonymous and definitive, rendering all possibility of retribution unthinkable. Revenge is a dish best served silently. Except with a few sniggers to yourself late at night in bed." He was correct, as always.

Celery: A surprisingly versatile vegetable, particularly at breakfast time, when you can have it with brandy or whisky or vodka or gin. Or even on its own.

¡Is a joke! ¡No one would eat it on its own!

Celtic Tiger: Not a tiger with hoops instead of stripes but a temporary spurt of the economy in lovely holy pissing Ireland that corrupted the country for a while with its materialism, atheism, and promotion of diversity, tolerance, and racial harmony. During my last Christmas in Ireland, I was watching the annual Toy Edition of everyone-in-Ireland's favourite television program, *The Late Late Show*, in which the insufferable presenter said to one little boy, "¿So, Lydia, what's out there for all the gay children this Christmas?" ¡I literally vomited with anger! And from that day forth, I prayed every day for a calamitous economic crash to smite the country and return it humiliated and grateful to a Fascist overlord.

I am still praying.

Censorship: Undoubtably a good thing. Is only because of censorship that the cinema-going public was prevented from discovering what happened to the rest of the horse in *The Godfather* and from seeing that blow-job scene in *The Crying Game*. Now that there is the Internet, censorship has become a thing of the past, and is possible to call up any image you want, whether "ISIS executions," "Third world girls, one world cup," "Dishwasher frenzy," "Small dog with slippers," or "Monkey shitting on a shovel." The only restriction is people's imagination, which is why we must do everything in our power to ensure stultification, conformity, and dim-wittyness. The best way to do this is to force people to work as many hours as possible at jobs requiring intense and constant concentration, such as in hospitals or air traffic control. If this is not possible, then they must be compelled to carry out boring and repetitive tasks but have someone standing over them with a stick. In this way, they will be too tired to do anything when they get home except sleep. Sadly, there is nothing we can do about their imaginations while they are sleeping, at least for the moment, but it will no doubt be possible to invent anti-erection devices, which we could require men to attach during the night as a precaution against unconscious pornography. I would call such a device "Night Censor for Men." "Night Censor for Women" already exists and is called a baby.

Centipedes: Centipedes communicate with one another through a signing system similar to that used by deaf people but fifty times more complex, mostly about lettuce.

Chameleons: Famously cunning but also loyal; they always stick together, although not in the way that stick insects do. For instance, if one of them eats all your beansprouts, you will be unable to identify the culprit; they will huddle together in the corner of the room trying to look like one another.
¡What cowards!

Charity: There is no point giving money to the Poor with no strings attached because they will only waste it on food and drink. Not a one of them will stop to think to invest it and live off the interest. Consequently, we would be forever giving money to them and they would never learn thrift or foresight, instead remaining dependent and parasitic on the respectable, moneyed, and soft-hearted, which is no way to run a country. Always say this to yourself when pity is tempting you to throw your money away on a whining beggar: Charity is Theft.

Chastity: In men, chastity is a good way to remain fertile. Is a way for them to hang on to their valuable juices rather than waste them by shooting them willy-nilly up every hole they see. The proof of this is demonstratable by the fact that there are so many priests who are having children. They are so fecund that they don't even have to have sex with a woman or a child for them to get pregnant.

Chicago: Much as New York and London gave us Nylon, Lesbos gave us lesbianism, and Los Angeles gave us lozenges, so the city of Chicago gave us the adjective "Chic," deriving from the abbreviation on the railway timetables of the Pullman Train Company. "Chic" was where all the American jet-setter elites alighted when returning from New York, having completed their nefariant business doings. "Chic" was also the location of the massive stockyards where pigs from all over the country was being sent for slaughter, hence the double meaning of the word "Chic": fashionable, on trend, and up-to-date but also swinish, wallowing in shit, and deserving of execution.

Chicken Vimto: Spain's top boy band. From Jerez, of all places. ¿Who says we need American culture and crip-crap hip-hop K-pop in order to create contemporary middle-of-the-road music that both girls and their grandmothers can enjoy?

Childbirth: Patently ridiculous. The one lesson of value taught by the Albigensian Heresy is that the physical world is evil and an occasion of sin, while the spiritual realm is the realm of salvation. Mortality rates in childbirth—of both mothers and children—and the incomparable and agonizing pain inherent in giving birth show without fear of contradiction that Mother Nature did not design human beings to reproduce. ¿¡Why do you think women are having clitorises!? Is because penetrative sex is unnatural. Nature punishes women for having penetrative sex by making childbirth as painful as possible. "¿Did you not get the message yet?" she is shouting at us in the maternity ward over the screams of the mother. "¡Stop having sex and you will stop having children!"

The biggest secret that hospitals hide from women is that Nature in her cruel wisdom has made certain that the female body will do everything within its power to destroy any foetus being carried. The foetus is an alien being inside the lady's body that will most likely kill her if she carries it to term, and the lady's body knows this only too well. Idiot Darwinists and sociobiologists have invented the *post hoc* justification that mothers make it difficult for the foetus to survive so that only the strongest babies are born. Not only is this in contradiction with all other aspects of their theory, according to which pleasure exists to encourage a particular behaviour and pain to deter it, but also it flies in the face of all history, from which is clear that the process of childbirth aims to kill the mother and ensure that no more children are born to a woman stupid enough to persist in her pursuit of making yet another human being. If Nature is able to kill the child during childbirth as well, this is a bonus, but failing that, it can at least eliminate the source of these monsters.

This also explains why birth rates decline in those societies where women have been gived the choice whether to be having babies or not. And this is why any society that wants to perpetuate itself must first subjugate women, to coerce them or con them into having children their bodies don't want. Patriarchy has learned this, which is why patriarchies endure while democracies do not—eventually democracies run out of people because women are given a choice about whether they want to live. In democracies, doctors have to be taught to lie without smirking when they tell mothers-to-be that the pain of childbirth is intended so that she will bond with her baby. I don't know how they keep back the tears of laughter. Probly they think about the money.

The case of childbirth also exemplifies a problem that Darwinism faces whenever there is a contradiction to its theory and why the Catholic philosopher Karl Poper called evolution a pseudoscience, since it always provides flimsy explanations that convince no one and serves only to prop up the ideological edifice of Patriarchy. Of course, is no skin off my nose whether people believe in Darwinism. I am simply explaining that the truth about childbirth is something Patriarchy has always known; is a necessary evil that must continue if civilization, with all its benefits (cheap labour, yachts, sex slaves, cocaine), is to survive. I am not condoning childbirth—the True Fascist has nothing but contempt for decadence, material comforts, and women's bodies, after all—but I *do* understand it, and I observe the deceit and deception with amusement. Or possibly bemusement. Life is a bemusement park.

They may have been sodomites and pederants, but the Albigensians at least understood that Nature is entirely designed for hedonistic, non-reproductive pleasure, and for this reason we should revile it as unholy. This is why we proper Christians believe in self-denial, self-sacrifice, abhorrence of the flesh, especially female flesh, and punishment of those who enjoy life. In a Patriarchal society, such people include lesbians and homosexuals, who are getting a free pass by ignoring the state imperative to provide the next generation of meat machines for the country's farms, factories, and battlefields. ¿If the rest of us have to go through the pain of raising bloody kids, why shouldn't they too?

Children, Shoot One's: A euphemistic expression for a solitary action that constitutes an abomination in the eyes of God. Used in such sentences as "I was watching the topless beach volleyball the other day through my binoculars when I accidently shot my children all over the patio." In several U.S. states, a much worse sin than actually shooting one's children.

Chimerical Weapons: Weapons that don't exist, like the ones Saddam Hussein refused to get rid of.

Christ, Jesus, Lord God, King of Kings (0–33): The son of God. Born to take away the sins of the world. 166 cm. Dark hair. Brown eyes. Circumcised. Left-hand over the wicket. Tattoo on right forearm ("Mother"). Carpenter by trade. First-time offender but still sentenced to death by crucifixion by the Judaeo-Roman conspiracy, who, whatever else we might say about them, at least understood the importance of law and order.

Christ, Keith (1948–): Electrical engineer in Bridgewater, Somerset, born Keith Judas. Changed name by deed poll in 1977.

Christmas: Christmas is the time of year to remind ourselves to open our hearts to Christ Jesus, Lord God, King of Kings. Also is a time not to forget that those who don't open their hearts to Him will burn forever in the fires of Hell with homosexuals and Buddhists. One thing Christmas is *not* for, Catalan scum, is shitting in the corner of the room.

Christo (1935–2020): Well-known wrap artist.

Christopher, Saint: Patent saint of tourists, travellers, gypsies, Wandering Jews, and cetera. Discovered America in 1492. Lucky numbers: 14, 92. Aquarius. 9:30 to 5:30 Monday to Saturday. Stone: Paper, Scissors.

Churches: Churches can be divided into two types: the correct Catholic ones and the heretical Protestant ones. You will need to be able to tell them apart to avoid accidently meeting any number of Antichrists. The difference is easy to tell. If a church is facing away from the road, this is a guarantee of Protestant evilness. Catholic churches always face towards the road because, as everyone knows, all roads lead to Rome.

CIA: As Michael O'Leary, the *jefe* of Ryanair, has correctly observed, the CIA are only able to undercut Ryanair because of government subsidies. On the other hand, at least the passengers on CIA flights do not expect to clean up after themselves before being taked off the plane. Plus, if the CIA say a flight is going to Tripoli, that's where it goes, not some other dark site you've never not heard of 700 kilometers away.

Cloistermouth, Saint (1977–2008): Not her real name but a pseudonym adopted while working undercover on behalf of the Vatican Police to investigate embezzlement and fraud by manufacturers of liturgical vestments in China. The Vatican had long suspected that the Chinese Communist Party was taking backhanders for certification and export licences of surplices, dalmatics, and cassocks, adding to the prices of said vestments, which they already were inappropriately taxing at the rates for secular garments. Saint Cloistermouth also discovered that the factory owners were adding a so-called "sacralization charge" and diverting part of the payments by the Church into offshore accounts in Taiwan (which should actually belong to Spain). Thus, both the Chinese state and the manufacturers were swindling the Church, which is a mortal sin. The Church could have had have been paying far less for the garments, which was their reason for relocating production to China in the first place; ¿what is the point of cheap labour if you are having a bunch of arbitrary tariffs sprancged on you by the very same cunning and inscrupable Orientals you are trying to exploit? Cloistermouth managed to infiltrate the inner circle of the local CCP mugwumps but was found out by virtue of her overfamiliarity with Party ideology, which rendered her suspicious—nobody in the Party gives a fuck about ideology. She refused to reveal her true identity under torture, which the Chinese are very good at, by the way, and went to her knicker-soiled death as a proud martyr without ever revealing who she was working for. Most of her bones were returned, in pieces, to the Vatican Bank, which is next door to the Vatican Police. Lucky numbers: 4, 206ish. Stone: Jade.

Coal: In my first year at school, was a boy in my class, Felipe Jimenez y Madrigal, who suffered from a very strange illness that gave me nightmares. Was not fair to inflict that on a small boy, I think, and they should have kept him out of school altogether. If I remember correctly, the illness was called Fibrodysplasia Carboniferens. This meant Felipe was very slowly carbonizing, which is, he was turning to coal. A strange-looking boy with dark skin and oily hair and black dandruff. Every school has one. He came into class each day on crutches. Also, he smelled funny. At playtime, he would ignite the gas gived off by his fingertips, although in the summer the school kept him indoors in the fridge because he was a fire hazard. The other children did not pick on him very much, but when they tried, he would defend himself by saying, "In years to come I shall be a giant diamond in the ground while all you people will be just wormfood." Or else he would argue, "I am the next logical step in human evolution." How we all laughed at him. If there was one thing we had learned in school, was that evolution is nonsense.

I Googled him once to discover his fate. He is a milliner in Seville.

Cocaine: Best friend of the riot cop and wife-beater (the Venn diagram is not quite a perfect circle). Whether throwing women, children, and elderly Catalans down the stairs of a voting station or mushing the brains of a student with their baton, is cocaine (but also the protection given by their personal armour, their comrades, and the state) that provides the riot policeman with the necessary courage (he is already having the motivation).

There is a downside to the widespread use of this popular mood enhancer, however. I have seen the indiscipline it introduces into Fascist street gangs and pro-life demonstrations, turning dimwit foot soldiers into unruly yobboes, deluding them into believing they are Nietzschean supermen able to achieve anything they put their mind to when in reality they are sad divorcés living in bedsits with restraining orders. Cocaine may well be a *sine qua non* for a nice day out with their mates and a chance to punch a lesbian, but for the Fascist cause such men are a liability who need to know their proper place, which is dead on a battlefield. Annoyingly, but also understandably, governments much prefer cocaine to be the drug of choice among white boys—rather than ecstasy and cannabis, which do nothing but corrupt the nation's morale with love, solidarity, and tolerance—because it encourages aggression and stupidity, but it also comes with a lack of self-control that constantly requires direction and distraction.

The True Fascist does not need drugs. Compare the amphetamine-soaked Nazis of Hitler's Luftwaffe with Franco's legionnaires, many of whom forswore the mechanical assistance of air support, running into battle drug-free and naked, a fishknife clenched between their teeth so that they might do battle *mano a mano*, see the fear in their enemy's eyes, and display their erect manhood at the moment of gutting. Such men did not need drugs, only obedience to their superiors, a God-fearing sense of human worthlessness, and devotion to a cause they didn't even need to understand. ¿Where are the men like that today? In prison, probly.

Cockneys: Is the name for Londoners born within the sounds of the Bow bells. Easily confused with Cuntneys.

Church bells are particularly important to Cockneys because the ringing helps them find their way home during daylight hours when they are blind drunk and cannot see. For Cockney children, there is a mnemonic nursery rhyme which makes it easier for them to remember which bells is which after a night on the tiles.

Oranges and berries
Say the bells of Saint Jerry's.

You owe me five guineas,
Say the bells of Saint Winnie's

¿When will I get them?
Says the old bell of Streatham

Whenever I fancy
Say the bells of Saint Nancy

¿Could you be more precise?
Say the bells of Pat Rice

When I am dead
Say the bells of Saint Fred

Here comes the bailiff to enforce the court order
Here come the heavies to carry out murder
Chip shop, chip shop, we all fall down.

Colonic Irrigation: The Californian approach to dieting, involving the evacuation of partially digested matter using hosepipes inserted rectally. Independently invented by my sister and myself during our childhood games.

Colonies: Like charity, a waste of good money and intentions. Was a mess before we went in, was a mess after we left. That says it all. Some well-meaning but foolish empires are *still* learning this fact of life about inferior races.

Colorado: In the U.S. state of Colorado, is illegal to pull faces at waffles.

Communion Wafer: Every Sunday morning before Mass, Candelaría would leap out of her basket and sing, "¡My favourite flavour crisp is Jesus!"

Communism: The purest and highest form of Masonic thought and ideology, aiming at the destruction of all nation-states so that the peoples of the world are made rootless and interchangeable. Communism devours countries from within by pitting class against class, attempting to dissolve borders between countries, like a cell-bursting virus, in order to produce a one-world government run by the "chosen people," namely, the Illuminati, including the False Pope, the George Bushes, Osama bin Laden, the House of Saud, John Le Carré, Emperor Hirohito, and the dairy industry (Big Cheese). Not all Masons are Communists but all Communists are Masons, except for the ones who are Cyclists. This is why the Communist flag is a hammer and cycle. There are seventeen billion cycles in Beijing.

Compromise: Only the weak seek compromise.

Condnoms: The brand name of flavoured condoms. Oddly, the most popular Condnom worldwide is spunk flavour.

Condoms: In talks with my old friend Frank Prendergast (DEP), I learned that Holy Scripture allows the use of condoms but only by mules, when they are traveling between countries. Frank explained to me one day over the bottom of a prostitute off whom he was snorting some of my lovely nose candy that this is an especial dispensation because the mules are sterile anyway and not able to reproduce, and also because they need to have some way to smuggle their drugs past customs; consequently, is acceptable for them to put drugs inside condoms and then swallow them or insert them into their rectum using their own or someone else's fingers. Otherwise, the use of condoms is strictly forbidden.

This is a shame. Think, for instance, of poor Saint Teresa of Ávila, who had to walk around all day with a mouthful of leper's diarrhoea. If only she had been allowed to put it in a condom or, better still, a condnom, she wouldn't have had to spend all her pocket money on Listerine.

Confession: ¡Think how much the CIA would love to be having such a reliable form of intelligence gathering as the confession booth! Priests don't even have to use the waterboard or the thumb screws or the rack to extract a confession from someone, although this also explains why the CIA gets more applicants than the priesthood.

Conspiracy Theories: There is a secret global alliance of Freemasons, Jews, atheists, and Communists, the sole purpose of which is to undermine belief in conspiracy theories.

Corrida: Alongside total war, the corrida is the finest cultural expression of the art of killing. Confined these days to animals, in order to spare the delicate sensitivities of our beautiful Spanish women, in the old days, before feminism reared its ugly head and we were forced to allow women into the bullring, was acceptable to make naked prisoners do battle for their freedom or else two oiled anarchist whores fight to the death with scissors. I saw my first dead man in Las Ventas, our local corrida in Madrid, at the age of nine. He was slouching in a corner of the toilets. My father brought me in to see him.

Courgettes: Fry them and drizzle them with palm honey to make a tasty treat, or strap two courgettes to your feet to support your weight in the snow, giving you a fighting chance of reaching neutral Switzerland.

Crisps, Cheese y Onion: Not just a superfood but also a life-saving comestible. Rustle a bag of cheese y onion crisps to attract the attention of an usher in the cinema if the person next to you is having a cardiac arrest or has a knife at your throat or his hand inside your bra. If that fails, eat the crisps and breathe on him.

Cronaldo, The Wizard: A grotesque man-child and therefore the embodiment of the ultimate sportsman. An ethereal wingéd wonder possessing the feet of a ballerina with Saint Vitus's Dance, a maniac diarrhoea of the feet that shits all over defenders. The closest I have been to heaven in my lifetime was receiving oral sex while watching a trade unionist being murdered at a book burning in Toledo, but the second closest was watching the Wizard Cronaldo dribble and spit on Barcelona in the Santiago Bernabéu, his sublime ugliness the epitome of Iberian Fascist manhood. We tend to forget that the leaders of the Nationalist crusade were without exception ugly men—Mola, Franco, Millán-Astray, and cetera. They reveled in their ugliness because it showed to the world that outward appearance meant nothing to them. They had no vanity whatsoever. Each was a Man of Action, a man with a job to do. They went from killing to killing, battle to battle, with no quarter or thought gived to the latest victim. Women were not to be seduced by good looks and charm but to be taked by force if necessary and also sometimes if unnecessary. So, too, Cronaldo, when he was scoring a goal, proudly displayed his lack of vanity and rubbed his enemy's nose in his contempt for them. Not only have you been humiliated, he would say, ripping off his cheap polyester shirt to show his deformed body, scarred by a million half-time flagellations, but you have been humiliated by *this*, by a Portuguese ladyboy with the legs of a greyhound and the face also of a greyhound, but a different greyhound, with the smile of a third greyhound inside the face of the second one.

He is the perfect messiah for the consumer age. Even his name says so, combining as it does the name of Christ, the chosen one, with Ronaldo, the McDonald's clown.

Cucumber: A useless vegetable frequently possessed by evil spirits. In Galicia last year, an entire field of cucumbers was found to be possessed by demons. A local schoolboy who ate one of the cucumbers for a dare was himself possessed and grew a pair of flesh spectacles and an external stomach. Ritual exorcism usually works on cucumbers, but when it does not, Catholic charities export them to Africa as food aid.

Cuthbun, Saint (1111–1155): The Sage of Reims. It was Cuthbun who proved that an ethical code lacking an epistemological foundation is just as valid as one with such a foundation, providing that its premises are sound. This allowed him to generate an entirely brilliant and internally coherent two-volume exposition on the soul and its obligations, *Do What God Says, Not What God Does*. Canonization was to follow from reports of his involvement in a number of minor miracles, including making a pea disappear and reappear under walnut shells, which miracle he used to demonstrate the resurrection of both Lazarus and Christ Jesus, Lord God, King of Kings; the miracle of the detachable thumb; and the Feeding of the Thirty, when he miraculously fed an entire funeral party with three loaves of bread, some fishes, two amphoras of wine, olive oil, *mayonesa*, and some more bread and fishes.

Cycling: Too much cycling can lead to erectile dysfuction and a decline in sperms counting. The reason is, apparently, that the bicycle saddle restricts the blood flow around the Scrotal Sac, which is in Derbyshire, and the penis, resulting in numbness, Blue John, and no fun getting it up. Of course, the research is inconclusive, having been carried out on hamsters in wheels and gerbils on tricycles, but there is a lesson to be learned here and I will teach it you.

As you might have had guessed, this is yet another problem for which we can blame Modernism. Thanks to the muddly thinking of Enlightenment ideologs which resulted in the so-called Scientific Method, the world has been inundated over the last 200 years by all sorts of new-fangled inventions and contraptions, such as the penicillin, television, toilet paper, the condom, GM food, helicopters, the DX4 T109 ruthenium oxide cryogenic temperature sensor, car parks, Jamie Lee Curtis, and bingo. This has led to people getting feeble and weak and soft and decadent. Nature no longer weeds out the infirm; thanks to "science," the inferior members of the species are able to survive burst appendixes, heart attacks, stroking, fatness, being American, and death. Thus, human genetic inheritance has been gradually enfeebilizing and our sperm are committing suicide rather than produce another lazy fat baby.

This is in stark contrast to the days when I was a young boy in the 1950s. How well I remember the cycle rides on which the priests used to take all the young boys around Teruel. ¿Do you think we had saddles back in those days? ¡We did not! No one had invented them yet. Instead, we had to sit on the upright post, which was inserted inside us by the priest using special holy lubrication, before we set on our way. And at the end of the day's cycling, the priest would also do a sperm count of every boy. Not one of us ever failed, and that was because of the fresh air, the harsh discipline, the lack of material comforts, and our superiors' devotion to piety. You would not see this kind of thing today, not even on YouTube. I know. I have done a search.

Cynicism: A defense mechanism: of the weak against hope, of the immature against discovery, of the powerless against their responsibilities. Not all cowards are cynics, but all cynics are cowards. Or the other way round. Whichever.

D

Dalí, Salvador: A wonderful Spanish painter and knockabout comedian. Also a fabulous raconteur and wit, a good patriotic Spaniard most famous for living in a house with eggs on top, sunny side out.

Dalí gave the world many surreal paintings, as well also many religious paintings, but always included in them a portrait of his gorgeous wife, Gala, whom he loved so much that one time he sodomized her in the grounds of the Prado. Round the back.

Some of the surrealists accused Dalí of selling out, and others accused him of cashing in. He did not mind because, by definition, whatever he did, he could claim he was being surreal, which made him very difficult to pin down, like a butterfly with a gun. Or a moth with shurikens. Like a moth with shurikens, however, Dalí could not resist the spotlight, which was how the Ninjas found and assassinated him to get their shurikens back. Which genuinely *was* surreal.

Dancing: Originally confined to the royal courts and nobility, where it served as an early form of "conspicuous consumption" (before the coin was phrased), a display of wealth which demonstrated to one's peers the possession of sufficient free time to learn steps, forms, and patterns of no practical use whatsoever. Only the very wealthiest was having the time to waste on pointless activities; thus, displaying adeptness in the dance was a way of claiming the right to membership of the elite, in the same way that a second home in the sun, skiing holidays, and a mistress later became markers of status among the professional classes; proof of money to throw away on frivolities. Such displays were reminiscent of the Native American potlatch, in which tribal chiefs burned all their worldly goods in the presence of other chiefs, not to demonstrate that material possessions meant nothing to them but to show how much wealth they could dispose of and replace through the fertility of their lands, labour of their minions, or prowess of their warriors.

Mechanization, modernity, and, most of all, trade unions was responsible for bringing music and dancing within the grasp of the proletariat, thanks to gramophones, radio, and a reduction in the 110-hour working week, giving the masses ideas above their station and transforming a marker of exclusivity into a mockery of their masters. Whenever a peasant or worker dances today, he is delivering a direct insult to his masters, rubbing their noses in his black bottom, jazz hands, jitterybug, gay gordons, mush pit, or boogie-woogie. No responsible person would ever be caught engaging in such undignified manifestations of proletarian preening and arrogance. And any dictatorship worth its salt would immediately stomp down on all such provocations. Non-rhythmicly.

Dancing, Latin: Is what middle-age women do rather than buy a classic sports car.

Dar Riffien: The location of the headquarters of the Spanish Foreing Legion. Is in Morocco. Was from here that El Generalísimo Francisco Franco launched his *cruzada* to save Spain. Is now a neglected site, but visitors can still go there to pay homage, sit out of an evening, and listen to the wind blowing through the hoopoes.

Darwinism: Is no wonder that Darwin saw so little difference between human beings and monkeys if all he had to go on was the English.

Deafness: In this day and age, a blessing. Like virginity, deafness is not something to be too readily surrendered. Deaf virgins are blessed twice over.

Death: No death could be more beautiful than that of a Spanish soldier surrendering his life on the battlefield for his Fatherland. Is true that this is a death afforded very few men these days and rarely even contemplated, yet one need only reflect for a moment to understand what we have lost. Picture yourself in your glorious hessian Spanish uniform, outside in the sunshine, breathing in the lovely fresh air, your hands desperately clutching for the Spanish soil that gave birth to you, the earthy smell in your nostrils of gunpowder, hot shrapnel, and excrement, your comrades lying around you bleeding their last, thinking of how their sweethearts will miss them or else crying for their mothers or trying to locate their thumbs. ¿What could possibly be more noble, more inspiring?

I pity the young men of today, who are not having the same opportunities as their ancestors. We could almost do with another civil war, like the one they are praying for in America.

Death, Black: Is always amusing for me the story of the Flagellants in middle-aged Germany, who was devout idiots traveling from village to village while flogging themselves, and possibly one another, in order to atone for their sins and lift the curse of the Plague, which God had have so righteously inflicted on them. Like all bed-wetting liberal do-gooders, the Flagellants sought to take the sins of others upon themselves in order to save them, asking the Lord to forgive each village as they passed through. At the ringing of the bell and the sound of flailing flesh, all the villagers would come out to witness the expiation, and in the process they all became infected by the illness that the Flagellants were unstintingly spreading around the entire country in the bloodspritz of their lashings and their sweat and also their tears. ¿Who says God is not having a sense of humour?

Similar to this, when the New Rabies arrived in Fuerteventura, the Policia Local went from door to door to tell people to paint a big X on their house if it contained a gambie. Although nobody was in danger of catching the illness through inhalation, this was a way of letting the neighbours know that they should wear gloves and thick coats when visiting to avoid being bitten. And also not to be having their cock out when knocking on the door. Mind you, this policy was only introduced after the hospitals had already filled up and the Ayuntamiento needed people to care for their gambies at home, arguing that people exhibiting only mild symptoms of rabies—frothing at the lips, convulsions, barking—could be cared for by their elderly parents or small children. Not until the unwiseliness of this policy was understood and whole households, and then whole streets, became rabid did the Ayuntamiento instead advise families to adopt a more hands-off approach, which is why infectious relatives were then taked to the city limits and left outside the towns until a cure could be found. And only then did they come to be called "gambies." Because under the unrelenting attention of the African Sun, they all turned bright pink like frying *gambas a la plancha* and because, in their delirium, they wandered the plains and mountains like zombies; hence gambies. They are not real, proper, authentic zombies, though, because rather than being dead they are only experiencing a kind of suspenseful animation. Their brains fry and frazzle under the Sun but they are still alive and resemble normal human beings, even to the extent of being a threat to others until either killed or cured. We must wait to see which is the lesser of two evils, kill or cure. I know what I think.

Democracy: A crime against God and Nature, and which always ends in tears or rule by morons.

There is no democracy in Heaven.

Descanso: One of the most horrifying aspects of rabies, new and old alike, and which often tips people's opinion on the "kill or cure" dilemma, is that every so often the victims of the illness experience a break in their delirium, a rest or lull that Spanish doctors refer to as the *descanso*, which translates in English literally to an "interval," "rest," or "pause." Normally, the *descanso* lasts only an hour or two, but is long enough for the victim to remember what is happening to them. When the disease first arrived on the island and the victims received treatment in the hospital and emergency medical centres, many victims tried to kill themselves during the *descanso* or else pleaded with the nurses to kill them. This was hugely traumatic for the patients but also for the medical staff, who were used to dealing only with mountain bike injuries or jellyfish stings. Thankfully, the influx of patients soon overwhelmed the capacity of the medical services to cope, and after the fiasco of the Ayuntamiento's at-home care policy, the decision was taked only to treat victims in the early stages of the illness in order to prepare them for release into the wild; nearly one quarter of the population was infected by that point, so dealing with the disease had become a matter of peaceful co-existence between the infected and normal people.

No doubt the *descanso* is disorientating and alarming for the gambie. Imagine suddenly coming out of your delirium and finding yourself lying in a grove of agave plants or squatting naked on a beach in the midst of a thousand rabid gambie surfers or awakening to discover yourself on the side of a mountain in the middle of nowhere beneath the statue of Miguel Unamuno, an individual unfamiliar even to the Spanish these days, let alone hydrophobic Belgian pensioners. No matter how idyllic the moonrise looks over Tindaya, you will drop to your knees with a howl and beg for delirium to overwhelm you once more. Even for someone like me, who has devoted his career to eliciting screams that will cut the blood of lesser men, the sound of those howls across the desert at dusk is shudder inducing. Which is why, despite the raging heat of this island, the double-glazing industry is doing so well here.

The word "*descanso*" also is having a second but no less pertinent meaning. It refers to those periods when the mourners carrying the coffin in a funeral procession place the coffin down on the ground to take a breather or smoke a cigarette. In some respects, this meaning is similar to the first, in the sense that, in taking a break from their labours, the mourners are having a chance to appreciate the full horror of their situation, to reflect on life and death, on the fact that they are transporting to his grave one of their number—perhaps one who had himself previously been their comrade in the transporting of other bodies—and thus that the next time they attend a funeral it might be their own. The French tubercular playboywrighter Albert Camus offered us a rosier analogy of the *descanso* in his work *El mito de Sísifo*, which he based on an ancient Greek tale. The ancient Greek gods had condemned Sísifo to push a boulder up to the top of a mountain in the Underworld for eternity, with no slaves, burros, or pulley mechanism to help him, and every time he reached to the top of the mountain, because the peak was very pointy, the boulder rolled all the way down to the bottom and Sísifo had have to begin all over again. Camus argued that even though an eternity of futile labour might seem like a harsh punishment, Sísifo was lucky because, as he ambled back down the mountain to retrieve the boulder, he had an opportunity to reflect on life, to enjoy the view, to engage in philosophy, and even to laugh—yes, laugh—at the absurdity of his situation. This is Camus' stupid message to humanity. Even though you have to get up every day and push your own particular boulder up the mountain, you are still having the leisure time, "on the way back down," in which to reflect on and even laugh at the absurdity and futility of your situation. Of course, what Camus forgot to take into consideration is that, for Sísifo, philosophizing is a way of occupying his time, an amusement, a distraction, because he had have been condemned to roll his boulder for eternity, whereas when the mourners put down their comrade's coffin and light up their Fortunas, the inevitable focus of their thoughts will be that they too will be dead soon and won't not be ambling *nowhere*. The *descanso* they confront is less like Camus' French festival of philosophical fun and more like American analfan William Burroughs's *Naked Lunch*, in which the innocent and naïve luncher of the title is suddenly confronted with "what is on the end of his fork," namely, dead meat. Which is, in truth, the fate of us all. The formidable Nazi anti-thinker Martin Heidegger referred to this moment as the *Augenblick*, a moment of searing clarity in which we see the truth of existence as it really is. A visceral claustrophobic terror rises up in the heart of the luncher, of the coffin carrier, at the realization that they are trapped, that there is no escape from this singular, contingent, absurd existence, except for their inevitable death. This is what the gambie feels, what the philosopher endures, what the coffin dodger attempts to deny.

For devout and devoted Catholics, of course, the *Augenblick* holds no such horrors. After all, like Sísifo, we have the promise of eternal life, guaranteed for us by God Himself, and with no boulder pushing involved. We are not afraid of death, whether our own or others'. ¡Indeed, we delight in it! Only those idiots who believe that God does not exist are forced to endure the consequences of their own flawed logic. And well for them. They deserve nothing better. Whereas, I have no doubt, that if I ever became a gambie, I would find the *descanso* nothing more than an inconvenience, perhaps even a curiosity: "Hmm, I wonder where I'm going to wake up today." Not that I encourage curiosity, you understand, and perhaps it would be better that there be no *descanso* at all, no time to pointless thinking or having of ideas. Those gambies who have been out in the Sun a few months, who remain in a state of delirium even when the *descanso* arrives, their brains having had been frazzled for so long with sunburn, sunstroke, heatstroke, breaststroke, and cetera, perhaps they are better off than the rest of us. Perhaps. Is always more preferable not to have to think, don't you think, since there is nothing to be gained from it but worry. A True Fascist never worries.

Deus Ex Machina: A Latin phrase which means "¿What would Jesus drive?" We know the answer because the Bible says he is in his Seat at God's right hand.

Dignity, Human: A myth, an illusion, a construct of the so-called Enlightenment. The human body shits, farts, sweats, exudes, oozes, ejaculates, vomits, bleeds, breaks, pisses, spits, coughs, wheezes, belches, hiccups, sneezes, and generates fifty-seven different types of pus, just like Heinz. ¿What is dignified about that? Dignity comes to humans only in the manner of their departing this life, best of all on the battlefield, dying a glorious death for the Fatherland (or Motherland if you come from one of those gay countries like Russia). Women, needless to say, never have this opportunity and so are always both without dignity and indignant. Especially at me for expressing this unplatable truth.

Dinosaurs: Absence of evidence of absence is evidence of presence. The historian Edward Gibbon once observed that we know the Koran is an authentic Arab work because not once is there any mention of camels. Camels was so much a part of the landscape that they didn't merit being commented on. Similarly, the absence of any mention of dinosaurs in the Bible demonstrates that there was undoubtably dinosaurs around in Jesus's time. Nobody taked a blind bit of notice of them because they was so commonplace. This is incontrovertible proof that men and dinosaurs once lived alongside each other. ¡Quod Erat Diplodocum!

Disguise: The famous theologian and logic chopper (although he used a razor and so took longer) William of Ockham famously argued that identities should not be replicated beyond necessity. This was his proof that there is only one God, the Catholic one. This proof also offers a lesson for spies: do not multiply your identities beyond necessity. The more disguises you are having, the more difficult it becomes to remember who you are. ¿Should you be wearing a moustache today? ¿Should your accent be Galician or Asturian? ¿How many legs are you having? Thus, while aliases are handy for banking and accumulating passports, too many disguises can render you vulnerable to exposure if people get to know one of you very well. To be a brilliant master spy, you must either be an instinctive and accomplished liar with a very good memory or else suffer from multiple personality disorder. Most spies are the former, but the latter require less training and thus are attractive to poorer countries such as Britain which like to spy on the cheap. And on the poor.

Disgust: The basis of all forms of civilization. The Polish language is not having a word for "disgust," which explains Polish cuisine.

Disgusting: The fundamental reality of human existence.

D.I.Y.: I have never been a great fan of Doing-It-Yourself around the house, both for practical and ideological reasons. Ideologicly, the D.I.Y. is an attitude synomynous with anarchism, exemplified by the punk rocking, fanzines, blogging, and masturbation. In Spain, this approach reached its apogee with the anarcho-syndicalist CNT and autonomous self-serving workers' organizations who didn't think it through and probly were expecting the landowners to pick their own bloody fruit. When D.I.Y. was revived in the seventies, despite Franco doing all he could to suppress it, it taked the form of ordinary idiot plebs deciding that they were no longer willing to pay self-employed plumbers, carpenters, builders, and cetera—the beating heart and fist of the Fascist demographic, let me remind you—for shoddy workmanship and a cunty attitude. Consequently, there was opening all these megastores such as Bricolemar, Leroy Merlin, Home Despot, Atlantic Homeboy, and, in Ireland, Hoodies, to cater for proletarian truculence. Also on the television was such shows as *Home Improvement, Tomorrow's World, Kitchen Impossible,* and *Upstairs and Downstairs,* all of which was intent on turning the men and women of Europe into atheist communist autonomous revolutionaries. Every Sunday, which is God's day, no less, men and women with hate in their eyes and dogs in their cars would drive to these suspicious out-of-town meeting places where they would congregate, plot revolution, buy nailguns and grout, and then return to their homes and put honest decent Christian small businessmen out of work. For this was their devious plan, the Why in their D.I.Y., a noxious conspiracy to break the petty bourgeoisie and draw them back into the seething proletarian mass, thereby polarizing society into decent God-fearing wealthy hacienda owners on the one hand and, on the other, the scum, the rabble, the mob.

Out of principle, therefore, I have never done a proper day's work in my life, choosing instead to employ others, lackeys of some sort or other, to do it for me. I have deliberately avoided learning how to turn taps on and off, change a plug in my bath, empty my jacuzzi, open an oven (¡or close it, obviously!), exchange lightbulbs, or flush a toilet.

I am also having a practical objection to D.I.Y., which is that it requires learning things: ¿Who has the time to learn things?

Doggers: Pound-Shop J. G. Ballards. I am having no idea what this means.

Dog, Washed: "A washed dog would look coquettish to a Protestant." Old French saying.

Domestic Bliss: The Beast with Three Fingers had no luck in Morro Jable. His assumption that I would attempt to hide among the throngs of South American immigrant workers servicing the bloated, decrepit German "expat" community was without foundation—reality defeating another CIA fieldcraft assumption. The realization that this impetuosity had not only cost him time but had also allowed me to initiate my defensive strategy must have been a source of much frustration to him. His partner, a retired MI6 pansexual of repulsive androgyny and obsequiousness, tried his best to provide consolation, but Americans are nothing if not petulant and persistent. I already knew he would not give up easily.

An essential element of Operation Oystercatcher, as I had called my plan, involved ensuring that Candelaría would be safely disposed of, by which I mean removed to a place of safety rather than buried in concrete like nuclear waste. Thus, that Sunday, after we had enjoyed our traditional roast chicken dinner, I pulled out her operational folder and proceeded through the steps we had agreed upon for her departure and concealment. Laying out a map of England on the dining room table — secured at each corner by an upturned *chupito* glass — I identified for her the principal towns and routes of travel. She frowned with attention as she followed my fingers.

"So, you can see here, this big dark area, this is London. Stay away from London. You might think there is safety in numbers, but you are more likely to meet and converse with Americans here, so your conversations will be insecure. Also, London is a stinkhole of sin and degradation, a colon of semi-digested detritus, a faecal feast, a bottomless pit of rotten, decaying, subhuman subcultures. Everything in London has a price, which means you must be using your credit card, and if you use your credit card, they can find you."

"I will avoid London. Stinkhole." She was saying it for her own benefit rather than mine. With a black marker, I wiped the Greater London area from the map. If only it were so easy.

"This area here, the Southeast Coast, the East Coast, this is where they will be expecting you to land. Dover, Felixstowe, Harwich. These are routes the refugees and asylum seekers use. The security will be tighter here, and facial recognition technology will pick you out at 200 meters, especially with your face. It would be better for you to arrive from the north or from the west. Through Scotland, Ireland, Iceland. Scandinavia. The Shetlands."

She sniggered.

"¿There is a place called the Shitlands?"

"Shetlands, you cretin. Islands north of Scotland. Not on this map. There are some security risks for you if you approach from that direction but there is not blanket coverage."

I blacked out the East and Southeast.

"This is Brighton. Full of homosexuals. Avoid."

"¿What is homosexuals?"

"¿You don't remember? I showed you last week." Blankness. "No matter. We decided you wouldn't like them. They will stick things in you and steal your soul."

She made her expression for horror. I blacked out Brighton.

"In fact, now I think of it, don't go to any of these places down here. Eastbourne, Hastings, Worthing, the Isle of Wight. Awful people. You will be sick."

I amended the map accordingly.

"Everywhere else here is okay. Full of English people, but okay."

"That is Fuerteventura," she said.

"Ha ha." I was surprised to hear her make a joke. "Yes, is similar. Full of English people, but fewer Germans and Italians, and much colder."

"No," she said. "The shape. Now you have oblit the right side of the map, the rest of the country is looking like Fuerteventura." I squinted.

"Hah, I see that. How amusing. Perhaps you can use that as a reminder. So long as you are in Fuerteventura, you are safe."

"And if I go into the black bits, I will drown, because that is the sea."

"Yes. A black sea of snakes and Cockneys."

"¿Cockneys?"

"The worst kind of knees."

"¿Really?" She looked confused. "¿Wouldn't that be cuntneys?"

"Cockneys, cuntneys. Same thing," I said. Is true.

Later, as Candelaría washed my penis in the bath—something my father would once have ovened me for, even though Candelaría never objected, calling it my "button mushroom" (I have always thought of it as more poisonous, like a toad's tool)—she recited for me, falteringly, since multitasking was new to her but a vital survival skill she would need to acquire, the addresses of all the safe houses available to our assets in the northwest and southwest of England, refuges of last resort should she find herself pursued by malefactors or lesbians.

"Gived what has happened with Brexit," I said calmly, "I recommend not speaking to English people unless absolutely necessary."

She handed me the bottle of bubble-gum-scented bath suds, bored with the conversation and with stretching my foreskin.

"Roll my boobies."

I poured the day-glo pink soap into one palm and smeared it over her hefty, bulging fatbags. Nipples woke up. I massaged the soap into a lather.

"You need to pay attention," I scolded her. "Is important that you don't attract unnecessary attention to yourself. The English like to think that they are tolerant, but they can sense foreigners at 400 paces. Is genetic. The unavoidable consequence of the inbreeding of an island nation. We normal people stick out like a ... erm ..."

"A penis in bathwater," she suggested.

"Penguin in a barnyard, I was going to say, but the analogy holds. The English don't like anything that tests their cognitive load. Their excuse is 'being practical' or 'common sense' but it's just indolence. Don't misunderstand me. I despise intellectuals as much as the next man, but we Spanish, our genius lies in not needing book learning or higher education in order to be original or to develop a sense of the transcendent. ¿What else is *duende*, after all? We are having the Church. We are having the Falange. Style, flair, flamenco, the Imperious Zidane: They are in our blood. ¿What are the English having? ¿Fucking rugby? ¡Pfah! Only the English could turn concussion into a sport. This is why they are such dullards. But also why they can spot us so easily. Anything that suggests novelty or difference is like a midnight car alarm to their sleepy brains."

I had carried myself away on an oratorical flight of fancy, failing to check whether Candelaría was following me. When my flourishes elicited no response, I realized I had lost her. She had lapsed into a state of near ecstasy, not from my rhetoric, nor even from my massage, but from inhaling the bubble-gum foam bath straight from the bottle. Her rheumy eyes had rolled back in her head as she contemplated some distant imbecility, soap running from both nostrils like pink snot where she had sniffed it.

"Of course. ¿What am I thinking?" I said, mostly to myself. "There is nothing to worry about. You will fit right in."

Donnybrook: The nice part of Dublin where I used to live in my fashionable *pied-à-terre*, the French word for foot-potato. Was a bit noisy and grimy, but that is Dublin for you. Donnybrook is famous for rugby and television, but also for the regular fights that used to break out on its market day; the word "Donnybrook" has even passed into the English language to mean a scrap, a bit of argy-bargy, like also the word "Fisticuff," after the violent port town in Brittany.

Donuts, Ring: If you break the rowlocks on your boat while sailing single-handily across the Atlantic, stale ring donuts will suffice for the first 300 miles, enough to get you to Iceland. Or away from Iceland.

Doo-Dah, Doo-dah: Camptown ladies sing this song.

Drains: In Greece, the drains smell of sex. In Amsterdam, they smell of abortions.

Drogo, Saint (1105–1186): The patent saint of cows, coffee drinkers, and the ugly. I am not sure that cows take up much of Saint Drogo's time because they are not fond of praying. The ugly, on the other hand, are notorious pests, and coffee-drinking ugly people must be the bane of his existence. Lucky numbers: 2. Stone: Coffee beans.

Drool: Women derive no sexual pleasure from seeing a man drool. Is why women invented the doggy-style position. She can get on with reading (or writing) her crime novels or knitting and doesn't even have to make eye contact with her slobbering husband, safe in the knowledge that he is completely hypnotized by her shitter.

Drugs: While I was running the main cocaine trafficking route through West Cork, twenty kilograms went missing from the main police station in Fermoy. At the time, it was under lock and quay in a van as part of a haul of 427 kilos taked from my main rivals—the Fowlers—as a result of a tip-off I had provided to the Gardaí. Because the van was in police custody at the time of the disappearance, the police had to interrogate each other as to their whereabouts on the day in question and then lead them to the cells for anal searches and beatings with rubber truncheons. Then, I am telled, they swapped round and taked turns.

If I recall correctly from my inside source, no one noticed the disappearance of the twenty kilos for four days. Which is easily enough time to get it up your nose. Or else up the noses of several construction-industry executives and high-profile senators in Knockmerry House. But I am only using that as an example, you understand. ¡I don't know nothing about where it really went!

Drunkirk: A small French coastal town where the British Expeditionary Force running away from the Germans discovered to their delight that French wine cost twopence a bottle. The British was forced to evacuate on fishing boats, so drunk that they couldn't stand up straight, puking all the way back to Dover. The British today herald the evacuation as a great victory, commemorating it every year by staggering en masse along European streets at two in the morning like they've been shot.

Dulux of the Light, Saint (1014–1034): Martyred by having his skin stripped off in one piece and then being dragged back and forth across the walls of Jerusalem. Real correct name: Matt Finnish. Reliquary of his skin last seen in Salonika, Greece, 1943. Mostly Aquarius. Lucky numbers: 70BB 21/147, 30GY 44/248. Stone: Horsehair.

Dutch, The: Science cannot explain why Protestant nations are taller than Catholic nations. The reason is so that their heads remain above the surface of the fiery lakes of Hell and the Pious in Heaven can revel in their screams.

Dylan, Robert "Bob" (1945–2012): Filthy 1960s protest singer, writer of such hits as "Wichita Grub Man," "Masters in War," and "All along the Clocktower." Dylan has been the recipient of the Nobel Peace Prize and also the more important Prince of Asturias Art Award, which recognizes extremely rich celebrities who the committee would like to be associated with. Other contestants the year he won included architect Frank Gehry and farming impresario Andrew Lloyd-Webber. Previous winners have included Yo-Yo Ma (violinist), Ricky Martin (crooner), and Adolf Hitler (painter).

The awards such as this always make me feel slightly queasy. Is inappropriate, I think, for royalty to be attempting to curry favour with their minions by attaching themselves to "popular" entertainers in this way. Once upon a time, singers would have felt themselves lucky to be performing in front of royalty. They was expected to wear Motley and make jokes and could even be garrotted if their performance did not please the monarch. Nowadays instead we are having the heir to the throne of Spain trying to be trendy and demonstrate his democratic credentials by pandering to the lowest common denominator and pretending to like foreingers.

The responsibility for all this stupidity lies with Dead Princess Lady Diana Spencer, who used her marriage into the British royal family as a way of meeting her heroes: Status Quo, Wayne Sleep, Steve Hillage, Captain Beefheart. In the process, she dragged through the mud the quiet dignity of a proud monarchy, including stoical social drinker/gambler the Queen Mother, plainspoken aristocratic Duke of Edinburgh, utter cunt Prince Andrew, and her fat-fingered useless adulterous husband, Prince Charles, the man who would be tampon.

¿Do you remember the big funeral they held to celebrate Princess Diana's death? Was the height of vulgarity. The fact that she was the

"People's Princess" tells you all you need to know about the people. I was not watching the funeral myself, but I am telled that Elton John sang his famous hit "Candle with the Wind," which went straight to number one in the hit charts because English people love funeral dirges and play them at all their parties. Then he followed up with "Rocket Man" and "Goodbye Yellow Brick Road," but he changed the words to set it in Paris.

Is ironic, I think, that Lady Di was funeraled in Saint Paul's Cathedral, the same place where she was married only months before, and also where she conceived her first child (which was required by an arcane British royal tradition, but the baby was a girl, so they killed it in a Satanic ritual and hushed it up). Of course, nobody remembers her for that. Everybody still thinks of her as an innocent and dim childminder slaughtered on the altar of *noblesse oblige* and *droit de seigneur*. What they forget is how she stained and besmirched the nobility of a once-mighty household with her low-brow culture and love of landmines. I only hope we are not too late to save the Borbóns from a similar fate, but I am not holding my breath.

E

Easter: In pious lovely holy pissing Ireland, it was always being a tradition at Eastertime to give a choice to selected petty criminals: 200 hours of community service or one day on the cross in the local pageant. A great many chose the cross; community service is a pain on the hole. However, the petty criminal was not telled until later that the traditional Irish public is also let throw rotten tomatoes and eggs at him on the cross, just like the Protestants did to Jesus (they cannot spear a stick in his side, though, because it would leave the council vulnerable to litigious messiahs).

Easter is the big festival for Christians, much bigger in a religious sense than Christmas, which was only Jesus's birth. However, you would not know this from all the kerfuffle that happens every December. ¿Why is Michael Bublé bringing out records at Christmas but not at Easter? I will tell you why. Because songs about tiny babies are sweet, whereas songs about blood, gore, and sacrifice are popular only with neo-Nazi skinheads and death metal acne-ridden teenagers is why. Perhaps the executives at his record company are so stuck-up that they think he doesn't need those demographics.

The reason for the choice offered to petty Irish criminals is in commemoration of the choice gived by Pontius Pirate to the crowd in Jerusalem. He asked them, "¿Whom will you have me release: Barrabarabbas or The King of the Jews?" (Barrabarabbas was an early exponent of surf music around Galilee, while Jesus was a sort of Aramaic Elvis.) The stupid moron unhip crowd plumped for Barrabarabbas, meaning no more gigs for Jesus, like the famous wedding cabaret at Cana or the open-air Sermon on the Mount, both of which was sellouts.

And herein lies the meaning of Easter, which everyone is forgetting, even though you will see it in all the football stadiums in America on handwritten signs held aloft by Born-again Protestant nutters: "John 3:16." This is a reference to a verse in the Bible:

"For God so loved the world, that he gave his only begotten Son, that whosoever believeth in him should not perish but be having everlasting life."

At least, this is what the stupid King James English version of the Bible says. What the original, Spanish Bible says is "For God so loved the world, that he *almost* gave his only begotten son ...."

¡Yes! ¡Is true! Because if you check your Bible, God clearly changed his mind after Jesus had been dead for three days and resurrected him to go up to Heaven in his Seat. If God had truly given up his son, Jesus would still be decomposing in his cave to this day, tucked up in the Turin Shroud like a good boy.

What actually happened but they don't like to tell you is that God was having second thoughts and said to himself, "These human beings, they are despicable pieces of shit. They don't deserve to be having my son to take away their sins through his death. Besides, I am missing Jesus. He was great fun at the parties and bar mitzvahs." So he made Jesus better again and brought him back up to Heaven.

This is the *real* true meaning of Easter: Human beings are despicable pieces of shit and generally not worthy of going to Heaven. They must repent for being born and engage in severe self-punishment, including a lot of praying and kneeling, eating fish, and abstaining from all pleasures of the flesh, especially sex, which makes people particularly unworthy of entering Heaven, where there is no sex at all and angels are androgynous fashion-model types with wings and unisex names like Leslie and Hilary and Moroni.

Some people say that Hell would be a much better place to go anyway, because there would be no U2 or Coldplay and lots of rock and jazz, but you wouldn't want to stay there either, because it would also be full of Protestants and Muslims. With all that rock music and jazz, Hell would be just like living in Holland. ¡Eurgh!

Ecosystem: On the Monday after the Rotgütts' visit, I taked what turned out to be a final hunting trip to the Malpais—the Badlands. As you may guess from the name, the Badlands is not the ideal location for a hunt: The unbroken broken terrain of sharp rocks and lavastone make it almost impossible to walk silently, even with the softest of shoes, and the softest of shoes are never a good idea when hunting on an irregular plain of roasting scree. An ankle sprain and cut knees are always a possibility. What is more, the volcanoes west of La Oliva are covered by a layer of sage green lichen, as though Nature was attempting to compensate for the absence of grass on the island by painting it with verdigris. This lichen is so choosy that, in all the world, it grows only in Fuerteventura and in the Swiss Alps, an attitude that is not conducive to proliferation, particularly gived the resilience necessary to survive in such locations. Cacti, aloe, agave, vicious spiny succulents that protect their dense, sticky, life-preserving juices with a callous hide and an armoury of needles: these are the typical denizens of Fuerteventura. They can be said to almost thrive here, since nothing else wants to compete. Yet this delicate, fussy, finicky, fungi-algae fusion somehow bucks the trend, offering a haven for geckos and gilas, which it so perfectly camouflages that they are impossible to spot until you are almost upon them—which only ever happens by accident—when you tread upon their hiding place, whereupon they dart into the crevices and cracks before the shock of their presence even has time to register. ¿¡What the Fuck!? you yell, your leg recoiling as though electrocuted, the lizard-shaped dust beneath your boot all that remains of another missed snack, evaporating like a will o' the wisp, its material form apparent for only the fleetingest of instants.

¿Why hunt in the Badlands, then? you ask, as if I am a moron. Well, in the first place, the greenery of the landscape is a relief from the monotony of the rust-coloured scabs that pass for mountains across the rest of the island. In the second place, safety. The rocks and stones that provide infinite hiding places for chipmucks, rabbits, and geckoes also prevent any gambies or rabid bardinos from sneaking up on you unawares. At the best of times, a gambie's sense of balance is laughable. Combine that with the relentless hellscape of a loose, angular, sharp, and pointy carpet of rocks and you have a recipe for slapstick at its bloodiest and least forgiving. I have seen slavering naturist gambies attempt to sprint along the crest of dunes stark bollock naked in vain pursuit of camels, the sand yielding beneath their feet in puffs like bursting dreams, but the hilarity is as nothing when you compare it to the efforts of a foamy-mouth purple-veined Yorkshireman stumbling over what might as well be broken glass, his eyes bulging and streaming, his neck red raw from the noonday Sun, his fists clenching and knuckles bleeding, his trousers shredded from a thousand trips and missteps, as he edges ever nearer—five meters an hour is the going rate—to sinking his teeth into your baseball bat, monkey wrench, or whatever defensive weaponry you have to hand.

Those of us who have been frequenters of the Malpais know one another's traps and general hunting areas, and on occasion, I confess, I had have been tempted to check other hunters' traps for prey, especially when hunger struck. But you must find them first, since only small traps are practicable on such terrain, and when you do find them they are only ever strong enough to retain their hold on the smallest of lizards or the most intellectually deficient chipmucks, barely enough for even a light snack. ¡You would have to be desperate!

My intention on this trip was instead to trap a few lizards and small mammals for pickling and laying up in case of a long-term siege. Once the home place was secure, and on the assumption that the Beast with Three Fingers would not find me for at least a week, I would be having enough food to survive any attempt to starve me out, providing me with the opportunity to take the offensive at the moment of my choosing. The best time to do so would be early on, before the Beast had have had sufficient time to assess the strength of my defences or had have been able to establish a *cordon sanitaire* around my perimeter. My plan, as I saw it, was to lay low and allow the Beast to exhaust his preliminary assays before attempting to meet him on terms that favoured me, the home team, with all the advantages of familiarity, preparation, and experience that my preferred battlefield allowed.

Was a very good plan indeed.

Education: A waste of everyone's time. Children should be taught to count and to read instructions. They need nothing else; even that much is more than Adam required to tend the Garden of Eden. The knowledge of one farmhand about the weather, how and when to use a spade, and the different applications of manure is worth more than the "erudition" of a hundred thousand Marxist college professors.

Einstein, Alfred (1879–1955): German-Jewish inventor of relativism, famous for his mad white hair, immortalized by C. S. Lewis in his book *Go Ask Alice*, which recounts the mad hair's adventures down the wormhole. It turns out in the end that everything was just a dream, like in *Dallas*. Alice had simply fallen asleep beneath a tree on the grassy knoll, and nobody was shot at all (everyone was actors, like Marilyn Monroe).

Elections: Ask any specialist whether he thinks his field should be democratic and he will laugh in your face (or she, if the specialism is make-up). ¿Why, then, should the running of society depend on democracy and not rule by the appropriate specialists, those born and trained to rule in the military academies, private schools, and polo clubs of our once-fine nation? Voting is all very well for gameshows or trivial TV competitions in which people's unimportant opinion about which singer is the prettiest is canvassed at €3.50 a pop. But when it comes to how many jobs to cut, whose turn is next to be mayor, and where do we build the hotel, these decisions are too important to ask the idiot public. You need to ask the specialists in job-cutting, mayor choosing, and hotel locations, whether that means the economist, the bishop, or the developer. This is how to run a society smoothly. A place for everyone and everyone in their place, like in a stage show or a singing competition. ¡Just not one you can vote on!

Elephant: People are so distracted trying not to talk about the elephant in the room that they forget the *real* elephant in the room, which is: ¿How did an elephant get in the room? ¿Is the room having special bi-fold doors? ¿Has the ceiling been especially raised to accommodate an elephant? Until they can answer these questions, the elephant in the room will be nothing but a huge, grey, wrinkled mystery, an enigma, inside a riddle, inside a room.

English, The: The English are the original Jews. The word "Saxons" is a corruption of the phrase "Isaac's sons." Far be it from me to second-guess God, but we are all now living with the consequences of His mercy. If only Abraham had been swifter with the knife.

Equinox: In Greek mythology, a half-horse, half-bull creature that spends the year chasing a menagerie lion around the equator. On two nights a year, its horns and penis are of the same length, but also, on one night a year, it has giant horns and no penis, like a French cuckold, and, on another night six months later, no horns and a giant penis, like late-period Simply Red.

Eucharist: ¿If a monkey eats a communion wafer by accident, does it still become Jesus inside him? ¡Answer me that, Mr. Darwin! (The answer is No. It becomes Monkey Jesus).

EuroDisney: A quasi-sovereign state-within-a-state, like Hezbollah in Lebanon or the Catholic Church in Ireland, with its own schools, hospitals, and judicial system, including police cells, prisons, law courts, and cetera. Any reprobate who breaks the Disney law may well find themselves in Disney court standing before a jury of their Disney peers, comprising Sleeping Beauties, Goofies, and Mickey Mice. Members of the public can find themselves conscripted into working for several years in the Disney kitchens or sweatshops, while anyone with diplomatic immunity will find themselves quietly asked to leave under cover of darkness even if it was just a case of innocent wrestling and the tweenage American girls were up for it and their deaths was entirely accidental and they deserved it anyway.

Euthanasia: Is when you have to kill old people because Nature won't.

Eve: The first lady, except for in America, where the first lady is a new woman every five years. In my humble opinion, vicious ungentlemanly misogynists have constantly maligned Eve unnecessarily for causing the eternal banishment of humanity from Paradise. What they tend to forget is that, although she was a grown woman and should have known better, she was actually *born* as a grown woman, and therefore, when Satan was tempting her, she wasn't even one year old. Misogynists should show some understanding. This is also why God condemned women to eternally be having the intelligence and emotions of a small child no matter how old they get.

Exorcism: What sneering septics and smarming scientists always forget is that exorcism only works on Catholic demons: They are the only ones who understand Latin.

Experts: Experts are always having an agenda, usually the protection of their status, which allows them to retain a monopoly over their so-called "intellectual capital," which is just a fancy name for command over the faculties, facilities, and jargon in use by their organization, whether legal, medical, or scientific. Foretunately, this exclusivity renders them vulnerable to Othering and resentment. A society that has an intellectual division of labor will always distribute its educational resources and opportunities unequally, making it impossible to conduct a genuinely informed debate across society at large, a *sine qua non* of genuine democracy, as evidenced by the sham that parades itself as such today. This state of affairs is advantageous not just to the experts, who possess and wield their intellectual capital successfully as a result of this inequality (in the form of autonomy, decision-making power, and control over legitimacy, for example) but also to any Fascists who know how to exploit the imbalance between those arrogant elite bastards who claim to "know better" than the rest of us and those who are on the receiving end of decisions for which they may not fully understand the rationale. In fact, we might say that we Fascists know "even better" than the experts, thanks to our lived experience and learning from the university of life. We know that the elites are never having the best interests of the people at heart and that any claims or evidence put into the public domain are nothing more than a smokescreen to hoodwink and intimidate the ignorant rabble. The hierarchy that separates the experts from the rest of society may not be necessarily of their own making, but they still benefit from it. If the so-called experts were genuinely having the people's interests at heart, they would attempt to close the intellectual capital gap altogether so that everyone could be at their level of knowledge. Instead, they protect themselves and their privileges, demanding that we trust and respect them and their bloated, smug, unaccountable fiefdoms. Foretunately, like any hierarchy, knowledge inequality is open to disruption by sowing distrust, and the so-called experts are only having themselves to blame when we cast doubt upon their *bona fides*, a Latin phrase meaning dog bones. They can flail and scream "¡Populism!" all they want but, properly framed, their screaming only confirms the threat we Fascists pose to their power and the legitimacy of our cause. Every time they wag their finger or raise their sneering lips they prove our point. Their expertise means nothing to us.

Exploitation: Imagine that you and I are living on an island where the only means of sustenance is a big banana plantation, of which you are the owner. Also, because all the fish in the sea around the island are dead from an oil spill or else are the inedible kind of fish, such as puffa-puffa fish, I will starve unless I get access to your plantation. The fact that I will starve is not your problem, obviously, but you are having more bananas than you can eat and there is the danger of them going off, so out of the goodness of your heart and because you do not like to see good food go to waste, you say to me, "Manuel, I will give you some of my bananas to eat, but in return, I would like you to harvest the bananas for us so that we can eat our fill and also maybe export the surplus before they go off." I am absolutely ravenous but also grateful and so I say, "Yes of course" but also, "However, I am having no energy to work for you since I am having nothing to eat." Therefore, being both a businessman and magnaniminous, you give me some of your bananas in advance to provide me with the energy in order to work.

At the end of the day, I have done much harvesting and you are very happy with my commitment, while I am proud to have done an almost honest day's work. However, you are struck the next day when I arrive at the plantation with a hangover and listlessness, and when you ask why I am stinking of the booze (banana beer), I explain to you, "Oh I was out last night at a local bar to celebrate having a job and got shitfaced. Was great fun. I would have had invited you, but I knew you was busy with the responsibility of managing your business." And this is true, but also beside the point. You are struck by surprise because you cannot understand where I was able to get the energy from in order to go out gallivanting. All the energy I am having in my body must surely have come from the eating your bananas, which contain lots of carbohydrates and sugars, as everybody knows, as well as potassium and mangnesium. But all of that energy from those bananas was supposed to have been expended on harvesting the bananas on your plantation. ¿Was that not the deal? You give me bananas, I harvest bananas. ¿Therefore, how am I still having some energy left? ¡That is not a fair exchange! All the energy I have inside me was coming from *your* bananas. ¡You are livid! I had have taked advantage of your good nature and trust and lack of rigid surveillance to smuggle some banana energy past the guards.

This iniquity is why the urban idiot Karl Marx was forced to invent the concept of "labour power": to conceal and obscure the thievery conducted by the proletariat every time they leave the factory under their own steam. As this example is proving, directly contrary to the disgraceful bullshit Marxist atheist communist ideology, which turns the real world upside down by mystifying relations between people, the workers are the ones who do the exploiting, rather than the reverse, stealing from their generous and naïve bosses. And this applies not just under capitalist relations but also in feudal and postindustrial societies. T'was always thus. People are cheating scum, but especially the poor.

Eyes: Not to be trusted. I am not saying that we should be like Doubty Thomas, who saw Jesus resurrecting from the dead but still had to see his hole to be certain it was him. Doubty Thomas was so called because he was lacking in faith, not because he had very sensible attitudes about optical illusions. What I *do* mean is that looks can be deceptive, especially the looks you get from a woman across a crowded bar. Also what you read in the newspapers is probly bumshit, and the news that comes from the liberal state media is always dodgy. Only children and fools believe their eyes, which is why blind children are always wiser than their classmates, as you know already if you have been paying attention. With your eyes.

F

Falangism: The only True Fascism.

False Friends: The German word for poison is *Gift*, so when a German woman tells you she is having a gift for you, you may be right to suspect she is a foreing services operative intent on your annihilation, not one of Saint Nicholas's sexy elves. Also in German, the word *also* does not mean "also" but "thus"; thus, the "also" at the start of this sentence would mean "thus" if the sentence was in German, but also the "thus" after the colon *does* mean "thus," not "also," while the "also" that follows the "but" means "also," not "thus." Also, the word for cancer in German is the same as the word for crabs, so if a German woman tells you she is riddled with crabs, you can safely be having sex with her, if you must, because the type of crabs she has is not the kind she can give you. Like a gift.

Fascism, True: The term "Fascist" is one that is much misunderstood, thanks largely to it being brought into such disrepute by the Nazis, who are having a high profile only because of their committed participation in the Second World War Two. The Nazis was very much a product of the decadent degenerate German Weimar Republic, and despite their clear rejection of that epoch, its degenerate influence on their behaviour is obvious. The Nazis, for instance, loved to dress up in leather or in women's clothes and were notoriously liberal in their membership criteria. Even today, you can be gay and be a Nazi. You can be a woman and be a Nazi. You can be a paedophile and be a Nazi. In America, there is an organization called the Proud Boys, a homoerotic group that spends most of its time grooming young men on the Internet (the clue is in the name; "proud" is a synonym in English for "erect"). Indeed, there are very few things you cannot be and still be a Nazi. You just need to like hurting people.

There is a well-known clandestine Liberal-Masonic conspiracy to confuse decent pious God-fearing right-wing citizens and lead them down dark alleys that are ideological cul-de-sacs while pretending to be proper genuine honourable Fascism. This is how they muddle the waters and how the conspiracy is able to discredit the hardcore true inheritors of Franco's legacy.

The other thing that distinguishes the Nazis from True Fascists is that despite all the militaristic posturing, the Nazis liked a lot the killing part of Fascism but the dying part, not so much. By contrast, the Spanish Foreign Legion ran into battle crying "¡Viva la Muerte!" knowing that, as the scum of the earth, their deaths would go unremarked upon by respectable society. The Legionnaires were True Fascists, with the proper attitude towards death: all humans deserve it, but only the True Fascist welcomes it. Is a shame, but no surprise, that so few of us are left today. The average human being is too pitiful and weak to face how pitiful and weak the average human being is. Which is a palindrome.

Fatboy Slim: The show isn't over till the Fatboy Slims.

Fear: Fear is the Fascist's friend. Make women afraid of the outsider, and they will cling to you for protection. Make women afraid of you, and they will be having no choice but to stay.

Feminism: An evil belief system constructed by the Judaeo-Masonic Illuminati in order to weaken the race by making ladies more masculine and men more feminine, thereby making ladies less able to raise children and men less able to fight wars without wearing lipstick. It tells women that their desires to kiss men and suck penises—carefully crafted by the Patriarchy over millennia—are learned behaviours, which is why so many women are shit at it. It uses the well-known tactic of divide and rule, which the Illuminati designed in their quest to create a totalitarian world government and reduce the resistance of mankind to their evil plan of international peace and harmony.

Fingers, The Beast with Three: A beast with three fingers can still hold a grudge.

Fish: The fish is the emblem of Jesus Christ, Lord God, King of Kings, and with good cause. Is because the fish is a miraculous creature, which can live all its time in saltwater and yet never dehydrate.

When we was at school, our teacher telled us never to drink the saltwater when caught adrift in a boat at sea because we would shrivel up and die, like *papas arrugadas*. I expect you was telled the same thing. But consider: ¡The fish is adrift at sea all the time, yet they seem to do alright! Indeed, is only when brought on board the boat and beaten over the head with a rock that they start to feel dead from all the bruising of their gills.

Jesus was not having gills, which is why he walked *on* the water rather than swim in it. Is also why the Romans crucifixed him rather than stoning him to death.

Fishes, Swims with the: A phrase invented by the Mafia as a polite way to refer to someone who is dead, e.g., "Robert Maxwell swims with the fishes." Origin unknown.

Fishwife: I am having been reliably informed that there are two words in the English language in which the word "fish" appears twice. They are "fishwifish" and "fishknifish," which mean "like a fishwife" and "like a fishknife," respectfully. The only phrase with a similar claim is Martin Luther King's famous "I haddock bream."

The word "fishwifing" should not be confused with "fishwifiing," which is borrowing a pike's mobile for their free Internet connection. Also note that a sheepwife is different from a fishwife and, confusingly, comes from animal husbandry, not animal wifery. I don't think there is such a thing as a sheepknife but there is a sheepshank, which is what they do to prevent overhusbanding by rams: they tie a knot in it. Is a bit unfair; the problem is usually nymphomaniac ram-paging ewes.

Fleas: Big fleas are having little fleas upon their backs which bite them, and little fleas are having even littler fleas, and so on until you get to the littlest.

Floaters: Is a piece of shit in your eye that won't flush away no matter how much you try.

Florida: Due to a trade agreement with Greece, in the U.S. state of Florida, a "continental breakfast" must include squid.

Fossils: Paleontologists have yet to understand that fossils prove nothing. God created the world in six days with the appearance of a pre-history. Science simply is wasting its time in tracing this fictional family tree. As the Irish Bishop Berkeley conclusively proved, your memory is only circumstantial evidence that the past ever existed. If the past exists at all, it exists only in the Mind of God. As a joke upon us all.

Fox's Glacier Mints: Not, as I once assumed, proper right-wing confectionaries manufactured by the Australian Catholic billionaire Rupert Murdoch, but rubbish English sweets made in Leicester, England, from foxes.

Franco y Bahamonde, Francisco: A quietly spoken humble servant of God who asked for nothing for himself but to rule Spain in perpetuity. A true Spaniard and a fine dancer (of the Quadrille). An example to us all. His achievements are beyond words, and I am humbled even to say his name. Franco.

Freemasonry: A secret society beginning in the sixteenth century as a result of a blood-seal compact between Protestants and Jews to overthrow the hard-won Catholic civilization. ¿Have you ever met a freemason? I haven't. Or maybe I have. There is no way of knowing. And that is the problem. They are everywhere and yet invisible. They are even more secretive than the World Economic Forum, the Trilateral Commission, and the Skin and Bones Society, which we all know and love. ¿And you don't never see anyone going into Masonic Halls or Lodges, do you? This is because they all live in the vaults beneath the buildings, in coffins, and only come out at nighttime to read books by candlelight, cast spells, engage in scientific research, and indulge in other "Enlightenment" activities. Is not fair.

French, The: Is strange that, of all the people in the world, the French are having the least *joie de vivre*.

Frogstorm: Not just a fictional device to end a crappy movie like *Mangolias* but also a genuine real phenomenon, as the Bible records, and an augur of the Endtimes, which is why the Spanish town of El Rebolledo, near Alicante, experienced a massive deluge of frogs at the turn of the 21st century, over the weekend (the technical term is not "Frogstorm," in fact, but "Anural Downpour" or "Amphibial Kermitation").

I understand, incidently, that the French are working on ways to combine the raining of frogs with electrical storms in order to pre-cook the frogs before they land. I hope they succeed, but in their own country, please. The people of Alicante have been perfectly happy living on a diet of paella for the last two thousand years, and although the addition of frogs will add a nice new twist to the dish, having French people come to visit is too high a price to pay.

Fuerteventura: As a result of tourism, all the goat herds on Fuerteventura are gone. Consequently, the goats have to herd themselves and return to the fold voluntarily at the same time every evening. However, they don't milk themselves, so the island's award-winning cheeses must be made by indentured labour. Which is why they taste so good.

G

¡Gambies!: Rather than park the Land Rover out front of Candelaría's house, in full view of the street, I was always being in the habit of driving it around the side farthest from the town, hiding it behind the wild ferns that array themselves along what might once have had been an arbour or al fresco dining area. This approach allowed me to scout the vicinity and spot any untoward activity suggestive, indicative, or significative of an ambush.

And when there *was* an ambush, this tactic did indeed work. From the Tindaya side of the house, I could see well before I pulled up that something was amiss. The front door was wide open and a southside window ajar. The all-clear signals we had prearranged that Candelaría was always to trigger—the Child of Prague on the trellis and photo of El Generalísimo beside the postbox—were absent, meaning her attention was elsewhere. Due to something.

Or someone.

¿¡Could it be?! I thought. ¿The Beast with Three Fingers already? I cursed myself for my strategic failure to imagine he would come for her first. She was my weak spot; he could find my location by finding her location. Or, at least, he might have believed this, not having a full grasp of the extent of her dimness. It would be just my luck, my defence planned so assiduously, to walk in on him just as he was extracting nonexistent information from my idiot sister with a pair of pliers and a bikechain. ¡What a travesty! ¡What misfortune!

Happily, was a false alarm. Was only fucking gambies attacking her. ¡The relief! One was sinking his teeth into Candelaría's plump and crusty thigh, while the other was gnawing on her left hand, the blood dripping slowly off the kitchen table, across which my sister was sprawled, face-up, her eyes sparkling with their usual absent delight, both of them still in their sockets, which I taked as a good sign.

Was at this point, I suppose, that I for the first time crossed the lines of legality without the protection of my especial judicial status as a former clandestine officer of Spanish Intelligence. Also without the approval or benign neglect of my superiors. Many have been the corpses I have had to wantonly discard, the limbs flensed, the jaws broken, the eyes gouged out, the skulls hammered, the calves skewered, the rectums pierced, all absent from my résumé but all in the service of my country and thus justifiable by their ends. And I have always been meticulous since my retirement to stay well within the bounds of propriety in order to avoid drawing attention to myself. Not for me the drug dens of Marbella, the casinos of the Maghreb, the sheep palaces of Limavady. Tempting though it might have had been to experience the mundane thrill of topping a gambie — there were rumours of an illicit club near Triquivijate where Majoreros paid in crates of Ocho Pies beer to wrestle with bloated German gambies in Death Matches. Such juvenile revenge fantasies were beneath me. I did not share their pathetic need for belated score-settling after years of Teutonic disdain.

Having anticipated the Beast with Three Fingers within the house, the safety was already off my Uzi before I entered. Upon seeing that the intruders was only gambies, I laughed cheerily at my own misapprehensiveness before unloading into the thigh-biter, a bronzed white rasta who pirouetted comicly across the room as the bullets hit home before colliding with the salvage sculpture of a lobster boat, banging what was left of his head against the wall and sliding to the floor in an ungainsomely pile.

The *frut-frut* of the Uzi failed to gain the attention of the second gambie, whose focus on Candelaría's left hand undiminished. I confess that anger had overtaken me by that point, since my relief had gived way to the realization that my idiot sister, if she was not already dead, was now likely to be a gambie herself, leaving me with an even greater burden of care should she survive.

The Uzi being empty, I strolled into the kitchen, where I assembled a toolkit of such gore-eliciting and blood-curdling horrificness—carving knives, forks, macerators, mallets, cleavers, corkscrews, and a whisk—that it would be unnecessarily and gratuitously gruesome for me to detail the finger assailant's demise. Suffice to say that my kitchenwork resulted in a stew that no human tongue should taste; there was no need, since human tongue was already in it.

But here my bad luck was only just beginning, for having cleared the zone of any enemy infiltration, I now turned to the care of my precious sibling to find, to my dismay, that her condition was inconclusive. Where there had have once been a clear, resounding heartbeat there was now nothing of note; where once there had have been a powerful, garlic-laden breath, there was now no more than a whiff of sulphur; and where once there had have been a full complement of digits on each hand, there was now only seven. Yes. Seven.

Genius: Is the intrinsicly Fascist concept that a few exceptional individuals are blessed with thought processes and insights that are beyond the capacity and comprehension of ordinary mortals. Due to the ongoing deterioration of the species, there are no longer any geniuses alive today, but the term is still bandied about willey-nilley with reference to scientists, who are nothing more than gatekeepers for the elite, paid to come up with new ways to bamboozle and confuse the public in order to protect their privileges; musicians, who are just the weird autistic kids who paid attention in music class; and chefs, who are merely psychopaths fortunate enough to be provided with a socially sanctioned outlet for their anger. Those who use the word "genius" today can be forgiven for daring to imagine that Fascism still thrives, but what they perceive is no more than a feeble simulacrum, an accidental resemblance generated by the process of social decay and decomposition, like seeing the image of Christ in a colostomy bag.

Georgia: In the U.S. state of Georgia, is illegal to play tunes on the elderly.

Gestation: The period during which the embryo develops in the womb. In human beings, the gestation period is normally nine months. Babies that are born prematurely are usually not fully developed and consequently suffer from a range of physical and/or intellectual debilitations. In my case, the period of gestation was roughly eighteen months (the difference between my date of birth and the last time my father had had sex with my mother). For this reason, despite being a small man, I have a huge amount of development packed into my diminutive body, making me both physically and intellectually more developed than the vast majority of human beings; my smallness can be explained by the compression placed on my eighteen-month-old foetus by my mother's standard uterus.

Whenever I asked my father how he could be sure about the date of my conception, he would simply say, "That was the week the circus came to town." Then he would stare at me momentarily before breaking out into huge guffaws, which he was careful not to hide from me even though I just shrugged my shoulders, assuming that this phrase was a euphemistic reference to my mother's menses. Seeing this only made him guffaw more.

Gin: Mother's ruin. Or one of them.

Gloves, Kid: What the police and courts use when handling anti-immigrant protests. Is important for Fascists to understand that it suits governments to allow such protests to make the country less welcoming to asylum seekers and refugees. By deterring immigrants, they reduce the need for new housing that would lower landlords' rents and absolve the government of any blame while permitting it to take the credit for solving the refugee crisis. Fascists thus render themselves liable to the accusation that their "local community groups" are in league with the state, doing the government's dirty work, a despicable slur, especially when all the funding actually comes from America.

Gold: The dairy farmers of Spain are having a saying, "*Dentro cada toro, hay oro,*" which is a clever play on words meaning "Inside every bull, there is gold." This expression tells you of the high esteem and importance in which rural communities hold bulls and their regenerative powers, since a good bull is much more valuable to a farmer than a dozen heifers. Some people, mostly foreingers, think that the saying is meant to be taked literally, as a reference to the bull's seed, but bull semen is not gold at all, merely a sort of orangey-beige, as any Spanish child can tell you from school trips. Instead, the reference is metaphorical, similar to the Irish saying "Every cow has a silver lining." In the case of Ireland, however, the cows are all sent to England, where the silver lining is stripped out before the meats are sold back to the none-the-wiser Irish consumer. Hence the famine.

Gomorrahmy: The sin so filthy that even the Sodomites was disgusted. The Bible, which usually goes into graphic, luxuriant detail when recounting sexual perversions, could not bring itself to describe this abhorrent activity. I suspect, however, that salt is involved in some way.

Grinkles: Wrinkles from too much grinning. Show me a man with grinkles and I'll show you an imbecile.

Guerra: "¡WAR! ¡HAH! ¿WHAT IS IT GOOD FOR?"
Is good for weeding out the weak, reinforcing orderliness and discipline, legitimating the necessity of authority, social cleansing, raising

the spiritual and moral health of the nation, and fertilizing the soil with the blood of martyrs.

Clearly this is a rhetorical question.

Guinefort, Saint: The only saint who was a dog, unless you also count Saint Bernard.

Guitar, Spanish: All forms of music sound better when you perform them on a Spanish guitar.

Gums, Fruit: A packet of fruit gums can keep an alligator's jaws busy for up to forty-five minutes. Just don't make the same hilarious mistake as the late Anthony Hempel of Stroud, who confused fruit gums with fruit pastilles. The alligators wolfed them down in seconds, and when Anthony ran out, the alligators suffered a sense of humour failure.

H

Haiku: The Japanese art of poetry folding.

Hangover: Sometimes, a hangover is all ordinary people need in order to see the world clearly, as we Fascists do. When you are drunk, you see the world like a pathetic simpering sentimental liberal, and everyone is your mate. When you are hungover, you see that people are shit, including yourself, and you call on God to make it all stop.

Happiness: Like human dignity, an illusion, the pursuit of which provides the fuel to drive the engine of decadent bourgeois liberal consumer capitalism. If a Fascist revolution can come only at the price of unhappiness for every human being, I think we can all agree that this is not too big a price to pay.

Hardware Stores: Is a big disappointment to many British immigrants to Spain, especially those from the north of England, to find that *ferreterías* don't sell ferrets. No, I tell them. If you want to buy an animal, you must go to the *farm-acia*.

¡Is a joke! The only animal that you can get in the *farmacia* is *perro*-cetamol.

¡Is another joke! ¡I am on fire!

Hawaii: In the U.S. state of Hawaii, is illegal to keep elephants and tigers in the same bedroom.

Hedgehog: Spiky-faced French mammal from whose droppings we get popcorn. During embarrassment, the hedgehog curls up into a tiny ball, then dies. Prey: sarcastic cats, dinner parties.

Hell: For all its downsides, Hell does at least come with the guarantee of eternal life. For this reason, I strongly believe that Hell is too good for some people. Especially some of the people I killed.

Hemisphere, Southern: Turds curl in a clockwise direction in the Southern Hemisphere and anti-clockwise in the North. Is a well-known fact.

Heresy: Is heretical to believe that the burning of heretics is contrary to the will of God.

Heterosexuality: As a red-bloody Spanish male, I naturally find all other men's bodies sexually revolting, even if they are smooth, rippling, and throbbing with urgent energy. Consequently, I find it totally impossible to understand how *any* woman could possibly want to be having the sexual intercourse with *any* man except for myself. However, sex with women is also not something that I could bring myself off to do because women's bodies are gunk, flob, and snot colonies. Neverthenonetheless, since the vast majority of women who *have* had sex have had it with men other than myself, I can only conclude that such women delight in demeaning and degrading both themselves and the men they are having the sex with. Even to contemplate such an activity requires them to be having an extraordinarily low opinion of themselves, albeit not as low as God's opinion of them. When the miserable and insightful poet Sylvia Plath said that all women dream of having the jackboot on their faces, it pleased me very much, since it demonstrated that the Patriarchy had have been successful in permeating women's consciousness to such an extent that heterosexuality and reproduction have become accepted as the norm, enabling the construction of mighty empires on the backs of willing slaves (and also unwilling slaves, but willing slaves mean a larger profit margin). The statement did confuse me, though. ¿If women dream of a jackboot on their face, why have they not all been lining up outside my door, where I would have been perfectly happy to give them the full Fascist experience? I can only assume that my deliberate anonymity worked against me, even when I was running Knockmerry House. The whores who lapped up my cum on a twice-daily basis would have probly forgot my name the moment they left the room were it not for my monomaniacal authoritarian control over their existence. Such is the curse of a life spent in the Intelligence Services: Nobody had the chance to get to know the real me.

Hindsight: With the benefit of hindsight, I realize now that I could have saved myself a lot of bother had I have gutted the gambie who was nibbling on my sister's hand in order to check his stomach for her missing digits. It would have confirmed or disspelled any concerns I might have had about the impending arrival of the Beast with Three Fingers. Frustratingly, in the moment, my priority was to save Candelaría, and the shock of seeing her mutilated hand was disconcertating. I recalled from a case we examined during a refresher course I had taked in Zaragoza prior to retirement that rabies bite victims need to be put into a coma and their core body temperature reduced to slow the progress of the virus to the brain. Also, I calculated that if Candelaría was about to die, I could at least preserve her body through the use of ice, so she could receive the correct Catholic rites, something I had have promised her mother on many occasions in the past, usually not long after one of a litany of death-defying acts of ineptitude.

"Your sister's diarrhead her bedroom again. She won't make it past thirty-five. Promise me you'll see to it that what's left of her gets a proper Christian burial."

"Manolo, that idiot sister of yours was found dancing in the lumberyard this morning. Please see that the priest blesses any remaining limbs when she dies."

I ran from the house with little thought for my own safety—a sniper sitting patiently atop the nearby kindergarten could have punched several holes through my head with an indulgent chuckle at my carelessness—and I sped off to the Hiperdino a kilometer away on the main street. La Oliva was on its lunch break, staff from the Ayuntamiento offices reclining on park benches with their *bocadillos* and sopping shirts, labourers and van drivers munching tortilla sandwiches and sipping cañas; all of them was too engrossed in their conversations to notice the fierce determination of the driver in the black Land Rover to buy every available bag of ice in the supermercado—cash be damned (I figured I could use my debit card now that all bets were off). I was a man with a mission. Like in that film.

It taked me three trips from shop to vehicle, twelve five-kilo bags of ice on each trip, enough to half-fill the Rover. There thus remained sufficient space for Candelaría's big-boned body and some fresh food, so I also bought bananas, some chicken, chorizo, a few cans of Cruzcampo beer, grapes, carrots, cucumber, tomatoes, onions, garlic, pasta (spaghetti, fettuccine, and fusilli), fillet of dorado, and five litres of Fuenteror sparkling water. I placed the food around the cargo hold of the Rover and padded them with the icebags, so that the interior was lined to form a bed for Candelaría, with a few spare bags remaining to conceal her body from flies and nosey parkas.

Even for a diminutive low-centre-of-gravity powerhouse dynamo like me, was a struggle to get Candelaría's body from the house to the pickup, but I had earlier spotted a pair of plantpot trolleys behind the fence at the back of the house—three wheels on one of them but adequate to the task—which I manoeuvred under her like a skateboard. In this way, I was able to drag her along while walking backwards, with her feet clutched under my oxters. I averted my gaze from her rancid bloomers by alternately looking over my shoulder in the direction of travel or fixating instead on the reversed escape map of England covering her upper half, glued by cakes of blood to her face, breasts, and belly—her body had have been lying across it on the table when I found her. Although a hot wind was tugging at it around her hairline, trying to pull it free, it refused to let go, determined to accompany her on whatever journey she was taking. Safe to say that it would not be to England.

You are no doubt aware of the apocryphal tale of the mother from Teruel who was able in a moment of desperation to call upon superhuman capabilities to lift with her bear hands a fully laden SUV off her pancaked child, thereby rescuing it for a proper Christian burial (in a pizza carton). The inverse scenario, equally implausible to the nonbeliever, turns out to be perfectly feasible, given sufficient adrenaline: a child-sized adult can lift a mother-sized deadweight into the rear of a car-sized car provided there is sufficient urgency, a decent run-up, and an improvised ramp made from garden debris and the discarded fibreglass cowling of a lobsterboat. ¡Explain that, Science!

Hindus: Are not having souls, even though they think they do, a bit like in *Blade Runner*. The Hindus have 15,000 different gods, the majority of them snakes or monkeys. Nobody is knowing the names of all the gods, so you can easily pass yourself off as a Hindu simply by knowing the names of a few main ones and then inventing the others. My favourites: Vishnu, Kali, Ganesha, Allah, Paranorman, Edwin Poots.

Hitler, Adolf (1889–): Single-handily gave Fascism a bad name.

Holiday: From the phrase "Holy day," so when Communist agitators and trade unionists tell you they are responsible for you not having to work twenty-four hours a day 365 days a week, you can point out that in fact the Church was responsible for introducing holidays, not the working class. Otherwise, they would be called "prolidays."

Holy Water: Indispensable for pouring down the back of your PC when demons possess it. Be aware, however, that your computer will still die.

Holy Water, Death by: When my Great Aunt Conchita was ill with the consumption on her death bed (although she did not know at the time that it was her death bed), my grandmother brought to her from the shrine of Lourdes a big bottle of the Holy Water blessed by no lesser person than Pope Pius Twelve. For the following five days, my great aunt was partaking of this sacred elixir, which my grandmother mixed into a glass of brandy (five parts Holy Water to one part brandy) three times a day, in the hope that in her boundless compassion and as the messenger of forgivedness, the Mother of God might intercede with Our Lord to give Conchita a little more time on Earth among her family while also releasing her from the agonies she was so clearly enduring. Alas, was not to be. Holy cryptosporidium present in the water infected Great Aunt Conchita and gave her appalling dysentery for the remaining two days of her life, so that she died a dry, shrively husk of a lady with barely a drop of water left in her body, holy or otherwise.

A number of septic and loathsome neighbours whom my family later drummed out of the village argued at the time that my grandmother should stand trial for killing her sister, pointing not just to the water but also to the subsequent marriage between my grandmother and Great Aunt Conchita's widower, Don Miguel. Pure jealousy. This was a perfectly common practice in the mountain villages in those days, and to suggest that God did not know that the cryptosporidium was in the Holy Water was tantamount to denying his omniscience. God of course knew, and therefore He it was who had decided the time and manner of Great Aunt Conchita's departure. If we had not given her the Holy Water as God intended, she would still be alive, a burden to her family, snickering away to herself in a fetid smelly corner of Don Miguel's palace, he wondering why nobody ever came visit and my grandmother denied my inheritance.

Home Makeovers: Is television for ladies. I only ever watched one episode: "Social worker and community activist Susan Jensen recently received a surprise home makeover when she returned from work to find all her windows smashed in and graffiti on her patio calling her a 'fucking grass.'" She decided to list it.

Homophobia: The very term carries negative connotations, as though there is something wrong with it, so I don't use it. I prefer Gaytred.

Homosexuality: The ancient Greeks have a lot to answer for: democracy, philosophy, homosexuality. Humanity has been unable to rid itself of these three plagues in the subsequent four thousand years. Indeed, things have only got worse, since we now also have plagues that the Greeks had never not even heard of, such as Covid, socialism, and tennis. If we are unable to develop immunity to these social diseases, the only option is social surgery. Fascism is the scalpel. The Internet is the anaesthetic. Golf is the rehab. I don't make the rules.

Honey: So my mother comes into the kitchen, and there is Candelaría with a big tablespoon which she is using to shovel honey into her mouth out of a big jar that my mother usually kept in the fridge but which Candelaría had put on the kitchen table. My mother went mad with the shouting, telling my sister that she was not just making a mess and spoiling her dinner but also getting all sorts of germs into the honey by transferring the spoon from jar to her mouth and then back again, thereby ruining a perfectly antiseptic and expensive jar of Manuka. In order to teach my sister a lesson, my mother taked the spoon off her, wrapped a cloth round the handle, then held the bowl portion over the flame of the stove. When the spoon was good and hot, she grabbed hold of Candelaría in a headlock and pressed the spoon against her lips while she struggled and screamed in pain until her lips was all blistered and burned. "That will teach you," said my mother to Candelaría when she ran off into the bathroom crying to get cold water. "If this is the only way you will ever learn, you stupid retard, then that is how it must be. Even if I have to kill you. Is for your own good."

This was a very important learning experience for both Candelaría and me. She learned not to eat honey from the jar, and I learned that a hot spoon will melt honey perfectly. And also that ruined honey tastes just as sweet as not-ruined honey.

Horoscope:

Aries: Intimidated by tattoos. Collaborators.

Taurus: Fearful and timid. Usually try not to be noticed. Deserters.

Gemini: Politicly active, initially as a matter of principle, until experience jades them. Often make the best and most cunning Fascists.

Cancer: Capable of great kindness and generosity but will never know it.

Leo: Cowards and weaklings.

Virgo: Willing executioners.

Libra: Credulous and gullible. Most likely to believe in horoscopes and prophecy. Natural allies.

Scorpio: Rapidly accommodate themselves to a Fascist state. Compliant.

Sagittarius: Will betray their own parents if necessary.

Capricorn: Lost Boys and Girls. Looking for guidance from a charismatic leader.

Aquarius: Butchers, psychopaths, and liars. Unreliable. Require domination.

Pisces: Eichmann was a Pisces.

Hospices: A handy source of drugs. When I lived in Dublin, you would be surprised how many nonexistent terminally ill patients I knew in hospices who desperately needed morphine or something a little stronger to see them through to the other side.

¡Yes, the other side of the weekend!

¡Is a joke!

Hull, Kingston Upon: A town in England. Not to be confused with Thames, Kingston Upon, or The Roof, Rod Hull Upon.

Hull, Rod: Dead children's entertainer, which are always the toughest audience. Hull himself died tragicly when he fell off the roof of his house while trying to fix his television aerial. He shouldn't never have taked that emu up there with him; he knew what it was like.

Humour, Well-Developed Sense of: A sign of failure. In life, is sufficient to be having enough humour to laugh at the misfortune of others while also secretly thinking that it serves them right. Anything else is intellectual gymnastics attempting to justify weakness. Life is serious and hard. Or if not, it should be.

I

Idaho: In the U.S. state of Idaho, identical twins/triplets must dye their hair different colours.

Ideas: Ideas are of use only to the extent to which you can weaponize them against your enemy. Their content matters less than who is expressing them; that should be your first point of attack. "Never mind the impending firestorm in Oslo, Greta. ¿What is your *actual* agenda? ¿Who is really behind Big Ecology? Thunberg: ¿Is that a Jewish name? I thought so."

Idiocy, Urban: The communist ignoramus Karl Marx once made some famous and fatuous comment about the "idiocy of rural life," even though the countryside was somewhere he had never not ever visited because he was spending all his time in the fucking library doing his own "research." Everyone who has ever lived in the country would have been able to tell him, if he had bothered to ask, that it requires a much higher level of cleverness to survive rural life than life in the city. On the contrary, the city is often a refuge for all those who can't hack it in the country. The city offers anonymity and security. So long as you are having the money to pay your way, the shopkeeper, landlord, or police officer will not ask where you got it from; your money is as good as anybody else's, and he couldn't give a shit who you are anyway. Consequently, life in the city doesn't come with the burden of negotiating the sophisticated and nuanced power relations of rural life. You don't have to stay on top of who is shagging whose sister or who has grazed his sheeps on whose land without them knowing this week, or which councillor gave the green light for building the spa hotel where the asylum seekers' playground was meant to go. In the countryside, you need to know not only who everyone is but also their current status in the parish hierarchy, and because this status is subject to change from day to day, you must stay abreast of all the gossip, you must go to church every Sunday (¡at the very least!) to hear all latest news (and also because your absence will put your own status in jeopardy). None of this matters in the megalopolopolis, where money rules and nobody need know their neighbours nor even speak to anyone except the barista or madam. Is thus urban life that is full of idiots, sound, and fury, signifying nothing. Rural life requires sharpness, cunning, social intelligence, and guile, which is why farmers are so rich.

¡Marx was such an urban idiot!

Iglesias Jr., Julio: Well-known and popular crooner and former goalkeeper, two talents that made him immediately attractive to women. Is also interesting to note that his father, Julio Iglesias Sr., was one of the first ever gynaecologists in Spain, before which the job was done just by men who had an interest in the area. Iglesias Jr. clearly inherited his father's ability with his hands and also his ability to get into women's undergarments, although, unlike his father, he did not use an anaesthetic.

Immigration: Immigration is the sincerest form of flattery.

Imperialism: A clever means of exporting immigration, allowing the people over there to remain over there while still working for Spain without anyone having to pay expensive bloody prices in the shops.

Incels: Anyone with half a brain can understand why, in an age in which women have free will and the right to choose who they talk to, there are young men who would prefer not to have to do the arduous work of developing empathy, listening and conversational skills, making themselves interesting, demonstrating kindness, and cetera, when they will *still* run the constant risk of rejection and failure, which could hurt their feelings and self-esteem. In Franco's day, women's choices were limited to having their babies in the hospital or the asylum, depending on their attitude. Moreover, men were not burdened in those days by the delusion that women's bodies were desirable or that their opinions mattered. Pity the poor adolescents of today who must live with the possibility of being judged by someone other than God. ¡Is no wonder they hide away like Quasimodo!

Inquisition, The Spanish: Unjustifiably persecuted by history.

Integration: If there is one thing worse than immigrants who will not successfully integrate, is immigrants who integrate too successfully. Immigrants need to know their place, and is not as the multimillionaire heads of fruit-picking businesses, condiment manufacturers, hotel chains, or videogame designers. They should be cleaning office toilets and grateful for the opportunity.

Intervention, Divine: I have personal experience of divine intervention and can therefore vouch for its existence. During a dispute over the rights to Fentanyl distribution for the women's prison in Mountjoy, I was jumped in the jax of an upscale restaurant in Portobello by Liam "Screwy" O'Toole, the notorious Dublin 8 pimp and cat worrier who had been storking me for several days. In an ill-judged strategy typical of the Southside petty criminal fraternity, O'Toole considered it smart to launch his assault just as I was mid-stool, forgetting the potential for weaponizing faecal matter that this afforded me. Much in the way that Iroquois braves tipped their arrows with animal dung so that wounds would fester and poison, or the way that British soldiers in the trenches shat on their bayonets prior to going "over the top," I was able to swirl Madonna in my own turds before plunging it through O'Toole's left cheek as he pounced. I had been aiming for his eye but his cheekbone performed its defensive function, directing my blade downwards into the fleshy cheek where it remained buried to the hilt as he turned and fled in painful embarrassment and infection. It was not by any means the first scar he had acquired in a public toilet, physical or otherwise, but is the one that he remembers the most thanks to the sepsis it caused and the nasty taste it left in his mouth. Not even the cats will kiss him now.

¿How is this divine intervention, you may ask, particularly since I always practice my knife skills with Madonna when I am defecating precisely because of the inherent vulnerability of the activity? I will tell you. When I sat down at home later to debrief, after I had taken a shower, I discovered in my own back trouser pocket a betting slip for the 4:15 at Fairyhouse some eight months before. ¿The name of the horse? Papa's Bag. I had no recollection of ever having placed a bet on such a horse, and a check of the course records showed that no such horse had raced that day at Fairyhouse, so is beyond doubt that this betting slip was some form of divine intervention, like a miraculous medal, inserted into my trousers by some supernatural power. The name "Papa's Bag" might under other circumstances be taked to refer to James Brown, but in holy pissing Ireland such a phrase can only be understood as a tribute to the Pope's scrotal sac, the most sacred sac in the universe and also the holiest for never having been used. What's more, before you scurrilously dismiss this anecdote as the shock-induced fibblings of a credulous nitcompoop, when I checked the contents of Screwy's wallet, which I had liberated during our contretemps, what should I find there but a slightly stained appointment card for the STD clinic in Harold's Cross. ¡Aha! ¿You see? ¡Not only did I have the Pope's balls in my trousers, but Screwy had the Devil's in his!

Ireland, Lovely Holy Pissing: Is my favourite foreing country, where I was living for a few years before retirement and where I sometimes sneaked back for clean weekends. Is one of the few places that still knows how to do proper Catholic devotion; at least, this is true up the country, where the statues still move and the Sun still dances for virgins. Occasionally. I fly into Dublin airport then drive in any direction except towards Dublin itself, although sometimes I end up in Dundalk, which is not so good. Wet, damp, minging rain and mud is one thing. Wet, damp, minging rain and mud and Dundalk is taking masochism to the point where it becomes venal.

Irish People: The salt of the earth. And also the vinegar.
When we was recruiting women for work in Knockmerry House, we was careful to avoid using Irish women because the last thing an Irish man wants is to be having the sex with an Irish woman. Some people might refer to what we was doing as "people trafficking," in adverted commas, but in reality was just what the market would bear. You can bring a whore to water, and cetera.

Iron Man: Is a typical example of cultural appropriation, symptomatic of the disgusting blasphemous heresies that occur when America gets it hands on the values and cultures of other, better civilizations and transforms them beyond recognition to meet the lubricious demands of its idiot public before re-exporting their debased version back to the source societies to corrupt and imperialize them. In this case, we see what can happen when Americans get their hands on the story of Jesus and make it into a story that Joe Public can identify with, turning the Messiah from a humble holy carpenter's boy into a megalomaniac savior of humanity through his industrial conglomerate (not the Catholic Church, incidently, but Stark Industries). Of course, Hollywood retained some of Christ's most notable features, such as the stigmata in his hands and feet and the Sacred Heart; also, like Jesus, Iron Man is able to fly. However, in the Hollywood version, he has have to wear a magic mitten, like Padre Pio, to use his stigmata power, and the ability to fly is the result of scientific technology, the religion of Americans, which has enabled them to do things like make the atom bomb, the motor car, and toothpaste. The whole idea is ridiculous and he doesn't even die in the end.

When we Fascists talk about our opposition to Imperialism, this is what we refer to: the way Hollywood spreads its evil ideas throughout foreing cultures, a subcutaneous implicit insidious liberal value system infiltrating and undermining locally constructed belief systems such as voodoo, Copernicanism, Creationism, heart-warming Fascism, and, in places like Australia, Bananas in Pajamas and penis puppetry. These long-held and much-cherished vernacular worldviews struggle in the face of the virulence of Hollywood liberalism because of its technological know-how, its shiny newness that appeals to all primitive, innocent savages, and its loud bangs and large-breasted women, all of which distract and confuse the former penis worshippers, with the result that they don't notice the sneaky subtext being slipped in underneath, namely, the sympathetic portrayal of Jews and Freemasons, the blatant feminism, the tolerance for inferior races, and the anthropomorphizing of Muslims. All of these things are there, if you look closely, but nobody does because they are all still recovering from the shock of seeing an elephant fly.

You are probably thinking, "Well that's all true, Manuel, and well observed, as usual, but tell me: ¿How does this fit into the correct Fascist view of the world? Surely inferior races with their stupid worldviews and religions will just be wiped off the face of the earth in the struggle for survival like that appalling race of human beings in the movie *Independence Day*." There is some merit in your uncomprehending response, but you must understand that the correct view, held only by those of us in the Falangist movement, appreciates and understands the importance of societies retaining their own cultures and sense of place. The peoples of all societies have developed their cultures and values so that they are appropriate to where they live—Islam for the desert, Buddhism for the rice paddy, Christianity for the battlefield, and cetera—which is why they should never commingle. While saying that, is also obvious that 1) Christianity is correct and therefore we are having an obligation to take Jesus's Good News to all human beings regardless of their ability to understand it, and 2) it follows that there is a natural hierarchy between societies, specificly those superior ones which received Jesus's message first, and the inferior ones, most of which are not in

Europe, including America. Thus, even though Christianity might be inappropriate for the geography and culture of the Trobriand Islands, for example, they will have to make the best of a bad situation and in the long run, if they obey hard enough, will (possibly) enjoy the fruits of Paradise (probably some of the lower-hanging ones).

Irony: The invention of lazy minds. There are *no* ironies in life. The reason why our reproductive and excretory organs are so close together is that sex is dirty and shitting is fun.

Irritation: The drive from La Oliva was fast and uneventful. Fast because I was conscious that the Beast with Three Fingers might be on my tail — though there wasn't no sign of him in my rearview mirror — and because the ice surrounding Candelaría would stay solid in such blistering heat only for an hour at most, gived the large surface area of the cubes, even with the Rover's aircon turned on. The roads were still smooth between La Oliva and Cotillo, having been resurfaced just before the Outbreak. Dessicated gambie corpses belittered the storm plain just past El Roque, the Egyptian buzzards having learned to avoid poisonous gambie flesh. Those fuckers are having cast-iron stomachs, but why take the risk when there are more succulent tidbits available: chipmucks, geckos, cardboard.

So I pulled up at the entrance gate to Cotillo in a relaxed state of mind but also concentrative and alert. The wooden barrier remained down as one of the two guards, in a Hawaiian shirt and Bermuda shorts but carrying a Winchester rifle, approached my side window. He nodded in recognition as I wound it down and a wave of dry heat surged in. I recoiled at the heat and quickly glanced back over my shoulder to check the ice.

"¿The contents of your vehicle, Señor?" He rasped it through brown teeth that appeared to be fighting each other, the tangled mass of his facial fuzz watching on excitably.

"Sixty bags of ice cubes. One map of England. Shopping." I was hoping my answer would be sufficiently precise to deter further curiosity. I was also conscious that I had the Uzi under my front seat, which, although empty, might have made him a tad nervous.

"¿You are a resident of the village?"

"I am. For several years now."

"But your accent is—"

"I am not having an accent." He gave an abrupt snort, like an incredulous sow.

"Is as clear as day. Is—"

"*You* are having an accent. What I am speaking is the correct Spanish Castilian. Is pure Spanish. Proper Spanish."

"Ha ha. Is gay lisping Spanish."

I did not rise to the bait. Instead, I clenched the steering wheel and looked straight ahead. Through the windscreen, I recognized his partner. It was Andres the ironmonger. This calmed me sufficiently to respond informatively and with equaniminity.

"Is the Spanish of the King. And not just this king. Of all kings. Going all the way back to Jesus Christ, the King of Kings."

"¿The Spanish of Jesus? You're an idiot."

"¿Is a Spanish name, no? You have read your Bible, I trust. In the original Spanish."

"That does not mean Jesus is a Spanish name. If I was reading *Moby-Dick* in Spanish, it would not be making Queequeg a Spanish name."

"Of course it would. If the book has been translated into Spanish, then the character's name in Spanish is Queequeg. I imagine schools in fishing villages across Spain are full of Queequegs. Were it not the case that we in Cotillo already name our boys after San Andres—"

"Open the trunk."

Well, that conversation did not go as I had planned it.

"I have already telled you what is in there."

"Forgive me if I don't trust you." He gave a supercilious smirk. "Is your accent."

I bit my tongue to distract myself from my seething contempt. Quickly, I said,

"Oh yes. Also, I forgot. My sister is with me. But she is sleeping. In the back."

"¿In the back?"

"Sí."

"¿With the ice?"

"Sí. *On* the ice."

His gaze lingered septicly as he considered my response. Finally, he gestured to the back of the car with his rifle and moved away for me to exit the vehicle. I clambered out.

"I will show you, but we must be quiet," I said. "I don't want to wake her."

It was mostly the thin runoff of blood and ice seeping between the bags and trickling onto the flatbed in runnels that elicited the overreaction I had forseen and had been trying to avoid from this Majorero halfwit. The moment he saw the mess, he swung around to train his rifle on me and grunted for his partner.

"¡Andres! ¡Cover me!"

"¡Shush!" I whispered melodramaticly. "¡You will wake her!"

"¿Wake her? ¡She's a gambie!"

I stepped toward him to close the distance, to imply intimacy, secret sharing.

"Not at all. She's just sleeping."

"She's missing three fingers. Look at all the blood."

"She was in a bit of a scrap, that's all. It tired her out."

I could see from the corner of one eye that Andres was nervous. He knew that I knew him and also that I knew that he knew me. He did not want to have to make a decision he might regret. His partner, however, was having no such qualms.

"You can't bring her into the village. We can't take the chance."

"She's my sister. I am bringing her home to treat her wounds."

"You take someone to hospital for wounds like that. ¿Are you a doctor?"

"No, but I am having military experience in treating casualties."

I thought that the word "military" might put him on the back foot, intimidate him a little. Instead, he stepped away from me to put space between us.

"If she's sleeping, wake her up."

"No. I won't do that."

This response was too confrontational. I should have tried to de-escalate, obtain his name from Andres so that I could address him personally. My own impatience defeated me.

"¿Do you want *me* to wake her?" he responded, raising his rifle to shoot into the air. This was the point at which I should have jumped him, gambling that Andres would decline to get involved. It would have been a risk; Andres's nervousness could have swayed him either way. Instead, I raised my hands in conciliation.

"There is no need for that. Have it your way. ¿But if you won't let her into the village, where can I leave her?"

"¿Leave her?"

"I still have to go to my home. To get my medical supplies to treat her. Get water, painkillers … drugs."

As I anticipated, their ears pricked up. These imbeciles will swallow or smoke anything: cow tranqs, baking powder, vasodilaters, beta-blockers, codeine, paint powder, dried dogshit. One time, when I was chasing an escaping pimp who had been trying to turn my bints in Sallynoggin, I bribed a nightclub bouncer to access the club's VIP section with a wrap of cyan printer ink. Daft bastard.

"Well, of course, you can leave her with us," Fuzz-face finally said. "We will take care of her."

"¿Are you sure?"

"With the car."

"But I need the car. I need—"

"¿How many drugs are you bringing?"

He was having a point. And there was no way I could have left Candelaría lying on the bags of ice out in the sizzling heat. She was better off in the Rover.

"Okay," I said. "I will leave the engine running with the aircon on. If my sister wakes up, there is paracetamol in the glove compartment. Put more ice on her hand. I will be back within the hour." I was tempted to add, "And you will wish I wasn't," but I didn't. I would let them find out for themselves.

Italians: All very well in theory, but in practice you wouldn't want them living next door, hence the Alps.

The old Italian Fascist leader Benito Mussolini was once very very popular among Italians because of his no-nonsense racism, his populist rhetoric, and his cheap beer. After the surrender and running away of Italian forces in the Second World War Two, however, he became a big figure of fun, ridicule, and loathing, and those demure members of the middle classes who once was thinking he was a source of embarrassment but at least he made the planes bomb on time now came to believe he should hang upside down from a lambpost and be beaten with clubs like a piñata until all his teeth fell out. Which is precisely what did happen. Except when all the children gathered up his teeth and bit into them, thinking they was sweets, it made their tongues bleed. Which served them right. Even in death, Mussolini had the last laugh. With no teeth.

J

James, Saint: Better known as Santiago, the patent saint of Spain, famous for his *camino*, or Saint James' Highway. For this reason, he is also the patent saint of highwaymen. In Newcastle, where their football team plays in the Parque de Santiago, or Saint James' Park, the Jordis pronounce it "howayman."

Japan: All residential care homes for the elderly in Japan are made of wood and, consequently, are prone to collapse in earthquakes. A disproportionate number of elderly people die in earthquakes in Japan, mostly from splinters. This, I think, is a most elegant form of social hygiene. The Japanese once again point the way forward.

Jellyfish: In America, the word "jelly" is used to refer to what the English call "jam" and what we normal Spanish people call "marmalade." A jellyfish is neither made of jelly nor does it taste of fish, discoveries that come as a very stingy surprise to idiot sisters who try to spread one on toast.

Jews: Notorious for their great erudition. If you know what "erudition" means, you probably *are* Jewish.

Joke, Basque: Q: ¿How do you keep a Basque in suspense?
　　A: First, you tape his hands together at the wrists. Then, you tape his legs together at the ankles. Then, you place a noose around his neck, throw the rope over a beam and pull it tightly so that his feet are barely touching the ground. Then you tie the other end of the rope to a secure, weight-bearing load. Then you go home.
　　¡¿What?! !Is a Basque joke!

Joyce James (June 16, 1904–unknown): Well-known Irish semiliterate writer, author of the books *Ullyses* and *Finnegans Wake*, books both simultaenously brilliant and shite. Joyce was very confused because she was trying to write books about Dublin without ever having had been there, notoriously spending all her life in Trieste, Paris, and Zurich, Switzerland, France. Famously said she hoped it would be possible to reconstruct the city of Dublin just from reading *Ullyses*, like an Airfix model village or Ravensburger jigsaw puzzle, but her hopes were unfulfilled because of her lack of mastery—or mistressy, since she was a woman—of the English language. This is often a problem for people who communicate primarily in their second language, like Samuel Beckett, Joseph Conrad, the Windsors, and even yours truthfully, but then I am not making any gradniose claims for my masterpiece the way Joyce did. I am fortunate in having a God-gived humility that she lacked.

Judaism: God's trial run.

Juggle: For many years as a child, I was not knowing what meant the phrase "I will juggle with your bollocks." It was something I overheard my mother say during a big outrageous argument with my father downstairs one night (I had crept down the stairs partly the way in my naked pyjamas) because they were having loud shouting about alcohol—my mother was saying she always drank because my father was never at home, whereas my father was saying that he was never at home because my mother always drank. Then the subject changed and my father said something about being very sad that women cannot multitask.

Later that same night I heard many strange noises coming from their room that may have been the juggling, I don't know, but when I used the phrase myself in a big row with Candelaría about whose turn it was to empty the fish-washer, my mother and father spat out their sangria in hysterical laughter. Then my father clipped both my ears, one for swearing and the other for dropping eaves.

Juicers: Men who pay money to watch other men fuck their wives and then they lick the other men's cum out of their wives' vaginas. Very popular among tabloid journalists, who use it as a form of networking.

Junk: I returned to the Rover with bandages and tourniquets, for the sake of appearances, but also bullets for the Uzi and a small jar of nutmeg, with the aim of convincing Candelaría's "minders" that it was a rare Mexican hallucinogen capable of inducing aerial flight. I place "minders" in adverted commas because when I arrived back at the barrier, Fuzz-face and Andres was nowhere to be seen and the rear of the Rover was open, blood-water pouring from the flatbed and spattering the dust below.

This was my chance to bring Candelaría and the Rover into the village. Or so I thought. When I cornered the back of the Rover to shut the trunk, what should I find there but a naked-arse Fuzz-face humping my sister, her bloodstained underwear hanging from her right foot. Several of my fillings came loose as I ground my teeth in infuriated rage, but my grinding was brief, precursory, and inconsequential. Before you could say "Goat vomit on toast" (a Gomeran delicacy), I had leapt onto the flatbed, the sudden increase in weight on the suspension hidden by the rhythm of his humping and my diminutive size. My legs either side of his, I whipped out Madonna's drop-point blade, shimmied up his spine, and pulled back his head by his hair. Before he could react, I made two quick, deep stabs into the side of his neck—¡Jab! ¡Jab!—puncturing his carotid. ¡Y voilà! Blood sprayed everywhere—all over the shopping, goddammit—turning the cabin of the Rover into a cherry black Jackson Pollock. To prevent any further unwanted redecoration of the interior, I clambered back down his body, grabbed his feet, and pulled him out of the car and my sister.

"¿Now who has an accent?" I asked sarcasticly as frantically attempted to staunch the wounds with both hands, gurgling with panic and disbelief. "I'm sorry," I said. "I cannot understand a word you are saying."

Within a very long minute—I timed it for something to do while waiting—he was floppy, all spent up, his worthless corpse sputtering final, pathetic ejaculations of blood onto the barren ground. I stood over him to gloat for a moment—gloating is a form of respect, if you think about it—but could not do it properly because my sister's whiny voice intervened.

"¡My pee hole hurts!" It was a comment that shocked me less for its content than its origin, since she hadn't given no sign of consciousness for at least an hour. And when I clambered back into the car to meet her gaze, there was no gaze to be met. She was still prostrate on the flatbed, eyes shut, mouth tight, suggestive not of a painful pee hole but rigor mortis. I quickly checked her pulse. Nothing. Yet it was definitely her voice.

"¿How did you manage to say that?" I said aloud, in case it required enunciation.

"The same way I always say things. With my head. ¿But why does my pee hole hurt? ¿Is there something in it?"

That was the moment when I truly regretted not gutting the zombie in Candelaría's house. Had I checked his stomach then, I might have found the missing fingers from Candelaría's hand and drawn the logical conclusion that her gambie assailants had been responsible for her mutilation. Instead, I was now faced with the prospect of internally inspecting her dirty organs on the off-chance that my pursuers had indeed tracked her down, tortured her, lopped off her digits, and inserted them where they did not belong, except in porno.

Foretunately, the option then occurred to me of asking her.

"¿Did someone put something in your pee hole? Besides this man just now, I mean."

"Of course they did. You know full well. There was you, Mama—"

"I don't mean *ever*. I mean today. ¿Has anyone else been inside you today?"

There came no response.

"Anyone. ¿Do you remember?"

Nothing.

"¿Do you remember the attack at home? ¿Was there anyone there in the house besides the nasty gambies? ¿How did you lose your fingers?"

Still nothing.

"Okay. Then we will have to play doctors and nurses again."

"Wash your hands first."

"So you *can* hear me."

"Yes. I was just *trying* to remember."

"Well, keep trying to remember while I drive us home. We can't hang around here all day. People will talk."

K

Karaoke: Is singing aloud to music in public, which, until karaoke, had not been thought of before. In terms of social hygiene, and not just because of all the different people who have been holding the same microphone and all the spittle flying everywhere, karaoke is a bad thing because it makes possible for men to sing women's songs and for women to sing men's songs. This can be the start of the slippery slope to gender fluidity, encouraging individuals to experiment with their personal identity and also with their genitals. The Japanese, who originated karaoke, did so as a way to winkle out employees with suspect deviant behaviour, nipping in the bud any thought crimes and non-conformities likely to fragment the social organism. The West, in its wisdom, turned it into a "fun night out with workmates," missing the point entirely and dooming generations of marketing teams to frivolous debauched etiolation, sapping morale, moral fibre, and sexual juices that would otherwise have been dedicated to national invigoration. But never mind. I will survive.

Kindling: Even before we had begun the descent from the top of the village, I could see a dense brown plume of smoke spiralling into the no-man's-sky separating earth and heaven. It was coming from whence I had have just departed but also whither we was heading, meaning that where I was having had been was now ablaze. My house. My redoubt. Either someone had followed me there or the perpetrators of the conflagration had lain in wait until I left in order to prevent me from returning and insulating myself against external threats, to drive me into the open by denying me the option of retreat.

"I smell burning. ¿Is it my hair?" Candelaría was reclining behind me, her comment testament to her still-working senses.

"Is my place," I replied, confirming the assertion by pulling up at the brow of Avenida los Lagos, which faced north and thus permitted me an unobstructed view of the upstairs floors of my house, where the reinforced windows remained intact but an inferno was raging within, the smoke, it was now apparent, escaping from the rooftop in swirls through the building's internal ducts and conduits.

I assessed the situation on the basis of the immediate information and my contextual background knowledge. ¿Who was being the likely perpetrators? Consider. For five years I had been trying to live under a radar, to enjoy my retirement as inconspicuously as possible, conscious of any action or distinction that might draw attention to my location. ¿Who on this earth might bear me any ill-will, what outrage could I have left imcomplete to deserve this? I consider myself an ordinary, passionate, principled, devout Spaniard living among other ordinary, passionate, principled, devout Spaniards. ¿How might I have caused offence? Sure, Andres the barber always rolled his eyes in despair when I entered his establishment, knowing that even though my head is small, it would take him more than two hours to trim my beard and moustache, cut my unruly thatch, tame my nostrils and ears. Certainly Rosa the pedicurist emitted a wail every time she saw me, having broken several pairs of clippers on my obstinate toenails. Andres the water-bearer may have borne not just water but also a grudge against me, I suppose, since I required him to bring my weekly supply of ten eight-litre bottles to the roof terrace every Wednesday—although I am wiry and strong, I am only small and not willing to play Sísifo every week, pushing them up the staircase one by one. Andres the boat builder had not forgiven me for making a *denuncia* against him for the smell of horse glue that hangs in the village air like an insistent taxman, banging on your head instead of your front door. Rosa the masseuse, yes, she always moaned about not being able to locate my flesh beneath my sleek black pelt. ¿But isn't that her own fault for using too much oil? And as for Andres the car mechanic, well, I am sorry, but if I want a replacement fan belt, I don't expect it to be made of his mother's corset lace simply because Andres the postman only opens an hour a day and it will take five weeks to source the parts from Dunf Ermline, wherever that is. Germany, I imagine. Andres the postman would have nothing against me in his capacity as the postman, since I have always been careful about what I order via the Correos. The only problem is that Andres the postman is also Andres the barber.

No. In general, I rub along with my neighbours very well. None of them have a good enough reason to burn my house to the ground. Thus, I concluded, this conflagration did not augur well.

I accelerated downhill, the speed bumps titillating Candelaría with their unexpected bounces, my eyes alert for any indication of human presence at my home—an open front door, a foot accidentally visible in the threshold, blue cigarette smoke at the downstairs window. An ambush was unlikely gived the obvious smoke signal that half the village must have seen, as well as the possibility of collapsing upper floors and the more probable tactical goal of depriving me of my stronghold. However, I couldn't take no chances. As I reached the bottom of the street, I passed Andres the Gossip Shop pushing Little Andres in a stroller. I waved nonchalantly before pulling the cushion from underneath me to sit low ... lower ... in the car and throttled the floor. The road was straight and short, with a clear eyeline from one end to the other, so it was easy to negotiate even with all the parked campervans and hire cars. It was also a one-way street, and so I sped down it the wrong way—in the hope of catching any assailant on the hop—past my front door—it was open, I saw instantly—before reaching the raised roundabout at the far end, which I had calculated would provide immediate cover.

There were no obvious signs of life as I raced by, which revelation gave me a clear choice. The first option: Don't stop. Drive on, seek shelter elsewhere, and make do with the weapons and kit which I was already having with me in the car and whatever else I could acquire. The second option: I could park up, venture back on foot, armed but not armoured, and see what I could salvage from the fire while also praying that nothing in the cache would explode while I was in there. For one thing, I could have done with saving my food supply. The pickled geckos would be baked but edible, providing the jars were intact. If the dried protein packs had survived, they would be no more inedible than usual. I was hungry.

"You stay here and keep your head down," I told Candelaría, who had gone quiet since we had passed the house. "I won't be more than ten minutes, but if I am, don't draw attention to yourself. Wait until after dark. You are safe enough within the village, and Andres the French baker will be passing by in the early hours. He will recognize the car. You can sleep until then."

"That's easy for you to say."

I pulled the Rover up outside the French bakery, around the next corner, and descended to the street, sprinting to the opposite wall and edging towards the front door of my home, the blade of Madonna's stiletto knife between the fingers of a clenched fist. It was ready to taste the thigh, first, of any doorway-hugger or sneaky-creep waiting to surprise me; then a puncture to the femoral artery, or at least to the meat of the muscle, blade in and out fast, before moving behind to the base of the skull, the assailant having been brought to his knees by the first strikes.

As I approached, the wind dropped and the road turned eerily quiet. The impermeability of my building's defences meant that little sound or heat was escaping the interior. The street slackened its tension, the twittering of concerned sparrows apart. Locals continued to recline on their daybeds on shady terraces unperturbed, tourists—those who still visited—sat pissed and sweaty in the nearby Muelle de los Pescadores, oblivious to the holocaust engulfing my beloved weaponry.

I threw myself across the threshold of the building at waist height—the waist height of an average Madrileño—and forward-rolled into the alcove of the stairwell. No one. As I had anticipated, the job, the foul deed, had already been accomplished. The first security door, on the mezzanine, was still unopened, meaning access had been gained via the back of the building, over the neighbors' rooftops, perhaps by zipwire, and with egress down the outside of the building via abseil or back through the neighbors' homes. My best guess was phosphorous grenades and/or incendiaries detonated down the service pipes; Molotovs would not have generated such an intense heat. I couldn't open the security door due to the risk of backdraft, meaning that I would not be able to retrieve my cache. No matter. I am nothing if not resourceful. Years of training as both a Fascist and a Catholic have had prepared me to endure, nay, enjoy, a life of hardship, bullying, obedience, and punishment. This would be like a summer holiday for me. In particular, that summer holiday in the Atacama Desert when our father left Candelaría and me in a broken wheelbarrow while he wandered off in search of a replacement strap for his travel humidor. Foretunately, on that occasion, I had been equipped with sufficient foresight—and childish sentimentality—to have brought the hipflask he had bought me for my tenth birthday, filled with Johnnie Walker—I was too young to appreciate single malt, according to him—which I used in conjunction with the deconstructed wheelbarrow to start a fire, enabling us to survive the freezing night huddled together until our father's triumphant return the next morning with a basket of dead long-tailed snakes, providing a heart-healthy breakfast, a makeshift humidor strap, a leash for Candelaría, and a story to entertain guests at Knockmerry House. You must never enbark on adventures you are unlikely to survive. Adventures that kill you cannot be embellished.

Kissing: A sign of betrayal. Also, very unhygienic. When Judas kissed Jesus, he not only betrayed him but also gave him herpes. ¡As if Jesus didn't already have enough to be worrying about!

Kissinger, Henry: "The United States is not having permanent friends or enemies. Is only having interests." This is not true. The United States is also having hobbies, such as eating, watching cartoons, and school shootings.

Knockmerry House: As you are by now aware, intelligence operatives are having an obligation to cultivate sources in all those places closest to power, be they boardrooms, barracks, basilicas or, as in the case of Turkey, bathhouses. This is a full-time job, there is not no two ways about it, but the canny operative, and I include myself in such a category, knows that you can kill two birds with one stone providing you have a particularly big stone or, failing that, with a shotgun, by conducting your intelligence gathering at a location guaranteed to attract the powerful from across the spectrum of social institutions, be they bankers, bishops, or brigadiers. I speak, of course, of the bordello, and I was most fortunate in this regard that one of Ireland's finest such establishments fell into my lap when Miss Whipcreme and Lady Jane Bondage, two of my high-class escort friends — it doesn't matter how I knew them — asked me to join their team. Over tea and scones in Bewley's Hotel, they explained to me that they had decided to set up on their own as entrepreneurial ladies, along with three or four other professional colleagues, operating out of a beautiful five-bedroom Georgian mansion just off the seafront in Dun Laoghaire, offering both take-away and eat-in services (¿or was it eat-out services? I cannot remember). Because of my useful contacts within the intelligence community but also because of my close work with the Gardaí and politicians of every colour, I was the ideal person, they said, to offer security for them but also the discreet publicity that they would require to drum up business in the right circles without bringing down on their heads the attention of the uninformed officer on the beat or the ignorant rabble-rousing journalist intent on highlighting the hypocrisy of the country's elite.

"Also, Manuel," they said to me, "We know you are a very devout and religious man, and therefore that you will ensure that nothing immoral takes place, such as clients trying to avoid payment or being rude to the girls or discussing communism or taking the Lord's name in vain and so on." Which was all true. And despite their reputations, working ladies are generally very God-fearing and upright-living people; even when they are flat-lying, they are upright-living. I was very glad that Jane and Miss Whipcreme asked me to be their moral policeman and could not think of nobody more suited to the job. It was the perfect symbiosis of the oldest profession and the second-oldest profession (the third-oldest profession is marketing). After not a very long time, I was able also to use my knowledge and position of power to take overall control of the business, through the judicious use of violence and blackmail against Jane and Miss Whipcreme, who soon realized that their natural position was under me and resignably accepted the senior madam positions I permitted them on pain of further pain.

Koala: Urinates far more than you would expect for a creature of such small volume. Does not understand the most basic instructions, even when spoken in the clearest Spanish, such as "Get Down," "Don't Urinate There," and "Stop Eating the Wasps." Tastes mildly eucalyptusy, with a hint of honey and urine. Not unpleasant but hardly worth the mess.

L

Lady Jane Bondage: Although, as I have mentioned, I was the manager of Knockmerry House, I did not devote the majority of my time to running it, since I was also the head of Spanish Intelligence for Ireland and thus also in charge of all administration, policy execution, and day-to-day decision making with regard not just to espionage itself, a minor aspect of my routine, but also the cocaine and ketamine distribution business, co-managed with Frank Prendergast of the U.S. Defense Intelligence Agency. My work at Knockmerry House was consequently confined to entertaining visitors whose interests were relevant to those other operations and also to afternoons of light relief in the dungeons below the building, where we interrogated transgressors and bill dodgers or tortured enemies of the state, drug rivals, and those who simply enjoyed being tortured and were willing to pay for it.

Miss Whipcreme and Lady Jane Bondage acted as the front-of-house staff, two of the most experienced but nonetheless least grubbedy of whores it has ever been my delight to encounter. Miss Whipcreme's main responsibilities were to supervise the "fucking team," as we called the whores who worked there (is important in any business that employees have a sense of team spirit), and to take care of the judges, police chiefs, politicians, and journalists with a penchant for BDSM, role play, food fun, diaper soiling, toilet bowl rimming, sphincter racing, *bimbonismo*, pneumatics/bubonics, juicing, flap-jacking, composting, thruving, wound play, seagulling, frothing, edging, vegetable play, brush snuffing, tappery, ball smoking, paralicking, nasal interference, muffing, chaircocking, scrote conduction, perineal plunging, knobotomy, bummery, knock-jobbery, corking, enemas (production and consumption), coprophilia/phobia/phagia, linging, jimming, pottling (light and heavy), pillowing, rag riding, smutty dithers, pompomming, mosaicking, jazzticles, scraping, anxious chocolate, panching, smearing, invisible painting, priapics, pump nutting, sour tots, opacity, noisy grapes, vasing, *jeux de corps*, felching, back cunting, and spaves. Lady Jane Bondage was responsible for the handjobs.

This division of labour may, on first viewing, seem somewhat imbalanced but, my word: ¡What handjobs Jane Bondage could give! I would venture that she had the supplest and strongest wrists this side of Christendom (the Christian side), and while Jesus himself would have had no need of her services, any of his followers would have considered themselves divinely touched were they to have spent no more than a minute (and fifty euros) in thrall to Lady Jane. She could have initiated a religion of her own had she so wished, but a vast crowd of regular, high-paying customers was sufficient and hardly any different.

I should also acknowledge that Lady Jane carried out other tasks in the business beyond her professional duties, such as bookkeeping and conciergerie. Was she who booked appointments, supervised and disciplined the girls (first-order disciplinary action; more severe punishments were dealt with by me or by one or more of my *bichos*), and welcomed and trained the first-timers (girls and clients). She also entertained various hangers-on and subordinates while I met with their superiors. For instance, whenever Frank was visiting, he would bring along the vacuous and useless Joseph Chambers, an appalling and disreputable CIA demotee who had been put in a holding pattern in Ireland while the Company decided how to dispose of him. He was also an old friend of Frank's whom he had been unable to shake off. Lady Jane was required to engage Chambers in conversation and diversion, keeping his focus on the pleasures of the flesh and away from too many questions about the clientele or Knockmerry House's extracurricular activities. On such occasions, her powers of manipulation always came in handy.

"Came in handy": ¡Is a joke!

Lady Lesbians: You would be forgiven for thinking that there is nothing more natural—and therefore more evil—than two naked nubile young ladies reciprocly enjoying the pleasurable sensations arising from the gentle touching and exploratory tonguing of one another's sweet pink grapefruity flesh, as seen on Fuckhub, Pornstop, and XBeebies. However, you could not be more wrong, since lady lesbianism, for that is what this is, is one of the mainstays of the Patriarchy, a gateway deviation that makes possible the undoubtably less pleasant but more necessary reproductive heterosexual sex that nobody can truly say they enjoy. To appreciate how this is the case, you need to understand that both of the outcomes of lesbian experimentation (negative and positive lesbian sexual experiences) lead to an increase in heterosexuality and therefore more children. On the one hand, if a normal lady is having a positive sexual experience with a lady lesbian, say during her experimental university phase or in prison, she will say to herself, "Wow, that was good. Imagine what proper sex with a man must be like. It will be amazing. I must give it a go." If, on the other hand, she is having a negative lady lesbian experience, she will say, "Ugh, that muffing is not for me at all. And the scissoring is a lot of effort. Therefore, I must be a heterosexual." Whichever experience she is having, the normal lady will then be keen to give the sex with a man a try. However, if all the Patriarchal laws are working properly, she will have to marry one first and thus, no matter how vile and disgusting the sex with a man is, the disappointment will be too late; the Patriarchy's no contraception/no sodomy/no divorce/no abortion rules will mean she cannot turn her back. Even if she discovers that the sex with men is much much worse than lady lesbianism, she will soon be with child and unable to nothing about it.

For those who are septical about this theory, I will point out that the lady lesbian gene is passed down (indeed, *must* be passed down) by the male. Lady lesbians are unable to conceive on their own, so they cannot pass the gene down themselves. The existence of lady lesbians therefore depends on sex between two heterosexuals, meaning that normal sex is necessary to produce them. Obviously, the man must be the one who is having the lady lesbian gene because if the woman was the one having it, she would *be* one. Is in this way that lady lesbians exist, functioning as the unwitty handmaidens of the Patriarchy.

Don't blame me about it. ¡Is simple biology!

Lajares: It was four years ago, at the otherwise underwhelming Saturday market in Lajares, home to Fuerteventura's surf/reggae/riffrafftafarian community, that I first met Doktor and Frau Rotgütt. While the other market stalls was nothing more than vehicles for supplementing the *paro* of 1960s acid casualties, smackheads, and cultural degenerates, manifested by the proliferation of tie-dye shirts, the aroma of patchouli oil—even in the open air, the pungency was oppressive—and the dirty-face urchin offspring, the Rotgütts' stall shone, like a pelican of discipline, order, and holesome civilization.

I should say that a deviation from my routine led to this encounter, lest you imagine it my wont to frequent such louche environs. My Saturdays typically involved the leisurely perusal of papal histories and three hours of determined self-punishment. The need to visit Lajares only arose from the absence of chloroform in my medical cabinet and the fact that my usual supplier in the north of the island refused to work weekends. I was thus being forced to visit him at home; why he had chosen Lajares for his residence was beyond human comprehension.

Parking on the main street meant that I had to cross the village square to reach his villa, passing through the market on my way. I found it easy to ignore the imploring cajolery of the near-destitute vendors: ¿Do I look like someone who would want to wear a threadbear hat? ¿An orange-braid bracelet made from fishing net twine? ¿Shoes which you recovered from the sea? No. I interrupted my traversal of the square only with the occasional stop to sneer. However, on this day, I couldn't help but be drawn to what I can only describe as a beatific vision, directly ahead of me, both in my path but also worth going out of my way for: distinctive, alluring, sirenic.

On one side of the cash desk was sitting Frau Rotgütt, a leather-skinned Brunhilde surrounded, almost adorned, by stack upon stack after stack of birdcages, within which fluttered, squawked, whistled, and screeched a kaleidoscope of avian life: parakeets, finches, canaries, toucans, budgerigars, hummingbirds, kingfishers, pheasants, cormorants, ducks, eagles, peacocks, and tits, each expressing its own particular god-given nature in the same way that nations and peoples do and for which reason must also be kept separate. Indeed, one might almost think of countries as cages, of many different shapes and sizes, some with cuttlefish and mirrors, others with nuts and seeds, but all fundamentally purpose-built to meet their inhabitants' needs and keep them safe and where God can keep an eye on them so that they don't try to fly. God in this case was Frau Rotgütt, who was supervising benignly while amusing herself with the large spider sleeping on her right shoulder and the patient, possibly narcoleptic, spider monkey on her left: "I always co-ordinate," she explained to me later.

In part, the brouhaha being generated by this colourful and exotic throng was no doubt the result of the smells emanating from Doktor Rotgütt's side of the stall, where he, ecto- to his wife's endomorph—lean, tanned, wizened—was presiding imperiously over an impressive charnelhouse of barbecuing meats of the world—sausages, burgers, chitterlings, blood pudding—and more than a few whole roast birds: chickens, pigeons, ducks, and some of the more insubordinate parakeets, finches, canaries, toucans, and cetera. The aroma of caramelizing flesh was, while not necessarily saliva inducing, a balm, a salve against the gutteral hippie stench around us. The Rotgütts' stall provided a veritable island of decency in a sea of turpitude.

While I munched on an ortolan empanadilla, the Rotgütts telled me their story, insofar as it explained the incongruity of their presence there that day. It seemed that their home was overrun, Durrell-like, by animals and that they toured the island's markets to dispose of their surplus fauna. Indeed, I was to meet them again only two weeks later at the Friday-night market in the Old Square of El Cotillo, an entirely new stock of creatures on display, including pangolins, capybaras, otters, moths, and owls. On that occasion, I expressed my septicism that anyone would want to buy, let alone eat, a bag of moths.

"We don't leave the wings on, obviously," the Doktor said, as if that resolved the matter. "We're not mad."

Once the market was over and they had packed up the surviving produce, we retired to the aptly named Corner Bar, in the corner of the square, where the owner, Andres the Corner Bar, plied us with Arehucas rum with bitter lemon, an odd taste combination but a favourite of the local fishermen and anyone trying to blend in.

"¿Have you gived thought perhaps to just ... releasing the animals into the wild?" I suggested and quickly regretted.

"We aren't running a charity," Frau Rotgütt said, keen to disabuse me. "Don't think just because we are Germans of a certain age that we are soft in the head. I know you see a lot of these idiot Krauts here who have 'dropped out' because they could not survive in normal society and come here to live on the cheap with their rescue dogs and their rescue fleas. This is not us."

"Besides, Señor Estímulo," the Doktor broke in, "We could cause an ecological meltdown were we to do so. We are trying to be responsible custodians of the wildlife."

"Hence the barbecue," said Frau Rotgütt, her shrug punctuating the self-evidentiary nature of her explanation.

"Of course," I allowed. "Most admirable." Andres the Corner Bar brought over *papas fritas* in a large bowl. Frau Rotgütt plucked one out for the spider monkey, which displayed no interest.

"We are not jewboy capitalists determined to make money any way we can," the Doktor continued. "We dispose of our waste in a sensible and self-sustaining manner. To avoid overpopulation."

"Is all about *lebensraum*," Frau Rotgütt elaborated, glass of Arehucas at her lips. "Our vaults and storerooms are vast, but they soon fill up in the face of such fecundity."

"Animals do what animals do," the Doktor explained. "They follow their nature."

"Good for the roses, though," I ventured, cheerfully. This seemed to perplex them momentarily.

"Ach, the *Scheisse*," said Frau Rotgütt. "Ja, we are full of it. Sadly, we are having no roses, though. Is too hot, this climate. They don't last."

"You must come to see our home one day," the Doktor said, "but is very remote. ¿Do you know Cofete?" I shook my head. "You would need a boat to get there. We are right at the very bottom of the island. The rocky terrain and desert make it difficult to reach, but the beaches are incomparable. They stretch over the horizon. Further than the sea. And there are no other people to be seen."

"Ja," said Frau Rotgütt, wistfully. "Just us and the animals. Is perfect."

"Sounds lovely," I said. "One day, perhaps. One day."

Lancashire Hotchpotch: A dark Satanic stew, which contains all the food ingredients to be found in the northern English county of Lancashire: tripe, gravy, poverty, Eccles cakes, grime, and clogs. Like the Basques, the peoples of Lancashire are very poor but proud for no reason. Also, like the Basques, the Lancastrians have their own cuisine and their own language, but any responsible parent would slap it out of their child's mouth upon first contact, be it a slice of Parkin or a fronted Y.

Laserian, Saint (d. 639): According to *¡The Truth About Carlow! Saints, Murderers, Sodomites, and Celebrities,* Saint Laserian miraculously healed a boy who had been decapitated, but the book does not say whether the Saint used his laser vision in a kind of cauterizing/welding operation or if he just did it by praying. I assume the former because he subsequently became the patent saint of shipbuilders, microprocessor manufacturers, and Bond villains.

History books state that when he arrived in Carlow, Saint Laserian first considered establishing his church in Bagenalstown but then had second thoughts when the first person he saw there was a red-haired woman, even back then thought to be a terrible omen. Consequently, he taked the rest of the day off to recover, like any sensible construction industry boss. However, the next morning, an Irish angel came to him and told him to sit in the stone chair on the top of Ballycormac Hill and to build his church on the spot where the Sun first shined that day. This turned out to be five days later, when a wan finger of light descended upon the village of Old Leighlin, although at the time it was not very old at all and was just called Leighlin.

Despite his laser vision, Saint Laserian was no match for his rival for the affections of the local virgin, Saint Sillán, of whom it was said that anyone who saw his eyebrow would die immediately. Although laser treatment is used these days for monobrows, Laserian stupidly tried to pluck out Sillán's eyebrow instead, conserving his laser power. Unforetunately, this meant he had to look to see what he was doing and thus it was curtains for Laserian. Thick black curtains.

There is a range of opinion as to where Saint Laserian's remains remain. Some say that they was put under his church at Old Leighlin whereas others say that looking at Sillán's eyebrow results in death by explosion and that Laserian has no remains other than those littering the fields of Leighlin and now well mulched into the earth that he once trod and ploughed with his laser vision. Still others wonder why Laserian didn't just use his laser power on Saint Sillán and evaporate him instead of using his normal vision, but the rules of engagement for saints in combat against each other preclude offensive use of holy weapons. Sillán's eyebrow constitutes a defensive weapon, and anyway it was Laserian who started it.

The virgin did not remain a virgin for long. Not in Carlow.

Law, The: No one is above the law. Not even Jesus, as was proved in the Bible.

When dealing with the law, always ensure that you are hiring a female solicitor and a male barrister. Female solicitors are more diligent because they think they have to prove they are as good as the men. Male barristers are better because most judges are men and will therefore treat your barrister with the respect he deserves.

Lawrence, Saint (225–258): Spanish-born saint who the Romans burned to death on a griddle. The river in America bearing his name separates the barbecuing from non-barbecuing states.

Leaving: After the destruction of my home, the most obvious source of shelter and protection was that being offered by the Rotgütts, at the furthest, most remote and most inaccessible part of the island. A journey manageable within a day, 130 kilometers by road or a mere seventy-five according to the crowflies. The roads were not an option because a) there is only one possible route to Cofete, making interception inevitable, and b) the map I was having was a map of England, and while what remained of England on the map resembled Fuerteventura in outline, the roads were not remotely similar. For one thing, the roads of Fuerteventura are either gleaming strips of pure driving bliss—thanks to EU subsidies—smooth, slick, silent, and traffic-free, or else dirt tracks of volcanic stone, discombombulating, unbalancing, irritating, enraging, and dangerous, with or without other drivers. The roads of England, by contrast, are cars and trucks as far as the eye can see, a nation on the move to nowhere. It matters not whether English roads are shiny or ruckety, nobody moves any faster than the tortoise beating Achilles.

The fastest route for us was a straight line south, down the west coast of the island, offroad, avoiding all the towns and ports, negotiating bird sanctuaries, *barrancos*, *arroyos*, and riverbeds as best we might could.

Foretunately, this was just the kind of journey for which my solid, stable, stalwart Land Rover was having had been built. We was sorted.

Leicester, Red: Coalminers always carry wedges of Red Leicester cheese when they are beneath the surface; in the presence of carbon monoxide it turns blue.

Leitrim, County: The home of Irish Fascism. A hotbed of the rural underclass, survivalists, hippie supremacists, Christian racists, and British ex-pat Nazis on the run. Its motto is "~~Welcome to~~ Leitrim."

Lemons, Sherbet: Everyone loves sherbet lemons, but resist the temptation to scoff the entire bag. When you are stuck under an avalanche, you will be grateful that you saved one to make into a whistle.

Lent: Every Lent, I always give up margaritas and baby lotion. It never lasts.

Lettuce, Romaine: Make holes for your eyes, nose, and mouth in a large Romaine lettuce leaf to avoid the police recognizing you at the Swiss border.

Lipstrob, Saint (1407–1444): The following are some of the messages, prayers, and petitions for intercession left at the shrine of Saint Lipstrob the Indifferent in Antwerp before the Second World War Two:

"Dear Saint Lipstrob. Please help my brother find his eyes."

"Blessed Saint Lipstrob, please let Bayern win the League this year. Failing that, let my wife die in an accident. Is our destiny."

"¿How can I tell if a prostitute is really interested in me?"

"Holy Saint Lipstrob, please give me my handkerchief back."

"¿Why are there ironmongers, cheesemongers, and fishmongers but not meatmongers? ¿Did Jesus have them all killed?"

"Dear Saint Lipstrob. I have done a painting of you in heaven. ¿Would you like to see it? I have gived you a monocle. It suits you."

"¿What can I do about my girlfriend's provocative candle collection?"

"¿Where are my arms? I can't feel my arms."

¡Long Live Death!: ¡Viva la Muerte! Is the battle cry of the Spanish Foreing Legion but also my very first words, which I proclaimed as I entered this world from my mother's womb, slick with mucous, blood, and shit (hers, not mine). Two of the nurses immediately fainted dead away. My father often said that he was never prouder of me than on that day.

Lorca, Gabriel Garcia: Degenerate homosexual poet and playwrighter with friends in high places but not high enough.

Is a well-known fact that if you read a poem by Lorca out loud, your breath will stink afterwards. If you read it silently to yourself, afterwards, your brain will stink.

Louisiana: In the U.S. state of Louisiana, every art gallery must display at least one dog portrait.

Loyalism: Like Nationalism, the substance and style of loyalism varies by country. In Spain, for example, loyalism refers to those who was loyal to the criminal Republican government during the Civil War and included liberals, socialists, Trotskyists, and other assorted nefarious scum. Loyalism was thus a very bad thing and symptomatic of the virulent disease of democracy which the Spanish nation was suffering at that time. By contrast, in Northern Ireland, loyalism is an openly homoerotic movement with all-male gangs, boy grooming, body-building, hard drugs, prison, and Tina Turner songs. Strangely, this is *not* regarded as a disease or an illness corrupting the body politic but as the legitimate cultural expression of a normal, decent, right-leaning, white supremacist, misogynist tradition. ¡Is very confusing but also explains why loyalists like to be (and should be) kept separate from everybody else!

Lucozade: Spray Lucozade into the eyes of an advancing tiger. This will stick its eyelids shut, giving you ample time to open another bottle of Lucozade and drink it for all the energy you will need to run away.

M

Madstone: A madstone is a special medicinal substance that, when you press it into an animal bite, will prevent rabies by drawing out the poison. The *Encyclopedia Americana* describes it as "a vegetable substance or stone." Researchers publishing in 1958 reported "143 cases of healing attributable to madstones" and "three authentic stones in the United States today."

What the researchers forget to mention is that the U.S. government has all three madstones and only lends them to its friends. ¡Typical!

Mafia: A term used to refer to any underground organizations, affiliations, coalitions, conspiracies, or actors lacking the legitimacy of state recognition, thereby distinguishing them from state-sanctioned criminal enterprises like the Freemasons, Illuminati, Big Pharma, Hollywood, NGOs, Big Ecology, the Post Office, academia, the mass media, and zoos, all of whom are in a symplegmatic relationship with the government, like two entwined lesbians with their fingers in each other' pies. But less fun to watch.

Magicians: Social pariahs whose shenanigans attempt to replicate the miracles of the Pious, the implication being that Jesus was a charlatan who pulled the wool over the eyes of the simple Galileean public with his walking on the water, turning fish into chips, and cetera. Foretunately, is no more acceptable today to be a magician than in the days of Harry Houdini, when members of the Magic Circle was outcasts, misfits, and lepers who the normal townfolk hunted down, humiliated, scorned, tied up in a strait jacket, suspended upside down, and lowered into a tank of water behind a curtain so nobody could see them. And then afterwards punched them in the stomach. Usually this was enough to kill them.

Mankind: The venerable and reliable newspaper *ABC* once reported that scientists had found a human tooth in Spain that was over one million years old. ¡Older than planet Earth itself! The idiot scientists was also able, using sophisticated prognosis forensic morphinology, to reconstruct the entire head, torso, and limbs of the first human being from this tooth. His name was Pablo Martínez Escudero from Valladolid.

This evidence conclusively proves what I and all the correct scientists who agree with me have been saying in the wilderness for ages: Human beings originally came into existence in Spain, where they wrote the Bible and killed off the dinosaurs. This tooth also showed that carbon dating is a totally unreliable method of testing the age of things like trees, planets, Turin Shrouds, and cetera, and that scientific learning requires a complete overhaul, as well as groveling apologies to the Church from Richard Dawkins, Alfred Einstein, Charles Darwin, and Galileo, who has already made one groveling apology but had his fingers crossed at the time and was not being sincere.

Pablo lost his tooth when he was twenty-five, probly the result of fighting Sable Tooth Tigers or a gang of Mastodons. We tend to forget that back in those days, prehistoric man was not having such weapons as the sword, lances, banderillas, or capes with which to defend himself against wild animals. He would have had to use fists, teeth, feet, fingernails, stones, bad breath, lies, the homeless, big sticks, or whatever else came to hand. Was a real proper struggle for survival, and very few dinosaurs was susceptible to the Word of God, so converting them to Christianity was out of the question, especially when they tasted so good.

There has been since more discoveries confirming Spanish primacy in the origins of humankind and showing the derivation of everyone else thencefrom. It therefore should come as some comfort to all those not fortunate enough to be Spanish to know that their ancestors were more lucky than them and of purer blood and better breeding; we current proper Spanish already know how lucky we are.

Marat, La Cloche du: A slang term which Parisian whores use to refer to the clitoris. "Ringing Marat's bell" thus refers to orgasm from stimulation of the clitoris alone, an experience rare among that demographic.

Marathon Man: A famous film with an unrealistic torture scene but a strong underlying message: You can't eat a lot of chocolate bars and expect to get off lightly at the dentist. Was recently remade as *Snickers Man*, which was shorter but cost more.

Marbella: Once upon a time, almost a heaven on earth, a place much-sought-after to live by gangsters, Fascists, and other lovers of golf. The town has gone a bit to the dogs in recent years, however, now that the Russian oligarchs have moved in with the wealth they expropriated from the Communist Party. Of course, there is nothing wrong with wealth, especially wealth from another country being spent in Spain, but in this case it brings with it the Russian oligarchs, who are just as loud and domineering as Americans but even more vulgar. ¡They don't even know one end of a three wood from the other!

Marcelino pan y vino: Every Spanish person's favourite film of all time (and thus a good measure of whether someone is Spanish enough). It tells the true story of a little foundling boy, Marcelino, who got his name from the film of the same name, taked in by a monastery of monks who raise him to be a little scamp (he has no mother or father to be role models). One day, Marcelino goes into the attic of the monastery during one of his escapades and who is he finding there hiding but Jesus. ¡Sí! Jesus had been there all that time in the attic, hanging from a cross, except he is also wooden, like the cross to which he is nailed.

Nevertheless, this being Catholic Spain, the wooden Jesus can talk and eat and drink, so Marcelino begins to steal bread and wine from the monks (even though this is illegal) to feed the crucifixed Jesus. The crucifixed Jesus is very grateful, so he grants Marcelino one wish; Jesus in this movie is a sort of Good Witch of the East, only without the wings or magic wand or nice pink dress. Marcelino says that his biggest wish is to see his mother, although he does not know when he says this that his mother is dead. Jesus *does* know, however, so to arrange for Marcelino to see her, Jesus kills him.

How delightful. Is a heart-warming tail about looking after Jesus, and he will look after you, a kind of religious protective racquet, like the ones they use in fencing.

Margarine (with plant sterols): Smear it across the floor of a shopping mall and it will provide an impassable barrier against small dogs and old ladies carrying small dogs.

Margarine (trans-fat-free): Far healthier than trans-fat spreads. Coat the inside of your coffin with trans-fat-free margarine when they have buried you alive and the slight translucent glow it gives off as a result of a chemical reaction with the wood in a low-oxygen environment should give you enough light to locate your mobile phone. Is a long shot, but it won't work with any other kind of margarine or butter.

Maryland: In the U.S. state of Maryland, is illegal to eat cement.

Mary, Typhoon: She blew through Kansas in a shitstorm of dysentery, the first case of nominative determinism since John the Baptist.

Marx, Karl: According to materialism, which is wrong, the ideas of the ruling class are in every epoch the ruling ideas. Marxists believe this hogwash to be true but therefore cannot explain how the ideas of Marxism have become the ruling ideas in modern society. Not unless, that is, *they* are the ruling class. However, they are not the ruling class: ¡They are just morons! Instead, the truth is that Marxism is pushed everywhere by the liberal intellectual elite, who are the real ruling class, not because Marxism is having any truth in it but because it meets their need to divide and rule the nation. When people self-identify or identify others as petty-bourgeois or working class or middle class, they are set in competition against one another, instead of uniting as a nation to overthrow the ruling liberal intellectual elite who propagate this nonsense. Only when you realize that every country is run by a liberal intellectual ruling elite can you begin to see the world clearly and shake off your "false consciousness," the only Marxist concept that *is* true.

Massachusetts: In the U.S. state of Massachusetts, schoolteachers must always pronounce the word "carapace" with a silent n.

Mass Media: Necessary for the manufacturing of consent, but also handy for manufacturing passivity, cynicism, apathy, fear, and cetera. In the perfect dictatorship, the mass media would be unnecessary since the masses' views would be of no consequence whatsoever. ¿Where, today, is such a paradise? If you find it, let me know.

Masturbation: In men, demeaning and pathetic, neither of which have proven to be a deterrent. In women, a sad fact of life, but often preferable to sex with men, who are also a sad fact of life.

Matilde, Waltzing: Just as Britain is having John Bull, the U.S. is having Uncle Sam, and France is having Pepe le Pew, so Austria is incarnated by the archetypal Aryan *Hausfrau* Matilde, a buxom, middle-age, sexually alluring blond in plaits and gingham who, when she is not baking the pastries, dances the waltz, which they invented in Austria, as is well known. Indeed, the song "Waltzing Matilde" is the unofficial national anthem of Austria.

Mediocrity: One day, when he was particularly frostrated with my lack of sporting achievement and had resigned himself to me never playing for

Real Madrid, my father sat me down for a heart-to-heart chat to encourage me in other directions.

"Hijo de Puta," he said, "You will never not be anything more than a mediocrity in this life. You are well below the average height, your limbs are short and ungainly, and you are no oil painting for the ladies. However, you must never not let any of this stop you from achieving your goals. The Generalísimo himself was a mediocrity, a small man with the squeaky voice of a whore on helium. Hitler was a mediocrity, a semi-literate autodidact with ideas above his station. Il Duce was a pompous bombastic blithering idiot. All three of them was, by any objective standard, total losers. ¿But do you know what else they were having?"

"¿Massive financial backing?"

"Well, yes, of course. The support of true patriotic landowners and industrialists goes without saying. ¿What else?"

"¿Aerial superiority?"

"Oh yes," he beamed. "That was essential." I had learned even at this early age that my domestic education was having more to do with my father's self-aggrandisement than the imparting of valuable information. "Without aerial superiority, there could have been no Guernica. But I was thinking of something else."

I frowned to indicate the difficulty of this test.

"Aggression. Drive. Hatred. As small men, they had learned the importance of teaching others not to try bullying, intimidating, or dominating them. Consequently, they regarded every encounter with a stranger as a challenge that they were determined to win."

I nodded my understanding.

"They had to struggle immensely against all odds to get whatever they achieved early in life, however meagre. But they were having the advantage over taller, better, more handsome men because such men are often ignorant of their own privilege. ¿Why should a smaller man not be having everything the tall man has when the small man has fought for his country? You too must develop such aggression. With it will come cunning, ruthlessness, guile. ¿What is playing for Real Madrid when you can own Real Madrid? This will be your revenge on the world. You might be small like a woman, but you must refuse to let others treat you like one. That would be the ultimate shame."

"Thank you, father. I will bear this in mind."

"Good. Now send in your sister."

Metro System: As my father used to say, "If you don't know the difference between the metro system and the metric system, you won't get very far in life. You won't even get across town."

¡Is a joke!

Michigan: In the U.S. state of Michigan, you must be over sixty-five years of age to use a yo-yo.

Miguel, Don: Was our great uncle, on my mother's side, a war hero (a member of the Infantry of Castile) and a very rich man (he did not become rich until after the war, obv) who raised grapes on his estate and was married also to our grandmother. A man of great daring but also insouciance, he once cut off the little finger of his left hand and throwed it into a furnace of 1,000° Celsius, just for the craic (as the Irish say). Was not even for some shoddy prosaic reason such as a bet or curiosity. He did it to entertain his grandchildren, two of whom died of shock (one of them not until three years later as the result of an unrelated incident).

Military Life: Contrary to weak-kneed liberal propaganda, the military life is one that promotes longevity and healthiness. Just pay a visit to your local war memorial on Remembrance Day and see how many old men are there marching. You will never see that many old surgeons or doctors or nurses or social workers or journalists marching because they are all dead. Probly it was these soldiers who killed them.

Millán-Astray y Terreros, José (1879–1954): Whereas Nazism is a homoerotic movement that delights in the zeal and physical beauty of young boys, the character of True Fascism is the defilement, degradation, and disparagement of the body, in line with the slogan "¡Viva la muerte!" which scoffs at the preening of pretty boys seeking to seduce and impress ladies using their superficial and ephemeral charms. Nobody embodied the True Fascist spirit better than Millán-Astray, founder of the Spanish Foreing Legion and scourge of communists, anarchists, Protestants, atheists, homosexuals, and liberals everywhere. I use the word "embodied" advisably, since what remained of Millán-Astray after his battlefield adventures was only part of his body, and yet he was more of a man than any of his peers, regardless of their limb count.

There is no truth to the rumour that Millán-Astray regularly rode around the parade ground in the middle of the night on the backs of naked Moorish soldiers on all fours while wearing a crotchless leotard. ¿And anyway, even if he did, what were you doing up so late to see it?

Milo, Venus de: Absolute proof that the Romans too faced the problem of terrible farm accidents that no amount of government regulation could prevent. Also clear evidence of an empire that did not shy away from disfigurement. So confident was the Roman Empire in the permanence of its power that it could even devote statues to amputees.

Minnesota: In the U.S. state of Minnesota, is illegal to stick Post-its on babies.

Minotaur, Milk: In Olde England, the milk minotaurs was misshapen children with human heads and the bodies of cows who distributed their milk to all their classmates at morning siesta time. In her wisdom, Margaret Thatcher had them all put down. You don't see them any more, which is why English children today are simultaenously more weak but also have fewer nightmares.

Misogyny: Not to be confused with gynophobia, which is "an irrational fear of women," misogyny is simply "hatred of women." There are two implications from this distinction and these definitions. The first is that hatred of women is *not* irrational. The second is that there is a fear of women that *is* rational, presumably one resulting from personal experience. Thus, it follows that both hatred and a rational fear of women are justifiable attitudes. When the unapologeticly Australian Germaine Greer said that "Women have no idea how much men hate them," she forgot to add, "¡And with good reason!"

To my mind, however, hatred is too strong an emotion to countenance toward women because it implies that they are worthy of such an extreme response. The belief that Fascists hate women is one of the reasons why Fascism is so often misunderstood. True Fascists feel not hatred for women but contempt, the same way we feel nothing but contempt for men too, including ourselves. As the IDF says, "Kill them all, let God sort them out."

Remember, though, suicide is a mortal sin, so you must let someone else kill you, preferably on a battlefield in the sunshine with God watching.

Mississippi: In the U.S. state of Mississippi, is illegal to use electric razors to scare children.

Missouri: In the U.S. state of Missouri, is illegal to share your toothbrush with an elk.

Models: Sales prostitutes. Models are human objects whose proximity to commodities is meant to enhance the desirability of those commodities. Spiritual and moral black holes. If I had labour camps, the first people I would imprison would be models. They would all starve properly then.

Mola, General Emilio (1887–1937): Initially the director of Spain's Nationalist crusade. In 1937, he died suddenly, selflessly, and not at all suspiciously in a plane crash in order to make way for his acknowledged tactical superior, El Generalísimo Francisco Franco. Some heroes don't wear parachutes.

Molinos, Los: *¡Puta de mierda!* ¡Fucking useless Rover! The British make cars the same way they make love: with no attention to detail or safety. Also, up the barranco. Because that is where the Land Rover ended after only fifty minutes of driving.

We was heading due South from El Cotillo, according to plan, along the dirt track that follows the clifftops before meandering haphazardly through the bird refuge. After six kilometers, we cut inland before the isolated hamlet of Taca to find the shallow crossing point of the Barranco de Esquinzo—no water was running down the barranco, but its southern ridge at the coast is steep, and I didn't want Candelaría tumling out the back of the car and rolling down into the ravine. I would have had to push her back up the slope, like Sísifo. Three kilometers inland was a junction with the narrower and shallower Barranco Encantado, which flows into the Esquinzo before the latter reaches the "Witches' Ballroom," la Cueva del Bailadero de las Brujas, where local witches used to pleasure themselves at midnight with fetishes, familiars, and unfamiliars, usually goats, either to bring rain and drown their enemies or else to stop rain and curse the farmers. They were happy either way, which is why they danced.

We continued along the track in a straight line past the sacred mountain of Tindaya, with its cat-shaped stones and rugged outline, peculiar for such an old volcanic island, where all the other edges and ridges have been softened by millennia of sand- and saltblasting into a landscape of reclining women, with soft curves, gentle undulations, and smelly crevices that look like you could softly part them to reveal dark, secret tunnels filled with bats. We skirted Tindaya village and crossed the

Barranco de Tebeto, not far from the old Mismorilla watering hole. In bygone days, this watering hole was full of leeches which used to bite the farmers' cows when they drank there, causing a reduction in milk output and bovine respiratory problems. In response, the farmers used eels to kill the leeches and were so successful that they was able to develop a sideline in eel breeding, taking the eels to other wells and watering holes or selling them to other farmers. Eventually, some of the farmers stopped cattle herding altogether when they cornered the market in eels. There is still a Calle Anguila, Eel Street, in Corralejo, and the Rosario adult cabaret act Andres the Eelboy is said to be a direct descendant of those farmers, although his act would make them spin in their eel-funded graves.

We briefly joined one of the coast roads from Tindaya that ran parallel to the Barranco Las de Pilas, keeping the Sun to our left at all times—I turned the visor to shield the side of my face from the glare and blazing heat. We crossed the barranco at the foot of the lava cascade of El Sobaco de Malpaís, behind Montaña Quemada, home to the Monument to Unamuno, and followed the lava flow almost back to the sea, weaving by the Barranco de Jarubio at the Playa del Jarugo.

Was just before the village of Los Molinos that it happened. My intention was to head away from the coast because the terrain after Los Molinos became non-negotiable by car: a terrain riddled with *arroyos*, crevasses, and steep impassable rifts. We would had to risk briefly joining the FV-221 between Puertito de Los Molinos and the Hermitage of San Andres to join the FV-207 and avoid the busy town of Tefía, but foretunately a side road followed the Barranco de Tao and crossed the Barranco de Los Molinos further inland, narrow but, with care, passable. Taking it would have had been a sound plan on any other day. On this day, however, San Andres was doing his rounds. The good pious folk of Tetir had gathered in procession with the statue of the saint held aloft afore them, taking him out to the fields to ask for his blessing and some rain pretty please and stop the witches. This was a problem for us, not because we ran the risk of being spotted by suspicious locals but because this particular saint, God forgive him, was always having a habit of answering such entreaties promptly and without reservation. He was such a crowd pleaser.

And indeed, just as the saint was reaching the first field, out of the blue—literally out of the blue, since there was no clouds to be seen—came the deluge. The sky burst open, a tear ripping across the blue, and the torrent was immediately upon us. Instinctively, I put my foot down on the gas and raced inland, up the barranco, in the hope of reaching the crossing before we could be washed away. But these barrancos were formed with such ingenuity by God, with His knowledges of gravity, physics, geology, and water, that they concentrate the sky's secretions with unfathomable efficiency, channeling even the most widely distributed precipitation into deep and powerful cascades, and woe betide anything in their path. The vast cerulean dome above us emptied its contents upon us and the cascade began, burling down the mountains before plunging without pause across the fields and plains, and straight down the barranco, sweeping along everything in its path: agave plants; dead cacti; palm fronds; lizards of various sizes splayed on the surface of its waters, slowly spinning; goat skeletons; three screaming gambies trapped further upstream; and one fully laden Land Rover Explorer, which it first rotated ninety degrees and then flipped onto its side before pushing it out towards the sea. I held onto the steering wheel for as long as I could, but the moment we hit a boulder, the airbag exploded, shooting me into the back of the car and onto Candelaría's chest, the compression of my weight forcing gas and liquid out of every hole (hers, not mine), ruining the bloody shopping. Always wear your seatbelt, kids. You will be happy to hear that I displayed more self-control than my sister, retaining most of the contents of my own internal bags—stomach, lungs, bladder—and was able to clamber down her fetid, shit-washed legs. Luckily for us both, the boulder had brought the car to a halt, wedging it against the barranco wall. Unluckily for us both, the car was on one side, half submerged, and rapidly filling with water.

Using Candelaría's body to brace myself, I was able to kick out the rear cabin window and clamber through, drenched to my bones. Candelaría's shriekings had been inaudible, due to the roaring water, but I could now hear them even though her mouth was closed and she was submerged, swaying with the relaxed ease of a giant kelp. Without hesitation, I stripped off my sodden clothes, opened the rear compartment door, and dived in to pull her head above the water—I was not having the strength to pull her entirely from the vehicle—for which she expressed no gratitude, only cranial fluids the colour of peach juice from all facial orifices and a wild exclamation.

"¡That was fun! ¡Again! ¡Again!"

"We are not having the time," I responded, struck by her capacity to endure suffering even with no discernible sign of consciousness other than speech. "¿Still in one piece?"

"I'm sopping wet. But I'll dry out quickly enough. ¡Look! The rain has stopped already and the waters are receding. Get me out into the sunshine."

She was right. As quickly as it had arrived, the flood was subsiding, allowing me to scramble over the back of the Rover to pull her out. She was askew against the internal wheel arch, one eye open, tongue swollen but held within a now half-open mouth rimmed by crust and spume. The vehicle was inclined enough to allow me to lever her over the arch so that she slid down with surprising alacrity onto the muddy ground.

"I think my collar bone is broken."

"¿Are you in pain? I can try to set it or strap it up." I squatted down beside her to check.

"¡Not at all! I was just making an observation."

"¿Has it pierced the skin? You don't want an infection."

"Not sure. I'm not bleeding. ¿Do you want to look?"

"It's okay. I can see it. In any case, we have to get on the move again as soon as possible. ¿Will you be comfortable here for a short time while I find another car? I will be back before it gets dark."

"Knock yourself out." I stood up to go. "Look. Here in my lap. The chorizo has survived. It only has a bit of shit on it. Take it with you. I won't need it and you might get hungry."

"Good idea," I said. "Chorizo is a man's best friend."

Money: *Radix malorum est cupiditas*: The love of money is the root of all evil. Something the poor would do well to remember.

Montana: In the U.S. state of Montana, is illegal to stop someone from throwing themself under a moose.

Moodswing: Music for manic depressives.

Moroccan Delight: Is like Turkish Delight, except with hairs in.

Morons and Imbeciles: Morons and imbeciles are having stronger libidos than normal ordinary Christian men and women, who copulate only out of obligation to God. This is why there are so many more morons and imbeciles in the world than the rest of us. I blame urban idiocy.

Mosquitoes: Is forbidden by the Catholic Church to swat mosquitoes that have been sucking your blood because doing so constitutes a form of mini suicide. Under canon law, however, you are allowed to eat them.

Motherhood: Although we revere the mother of Christ, is only possible because we know that when Jesus was born no human penis had been anywhere near her, rendering her unsullied. All other mothers are dirty.

Moustache: According to the ancient proverb, kissing a man without a moustache is like eating a boiled egg without salt, or even is like Good without Evil. Therefore, two men with moustaches kissing is two evils, and the one with the smaller moustache, say, Hitler, is the lesser of two evils. Don't get me started on beards.

Muncle: Is a combination of your mother and your uncle. Is what happens when your sister's brother-in-law's father marries your father's sister's mother-in-law. Is a lot of them in Aragon.

Music: As I always say, you can't beat a good speech.

Music, Irish: Those for whom Irish music is epitomized by the *seisiún* or the *céilí*, featuring a bodhrán player, a guitarist, a fiddler, a tin whistler, and Shane MacGowan, will be surprised to know that most of the components of traditional Irish arrangements can locate their origins in the Iberian peninsula, with the exception of Shane MacGowan, who is as Irish as Pontefract cakes and seaside rock. Everyone knows that the guitar is originally Spanish, which is why they call it the Spanish guitar, which distinguishes it from the much-inferior banjo and ukulele, much later inventions of slaves in America and Hawaii working in sweatshops making knock-offs.

According to musicologists, Irish music was brought to Ireland by Saint Iberius, who lived on the island of Beggerin in Wexford harbour. Saint Iberius drew many disciples to his modest church, mainly wanting to learn to play the guitar or the organ; there wasn't much to do in Wexford in those days. We also know from the story of another saint, Saint Veoc, that Wexford was a desolate, barren place, just like today, qualities that attracted Veoc there from Armagh in the hope of a hermitic existence. Imagine his disappointment at finding the place full of spotty novices learning the first chords of "Smells Like Teen Armpit." Consequently, he stormed off in indignation and built himself a walled-off hermitage at Carnsore Point, the sore point being that they never didn't invite him to their parties. For this reason, he is the patent saint of incels.

Mustard, English: A strong-tasting emetic and powerful anaphrodisiac, English mustard is popular among restaurant chefs in London, who most commonly use it in powder form, which they mix with water and smear on the seats of rival restaurants' toilets.

Mustard, French: Milder and more delicately flavored than its English counterpart, delicious French mustard is invaluable when you need to disguise the taste of arsenic.

Mustard, Spanish: The best mustard in the world. Carry a jar of Spanish mustard with you whenever you are abroad in Europe or America; otherwise, you will starve to death.

N

Name of the Beast, The: The name of the Beast with Three Fingers is Joseph Chambers, formerly CIA chief of station Athens and subsequently the Dublin head of a CIA front company. Set up as the patsy for a false-flag terrorist attack on one of Dublin's main railway stations. Remarkable only for his inclusion in the augurs of the Spanish Catholic nationalist mystic Margarita of the Perpetual Migraine.

Narwhal: No more proof of God's existence is necessary than the astounding narwhal, which can live for three years on the starch in a mouthful of human spittle. Collective noun: a weft.

Nebraska: In the U.S. state of Nebraska, all bank robbers must be accompanied on jobs by their parents.

New Mexico: In the U.S. state of New Mexico, recovering alcoholics cannot become psychiatrists, and vice versa.

Nietzsche, Friedrich Wilhelm (1844–1900): German anti-philosopher, whatever that means, who correctly pointed out that Nature is characterized by richness, proliferation, surplus, bountifulness, abundance, and sexual promiscuity, although he seemed to believe that these were all good things instead of conclusive evidence for the evilness of the world. ¡Were it not for the State's sensible implementation of scarcity and austerity, people could not be cajoled, persuaded, blackmailed, or forced into the workplace at all! This is why all common lands must be sold off and privatized; otherwise the plebs would help themselves to Nature's bounty and have no incentive to endure the cold, hard, miserable life of poverty God intended them for.

Despite his exuberant celebration of the life force, Nietzsche spent his entire adulthood in the bedroom where he grew up, in his parents' house, never daring to venture outside. This suggests that anti-philosophers are just like all other philosophers in not believing the *majaderías* they concoct. What a div.

Nine-Eleven: In 2018, eighty-eight percent of American teenage boys shown film of the 9/11 attacks on the Twin Towers thought the attacks were "cool." Of course, given the vagaries of teenage jargon, the meaning of "cool" has metamorphosed into its opposite since the 1970s. In 2018, the adjective "cool" meant "Hot, attractive, sexually arousing."

Nipples, Nuns': Serve neither reproductive nor recreational purpose. The existence of nuns' nipples therefore provides further evidence that Darwinism is nonsense (I have not done the necessary practical research to ascertain whether all nuns are having nipples because it would be against the law, but there are certain Internet sites you can go to where you will see nuns clearly displaying breasts with nipples on).

Nostradamus: A true visionary, able to see through the midsts of time, piercing the veil of illusion to access God's omniscient mind by means of divination techniques beyond the capacities of the ordinary middle-aged peasant. Achieving a trance-like higher consciousness through the expert use of smoke, closing his eyes, and special tree bark, Nostradamus was able to predict helicopters, top hats, avocadoes, and the rise of Hitler, getting only the spelling of his name wrong (mistakingly predicting the rise of Adlof Hister of the Narxi Party). Although he did not predict Napoleon, he *did* correctly predict the name of his horse, Marengue. He also correctly predicted escalators, vaping, Macchu Picchu, VAR, 5G, and fell running. Moreover, he also predicted the materialist scientists who would scoff and mock him, which meant that their subsequent scoffing and mocking constituted a self-fulfilling prophecy, the first of its kind.

Not Far: Although haste was imperative, there was too much risk involved in taking a vehicle from the car park at the Hermitage because there was still many lots of pilgrims milling around, as well as children who had never seen rain before, splashing through the puddles, checking out their reflections—¿¡who knew?!—drinking from the gutters and spouting mouthfuls of rainwater at each other, so instead, to avoid being seen, I decided to follow the inner curve of the Barranco de Tao back inland on foot and cut across the road from the Hermitage before it met the main highway. I considered holding up a car but rejected it on the grounds that, one, I would have had to drive back to the coast to retrieve Candelaría and then, on the return trip, pass the scene of the crime, and two, I was not having a gun; my weapons cache in the Land Rover had been mudfucked along with all the food. In any case, most of the vehicles traveling this road would have been off-roaders and most likely carrying at least four passengers. I am not having any qualms about killing four people, but it did seem like an unnecessary complication. ¿What if one of them made a run for it? ¿And where would I conceal the bodies to avoid their rapid detection? You can't just go killing people like it's a Friday in Mississippi. You have to think these things through.

However, thanks to the 1960s and its liberal, do-gooder, back-to-nature, hippie-hugging philosophies, I had ventured no more than a couple of kilometers eastward before I spotted in a depression between two hillocks—just like the humps of a camel—a long lavastone wall around the lot of a ranch, behind which were the humps of several actual camels. Here, in the middle of nowhere, a camel sanctuary, which was great luck, both for the camels and for me, its existence another example of divine intervention, I am in no doubt. ¿Who else but God would come up with such a bizarre concept?

O

Oasis: A place of calm and succour in the heart of a desert wasteland. Also a racist Irish Beatles tribute band from Mayo. Not to be confused with Meiosis, a racist Irish Oasis tribute band, also from Mayo, whose songs are all about splitting up.

Obedience School: I was once unreliably informed that, unlike llamas, camels are timid, shy, reticent but inquisitive creatures that are easy to dominate and tame to the touch providing you act decisively and boldily in taking charge of the training encounter. And also that female camels are impossible to train, which is why all domesticated camels are male. I was fortunate on this, my first encounter with adult camels, that there was only a handful resident in the compound and one baby, a male, which was neither intimidated nor deterred by my nakedness. I quickly calculated that my chances of heaving Candelaría's bloating body onto the back of one of the adult camels to be less than zero, regardless of their willingness to kneel down upon instruction, and therefore I focused my attention on enthralling and ensnaring the baby camel—more my size, after all—with a view to lumbering it with my sister's hefty load. She is heavy: She's my sister.

Many and diverse were the life-threatening predicaments I faced in my career, from refractory drug dealers requiring a reminder from Madonna to cough up my cut, to filthy whores reluctant to fuck during their period owing to some outlandish sense of decorum (by life-threatening, obviously, I mean threatening to their lives, not mine). None, however, could compare with the challenge of kidnapping an infant camel from its mother while naked and armed only with a baton of chorizo, particularly since camels are herbivores, meaning the chorizo was having no value as a foodstuff with which to lure said infant away; it could only be used as a cosh against the mother should she stand between me and my quarry. Saddle was there none in the small shack between the compound and the administration block, in retrospect perhaps a fluke of good fortune since I could not have had held saddle, harness, and chorizo simultaenously while also effectuating my plan.

I had also been once unreliably informed, by the same malefactor, now I come to think of it—in Dublin's Palace Bar at four in the afternoon— that camels are quickly subduable by approaching them from behind and sharply yanking down on their tail. This will bring them to their knees and allow the prospective trainer to leap aboard, from behind—assuming the necessary dexterity and preparation—to implement the second stage of instruction, viz., teaching the camel rudimentary directions such as "left," "right," "walk," "walk quicker," and "stop." What I did not know then and have subsequently come to understand is that the Berbers widely recommend this technique to Western adventurers in revenge for centuries of demeaning Orientalism and bewildering exoticization. In fact, although this so-called "rear entry" technique *does* work eventually, its first result is a phenomenon known as the Tamanrasset Sleighride, in tribute to the Tuareg city of that name in Algeria where camel training reached its apogee in the thirteenth century. The application of this appellation stemmed from Tamanrasset's location at the heart of soft, undulating drifts of the finest Saharan sand, across which trainee camels was wont to bolt in response to the yanking of their tail. The novice trainer (also known as the "mark" or "sucker") was required to lean back and dig his heels into the sand in order to last the exhilarating but harmless roller coaster ride across and around the endless dunes. He must needed hold on only until the camel tired and conceded, broken by the superior determination and courage of its new master.

Fuerteventura has similar soft, undulating drifts of the finest sand, indeed, finer still than those of the Sahara, composed of silicate biogenic fragments, crushed coral, and marine shells, far smaller than the quartz grains of North Africa. Unforetunately, they are concentrated in the great Dunas Park reserve outside Corralejo and in the South of the island, in

Jandía. One place where they decidably are not to be found is in the camel compound just outside Tao, where the surrounding ground could best be described as "jaggredy." Try to dig your heels in here and your rude awakening will include (but not be confined to) severe lacerations of the forefoot as you are pitched forward and dragged at full pelt across the hard, gritty surface, the only blessing being your failure to fall flat on your face thanks to your continuing and desperate grip on the camel's tail.

Lacking the brakes that the trainer's heels typicly provide in the sand, a trainee camel in this sort of arena will take longer to tire, meaning greater wear and tear on the trainer's limbs and louder ejaculations of pain, which only serve to further alarm, enliven, and motivate the animal, pushing him on to greater efforts at escape. As if this were not enough of a deviation from the original "ideal-type" camel-training scenario, consider also that the standard Tamanrasset Sleighride takes place in the open desert, allowing master and camel the privacy of boundless space, with little chance of interference from extraneous fauna. By contrast, my first effort at camel domination was taking place in a highly circumscribed area and in the company of creatures not only of the same species as my prey but also larger and less amenable to instruction. As the baby camel became increasingly agitated by my high-pitched, yodellous, but still manly screams, so it increased its speed around the perimeter of the compound, drawing the attention, inevitably, of its fellow ungulates, arousing at first their interest, but then their concern, and finally their outrage, with the result that they was all soon giving chase, expressing said outrage by relentless, interminable, and aggressive spitting in my direction, depleting their humps, so it seemed to me, only when I was sufficiently soaked in slime and saliva to loosen my grip on the tail of Humpty Minor (as I later came to call him) and drop to the floor, breaking my fall with my chin. I was fortunate in avoiding a good trampling, but I ceased to be of interest to the angry bastards the moment my grip slipped and Humpty's agitation waned.

Despite the personal humiliation and the severe pummeling that my shins had received, I am not the kind of Fascist that gives up easily in the face of a recalcitrant baby camel. I have long known that there is more than one way to skin a rabbit—starting with the nose, for instance—and that if Plan A should prove an unmitigated failure, then Plan B need differ only in respect of Plan A's shortcomings to be having a chance of success. That is to say, I opened the compound gate and shooed out all the camels so that my arena of pursuit was no longer so small. That done, conscious that the owners of the camels might soon notice their emancipation, I proceeded at my fastest possible hobble in further pursuit of the baby camel—it appeared to believe me incapable of another assay upon its dignity—and my hands, the camel sputum already a crust in the heat, now took a firm hold for a second time. I braced myself and gritted my teeth in preparation (and True Fascist enthusiasm) for the pain I was about to endure and then yanked down hard once more. Remarkably, Humpty Minor, whether from pity, a lack of energy, or disbelief, abruptly and without curse or whine kneeled down before me, clearly acknowledging me as his one true lord and master. "¡Now that is more like it!" I said out loud to myself. Quickly, I stripped some fronds from a nearby aloe vera plant and wrapped them round my bleeding feet to act as both a balm and spurs. The other camels, no less remarkably, merely looked on in bemusement or began to wander away, apparently respectful of Humpty's freely chosen fealty.

Once I was completely ready, I climbed aboard Humpty's back and grabbed the long hairs on his neck. Ever-mindful of the symbolism inherent in the conclusion of every struggle, I naturally understood the need to mark this moment. Chorizo raised aloft, I dug my heels into Humpty's flank and, as he gingerly rose and then advanced, I launched proudly into the Falangist anthem, "Cara al Sol." I am sure that, had my father been there to see it, he would have been crying uncontrollably with virile paternal satisfaction at his son's magnificent achievement, in contrast to the only other time he cried, which was when I broke his bugle.

Obese Alligators: Live in the sewers of New York, eating fatbergs and obese Americans.

Oderick, Saint: Strangled with his own tendons. Patent saint of yoga.

Oil: Oil makes the world go round.

Oil, Olive: Olive oil is renowned for its anti-inflammatory qualities and as an emollient, good for the heart, muscles, cardiovuncular system, and libido (if you don't believe olive oil is good for the libido, you should try washing your genitals in it for half an hour. ¡It works a treat!). Spain makes the best olive oil in the world but exports only the inferior, non-alcoholic versions abroad to foreingers, who don't know what they're missing.

Oil, Palm: Not oil you massage into your palm before masturbation but oil that comes from palms, which is a kind of tree that looks like the trajectory of a firework or space shuttle. Palm oil plantations, which are now replacing the global rainforest, are important for the production of such necessary commodities of modern life as candles, corn syrup, dirty bombs, and mobile phones. The danger for humanity is that as the rainforest gradually disappears, the orang-utans who live there will be forced to migrate into the nearest towns and cities to find work, bringing with them who knows what sorts of diseases and ideas. Is bad enough that they don't believe in holy matrimony. Just wait till they move in next door to you, with their odoriferous rooftop nests, their old-school Islam, and that bloody Gamelan music which will drive you round the bend. "How I wish I had proper Spanish olive oil to light my alcove," you will shriek, but it will be too late. Those party-loving thieving shit orang-utans will have already drunk it.

Older Women, Sex with: If you really must have sex with a woman (in a hostage situation, for instance), sex with an older woman is far more preferable because they are more grateful, more experienced, and more eager to please. However, there is also no chance of pregnancy, which is why the Patriarchy finds it necessary to present gerontophilia as abhorrent, disgusting, and immoral. True, sex with older women is all of these, but no more so than sex with a normal woman.

Olympics: Even though many things in life change—empires fall, popes die, dogs fart, women faint, history books are rewritten, and cetera—one eternal truth is that the Olympic Games will always be run by Fascists, Fascist lackeys, and Fascist collaborators. Has always been a source of great comfort to me that what was once a moronic French Communist idea about promoting peace among countries through sports events in which random citizens would participate as amateurs has been transformed into a powerhouse steamtrain of propaganda for competition, professionalism, nationalism, drug cheating, winning at all costs, and ostracism of the weak. The Olympics is like a vast mobile floating Fascist ark, docking in different ports every four years to subdue the natives under the weight of their own ignorant enthusiasm for bankruptcy.

One-Legged Men: Are having larger penises than normal men. There is nowhere else for the blood to go.

Oregano, Saint: Became a martyr after curing both teams (but not the crowd) at the Leprosy World Cup Soccer Final in 1931 between Belgium and Egypt. He was torn limb from limb, proving that soccer fans *do* possess a sense of humour. His neck and forearm was on display in a church in Gent, although there was some doubt about the latter because of the tattoo of a Tahitian concubine. His shins was stored in the catacombs of Leiden, whence they disappeared in 1941.

Organ Donation: Against God's will, like so much else. People's reluctance to donate organs is an indication of both their incipient common sense and their natural Fascist inclination. The lack of organs for donation could easily be remedied by introducing organ swaps: If you receive a kidney, you should be required to give an eye, for example. Or vice-versa. Is one way of halting the trade in cheap, low-quality kidneys from the Third World.

Orgasms: Q: ¿How many orgasms was the Virgin Mary having when God fucked her? A: None. ¡It was the coming of the Messiah!
Joking aside, according to sex doctors, women are capable of having as many as fourteen orgasms in six minutes, whereas, at best, a man can only experience one orgasm every two days. This proves that Nature designed women to take hundreds of lovers in the same amount of time as men take one, so that if a baby happens by accident, nobody will know who the father is and the entire male community will have to take collective responsbility for its upbringing. Nature is truly disgusting and communistic in its design, which is why it must be thwarted at every turn and why women's wild sexual urges must be kept under control; the best invention so far for this purpose is marriage.

Orgy: Only bisexuals are comfortable with the idea of an orgy. Consider: ¿Who else except a bisexual could see another man's erection and not puke? Even women cannot bring themselves to look at it, let alone touch it, even if I wash it. Normal heterosexual perverts have to resort instead to the rustic English pastime of dogging, which goes back hundreds of years via the noble tradition of having sex outdoors with people watching (for example the Great Exhibition, George Michael, Cottage Loafing, and cetera). Orgies are just unadulterated pornography (although also no doubt they include adulterers, so also adulterated pornography).

Orifice, Saint: The holiest of all saints.

Ornate, Charles the: According to the apocryphal *Scrapbook of Mary*, once Joseph had have got over his intimidation at the fact that the Creator of the Universe had impregnated his just-pubescent wife ("¿¡How am I supposed to follow that?!"), he was eventually able to stiffen his manhood and generate a family with her. In line with the standards of contraception and mortality of the time, we are telled that Jesus was having twelve siblings, eleven of which died within the first two years of birth (the terrible twos) of the usual illnesses (head cramp, sugarknees, dysburbia, clinical hiccups, the bumps), leaving one surviving brother, Ignog the Sturdy, who, despite being outshone by his older brother in the messiah stakes, was nonetheless superior to other humans because his mother was blessèd by God, as was her womb, of which Ignog was also a fruit, albeit a lesser one (a clementine to Jesus's Seville orange, if you will). According to the *Scrapbook*, Ignog set out on his own adventures (*The Adventures of Ignog the Sturdy* exists now only in fragments but is incontrovertible in its verisimilitude), sending back missives that recount his establishment of the nation of Iberia, of which he was sole founder and proprietor until he could persuade a local girl to procreate with him, using his good genes and family connections as a lure. It was thus his line that established the Iberian people, of whom the first king was Charles the Ornate, in about 320 AD, not long after Ignog's death at the age of 299 (¡what bad luck!). Charles himself was a victim of the usurper Visigoths in 417 AD, in his prime, at the age of 133, but not before siring 200 children (not all to the same woman), and these offspring constitute the original and true and only Spanish people, direct descendants of the Virgin Mary and the true heirs to the Iberian throne. In this day and age, monarchy is something of an anachronism, and there is only one true King (in Heaven). However, if we wish to say that there is a hierarchy of countries, we can surely say that the Spanish people themselves are the King of all nations, divinely chosen by virtue of their origins in Ignog's ballbag.

O'Ryan's Belt: As seen in the sky and the movie *Men in Black*. O'Ryan was a Kilkenny hurler who is commonly shown in astronomy books holding his shillelagh over his head about to duff up Gary Owen, from Tipp.

Osteopath: Like a psychopath, but mad about bones. An archaeologist of the human body, the osteopath likes to dig beneath the surface to discover what is holding everything up. As the Irish band the Sawdoctors sang, "The pain in our bones is the writhing of our ancestors' souls." It was in fact a Sawdoctor who killed the journalist Jamal Khashoggi in the Saudi embassy in Turkey, home of the Grey Wolves. ¿Is it any coincidence that Ali Agca tried to kill Pope John Paul Mark Two with an N-17? Everything connects if you know what to ignore.

Our Lady: The responsibilities which Our Lady taked upon her shoulders at the tender age of twelve highlight how modern society has let its adolescents get away with an overlong childhood. Once upon a time, all children was working by the age of ten. My first job, for example, was in the media, working as a paperboy. Sadly, there are so many unnecessary protections today that children's characters are weak and craven, rendering them useless for anything but jobs in the theater.

Oven: On a lighter note, I think I was five years old when my father first ovened me. I cannot remember specificly what infraction I had committed to arouse his ire, but it must have been significant, though not heinous enough to deserve a belting or child garotte. He raised me up by the hair so that he could look me in the eye—I suspect that I had been nose-picking during the preprandial prayer—before turning me in the direction of the oven (we had been dining *en famille* around the kitchen table).

"I have been saving you from this because your mother is soft and still makes me hard, but there's a time and a place for everything. It's the oven for you, my boy," he said.

Quite possibly I then compounded my crime by urinating in my trousers, which my father would have taked as a deliberate provocation. In any case, was not many weeks before I managed to commit another serious crime—laughing when my father cut his knuckle on Candelaría's baby teeth—and again it was into the oven I went. No amount of kicking and screaming and crying and not laughing anymore could dissuade him, so enraged was he by the failure of my mother to discipline us properly with shaming and scolding the way only Catholic mothers can.

My continuing existence and narration of this episode is evidence enough that my father never turned the oven on, but I was left remaining in that dark, cramped cell each time long enough to learn my lesson, albeit not the lesson that my father intended. The lesson I learned was that once you have found your persecutor's limit, he cannot harm you anymore. In this respect, my mother was a far better torturer than my father, since her punishments was psychological—you carry them with you wherever you go in the form of guilt and morbid embarrassment. Plus, my mother was able to demonstrate that she had no limits. She was willing to kill herself and take us with her if that was what was needed to stop me masturbating into Candelaría's sippy cup. My father's punishments, by contrast, suffered from diminishing returns, though I was careful not to let him know it. He clearly suspected as much after nine months or so of ovening—despite my protestations when he throwed me in, the oven was having no effect on my levels of recidivism—and so he contrived to find some bones when cleaning out the oven one Sunday morning in the hope of convincing me of his capacity for infanticide.

"¿Do you know what this little boy did to make me put him in the oven, Hijo de Puta?"

"¿Was it worse than inserting a balloon in a cat and inflating it?"

"¡Hah! ¿The cat or the balloon?"

"Both. A boy at school told me you can inflate a cat by putting your lips to its asshole and blowing, but thanks to you, Papa, I have learned not to get caught out like that again. I realized you can put your finger inside a balloon inside a cat and still eat your tortilla on the way home. Neither your lips nor your fingers need touch the cat's asshole unless you want them to. Fool me once, shame on you. Fool me twice, toxoplasmosis."

"¡Huzzah! When I was your age, the Guardia Civil brought me home after they caught me planting iron spikes in the flower beds of the Retiro. As I telled them at the time, 'People need to keep their toddlers on a lead.'"

"I agree, Papa. ¿Did Granpapa punish you for it?"

"Of course. That is what fathers are for; to teach you how to be a man and to punish you when you get caught doing it. ¿Who would you rather learn to be a man from? At least you know that even when I scare you, I am still on your side."

"You are cruel and vindictive and wise."

"As any man should be. You are having much to learn."

"I know. I am only five. Tell me more."

"I will. But first, the oven."

P

Paedophilia: An important weapon in the hands of True Fascists. Nothing disgusts the general public more than paedophilia, and True Fascists know that the generation of disgust is key to driving a wedge between the public and any minority, whether the elites, celebrities, homosexuals, drag queens, clowns, or foreigners. Consequently, the accusation of paedophilia is the weapon of first resort, perfect in every way because it relies upon the ever-present suspicion that all majorities are having for minorities simply by virtue of their difference. No evidence is necessary, only the pointing of a finger and a whisper: "¿Haven't you always thought there was something odd about them?" Moreover, anybody from the majority who leaps to the minority's defence will risk being tarred with the epithet "Protector of paedophiles," which nobody wants, thus intimidating those with any thoughts of courage and "doing the right thing." As one famous clergyman once said, "First, they came for the paedophiles, but I didn't say nothing because I was not a paedophile. Also because I knew the bishop would move the paedophiles to another parish."

Josef Goebbels advised, "Always accuse your opponents of doing that of which you yourselves are guilty." This is not helpful advice when it comes to paedophilia, however. As Minister of Propaganda, he should have known when to keep his trap shut.

Pain in the Hole: Is an Irish dish, like toad in the hole but with potatoes instead of sausages. Not to be confused with *pain* in the hole, which is a French dish that replaces the sausages with baguettes.

Palace, Memory: As my grandmother's Alzheimer's advanced, she resorted to a variety of measures to help her remember information of importance to her, such as leaving notes to herself on the mirror and tattooing on her body the names and faces of all the actors who my family had employed to visit her in their stead at the exclusive residential home in Pozuelo de Alarcón (such homes are rare in Spain and cost a pretty penny; nothing but the best for grandma, even if she couldn't appreciate it). My father, too, cogniscent of the genetic component and fearful of inheriting the disease, taked every step he could to prevent but also prepare for any deterioration in his memory, ingesting daily gingko biloba supplements, red wine enemas, amphetamine sulphate, Viagra, and other, less scientific steps, including the use of a Memory Palace, a technique of thought association that goes back to the ancient Greeks.

"This is how Homer, despite being blind, was able to recite the contents of the *Odyssey* and *Aeneid* from memory," he explained to me incorrectly one day. "Is also how Joyce James was able to remember the layout of Dublin despite never having been there while writing her book *Ullyses*, which was based on Homer's *Odyssey* but which featured instead of Odysseus the travels of the Wandering Jew Bialystok Bloom."

"¿Why would anyone need to remember where the Wandering Jew went?" I asked, intelligently.

"Idiot child. You must always keep an eye on him. You never know what he's up to. Besides, Ireland was not having a proper secret police in those days; they had to import one from England."

You are not having to have ever visited a real palace in order to build a memory version. You can use any familiar geographical location, such as the interior of your home, monastery, ship, or, for ladies, kitchen. You don't even have to use an interior; it can be an entire city, such as Dublin, or your own garden, prison yard, or playground, provided that the location is familiar enough for you to recollect easily and there is enough space for you to attach the necessary memories to its walls, floors, ceilings, and cetera. Thus, for example, say you want to remember the players who won the Champions League for the brilliant Real Madrid against Valencia in 2000, then you would imagine going in the front door of your house, and where normally is your coatstand, there is Iker Casillas with his gloves on and arms held out like a coatstand and wearing your hat; Helguera is hanging from the ceiling by his legs with a light bulb in his mouth; your dog comes running to meet you from the kitchen, except is Ivan Campo, so your dog is a poodle; and your wife is Steve McManaman in a bikini. And so on. You get the idea. By associating a familiar place with the information to remember, but doing so in a deviant or perverse way, you can easily remember vast quantities of useless facts and figurines. Although I myself did not master this technique as a young man because I am naturally averse to perversion, especially Steve McManaman in a bikini, I highly recommend it for those who require it. Both my grandmother and my father are dead now and I cannot remember what they look like, but I remember the memory palace all about them.

Pamplona: The running with the bulls provides lots of good clean fun for Spanish families, in particular for everyone who likes to watch middle-age American Hemingway "disciples" getting a good goering. I always say, "¿¡If they are such Hemingway fans, why don't they just stay at home and shoot themselves?!

Pan, Frying: The mere idea of a frying pan is often enough for people to jump into the fire.

Parthenogenesis: Reproduction without having the sex. According to one famous conspiracy theory, parthenogenesis explains the Virgin Birth because Mary was a lizard. This is why there are lizard people running the country and why Joseph had a coat of many colours (he was a chameleon). Only a complete moron would believe this sort of rubbish instead of the truth that God insperminated Mary with His invisible shaft of light penis while she was married like a teenage hillbilly to an unsuspecting cuck with a love of donkeys.

Pasta, Penne: Always keep a bag of dry penne pasta around your neck for emergency tracheotomies.

Patriarchy: Simply a way to ensure that women are having babies they don't want. Is the basis of all civilizations, governments, monuments, monolithic testaments to human creativity (pyramids, hanging gardens, Heathrow airport, and cetera), religion, hierarchies, and armies, without which humans would be no different from flies. Except also for the lack of wings and compound eyes.

Peacetime: Much as I despise peace, the interwar years of the twentieth century demonstrated conclusively that the peoples of Europe are naturally Fascist. There was a massive efflorescence of Fascist movements in all the best societies: Germany, Italy, Spain, France, Hungary, and cetera. Fascism was only defeated because Oriental atheist communism and the corrupt bourgeois democracies were able to come to an understanding; neither of them could bear to see it persist and thereby set an example to the rest of the world. They would sooner prevent Europe from achieving its natural destiny. The course of history was set back hundreds of years, but sadly not far enough.

Peanuts: Shake a tin of peanuts at random intervals to convince myopic predators that you're a rattlesnake. (Note: Does not work with peanut butter).

Pennsylvania: In the U.S. state of Pennsylvania, lap dancers must give fifty percent concessions one day a week to the unemployed, pensioners, and the blind.

Perch: When I arrived back at the Rover on Humpty Minor, an Egyptian buzzard was perched on Candelaría's shoulder and tearing a strip of bloodless flesh from her left cheek. With some alacrity and no thought for my own well-being or the pain that would result from landing on skinless feet, I leaped down and unintentionally screamed my loudest banshee wail. The buzzard immediately taked flight, flesh in its beak, pulling Candelaría's head sideways as the flap initially refused to tear and then raggably ripped free. To avoid further unnecessary agony, I crawled over to her on my knees to inspect the extent of the damage. Her left eye was already gone, most likely the buzzard's hors d'oeuvre.

"Ah, here he is. My shite in nighning armour," she said.

"You're delirious," I replied.

"A combination of organ loss and heat stroke. Nothing to worry about. It will be getting dark soon. ¿What kept you?"

"Some complicated connegotiations." I was hoping that the use of long words would stifle her curiosity.

"Your clothes should be dry by now. Put them on. You look ridiculous."

"This is how I always look."

"No comment," she said. Which was a comment.

With the night drawing in, I pulled Candelaría's body back to the vehicle and drew Humpty close by to provide extra body heat. The chorizo would provide enough sustenance to see me through, but the absence of freshwater compelled me to suck the aloe vera fronds from my feet, a slimy, sticky gel with a taste reminiscent of non-human sweat, but happily, on this occasion, my ankle blood disguised it.

I could not risk building a fire since it might have attracted the attention of my pursuers or simply the inquisitive, who would quickly blab our whereabouts upon reaching the next pueblo along the route. In any case, Candelaría's body appeared to benefit from the cold night air— she didn't smell as much—and Humpty Minor offered sufficient shelter from the chilly north-westerlies skimming the mountains and scattering among the rocks. I calculated, using my head, that we could make the remaining sixty kilometres in two days, assuming no interruptions or interference and allowing for tapas breaks. I could eke out the chorizo and, while I would have to minimize contact with others, could plunder the fields for tomatoes and potatoes or prevail upon a benevolent farmer for milk or cheese. Survival in harsh conditions poses no challenges for me, but harsh conditions had not topped my list of desirable retirement ambitions. They are something you must always anticipate, of course, but all the same you do not want them, like the onset of dementia or another royal baby.

Pet Food: Food for pets. Not to be confused with Pet/Food, such as potbelly pigs, chow dogs, Mary's little lamb, mulligatawny owls, and cetera.

Pickle, Mustard: Avoid hypothermia by covering your body in Piccalilli. Don't eat any of it, however, because the temperatures of your interior and exterior will equal out and you will die of flumonia, a.k.a. gherkinfluenza. Which is definitely a thing.

Pill, Red: A drug, bought with Dunning-Krugerrands, that gives gullible, vulnerable young white men the vivid illusion that their inexperience and ignorance are (1) not their fault, (2) no impediment to their right to express their opinions on every matter, especially those relating to women, (3) a permanent feature of their character that they will never transcend, and (4) all they will ever need to understand the world. Is also a powerful aphrodisiac. ¡Which is the last thing they need!

Pinochet, Augusto: Saved Latin America from socialism back in the last century so that indigenous peoples there could breathe the same air of freedom as the civilizing West that had once been their colonial masters. In particular, the Chilean people got to breathe the same air as the people of Chicago, who supplied the ecomonists to run Chile according to a special experiment, which they carried out in the country's banks and football stadiums. Pinochet was not an archetypal proper Fascist, however, because the return to feudal society was never the plan of the

Boys from Chicago, regardless of how much inequality they were able to restore. Neverthenonetheless, good Fascists are few and far between these days, and we are wrong to pick and choose which of them don't come up to scratch. I am also having a very soft spot for Pinochet personally because, even when he was sick with the Alzheimer's, he was still able to outwit the English judicial system. ¡There is hope for us all!

Pisa, Leaning Tower of: A listed building in Italy.
   ¡Is a joke!
   ¡But also true!

Pomegranate: The pomegranate is nature's hand grenade. If you usually eat yours with a pin, remember to take the pin out before throwing it.

Populism: The Western Liberal Elite is shitting and wetting its pants simultaenously because finally its so-called objective truths and impartial observation statements have been identified for what they are: fake news. Although the elites lament that this is the post-truth era, implying that what came before was an era of truth, what they are actually lamenting is that their voice is now only one among many and that what matters in the new regime is only whose voice is loud enough. Although they proclaim to love democracy, they hate the people and their opinions and do everything they can to ensure that the people's will does not prevail. Even though it was the Jew Alfred Einstein who showed that everything is relative (and therefore that you would have to be God to see and know everything, which is correct because He does), it follows logicly that Einstein's statement is itself only relatively true, a Jewish truth that does not apply to other nations. We Spanish are having our own truth, one that no amount of internationalism, cosmopolitanism, and liberalism will overthrow. You may not like our Spanish facts, but they are objectively true for us, and no elitist tears will make it otherwise.

Pork Rinds: Also known as pork scratchings to the English and *Scabbes Danoises* to the French. The shape and strength of organic farmhouse pork rinds make them ideal replacements for crampons when you are stuck half-way up a mountainside with nothing but a 300,000-meter drop between you and your maker, Geppetto.

Pornography: Is in the hand of the beholder.

Potatoes: If a pitbull is clamping its jaw around your forearm, shove a spud up its hole and its jaw will release. An Irish farmer discovered this by accident (i.e., he was not under attack at the time.)

Pregnancies, Phantom: Extraordinarily common among underage girls aspiring to be nuns and who spend a lot of time around the local priest. Phantom pregnancies are treated as symptomatic of the girls' religious fervour and their desire to be the Mother of Christ. Religious orders normally treat such pregnancies with some indulgence, even though the wider community often regard them with some embarrassment, and the parents of the young lady in question even sometimes try to hush it up. Is stupid. ¡You would think they would be proud of their daughter's devoutness!

In any case, within a few months of the young lady in question entering a nunnery or similar such house of confinement, the pregnancy disappears, and there is never any subsequent mention or appearance of a baby at all. Indeed, everyone will pretend the pregnancy had never even happened. They will tell you that it was just wind.

Sí. ¡Divine wind!

Prejudice: What Pride comes before.

Presence, Command: You are either having it or you are not having it. Command presence is the charisma exuded by those who are natural leaders; the way they enter a room, dominate everyone in it, and control what happens there.

¿Is it possible to develop command presence? Yes, of course. The police and military train it into officers and men, both explicitly and implicitly. It manifests itself in the quiet confidence that, if necessary, you could kill everyone in the room; and I mean here not just the skill-set to do so but also the self-knowledge of your capability to see it through, a serene and unshakeable capacity for slaughter. After a while, once you know yourself well enough, this attitude becomes second nature. Much in the same way that governments explore the military and repressive potential of every new invention, be it the thermos flask, the microwave, or the smartwatch, so too, whenever I enter a room, the first thing I do is figure out the means by which I would kill everyone in it. If I am having no weapons on me, I look to see what alternatives are available: standard lamps, electrical items, stabby chair legs, glass windowpanes, curtain tiebacks, vases, bottles, mirrors, cables. Also, who is the strongest person in the room; they must be taked down first. It will often be enough to subdue that one individual to compel obedience or flight in everyone else; death is not normally necessary but can provide an additional incentive. If I am honest, only once have I been required to kill everyone in the room, but I don't count it because (1) I was off-duty and (2) it was in EuroDisney.

Priests: Contrary to many of the malevolent rumours spread by the Masonic media, priests and children repel each other, like two magnets which are identicly polarized. You will have seen for yourself that no matter how much parents try to push their children towards a priest, the child pushes back. This is the result of a powerful metaphysical force that science will never understand.

Prison: Prison is a necessary evil in contemporary modern society, required to produce the criminals who will keep the general populace in a sufficient state of fear, panic, and desire for security. There is besides a huge industry of police officers, social workers, counsellors, and cetera, not to mention the prison service itself, whose jobs and resources depend on the continued generation of a criminal class and a guaranteed rate of recidivism. Only an idiot says, "Prison doesn't work." It works perfectly well, thank you very much. Moreover, prison makes sure that do-gooder liberal wet-willy types spend all their time trying to reform career criminals instead of trying to reform society; I think everyone can agree that prison is the best place for both the criminals and their "saviours."

Property, Violence against: You would have to be severely naïve or retarded to believe that violence against people is always worse than violence against property. Reality is far more nuanced than such dogma. I am not saying that all violence against property is worse than all violence against people, such as some murders, but consider this: All violence against my property costs me money because I must fix or replace the violated object, and money, ultimately, is time, the time it has taked me to earn it, which is something I can never get back. Thus, crime against property is also a crime against the person. What is more, crime against property is a crime both against the workers who made the object and also the customer who bought the object, since neither will ever get the time back that was necessary to produce or earn the money to procure the object. Violence against the person, on the other hand, can be a blessing in disguise because people, unlike objects, can heal. ¿Do you know the saying "That which does not kill me makes me stronger"? The experience of violence can be a learning experience for the victim, rendering them less gullible, more wiser, and more resilient. In addition, people who have been physicly assaulted become less trusting, more wary, and more suspicious of outsiders, and also less willing to tolerate foolish generosity without proof of reciprocity. All of this is eminently sensible. If the world was perfect, we would all be born with instinctive xenophobia; instead, since Man is fallen, such wisdom must be acquired through misfortune at the hands of others. ¿What reasonable man or semi-reasonable woman could therefore dispute the virtue of such common-sense suspicion learned the hard way? The benefits of violence against the person are both under-rated by the populace and rarely admitted by politicians, but in secret, under their breath, they say "Good," when they hear of knife crime.

Prostitutes: Rarely virgins, though many a dominatrix maintains both her virtue and a pristine home thanks to the submissiveness of law-and-order politicians willing to pay to lick her carpets.

Protestantism: Not a fake religion like Scientology or Mormonism but rather a travesty, a monstrous outgrowth of the One True Religion, brought about by too much reading. Protestantism is a direct consequence of the printing press, the ultimate demonstration of the dangers of technology. The people of Spain had no need of literacy for thousands of years, happily tilling the soil, obeying the priest, praying to God, dying at thirty, and going to heaven for eternity without ever requiring the comforts of learning or the indulgence of curiosity.

Protocols of the Learned Elders of Zion: Everyone "knows" the Protocols are a fake. ¿But how many have actually read them?

Proverbs: Proverbs are the secular equivalent of stain-glass windows, a short-cut to the truths of life for the illiterate. They comprise concise, pithy sayings in frequent and widespread use and offer a moral guide to practical living for the masses. They are very popular in Spain, where they take the place of philosophy. The most commonly used proverbs of today express the Spaniard's natural sensitivity to life's lack of irony and readiness to generalize without justification:

- o He makes paella in the evening; she makes love in the morning.
- o A pauper is not a criminal until he becomes hungry.

- A stupid man brings me money, a wise man brings me luck, but my ass brings me both.
- God smiles on the goose that lays the golden egg but also the goat with cankers; neither will be eaten.
- Bells ring of their own accord when a saint is born, a whore repents, and a virgin dies.
- Oranges *are* the only fruit.
- The bell whose ring is cracked, Jesus heals with oil; the girl whose face is cracked, Jesus heals with modesty.
- Never trust a Basque.
- Give a donkey water, he will work all day. Sell a donkey water, he will work all week.
- Paella makes a man thirsty. The remedy is beer and more paella.
- The four essentials in life are an ass, a shovel, a knife, and a priest. They will satisfy all of a man's needs.
- Chorizo is a man's best friend.
- He who shops with Catalans must take two wallets.
- God will look after the blind driver. Those who can see must look after themselves.

Pudding, Christmas: Nutritious and full of fruit, a medium-sized Christmas pudding in a stocking makes a handy improvised bludgeon that can fell a reindeer with a single blow.

Pudding, Yorkshire: Strap a giant Yorkshire pudding to your chest when driving through Leeds in case your airbag fails. Following a collision, locals will eat you out of the wreckage.

Punch to the Face: If there is one thing that should be taught in schools, is how to take a punch to the face. Once a child has realized that it will not kill him (statisticly some will die, no doubt, but then the lesson need not be learned by those particular children), he will be more able to endure in conflict, in the ring, and in the street. Knowing that you can take a punch builds confidence and character because you cease to be afraid of the potential pain that a bigger man might threaten you with. Take me, for example. Most men are bigger than me, but I have always known that however much pain they might try to inflict on me, I will be able to stomach it and, in the meantime, inflict pain on them. Winning in combat is never a case of who can inflict more damage but who can withstand it. Because I never cared about being handsome—¿¡why let your life be controlled by your attractiveness to women?!—and I knew that noses and jaws can be fixed, I was relentless in battle and admired and respected by all men who understood pugilistic science and the importance of not giving a fuck.

Many so-called professional "comedians" recount an origin story in which they became "funny" as a way to avoid being beaten up or bullied at school. If only they had learned to take a punch to the face, the rest of us would be spared the narcissism they failed to grow out of. Perhaps all is not lost. The next time you see one at large, out in the street or shopping in Lidl, consider it your duty to society. There is only one thing you need to remember: The secret to punching a comedian is timing.

Putin, Vladimir: The Russian Franco.

Q

QAnon: Was a U.S. version of the fantasy game Dungeons and Dragons, but all the dungeons contained kidnapped children and the dragons were powerful menopausal women.

Queen: Usually the wife of a king but not necessarily, if she is ugly or a lesbian (see, for example, Boadicea, Elizabeth I, and Camilla of England; the English specialize in ugly lesbian royalty, which is why they had to kill Diana). The reigns of queens usually coincide with economic prosperity but also with plagues, comets, triple-headed pigs, and other unnatural events; in the case of England, these anomalies included winning the World Cup and beating an under-the-weather Armada. Foretunately, Mother Nature has an inbuilt stratagem for dealing with reigning queens. If they are ugly lesbians, they will be having no children, so the next in line can be chosen by parliament or war. If she is a married queen, then the king is the ruler or else, if he is an emasculated king, such as England's Duke of Edinburgh or Charles III, he will try to demonstrate his masculinity by breeding male heirs, making sure the queen keeps having children until she gets it right.

Queer: The English are having a well-known but underused and underrated saying, which is "All's queer except me and thee, and even thee's a little bit queer." So long as you understand that, by "queer," the English mean "strange, odd, different," and not "sexually disgusting," nothing could be closer to the truth, and everyone in their deepest, darkest heart feels this way, although if you say it in public they will call you a bigoted cunt. This just exemplifies the hypocrisy of Western Liberal society, which is as eternally suspicious of the Other as every other sensible "civilization" but suppresses it at the altar of globalization, cosmopolitanism, diversity, openness to novelty, "progress," originality, and relativism. There can be no rest or stability in a society that tolerates difference.

Queers: They used to say that there's nowt so queer as Folk, but that was before Disco.

Quemada, Montaña: On my unremarkable and remote Canarian island, this would be just another remote and unremarkable mountain but for the deleterious presence of a statue commemorating the Spanish Liberal Elitist writer and "philosopher" Miguel de Unamuno, who was exiled to the island by Spain's first True Fascist leader, General Primo de Rivera. Unamuno is sometimes being referred to as "Spain's existentialist," the equivalent of Sweden's Kierkegaard or Brazil's Socrates, thanks to his book *The Tragic Sense of Life*, in which, like Kierkegaard, he considers the struggle to find meaning within a finite existence in which reason and faith fail to provide definitive answers. So they tell me. This explains why the statue itself is also tragic, meaningless, and unreachable except only by the most dogged and stubborn of pilgrims or by gambies who happen upon it by accident. In fact, Unamuno was on the island for only a few months before Primo reprieved him, realizing that such a banal and adolescent philosophy was of no threat to the dictatorship. However, Unamuno also recognized this reprieve as the insult that Primo intended it to be and so, before he could be released, he had himself "rescued" by friends and "escaped" to France, the dick. To the day he died, he exploited his brief experience of exile to an extent that would embarrass any genuine expellee. From the luxury of Paris he was able to look back and romanticize the austere subsistence of life on the island, which he described as the "concentrated form of the Spanish soul," even deeming it appropriate to write a poem—oh yes, he was a poet as well, of course he was—about this very mountain, which he published in his book *From Fuerteventura to Paris*. He describes the mountain as a "heap of volcanic ash" (its name in English means "Burnt Mountain"), which makes it sound more impressive than it is. Apparently, Unamuno wanted to be buried here and yet, if you visit, you will see that his statue has its back turned to the mountain, looking instead at the Montaña Muda opposite and the FV-10 that separates them, almost as though Unamuno longs to join the holidaymakers driving by obliviously on their way to the airport. In 1980, when the council in Puerto de Rosario commissioned the sculpture, the sculptor decided to waive the fee, presumably on the basis that nobody would ever see it.

Quixote, Don: It was no mean feat to pull Candelaría's increasingly liquefaceous body onto the back of Humpty Minor. I had to drag her on her back to his flank, then turn her over and pull her up by the feet so that she lay face down over his hump, squeezing gases, liquids, and chunks of unidentifiable matter out of every available orifice, including the left eye socket. She didn't complain—and neither did Humpty Minor, surprisingly—but engaged in light ridicule and banter at my lack of strength and unseemly attire. My clothes were dried out entirely from the flood but caked in an auburn mud that no amount of banging against the lavastone rocks adjacent to the Rover could disperse. Clouds of red dust enveloped me but refused to do anything but enhance the rusty appearance of my shirt and trousers.

"You will be taked for a gambie with those clothes on," she said. "Or without those clothes on, for that matter. Or, even worse, a Commie."

"Communists do not generally wear red," I said to correct her. "It's too flamboyant."

"A flamenco dancer, then," she retorted. "But with no castanets."

"¿Is that a veiled reference to my lack of virility?"

"Nothing veiled about it."

"¡Hah! Joke all you want, but you didn't see me fighting off an army of full-size adult camels. Single-handily and without weapons."

"You had a baton of chorizo."

"It was ornamental."

"*You're* ornamental."

I roused Humpty to his feet. Gingerly, he rose, having been roused, with Candelaría flopped over him, her purple mottled arms swinging freely.

"There. We are all set."

I wiped my brow, smearing dust across my forehead, as I looked South along the shore.

"We will have to cut inland when we get to any villages to avoid attracting attention."

Candelaría harrumphed.

"Shouldn't be too difficult," she said. "I am blending into the environment even as we speak."

R

Rabbi: Better a retarded priest than a wise rabbi.

Racing, Horse: The principle purpose of the horse racing is the horse betting. ¿Why else would men on horsebacks run around in circles? ¡Is not even erotic! Mind you, is better than the alternative, which is men being ridden by horses. I have seen it.

In Peru, they are having this mad festival where the local indigents tie a condor to the back of a bull and then set it loose so that the bull runs like a mayhem all around the town while the indigents place bets on whether the bull will kill the condor or whether the condor will take off into the air and carry the bull back to its nest. ¡Imagine that! No umbrella made by man could ever protect you from the bullshit rain.

I am surprised that this practice is not more widespread. ¿Instead of jockies, why not tie condors to the backs of horses and let them race around the track? ¡Would be like a race of Pegasuses! Marvelous. Condors are such magnificent and powerful creatures, so this would be a far more exciting and uplifting spectacle than the antics of little Scottish men on horses, which is faintly ridiculous and comedic and lacking in gravitas; you would think jockies would be having a bit more self-respect and would try to find a proper job instead of prancing around in silk all day like a flouncing tart. Perhaps a job as a chimney sweep or a string puppet or child actor; proper, gainful employment.

Many people in the effete decadent bourgeois western "First" world object to activities that superficially look like cruelty to animals such as this, but I remind them that (1) it makes perfect economic sense to replace humans with animals in the workplace; (2) animals may seem to be screaming in pain but actually they enjoy much of what we ask them to do, such as smoke cigarettes, chase hares round in circles, fuck porn stars; and (3) animals are not having souls, so is alright anyway. In the case of the Peruvian festival, incidently, it ends with the best beefburgers you will ever taste. And condor.

Racing, Cockroach: What Catalans do in their kitchens for the rest of the year once Barcelona are knocked out of the Champions League (¡again!).

Racism: There is no racism in Spain, except from the fucking disgusting Basques and filthy Catalans. Everyone else in Spain is perfectly normal, hospitable, and tolerant of any outsider who comes to our country and is willing to learn the language, follow our customs, shine our shoes, peel our tomatoes, fix our plumbs, and cetera. They don't even have to be white (although it does help).

Ravioli: ¿Aqualung running low? No worries. Extra air can be found inside ravioli.

Reading: Over-rated. We tend to forget that Jesus himself was illiterate. If just looking at the pictures was good enough for him, is also good enough for the ordinary man on the Gran Via. I am not saying that if pornography had been available in Jesus's day, he would have been an avid consumer, only that he certainly would have preferred it to pulling himself off to recitations of the Talmud.

Real Madrid: God is a Real Madrid fan. Is why Jesus wears white.

Realists, Race: Pseudo-scientists charged with the task of producing justifications for discriminatory housing and educational policies that will prevent black and other minority children from accumulating the cultural and economic capital necessary for them to compete in the job market with white middle-class kids. Members of the professional and managerial classes claim to despise and revile such crass ideological eugenicism but secretly harbour a sense of relief and gratitude when those policies are implemented; school fees are already through the roof as it is, and their dunce of a son would stand no chance on a level playing field (unless it's a rugby pitch) against lean and hungry chavs with a sense of self-esteem and an equal opportunity to make something of their lives. "That isn't what we made their grandparents fight the war for," they say, and they would be right.

Rebellion, The Trilobite: Catholic arachnomorph uprising against the Glorious Permian Revolution. Hidden from history under multiple layers of Protestant sediment but slowly coming to light as God implements his Endtimes agenda.

Regulares **(First Blessèd Atrocity, The):** Wobbling in the heat haze on an isolated plateau outside and below Triquiviate, it looked at first like an oversize raspberry blancmange. On approach, it became a glistening pink hillock of soapy fat, with a grey cloud hovering above. Closer still and what I at first taked to be spikes or grating around the base of the hillock inclined me to wonder whether this wasn't some kind of hallucination produced by my sizzling, demented brain. Was only as we came within a stone's throw and the haze dissipated that I was able to resolve the indeterminate shapes and identify the debris as human ribcages and assorted limb bones—femurs, tibias, ulnas—haphazardly scattered like storm-felled branches, the grey cloud a dense mass of flies that couldn't believe their luck.

My recognition of human bones was revised to greater specificity by closer examination of the mound. These was all female bones, and the decomposing bodies all those of women, since the "mound" comprised their breasts, sliced off, collected, and agglomerated as if for display. I recalled straight away that this was being a favourite mutilation of the *Regulares*, the volunteer infantry units of the Spanish Army based in Africa, both during their North African campaigns and as they marauded across the Iberian Peninsula during the Civil War, putting down the vermin of the Republic: communists, anarchists, trade union members, peasants, red scum. Breasts removed with bayonets, prior to death and always preceding loss of consciousness.

¿Who could have had been gathering so many female gambies in one place to mutilate and execute them in this way? ¿Who today would be capable of such cold-blooded and gratuitous misogyny? Ukraine's Azov Battalion, perhaps, or the criminals of the Wagner Group. This was certainly not the work of the local council, who would not dare the expense or risk of exposure. ¿What in any case would be gained by such mutilations? It would require the complicity of a sadist—or sadists—who had no desire to send a message to anyone, only to gratify their own vindictiveness. ¿Did they round up the women and drive the men away? Impossible to say at short notice, but gived that this was a natural site of accumulation for gambies descending from the mountains, perhaps they all stalled here and the perpetrators happened upon them, dispensing with the men before indulging in an orgy of violence against the women, breasts reaped and accumulated to no purpose.

Candelaría found the vista equally perplexing.

"¿Why are all the boobies over there?"

"I am not having no idea."

"¿And why are there no buzzards?"

"Good point. They must know to keep their distance. This pile is still fresh. Whoever did this isn't long gone."

"We should make a move then." She wasn't entirely brain dead. "I am not adding mine to that pile."

"Don't worry. We aren't stopping."

While I was impressed with the scale of defilement, I had no desire to meet the perpetrators. I doubt they did it to be admired, and in any case, I didn't want Candelaría picking up a following among the fly community that had gathered there. This isn't a fucking Sartre play.

Reproduction: The foundation of any civilization is control over the reproduction of people, not just in terms of sex and who is permitted to participate but also in terms of the type and number of people reproduced, since these factors shape the size and structure of your society. Indeed, True, Traditional, Catholic Fascism and Rubbish, Derivative, Modernist Fascism can be distinguished by their emphasis in this regard. True, Traditional, Catholic Fascism focuses on number over type, which it does by restricting abortion, encouraging women to stay at home and make as many children as possible, and saving souls for the Church, Jesus, and working the land; the more hands the better. Modernist Fascism, by contrast, focuses on the type of person over the number, hence its notion of a Master Race and the threat of miscegenation, the importance of eugenics, and so on. There is thus an Enlightenment and, dare I say, Protestant, scientistic taint to Modernist Fascism, a strain—and stain—of modernism that is absent from True, Traditional, Catholic Fascism and which renders the former susceptible to scientific counterarguments. Supporters do their best to fight back with scientific arguments of their own, but the problem with traveling down that road is the need for coherence, and if one part of your argument falls, it becomes necessary to evade the counterevidence with Ptolemaic epicycles that take you further and further down the rabbit hole until no-one can follow you unless they too become as small as Alice. Catholic Fascism is not having this weakness of susceptibility to evidence; our faith and willful ignorance are all we need.

Rhode Island: In the U.S. state of Rhode Island, all homes built after 1957 are required to feature four more doors than windows.

Rhubarb: Useful to fend off an attacking shark by poking it in the eye. Don't use asparagus, which is too short and floppy.

Rice: Everyone knows that rice swells up in contact with water and that this can be used to plug a hole in a car radiator. Fewer know that it also works for a gaping stomach wound. Most surgeons prefer long-grained rice all the way from America.

Rock and Roll: Popular culture for psychopaths. A music that encourages hedonism, lack of consideration for others, abandonment of self-restraint, contempt for society, and self-indulgence. All these characteristics are typical of the psychopath. ¿Have you ever met a rock star? They are wankers.

Rolling Stones, The: Wankers. The Rolling Stones is a well-known racist Irish pop band from Liverpool, comprising Mick Jaggre, Ronnie Wood, Keith Harris, George Orwell, and Curlie Watts. Discovered playing in a marquee, which is a big tent in London, their biggest hits were "Honky Woman," "Brown Sugar," the theme tune to "Neighbours," and "Sticky Fingers," about a boy with twiglets for hands. Died in a swimming pool, which is a Californian religious shrine, as part of a Moonie ritual.

Roscommon: An Irish county and kind of illness. The Roscommon Tourist Board has a memorable slogan: "¡See Roscommon and/or Die!"

Roses, Smell of: Our Lady's perfume. People say that when a pious or blessèd person dies, the room fills with the smell of roses, rather than faeces. Usually, though, the explanation is Air Wick Ambipur: Catholic hospitals buy it in bulk.

Rugby, Women's: Increasingly popular in Spain and indicative of national decline. However, whereas the die is already cast for countries such as England, with its feminism and lesbians and weak-chinned men, Spain may still be saved. The women in England are already too strong and powerful, wearing the trousers, smoking the cigars, and sweating the sweat. In Spain, the women (by and large) are still natural, delicate beautiful flowers who do as they are telled and are kept indoors for their own protection (outdoor Spain is vicious and hostile). Like many of the best ideas but also the worst ideas, women's rugby works in principle, but not in practice. In fact, it does not even work in principle. For one thing, no Spanish man would let his girlfriend play. I know I wouldn't, if I had one.

S

Saint, The: A 1960s British Television show starring Roger Moore in which he traveled around the country converting people to Christianity or he shot them. Based on a book about Cecil Rhodes.

Saint John the Octopus: The Vatican-insider nickname for John the Baptist, derived from the fact that eight churches across Christendom purport to possess the hand he used to baptise Christ. Either some or all are fake or else the saint was more at home in the water than we generally assume.

Saint Patrick's Day: Is March 17, the day when everyone in Ireland dyes their hair green, drinks lots of porter, and hits in the head people whose accents they don't like. Is also traditionally when snakes are driven out of Ireland: Irish Ferries make it much easier than in Saint Patrick's day, whence the name.

Salmon of Knowledge: A know-it-all fish from Irish mythology whose expertise and brilliance didn't prevent it from ending up being roasted on a griddle with its guts pulled out. Not to be confused with the Sole of Discretion, the Ray of Hope, the Plaice of Execution, or the Fickle Fish Finger of Fate.

Sartre, Jean-Paul (1905–1980): The cross-eyed never see the world properly. ¿Is it any wonder, then, that this man, who thought he was being followed by a giant lobster when it was only Simone de Beauvoir in a red beret, was filled with frustration and despair and could never decide which was the real bottle of beer in front of him? The so-called dilemna of existential choice doesn't exist; is just the result of seeing double.

Satanists: There are a lot more around than you might think. Most people are Satanists and don't even realize it.

School: In Spain, the school is a very happy place, which is a sign of the times. In my day, the schools was being run by the excellently disciplined Opus Dei, who crammed lots of education into my body and made me very cunning and aware of what a dangerous and evil place the world can be, but also how tolerable it can become providing you make lots of prayers, chastise yourself regularly, feel lots and lots of shame and guilt about your personal habits, and learn Latin. This is what education should be. I grew up to be a well-balanced, normal, and rigid man thanks to the focused schooling I received at the hands (and sometimes the feet) of my stern-but-fair teachers, which disabused me of mass media lies and communist Satanic distortions about the Inquisition, El Generalísimo, and the human body. Many times now, when I look at the state of the world and its laxity, I wish I was back in school, where my main responsibility was to wipe down the chasubles.

If conducted correctly, education can be a valuable torment in which children are shaped and trained to lower their expectations and be realistic about their life chances, resigning them to a useful slot in the social organism and stop bloody complaining. Were it not for modern-day teachers and their lofty ideals about "knowledge" and "opportunities," school would be a perfect social institution, just like the army.

Anyway, school didn't never do me any harm; ¿and in any case, what's wrong with a bit of harm?

Schoolgirls: There wasn't no schoolgirls when I was growing up, and like most new-fangled inventions, this one has come at a price, in this case the price being educated women. The upside, of course, is the uniforms and the wrestling and knife fights. I still can't watch two crouching schoolgirls circling each other outside the school gates, flick knives in hand, without wanting to reach into the back seat for a box of tissues.

In Fuerteventura, girl fights are very popular and more sexy than the Lucha Canaria, although both draw big crowds of teenage boys watching and shouting, "¡Fight! ¡Fight! ¡Fight! ¡Fight!" There aren't enough police in Fuerteventura to control the crowds, so the teachers' trade union is always whining about being the bad guys and having to break up the fights and hose down the audience.

One teacher being interviewed for the papers after breaking up a fight was quoted as saying girl-on-girl violence can be "especially nasty." Ha ha ha, I thought when I read it. The proofreader has made a big mistake; the sentence should clearly read "especially tasty."

Scottish Enclosures, The: After war, golf is the pinnacle of human civilization, and the easiest wars to win are those against the poor, which is why ruling classes ever since the Spartans and the Samurai have used the poor for practice, just to keep their hand in. One benign consequence of wiping out or even just dispossessing the poor is the opportunity to optimize the potential of the land on which they was subsisting through the design of golf courses. This is why Ireland, Scotland, Japan, Spain, and Sparta are having all the best golf courses in the world. There is no golf/civilization without class war, a universal truth that all golfers know and all poor people understand and accept at gunpoint.

Second Blessèd Atrocity, The: "¡Willies!" said Candelaría, delighted with herself. "Lots of willies and balls."

She had have never seen so many before at one time, a surprise to me, gived our parents' at-homes.

A rarely talked-about side-effect of rabies, passed over by doctors in polite conversation with the victims' relatives, is the constant horniness of the sufferer. In a hospital context, standard practice was always being to conceal the patient from the family as much as possible, on the pretext of possible contagion but in reality to avoid presenting them with their relative in one of their frequent periods of fervent masturbation during their delirium. Few daughters want to see their father close to death, and even fewer when he passes his remaining hours tossing himself off, foam-flecked lips and wide wild eyes staring through her (unless the daughter is a nurse, of course, in which case she just gloves up and gets on with it like she would for any other terminal case).

These willies, however, was wilted willies, draped like sad Christmas decorations across a stand of spurges, sliced from their gambie owners no doubt by the same bad pennies responsible for the mound of breasts outside Betancuria. *Momentito.* "Draped" perhaps implies too great a degree of intention. The distribution of penises around the stand was too random, suggesting instead that they had been thrown aside wantonly, with force, and had stuck to the spurges like Velcro. Whoever had did this was as contemptuous of men as they were of women, meaning that my earlier inference of misogyny as their prime motivation, while not unwarranted, was presumptuous. It seemed instead that they were equal opportunity slaughterers, merely segregating their victims prior to despatch, indicative of an Olde Worlde propriety, a sense of decorum lacking in most mass killers; it's an observation rarely made that the Nazis frequently used unisex gas chambers, further evidence of their corrupt modernity. Whoever our perpetrators were, at least they were classy enough to show some decent Spanish courtesy.

Seneca: Spanish Roman who correctly observed that Spain was Christian before Christ.

Senses: Is supposed to be true that if you lose one sense, then your other senses improve in order to compensate. Is rubbish. I once creeped up on a blind English tourist walking along the promenade in Corralejo and vigorously slapped him round the chops from behind. ¡He didn't expect it at all! (I also learned some of the secret blind swear words that they usually keep to themselves in their Braille books.)

Sex: Like beer, an acquired taste. Most people would not instinctively or voluntarily engage in sex; indeed, it requires training from adolescence for young boys to overcome their natural disgust at women's bodies. Perhaps the greatest triumph of the Patriarchy and the State has been to repackage sex to the masses as the purpose of existence, so that the stupefied fools provide an endless source of meat machines for the nation's pyramids, plantations, and wars. This is why the clitoris had to be concealed for so long, both literally and metaphoricly, and why pubescent girls could not quite place their finger on why it was that they enjoyed riding ponies so much.

Shoes: You can always judge a woman by whether she judges a man by his shoes. Such women believe that shiny shoes are a symptom of style and grown-upness, but they forget that Jesus himself wore sandals and that Franco wore riding boots or, at home, high heels.

Shoes are named after their inventor, Elizabeth Shoe (874–1520). So popular and fashionable among the well-to-do were the wooden "foot-substitutes" that Shoe originally designed for war amputees to disguise their leg-end deficiency that perfectly able-bodied members of Europe's royal courts would cut off their own feet and seek her out purely in order to be *au courant*, another example of conspicuous consumption, the pointless spendthriftery that enabled the wealthy to set themselves apart from the two-footed hoi-polloi. Conscious of the limited market that her product catered for, Shoe began designing her foot-substitutes in a range of colours, with different heels, and from different types of wood. Her breakthrough came, however, when she realized that it was possible to construct a form of "imitation" foot substitute that would cover the foot rather than replace it, and this led to her early experiments in wooden shoes later taked up and developed by Hans Clog in the Low Countries.

Shoe also discovered that animal hides offered the option of a cheaper and more flexible product that could be made in a range of sizes that might, in principle, fit anyone's feet, but when this news became widely known, the "foot substitute" lost all of its exclusivity and cachet and people returned to stumps and naked feet for the next 200 years. Whence the movie *The Barefoot Contessa*, based on the film of the same name.

Shropshire: A fictional English county, like Thomas Hardy's Wessex or Tolkien's Shire, made famous by e.e. housemate's novel *My Shropshire Lad*. If you go online, you will find that there is an entire subculture devoted to this artificial world, with professional-quality sites carrying authentic-sounding names such as "Shropshire County Council," with complete electoral registers, histories of the county's towns, updates of traffic news, and cetera. Is proof that people are having too much time on their hands.

Shrove Tuesday: When I was being a child, all the other children ran and danced in the streets every carnival Tuesday and ate their meat mittens, a traditional Spanish savoury gived to kids before they begin the fasting.

Normally, the children would put their meatens on after their breakfast of cheese and chicken with yogurt and then dressed themselves, usually in clothes, meaning that they smeared animal fat all over themselves for the day. Then they was allowed out into the street to gambol, eat one another's hands, drink wine, and run away from dogs. Was all great fun and totally exciting, especially when a pack of dogs caught up with a disabled or fat child and overpowered him. ¡How we all laughed!

When the children had finished their meatens and wine, they would need a lie-down, which was how they learned the tradition of the siesta. In the old days, they would just fall asleep in the middle of the street in the warm Spanish Sun, and the parents was happy to just leave them there until they came round with a blinding hangover and meat-ache, but nowadays there are too many cars on the road and women are allowed to drive, so is much too dangerous. Instead, the local police truck picks the children up and takes them to the station, where parents can go to retrieve them. ¡If they remember! Sometimes the children are left in the station for weeks, with no food and only a cheap prostitute or two for company. ¡Which would not be so bad if it was not Lent!

Siesta: The traditional time for Spanish people to enjoy a small sleep and orgasm. In French, is called *le petit mort*. In English, *death in the afternoon*.

Silverware: In 2021, Atlético de Madrid did not win a single trophy. In fact, someone even stole some of the spoons from the players' lounge, so the club was actually down on silverware that year. ¡Is not a joke!

Sisters: More trouble than they are worth.

Socialism or Barbarism: Bear in mind that, under socialism, you would not be given the choice.

Socialists: Motivated by envy, jealousy, spite, a sense of personal inadequacy, and a lust for power, all of which they disguise with a paper-thin altruism. They are such unpleasant people that the working class would be better off enduring the worst oppression, exploitation, and injustice than for the socialists to be in power, as the people of Spain have learned to their cost.

Soup, Leak y Potato: A nutritious and warming winter beverage, there is sufficient starch in leak y potato soup to plug the blowhole of a dolphin, finally wiping that smug smile off its face.

South Carolina: In the U.S. state of South Carolina, is illegal to sleep in the same room as spaghetti.

South Dakota: In the U.S. state of South Dakota, is illegal to be drunk in charge of a hair dryer.

Spain: Is no surprise that Modern Fascism, that is, the inferior version of Fascism, appeared in countries that had only been unified fifty or sixty years earlier, around 1870. These were states without empires, without a homogeneous history, and thus which required an invented tradition, looking back to ancient Rome or Germanic, Aryan warriors. Moreover, because their nations hadn't got no genuine collective past, their ideologies was inevitably forward-looking. The Nazis envisioned a Reich that would last a thousand-years. Mussolini's Fascists dreamed of a dynamic, thrusting Italy of Futurism, of steel and chrome, of bullets and fast trains, rather than a revival or retrieval of past glories. As products of modernity, neither Germany nor Italy could escape the Enlightenment ideological straitjacket of Progress, Science, and Knowledge. Their paradise lay ahead of them, to be created by the New Men, the *Übermenschen*, shaping not the world but their own corner of it, a walled enclave impervious to the Chaos beyond, an ideal of Order, Health, Conformity, and Law inhabited by yet-to-be-perfected Aryan or Roman subjects.

True Fascism, which is to say Spanish Fascism, isn't so foolish, not so deceived, whether as a result of good fortune or divine decree (I prefer to think the latter). We don't look forward for our utopia. We look back, to the Garden of Eden, and know that it is gone forever. Like Emmanuel Kant, we understand that nothing straight can be made from the crooked timber of humanity. Man has been banished from his Paradise on Earth forever and is incapable of re-creating it. He is a fallen wretch, endowed with the faculty of knowledge—thanks to one act of Disobedience, the *original* Original Sin—from which can come nothing but Evil, an Evil that takes him further away from Eden the more he employs it. Moreover, we understand the folly of an Enlightenment-tainted Fascism which imagines that Paradise can be reproduced within a single nation-state. This is because Spain is, was, and always has have been something *more* than a nation-state. Indeed, Spain is something more than a country, which is why it can contain within it many smaller, inferior countries: Cataluña, the Basques, the Canarias, Peru, Chile, Uruguay. Because Spain is, above all, an idea, an ideal Catholic idea, the only idea that can save humanity, and hence the need to spread it everywhere. Only when everyone is Catholic and Spanish—though not, of course, living in Spain: ¡That would be stupid!—will humanity be correctly reconciled to its fate of eternal frustration and sin.

Spartans: Is well known that the ancient Greeks was the first to invent democracy and therefore have had more time than everyone else to realize that it doesn't work. But some Greeks figured this out sooner than the others, most notably the Spartans, who ran their society on the basis of militarism, with all the good things this entails. The citizens of Sparta engaged full-time in military training, and to keep themselves sharp and ready for war, they periodicly declared a practice war on their own underclass, the Helots, who was the peasants and slaves that provided the food for the society but also who wasn't allowed to possess weapons or to receive military instruction. What is also interesting about the Spartans, and something still pertinent in this modern crazy world what we are live in, is that the army was organized in such a way that every fighting man was gived a partner, who was another fighting man, and they often went into battle tied together like Siamese twins. What is more, the Spartan society encouraged the fighting men to love one another in a disgusting carnal way, so that they would be prepared to kill for one another, but more important, die for one another, on the battlefield.

Of course, this would never work today because we are not Greek and the last thing we want to do is train homosexuals in how to kill normal people. Anyone who recommends such a thing would deservably receive flak, and possibly shrapnel, from right-thinking Falangist critics for suggesting that the Spanish army's proud traditions of vigorous heterosexual brutality should be besmirched in any way, like a dark turd smeared across the Spanish flag. Homosexuals belong in an institution, those critics will say, but that institution is not the army.

After both the World War Ones and Twos, the countries of Europe came close to revolution, in part because the masses were still not reconciled to the idea of pointless suffering and brutality, but also because the governments had made the stupid decision to arm the workers and teach them how to shoot. It taked a long while to dawn on the slow demented inbred ruling classes that this is not how you run an army, let alone a country. Instead of conscription, you need a cohort of idiot volunteers from the peasantry who are suitably indoctrinated with patriotism, and above them an officer hierarchy which is entirely drawn from the ruling class. This is why now all the private schools in England teach their pupils officer training and why the aristocrats go hunting. They have learned from the Spartans that they must stay in tip-top military form and peek conditions, while the workers are all sat in front of the idiot-box and eating fishes and chips and pizzas and don't even know how to use a fork, let alone a knife or pikelet. In America, the last time they tried conscription it was for the Vietnam War, and that resulted in hippies. They won't do that again.

We are being lucky in Spain that we learned long before the rest of Europe the importance of having a volunteer army of professional killers rather than a conscript army made up of insubords and hoi pollois. ¿What are you doing when you train the working classes how to use weapons if not producing your own executioners? Far better to produce an army that is loyal to the state, with an officer class entirely from your ruling families, willing to come home to brake the strikes, teach the unions a lesson, and govern benighnly, like the way Franco did. How the Spartans would have envied us then. ¡Although they would probly also fancy us as well!

Sphagnum: Surprisingly, is not a rude thing at all. I looked it up. Is a type of moss.

Sport: The most right-wing elements in any society are its military brass, its organized crime, and its professional sports people. The reason for this is obvious: These are the people who are naturally superior to everyone else in society, thanks to the many hours of hard work they have had to put into perfecting themselves and also triumphing over and/or eliminating their enemies. They are the best of the best within professions in which there is no room for pity and in which coming second is meaningless. Also, in the case of sports, lots of running around in the fresh air and exercising in the gym leaves no time for reading the books, getting a liberal education, and cetera, with the result that sports people are entirely lacking in imagination or curiosity and display a greatly stunted intelligence: Would that we could all emulate them. Of course, we cannot, because every society also requires its bakers, cobblers, toilet attendants, accountants, cabaret singers, and petshop owners. Neverthenonetheless, I would argue correctly that, in every civilized society, sport should be made compulsory for all its subjects. This is for three very good reasons: (1) in order to inculcate a sense of patriotism; (2) so that the public can develop an appreciation for sporting prowess and therefore a love of watching sports; and (3) so they can understand just how physicly superior professional sports people are, thereby reconciling them to their lives of tedium and inferiority. In this way, they will realize that even if they wanted to leave their factory, farm, office, or hovel for a life of sporting or military excitement, they lack the ability to hack it out there with the big boys. The best they could aspire to is the glorious death of an ignorant foot soldier, blown to pieces on a foreing field that is historicly part of Spain.

Starch, Husky and: A humorously named Korean dish featuring rice and poodles.

Stockhausen Syndrome: Is an illness that happens when people who are being attacked by terrorists identify with the cause and interests of their attackers. Named after the German music conductor notorious for having described the 9/11 attacks as a work of art when in fact they was a work of craft: aircraft.

Stoics, The: There were more suicides amongst the Stoics than any other school of philosophy.

Storker: Let us be magnaniminous and call Seymour Stiveley a fly in the ointment, the ointment being our mellifluous, mollifying, medicinal solution for the Irish body politic's decrepit constitution, the strategy of tension that Frank Prendergast and I had so lovingly and cunningly nurtured through the considered and coordinated deployment of explosives in public spaces, of hard drugs among the military and judiciary, of blackmail, extortion, and sedition in the press and mass media. ¡Glory be! The more I remember, the prouder I am of our edifice, our artifice, our designs. ¡Such cunning! ¡Such deviousness! And was all the more galling, then, that it should have had been brought low by the unrequited love of a homosexual buttock boy—¿Have MI6 still not learned the lesson of the Cambridge spies?—for the insipid and useless Joseph Chambers, an afterthought, a nobody, a minor detail in our plans.

We were aware of Stiveley's identity, of course, because embassies' espionage operations all know each other, if not by sight then by name and reputation. We also knew that Stiveley, a former academic with a background in archaeology and ancient Mesopotamian languages, had a history with Chambers, who had once managed to have Stiveley deported from Greece after ancient relics from an Athens museum were discovered in his hold luggage on a routine embassy flight. After Chambers was similarly removed in disgrace from Greece for a separate scandal involving the prime minister's wife, a bottle of brandy, a tub of ice cream, and cardiac arrest, Stiveley pursued him to Dublin, obtaining a transfer and, we always assumed, seeking revenge. Indeed, one of Frank's agents, who had been assigned to befriend and betray Chambers, spotted Stiveley taking photos of her with Chambers as they promenaded through Dublin's Phoenix Park. Not for one moment did we imagine that, rather than seeking vengeance, Stiveley was not only seeking redemption, having seen the error of his ways, but had also taked it upon himself to educate Chambers about his own lack of professionalism as an act of devotion and homosexual benevolence. My failure and inability to empathize with and thus understand Stiveley's motives can undoubtably be ascribed to my strong and unequivocal heterosexuality. Sometimes, our greatest virtues can be our undoing.

Stroessner, Alfredo: Presidente Stroessner ruled over a country of ingrates, the Papaguayans, even though he made the eggs runny on time and put an end to all nonstate terrorism and crime in his country. History records that when Stroessner was president, no one locked their doors at night in Asunción. This was because (1) nobody had nothing worth nicking, (2) nobody could afford to buy locks, and (3), as the chief of police said, "Only those with something to hide are having anything to fear." This totalitarian logic remains unassailable to this day.

Stupid Bus: "The stupid bus is late."
 "¿Why are you on the stupid bus, Hijo de Puta? You should be on the smart bus with your sister."

Suits: The suit maketh the man. My favourite is a suit of armour.

Sun, Catch the: ¿Why do people say "You have caught the Sun," when they are commenting on somebody's sunburn? They have not caught the Sun. The Sun has caught them. Is typical human self-aggrandisement.

Superheroes, Spanish: As a teenage boy, I loved very much to visit the Museo Nacional de Superhéroes, which had on the first floor a wonderful and fascinating diorama featuring characters from Spanish comics who made just one appearance, never to be seen or mentioned again. This was my favourite part of the museum because no one else went there but me and I could finger the mannequins with no one watching.

El Snob
"¿Drive myself? Surely, you're joking, Señor Lario."
(*Tales from the Haçienda* #12, second series, 1962)

Hoarse Girl
"I'm sorry, Hoarse Girl. I didn't get your message."
(*The Listener* #363, 1966)

Mr. Digestive
"Wait while I pass these documents through my body. Then I'll tell you everything you need to know."
(*¡Spazam!* #2, 1973)

Go Girl
"¡When Trouble Arrives, She Goes!"
(*Disempowering Legends* #1, 1964)

Epileptico
"You never know when he's going to spring into action."
(*The Disabled Four* #208, 1978)

The Stool Pigeon
"Your bicycle seat is very moist, Luis. ¿What do you think that means?"

(*Erotic Tales for Kids* #5, 1974)

Luke Warm, a.k.a. Señor Tepido
"Ach. Let them die. I haven't finished the papers yet."
(*Capitán Salamanca* #19, 1967)

The Human Stain
"¡Hold on! ¡We're All Going to Dieeeeeeeee!"
(*Short Stories for Children about Mortality* #4, 1973)

Judge Liberal
"It could go either way."
(*Criminal Crackers* #15, 1975)

Lady Pentangle
"¡Margareta! ¡To the Ouija Board!"
(*The Sapphic Occultists* #1, 1968)

New Foetus Army
"Our limbs may be short, Archbishop, but see how many of us there are."
(*Catholic Odyssey* #40, 1970)

Hitler Youth*
"¡Let's Make Germany Great Again!"
(Strip removed from *Science Fiction* #17, 1939)[4]

---

[4] An intended sidekick for Falange Boy, Hitler Youth was created in 1939, just before the start of the Second World War Two, at a time when it was not clear whether Spanish interests was best served by collaboration with former comrades-in-arms Nazi Germany or sucking up to the despised Allies.

T

Tamasite, Battle of: A glorious battle near Tuineje in 1740, in which the courageous local Spanish indigents beat the vicious invading British pirates who wanted to colonize the Canarias like they had done the rest of the world. Is perhaps not an overstatement to say that this was the moment when Spain put an end to the slave trade forever. The battle is also noteworthy for the fact that one of the stout-hearted locals killed fifteen of the evil British plunderers using just his spontoon. ¡Imagine!

Tattoos: Forbidden for members of the intelligence services, tattoos are means by which those with no distinctive or distinguishing psychological features express their individuality. In my correct humble opinion, the only bodily modifications worth having are those earned in combat (scars, amputated limbs, lost eyes, swollen goolies, and cetera.). Millán-Astray did not need a personality. You could judge him by his deeds and disabilities.

Technology: Everything went downhill after the invention of the wheel. Before then, it had all just stayed where it was.

Most people have forgotten that the telescope was originally invented for use by the Inquisition to extract information from taciturn Jews and naysayers who refused to convert to Christianity before dying. The instrument was lined up so that the Sun's rays would be concentrated and then burn a hole in the eyeball of the Inquisitee, and anything they had witnessed and not squealed about would then be visible in the shapes of the smoke that arose from their smouldering orb. The Inquisition obtained many almost unbelievable confessions in this way: As they peered into the black streams of gas and particulate matter escaping the victim's charred ocular orifice, and once they got used to the smell, they were able to discern dragons, witches, cats, smoke, people's faces, incubuses, hellfire, demons, Catalans, airplanes, and lots more. They naturally regarded the telescope as a wonderful invention gived by God for the winkling out of Satan's minions. Only when one of the interrogees, Galileo from Galilee, looking up the wrong end of the telescope, said "Hey, I can see your house from here," did malefactors realize that the telescope could be put to the nefarious activities for which we know it today, namely, voyeurism and astronomy.

    The rest is one long story of civilizational decline as the so-called "thinkers" of the Enlightenment began to ask themselves "¿What else can we do with the Inquisition's interrogation devices other than that for which God intended them?" In this way, the pure and holy instruments of confession became weapons for so-called "science and industry." The rack became the loom, thumbscrews became the carpentry vice, and the Iron Maiden became a seminal source of Satanic rock music. It thus behooves us all to be circumspect when we go around inventing things. Before you run off applying for trademarks and copyrights or whatever, be sure to run any novel instrument of practical innovation by your priest first, and he will seek advice from the Church on whether your intervention in the natural order of things is going against God's plans and you should be put to death.

Television: A source of putrefying degenerate rubbish. I don't even have to watch it to know that much. Even sitting there turned off in the corner of the room, it oozes feculence and corruption.

Tennessee: In the U.S. state of Tennessee, is illegal to wash stones.

Tennis: Tennis turns people into homosexuals, as proved by the fact that there are seventy-three homosexuals in Madrid, and they all play tennis. You may say that correlation is not causation, but none of them was homosexuals when they started playing tennis, so you can draw your own conclusions, provided they are the same as mine. All tennis clubs should be razed to the ground and replaced by churches or golf courses, the home of Spain's two main heterosexual religions.

Texas: In the U.S. state of Texas, anal sex is only permissible between women.

Theology: I can think of no chore more tedious than that of listening to people argue about the existence of God. Is absolutely stupid. This is a subject that is simply not open to rational debate or argument. The existence of God is a fact the proof of which requires the all-important act of faith, without which all other actions are meaningless. The search for evidence is indicative of a Doubty Thomas, one whose faith is not strong enough to endure on its own and which also tells the Church he is a potential trouble maker who must be stomped on before he infects anyone else with his poor attitude.

Thermometer: A glass tube containing mercury which is used to measure the temperature of fridge-freezers, Sun terraces, and human bodies. Should not be confused with a barometer, which also contains mercury and can also be accommodated comfortably under the armpit but which cannot be inserted orally or anally without some discomfort.

Third Blessèd Atrocity, The: To tell the truth, I had no desire to discern with any clarity the nature of the third atrocity. From a distance of several hundred meters, I could already make out brutal, swift hacking with machetes and cleavers, like a Salvadorean death squad dismembering dissidents, and limbs tossed into the air like chicken bones at a banquet. Thankfully, "a distance" was as close as I needed to get, because I had stumbled first upon two microlites—keys in the ignition and with somewhat oversize pilots' seats—and thus had considered it wiser not to interrupt their owners' frenzy but to borrow one without seeking their permission, lest I become involved in some contretemps against my better interests. As quietly as I could, I lifted Candelaría from Humpty Minor's back and dragged her to one of the microlites, all the while with one eye on the butchers at play in the heat. My grunts and heaves were restrained, and Candelaría resisted the urge to inquire about the men with the blades, resigning herself to dwell in ignorance, as she had for much of her life, this attitude having had kept her safe thus far.

I assumed that starting up the microlite would attract the executioners' attention but calculated that they were far enough away for us to get airborne before they could reach us, even though take-off would require turning the microlite into the wind, in their direction, and taking a run at them in the hope of enough lift to avoid their reach. Foretunately, they was so engrossed in their dismembermenting that they failed to notice our larceny, and the wind direction meant that the microlite's whirring and purring carried away back north, behind us. Otherwise we would have had had to deal with two very angry psychopaths.

Two very angry *massive* psychopaths, I should say, like the giant statues of the ancient kings Ayoze and Guise that guard the road through the mountains to Betancuria. No wonder they were making such short shrift of the gambies. Giants ripping apart torsos with petulant exuberance, separating limbs without apparent exertion. Monsters of men. Masters of men.

They raised their heads in our direction only seconds before we passed above them, and Guise came close to swatting us down, machete still in hand. It was a leap of several meters by a man at least three meters in height, with the legs of a Miura bull, his swiping arm like a windmill sail, catching the air but, I am glad to say, nothing else. It did not seem to register with either of them that the microlite I had commandeered was their own, since they did not look back to where they had have left them. Rather, their aggression in our direction was entirely instinctual; we had intruded upon their domain and had thereby triggered their natural response, like the bite reflex of a crocodile or the anal wink of a whore. I gave a huge big sigh of relief and determined to never cross their paths again.

Humpty Minor, disturbed by Guise's leap as an example of sublime power, instantly understood the perils of curiosity and advantages of discretion. He turned tail and exited left with a casual lollop that only gathered speed once he was below the brow of the plateau. With such an attitude, he will no doubt live long and prosper (this is the true meaning of Mr. Spock's injunction, incidently: keep your nose out of other people's business and know when to run away).

Thoughts, Impure: All thinking is sinful and impure, the result of disobeying God and eating the apple from the Tree of Knowledge. Many smart-arse septics have asked why on earth God placed the Tree of Knowledge in the Garden of Eden if he didn't want Adam and Eve to eat from it, but this kind of smart-arse questioning is just the sort of sinful, impure thinking caused by the eating of the apple in the first place, which thereby proves God's point.

Torture: Sometimes a necessary evil, *pour encourager les autres*. On other occasions, a means of initiation for new recruits into the police or military, compromising them by virtue of their participation and thereby committing them to de facto allegiance to the group; one might consider it a form of hazing, not for the victim, from whom nothing is expected, but for the novitiate, who cannot be permitted to join the group without some form of sacrifice or opportunity for blackmail, and who cannot subsequently leave the group without tarnishing his own name or leaving himself open to discredit. Torture is just one of the many bonding rituals employed by military organizations, but is made all the more potent and poignant by its taboo status. Mewling liberals typically object to torture on the grounds that the information gained as a result is likely to be unreliable, suggesting that they would in fact be happy to condone torture if it could be shown to be effective. This is to miss the point entirely. The victim is merely a tool, like a stripper at a bachelor party or a pig's head in an Eton boys' club.

This is not to deny that there are out-and-out sadists who enjoy torture for its own sake or that oftentimes an interrogator may be driven by anger or revenge to engage in less-than-professional methods, but these are generally the exceptions and usually only a prelude to the victim's death. Such individuals are the bad apples that lead to torture's negative public profile.

Frank assured me that he would take care of the rival drug gang supplying Chambers and also that he would deal with Chambers himself into the bargain, blowing him to bits in the remotely detonated bombing of Connolly Station. The first part was achieved smoothly and without fuss—Frank even played me an MP3 of the ringleader's execution, which he carried out with his own manly hands and recorded on a digital device in the shape of a crucifix that he always wore around his neck. The second part, however, was undermined by Frank's ridiculous sense of honour. Rather than eliminate Chambers, Frank opted to blackmail him with compromising photographs from a party at the American ambassador's residence in the Phoenix Park—compromising photographs of Chambers in various sexual positions with the Connolly Station "bomber," codename Yasmina Yıldırım. Chambers refused to be cowed, and when he discovered that Frank had executed his drug source—his only route, as he saw it, to avoiding repatriation—he confronted Frank on a windswept Killiney Beach and demanded an explanation. At this point, sentimentality got the better of Frank, who, confident of his own superior strength and pugilistic skills, chose not to use the Heckler & Koch in his pocket and was found himself instead on the receiving end of a bludgeoning with a particularly rocky rock.

Well, as the old say is going, if you want something doing, pay a whore. I therefore contrived a plot with Lady Jane Bondage to lure Chambers to Knockmerry House—¿¡to rescue her, would you believe?!— and when he arrived, we chloroformed him and brought him down to the basement for a bit of fun and murder. I was wanting also to know why Frank had not killed him, suspecting that perhaps Frank had double crossed me and was planning to take over the rival distribution network with Chambers as his partner. ¡I should not be so mistrusting! Chambers was woozy but insistent, even after seven fingernails, that Frank had threatened him with blackmail and had ended up as dead as a doorknob, blank eyes looking in different directions—one toward Bray, the other at his chin—buried up to his waist with only the beachlice for company. I did not believe him at first, but eventually sent two of my *bichos* down to Killiney Beach to confirm the kill. Chambers was telling the truth after all, and not because he was tortured, mewling liberals, but simply because there was no advantage to lying.

He put my mind at rest, which was very decent of him, but I could not allow some blabbermouth loose on the streets of Dublin who was knowing all about our operation, the false flag bombing of the train station, and with nothing to lose by going rogue. Chambers would have to die that afternoon regardless of how helpful he had been. And while there was no new recruits to haze through inclusion in his torture, Chambers was unfortunate in that this was one of those cases not only where revenge felt justified but also where the interrogator was one of those out-and-out sadists who enjoyed torture for its own sake.

That all being said, we was not excessively extravagant in our actions, and I did express my personal gratitude to Chambers for his honesty. Nor did we wheel out the electronics or the water board. Not when I had Madonna to hand. It was she who sliced his nipples, one clean off, the other left hanging, partially attached, of use to neither man nor babe. "¡Suck on that!" I joked, and my *bichos* all laughed at my wit. Chambers merely gagged and drooled through broken teeth. "Stop drooling," I told him. "You will never get a lady that way. They *hate* it."

We taked off also his foreskin for amusement but left him one of his thumbs, an oversight in retrospect, never imagining that he might have an opportunity to use it again one day. ¡Quite the misjudgement! Having tipped him out of his chair and bent him over, we were in the process of inserting the other thumb into his rectum, in pursuit of two of his fingers, when who should appear in the doorway but his fucking queer fanboy, Seymour Stiveley.

"Perfect timing," I quipped, ever cool in the face of interruption. "Lend me your cock to ram this home."

But Stiveley was not alone. He had come mob handed with armed Gardaí, none of whom I recognized—this is why the cunts wear ski masks and helmets—intent on being Quixote to Chambers's Dulcinea. They put my *bichos* up against the wall and me face down on the floor, knowing full well that I had diplomatic protection—and in the basement of my own fucking brothel; ¡The sheer nerve of it!—before they dragged Chambers up and out via the back passage we had intended to use to dispose of his corpse.

Thanks to Stiveley's rudeness and lack of etiquette—he didn't even knock—early retirement became an inevitability for me on that day. Following the appropriate protocol, no questions was asked by my superiors about fortunes squirreled away in offshore tax havens, but I *was* expected to carry the can on this "scandal" and accept being spirited out of the country. I was allowed to hand over my intelligence assets to my successor, and I received extensive advice on how to cover my tracks, since I was after all stepping out of the shadows, but Knockmerry House was liquidated and its employees literally put back out onto the streets where I found them. ¿What has become of Lady Jane? No one knows. No one cares.

I was also permitted to keep some of my security *bichos* on my private payroll, on the black economy, purely to ensure a peaceful retirement in the inhospitable backwaters of Fuerteventura. They were detailed to keep an eye on the airport, on the docks, on the fishing boats coming in late at night, just so I could sleep with both eyes closed. Not that the ghosts of my torture victims have ever given me restless nights. Only the ghosts of those we failed to kill. There is a lesson in that for us all.

Trains: An unnatural and Satanic form of transport but a necessary evil for every government, which it uses to move illicit, secret, or sensitive materials around the country during the night without arousing suspicion. For example:

- Boxes of amputated limbs for placement at crime scenes (weeknights only)
- Sealed carriages of illegal immigrant impersonators
- First-class carriages of agents provocateurs: trade union infiltrators, ISIS moles, archbishops
- Sex toy snatch squads, sowing distrust by breaking into multiple-occupancy homes and moving vibrators from room to room
- Prisoners eligible for early release but who the government doesn't want back in the community
- Tanker after tanker of pure, clean drinking water, uncontaminated by Prozac, fluoride, Viagra, microplastics, hormone replicants, or *Streptococcus* bacilli, supplied to the underground bunkers where the "other civil service" and the Deep State live and work
- Boxes containing the Air Force's supply of amphetamines
- Parcels containing the Army's supply of cannabis resin
- Crates containing the Navy's supply of poppers and ecstasy
- Copies of ¡*Hola!* magazine

Travel, Time: We are all time travellers. Each one of us travels forward in time every day, whether we like it or not. So-called quantum scientists have "proved," moreover, that the problem with traveling back in time is that you cannot go back in time any faster than you can go forward. Thus, to go back one week in time takes one week in time. If you are forty and go back in time twenty years, when you get there, you will be sixty. ¿Who wants to be eighty when they are born? I expect this is why no one has done it.

Trombone: Should never be played by women. Could burst their lungs. Also, watching them play gives men unnecessary erections.

Trout: An oily meat that is good for the complexion, the hair, and the nails. Also, large slices of trout can be fashioned into a parasol to shade you from the Sun when you are in the middle of the desert and there is nobody in the vicinity who minds the smell of trout.

Tumours: God's way of telling you to die.

Tuna: Tuna always know where the guns are kept.

Turducken: Is a tradition among the Catalan diaspora analogous to the Caganer, involving the throwing of frozen shitballs at one another every January 6. The word is a corruption of the phrase "turd ducking."

Twenty-three seconds: The official length of time you have to get into heaven before the Devil knows you are dead. I hope you can run.

U

UEFA Champions League: A slang term used by whores in Cataluña to refer to vaginal sex.

UEFA Europa League: A slang term used by whores in Cataluña to refer to anal sex.

UEFA Europa Conference League: A slang term used by whores in Cataluña to refer to Gomorrahmy.

Umbrage: A small English town in the shade where they are making the traditional English radio program *The Archers*. Probly near the fictional Sherwood Forest.

Unamuno, Miguel de: On October 12, 1936, the patriotic Fiesta of the Hispanic Race was being celebrated at the University of Salamanca with a major political/religious ceremony in the morning and then a less important, almost repugnant, academic celebration in the evening, the host of the latter being the liberal philosopher and writer Miguel de Unamuno, who had recently been reinstated as the rector of the university by El Generalísimo Francisco Franco, having had have been ignobly removed by the Republican government of Manuel Azaña. Those present on that memorable night included the Archbishop of Salamanca; General José Millán-Astray; Carmen Polo Martínez-Valdés, the wife of Franco; numerous Falangist supporters; middle-class liberal students of the university; and other motley alumnis.

According to the account written by Luis Portillo Pérez, "Unamuno's Last Lecture," which was published in the December 1941 issue of *Horizon* magazine, the evening began with a speech from professor of literature Don Francisco Maldonaldo, who provided a bland, bien-pensant speech of no consequence, as you might expect from a milquetoast Janus. Following him was Don José Maria Ramos Loscertales of Saragossa, who obsequiously but convincingly argued that Spain would emerge from the white heat of the Civil War like gold from a crucible, purified and without stain, in her true proper colours.

Next came General Millán-Astray, his Legionnaire's uniform bedecked with the finest medals and honors the Spanish Army can buy. He opened his address uncontroversiably by declaring that more than half of all Spaniards—those loyal to the government—were criminals, guilty of armed rebellion and high treason. From one audience member incapable of restraining himself in the presence of such a war hero there immediately came an enthusiastic but premature ejaculation—"¡Viva la Muerte!"—but Millán-Astray was not ready yet to be distracted or flattered. "Cataluña and the Basque country," he continued, "are two cancers in the body of the nation. Fascism, which is Spain's health-bringer, knows how to exterminate them both, cutting through to the live, healthy flesh like a resolute surgeon free from false sentimentality. And since the healthy flesh is the soil, and the diseased flesh is the people who dwell on it, Fascism and the Army will eradicate the people and restore the soil to the sacred national realm. Every Socialist, every Republican, every one of them without exception—and needless to say every Communist—is a rebel against the National Government, which will very soon be recognized by the totalitarian states that are assisting it, in spite of France—democratic France—and perfidious England. And then, or even sooner, whenever Franco decides, and with the help of the gallant Moors who, though they wrecked my body only yesterday, to-day deserve the gratitude of my soul since they are fighting for Spain against the Spaniards ... the bad Spaniards ... and they are giving their lives in defence of Spain's sacred religion, as is proved by their attendance at field mass, their escorting of the Caudillo, and the pinning of holy medallions and Sacred Hearts on their burnouses ..."

He was interrupted at this point by another zealous Falangist, who shouted from the audience, "¡Arriba España!" This time, Millán-Astray responded with the well-known Falangist cry:

"¡Spain!" To which the correct response was gived by the throng:

"¡One!"

Again,

"¡Spain!"

"¡Great!" came the second correct response.

"¡Spain!"

"¡Free!" This call-and-response was a voluntary and joyous expression of Fascist camaraderie and an appreciation of the General's commitment to the cause. Several Falangists was now standing and saluting enthusiastically in the direction of the giant photo of the Generalísimo on the auditorium's front wall.

"¡To Franco!" they shouted. The rest of the audience now rose from their seats, almost in unison.

"¡Franco! ¡Franco! ¡Franco!"

I am saying "almost in unison" here because the liberal bed-wetter Unamuno remained seated, possibly peeing himself even then, waiting for the hubbub to subside, knowing also that once this celebration had died down, it was his turn to speak. Eventually, the glorious enthusiasm of the true Spanish people assembled there that night abated, and slowly, because he was already an old man, Unamuno stood to speak.

"You are waiting for my words," he began, straight out of the trap with a lie. "You know me well and know that I cannot remain silent for long. Sometimes, to remain silent is to lie, since silence can be interpreted as assent.... I will ignore the personal offence to the Basques and Catalans. I myself, as you know, was born in Bilbao. The Bishop," he gestured in the direction of the Archbishop of Salamanca, "whether you like it or not, is Catalan, born in Barcelona. Anyway, tonight I have heard this insensitive and necrophiliac oath, 'Viva la Muerte,' and I, who has spent his life writing paradoxes that provoke the wrath of those who don't understand me, and being an expert in this matter, find this ridiculous paradox repellent. General Millán-Astray is a cripple. There is no need for us to say this with whispered tones. He is a war cripple. So was Cervantes. And unforetunately, today, Spain has too many cripples. And if God does not help us, soon it will have very many more. It torments me to think that General Millán-Astray could dictate the norms of the psychology of the masses. A cripple lacking the spiritual greatness of Cervantes is hoping to find relief by adding to the number of cripples around him."

This insult was too much for the good General. Immediately, he leaped to his feet:

"¡Down with Intelligence! ¡Long Live Death!" The Falangists in the audience again rose to their feet and responded with rapturous applause. Unamuno, however, was unfazed.

"This," he said, referring to the university, "is the temple of intelligence, and I am its high priest. You are profaning its sacred domain. You will win the Civil War because you have enough brute force. But you will not convince. In order to convince, you must persuade, and to persuade you will need something that you lack: reason. I can see there is no point asking you to think of Spain. I have spoken."

As he finished, several officers reached for their pistols, ready to teach a lesson to this educated idiot—an educated idiot who had clearly learned nothing from his exile to Fuerteventura by the Rivera regime—but Millán-Astray was the model of restraint and old-fashioned honour, as you would expect. He intervened and taked charge, instructing Franco's wife to escort the clearly delirious old man out of the building for his own good. Although Unamuno was booed by the crowd and called a fucking moron and dotard by the rightfully outraged throng, no harm befell him as he was led out to his car, which then sped him away to his home on Calle de Bordadores in Salamanca. Was not until ten days later, when word got back to Madrid, that Franco signed a decree dismissing Unamuno as rector of the university, and by the end of December he was dead. In one of his last letters, dated December 13, Unamuno again recorded his famous sentence in response to Millán-Astray: You will win, but you will not convince.

Recent years have seen attempts at revisionist history to deny that this event taked place in the way described by Portillo. Severiano Delgado, a librarian at the University of Salamanca, has argued that Unamuno's speech is a fabrication and that Portillo's account of the night included many exaggerations. However, if you want my opinion, which is the correct one, such well-intentioned efforts to downplay the significance of that night are an affront not just to historiography but also to the memory of Millán-Astray himself. ¿Are we to believe that Millán-Astray did *not* shout "¡Down with Intelligence!" or "¡Long Live Death!"? ¿Why would we deny him his characteristic battle cries, the very slogans that have rendered him a hero, a role model, an archetypal True Fascist and Man of Action? ¿Are we to imagine that it might somehow be shameful for him to declare such principles? This is typical of modern-day Fascist apologists, feeble posturing fratboys who are secretly desperate for girls' attention. ¡They miss the point entirely!

Indeed, if Millán-Astray did not say "¡Down with Intelligence!," then he damned well should have. Unapologetic opposition to intelligence is the only solid foundation for a True Fascism. True Fascism is an absolute. Anything else, like a Christianity that opens itself up to falsification, immediately and unavoidably concedes the choice of battlefield to the enemy and will end in defeat. And Unamuno, if he had not said, "You will win, but you will not convince," would not have been the typical idiot liberal that history has shown us he was. This phrase is the perfect, archetypal response of the willy-nilly liberal to the Fascist, proof that liberals think that being right is more important than wielding power. We Fascists laugh in the face of such liberal posturing because we know perfectly well that we will not convince. The True Fascist does not care one jot if he convinces because, once he has triumphed, the opinions of his victims will count for nothing. ¿Who are the vanquished for him except slaves and scum? The True Fascist does not debate in order to convince.

Argumentation and rational debate are the enemy's preferred arena, and the True Fascist knows he cannot win there. The True Fascist will only engage in debate as a strategy to ridicule his enemies, to undermine the respect paid to debate, to cast aspersions on his opponents' motives, to suggest they have a hidden agenda. The True Fascist laughs at your "reasoned debate." ¿Who imagines that Millán-Astray would have hung around the galleries and cloisters of Salamanca to engage in rational discussion? Only is a liberal idiot.

Q: ¿Why did the Fascist go to university?
A: ¡To burn its books!

¡¿What?! ¡Is a joke! (But not really.)

Underwear: The French refer to their underwear as their "unnecessaries," which tells you all you need to know about the French. Is also the source of the English phrase "to come over all unnecessaries," which means that you have shot your children in your pants.

Unicorns: The answer to the question "¿What did Noah and his family eat?"

Up in the Sky: The ability to fly makes a man feel like a God, or at least like an *Übermensch*. As Candelaría and I soared above the vast swathes of semi humanity farting about far below us on the flat plains of Morro Jable, the wind at my back producing a sense of calm and stillness as I pushed on toward the cactus forest, I understood now why my father had spent so much time in the air and away from home. We must have seemed like puny and ridiculous nonentities to him, he who had enjoyed complete dominion over the land and seas, the cities and fields, the rivers and roads, the cathedrals and hovels, the jungles and deserts. The gambies who aimlessly mingled and moshed beneath us, like an amorphous cloud of agitated atoms bumping and colliding, were ridiculous and laughable, just as my family and I must have been for my father, *hors de combat*, above the fray of teeming, pathetic, petty humanity.

As the microlite cleared the mountains, it dipped slightly and I struggled to keep her level for fear of dropping Candelaría. It meant also that I did not initially take note of the vista before me, the broad flat desert plain of Morro Jable, perilously close to sea level, begrimmed with a seething mass of gambies. Thousands upon thousands of them. I truly had not realized before this moment how many this small island could hold. I had read the statistics, seen the graphs in the media, heard the results of the polls, but I had been victim of the assumption that the gambies were evenly distributed and had extrapolated from my own encounters with a mere handful. It had never occurred to me that they might have a propensity for a particular climate or habitat. Was almost as if they had congregated together on purpose as like-minded citizens to begin society afresh, to attempt the construction of a New Man in their own image, conjured from their fervid dreams.

However, the real reason for their assembly was much more prosaic: Gambies don't do mountains. Climbing uphill is an act of will, of determination and purpose. Gambies are having none of these. Gravity dictates their direction. If they are struck ill on the beach, at sea level, there they will remain, perpetually hemmed in by hydrophobia on the one hand and an unwillingness to walk uphill on the other. If they are bitten and struck down in the mountains, by contrast, they will remain there only as long as they don't accidently discover a route down, usually arse over tit, as my English nanny used to say. There are, no doubt, valleys in the mountains of the interior, around Betancuria, for instance, that are home to major gambie populations simply for the lack of interest in whatever is over the hill. Gambies are not an inquisitive demographic.

Urban I, Pope (222–230): The first pope to be driven around in a Popemobile, whence the phrase Urban Transportation. Was beheaded in Rome, probly while trying to go under a very low aqueduct.

V

Vaginas: The original meat bucket™, although I don't think this is where KFC got the name. Vaginas are a dangerous place for men, women, and children. Successful transit in either direction is a challenge. A gentleman does not discuss a lady's vaginas in public, but every gentleman knows that the purpose of the vaginas is to lubricate the clitoris in order to prevent soreness from over-rubbing. However, for the sake of reproduction of the nation, women must be telled that the role of the vaginas is to facilitate the sick-making entry of the penis inside so that children can be made. Of course, if Nature genuinely wanted humans to reproduce, the vaginas would lubricate not only for the penis going in but also for the baby coming out. But no. You just have to hope the baby has a lot of spit.

Valley, Silly Cunt: Where Elon Musk lives.

Vampire: Any fool knows that vampire bats are not real. They were invented by the Irish showboater Bram Stokoe for his novel *Dracula: The Count of Monte Cristo*. Is a brilliant story and a metaphor for how the parasitic British landlords sucked the very lifeblood out of the honest Irish peasants of central Europe, praying on them while they slept, which meant that they were not aware that they were being exploited until the day they woke up and found that they too had become British. ¡Is a very scary story!

Foretunately, help is on hand for the honest peasants in the form of Jonathan Van Damme, who leads a pogrom of villagers and burns Castle Dracula to the ground, which is how Tayto Crisps began.

Veno, Saint (1774-1820): Her false fingernails were stored in a reliquary in a well-lit, spacious two-bed chapel in Bruges. Her tibias were also on display in an adjoining convent. "I suppose I should be flattered," she was quoted as saying, "But I do wish they had waited until I was dead before removing them."

Vermont: In the U.S. state of Vermont, is obligatory to pray to the milk God before starting breakfast.

Villa Rotgütt: "¡Manuel! ¡What a surprise!" Doktor Rotgütt must have seen me landing on the airstrip because he was halfway across the gravel from the villa as I taxied toward him. "We had have been waiting many months for you to visit, but we thought you would come by boat. Finally, we can return some of your hospitality."

Rather than descend from the microlite, I reduced its speed to walking pace so that the Doktor could come alongside. At that point, he noticed the cradle carrying my sister.

"It would appear you are not alone, Herr Estímulo. Or at least that you have come with cargo."

"My sister, Candelaría. Candelaría, meet Doktor Rotgütt."

His eyes met mine with a look of uncertainty.

"I am sorry I could not have called ahead," I explained, "but I departed in something of a hurry and was forced to conduct a rescue mission."

"¿Rescue?"

"My sister. She was assaulted in her own home. ¿Would you believe it? ¿What kind of country are we living in, Señor Herr Doktor?"

"¿Assaulted? ¿By whom?"

"By gambies. ¿Who else? They were eating her fingers. Her thigh. She was lucky I arrived in time."

The Doktor appeared septical. He continued to eye my sister as I steered the microlite toward the villa. I tried to ease his doubts.

"She looks much worse than she is. All that blood she is caked in isn't hers. I was planning to take her to my house for safe-keepimg, but there were ... complications."

The Doktor nodded.

"Even so, Herr Estímulo ... There is a ... an issue of hygiene."

"I understand. Of course. If you can supply me with a hose, I can wash her down, strip her. She won't mind."

"¿Mind?"

"She is a moron. No sense of shame. If you tried to explain it to her, you would be wasting your time."

We was by now approaching the main entrance to the Doktor's home, a Spanish-style archway set into the high stucco wall surrounding the villa. The whole compound was most peculiarly located, perhaps a third of the way up a gently inclined mountainside, which sloped down behind me back to the airstrip and the beach. A level platform had been carved out of the mountain to provide the base for the villa and surrounding garden, a winding dirt track leading through the archway to the villa's imposing oak door, disproportionate in size and grandeur to an otherwise nondescript and plain facade, which neverthenonetheless stretched to four windows on either side, a round Norman-style tower and turret at the northern end. Perhaps I did not take everything in and I am not easily impressed, but in light of the Rotgütts' previous descriptions, I had expected more.

"You misunderstand me, Manuel," said the Doktor as I brought the microlite to a halt at the end of the dirt track. "I am afraid your sister cannot possibly come in with you."

"¿What? Is not like she's a Jew or something."

"She is dead, Herr Estímulo. ¿Can you not see? The lolling tongue. One eye is missing. The birds have had been at her. Possibly bardinos in the night. The ripped flesh. ¿You cannot tell?"

"¿Then how come she still speaks to me?" He had no possible retort. "Tell him, Candelaría."

"He is an idiot," Candelaría said. "You should box his insolent ears."

"That's right," I said.

"And kick him up the Shitlands."

"Shetlands," I corrected.

"I know what I mean."

The Doktor continued to look nonplussed, uncomprehending, almost as if he could not believe his unboxed ears.

"¿You see?" I said. "She is fine. She just needs a hand with her mobility until she heals. No doubt the assault by the gambies has have left her out of sorts, but is nothing that a bit of rest and recuperation will not fix. Is that not your specialty, Herr Doktor?"

I could sense that he was following only vaguelily.

"¿The what?"

"R&R. Recovery. I remember Frau Rotgütt telling me that your villa once provided sanctuary for German submariners during the war."

"Ach, Ja. That's right. A very long time ago. I will tell you all about it inside. But please, Herr Estímulo, consider Frau Rotgütt. She is having a sensitive disposition. We can bring your sister over here into the shade, see, and I will arrange for her to be looked after by the locals."

"Thank you very much but no thank you," Candelaría said. "I have already had experience of what means it to be 'looked after by the locals.' I would rather be left alone."

"There," I said, a sweep of my hand offering Candelaría's own words as sufficient justification. The Doktor just stared blankly. I was getting nowhere with him, and time was short. I shook my head.

"Very well. Just leave her in the shade. No locals."

"*Naturlich*, Manuel, *Naturlich*. And we can give her a blanket so that she does not get cold. In case the wind changes direction."

Nodding my assent, I restarted the microlite, rather than carry Candelaría all the way to the villa. I halted at the archway, and the Doktor, somewhat reluctantly I felt, helped me lift her from the cradle and sit her on the northern side of the villa, contemplating the succulent garden.

"Please, Manuel, come in. Frau Rotgütt will be so, so happy to see you."

"I will be so-so happy to see her, too," I said, displaying my superior wit. It was, how you say, a pearl before *schwein*.

The path through the archway led into a courtyard neither more nor less impressive than the exterior of the villa. To left and right, corridors to the wings, above, a gallery around three sides, bedrooms, I presumed, lining the periphery. In the centre of the courtyard stood a stone fountain in the shape of a goat, rampant, water jetting from the spout in its mouth in a steady stream. The effect was absurd rather than noble. To my knowledge, there are no goat fountains in the Escorial, although I am open to correction. And providing it, as Lady Jane can testify.

Villaverde: The highest town in the north of Fuerteventura. They say that water travels uphill in Villaverde, but only in eight-liter bottles. Which is why the main sport there is suing the council.

Vinegar: An astringent, which can be used to accelerate the healing of open wounds in the side and also to hydrate a messiah during his crucifixion. He will still die, though.

Virgin Islands: Is where Islamite terrorists believe they go if they kill tourists.

Vitamin C Sharp: Vitamin C Sharp travels through your body's organs, mopping up all the oxygen free musicals.

Voodoo: Not just a religion but also a form of medicine, usually involving chicken blood rather than lamb's blood, which is why it doesn't work.

W

Watercress: You can disarm a suicide bomber by sneaking into his room the night before an attack and replacing all his explosives with watercress.

Who, Doctor: An utterly transparent propaganda vehicle for the Illuminati's World Health Organization, poking its nose into everybody's health and fixing it with their sonic screwdrivers, vaccines, quarantines, and sidrats, the perfect place to hide the elephant in the room.

Who, The: Well-known racist Irish pop band from Acton, comprising Roger Daltrey, Sir Peter Townsend, Keith Burkinshaw, George Harrison, Dave Dee, Dozy, Beaky, Mick, and Titch. Discovered in a Parka, which is a big tent in London, their biggest hits were "Rock on, Tommy," "Quadriplegia," "Pinhead Wizard," "Salmon Fishing in the Falklands," and "I Can See Our Miles," about The Police. Not dead, just deaf, dumb, and blind.

Wicked, The: There is no rest for the wicked. Also, a woman's work is never done. ¿Do you need a Venn diagram?

Wilgefortis, Saint: Crucifixed for growing a beard. And rightly so. Women with beards belong in a circus, with clowns and cross-dressers, not in a church with priests and bishops.

Wilkommen: Blocking my path to the courtyard was Frau Rotgütt, looking matronly in a smock and blue gingham apron, spiralled plaits on either side of her crinkly, mahogany face, a giant raisin between two caracole buns. Like Waltzing Matilde herself.

"¡Wilkommen, Manuel! ¡How wunderbar! And such a surprise."

She taked my hands in hers and shot a look that I understood to be reproof combined with disappointment and dyspepsia.

"I am so sorry, Frau Rotgütt. I had no way of giving you advance notice. I left home in such a hurry. I am not even having a gift. Unless you would accept a microlite."

"I think we are already having one," she said, her attention briefly flitting to her husband for confirmation. "But no matter. ¿Is the thought that counts, is it not? I appreciate the gesture. ¿Would you care for some refreshment? ¿Some tea, perhaps? Or juice. You look like you have been through the wars."

I was tempted to say, "You should know," but politeness prevailed.

"Brandy. I will take a brandy."

"Please, come this way. The Doktor will fix your drink. Let me show you around."

I was expecting the briefest of tours, the exterior of the villa giving me no clue to the expanse that lay beneath. Instead, I was ushered down a long corridor that finished with what looked like a bank's security vault, a thick metal door barring our way.

"The world is at your feet, Manuel." As a statement, this could not have had been more banal, yet she said it with such gravity and self-importance that I could not but be intrigued.

"This door requires my fingerprint, voice print, and number. No one can enter the world beyond without me. Cabracadabra."

With a wave of her hand, the door slowly eased open toward us, revealing a glass-fronted elevator. The interior smell was musty, old people and urine, and accompanied by a chill.

"After you," she said, as if she was doing me a favour.

The descent into the island's bedrock was smooth, rapid, and soothing, rendering it difficult to judge the distance traveled, but it was thirty seconds or so before we came to a stop. I stepped out of the elevator and found myself on a raised viewing platform, beyond which lay a vast underground warehouse brimming with treasure, merely the beginning of the Rotgütts' hoard as I subsequently learned, goods sacred and profane, arrayed into the distance in rows of stacked pallets.

"Behold, Manuel. This is our Noah's Ark."

But what I beheld was much superior to Noah's Ark, which was only having shitty animals. Statues, paintings, vases and amphorae, reliquaries, skeletons (reclining and standing), caskets, baskets, mannequins, figurines, furniture, bullion, and body parts was the first items to catch my eye, and only because they was closest.

"The last remnants of the *Reichsraub* ... the Reich's plunder," Frau Rotgütt explained as we taked the steps down from the platform to the floor and began to walk through the hoard. "The treasures of Europe liberated by the Führer, now in transit to their final destination, awaiting only a forwarding address."

"¿Address?"

"To their rightful owners. Most of them in South America. Some in Panama or Ecuador. Babylonian, Phoenician, Roman jewels. Icons from Carthage and Corinth. Judea. Look, here are the hands of John the Baptist." She lifted a glass case from one of the shelves to my right. "Remarkably good condition."

"Indeed," I said. "I imagine you could fingerprint them, if you were of such an inclination."

"We leave such speculation to the septics, Manuel. There is no question of such holy relics ever being subject to contamination by the touch of mere mortals."

"I only mention it because I notice another box here also with the label 'Hands of John the Baptist.' Some might wonder as to their authenticity."

"Let them wonder. The Good Lord moves in ways beyond the comprehension of mere men."

"That much is true, I grant you."

"Besides, each pair belongs to a different owner, each of whom is having a certificate of authenticity from the Vatican—separated by centuries, I admit—but if anyone is an authority on how many hands John the Baptist was having, I imagine it would be the Church of Saint Peter."

"No doubt."

"Here are the kneecaps of Saint Filbert. All three. ¿Do you contest the Church's imprimatur?" I tried to look aghast at the mere suggestion.

"There might even be one missing," I said. "So multifarious are the saints that I have failed to keep track of all their peculiarities. Saint Grampus grew back an arm that he had lost trying to convert the sharks, that much I know. ¿So who am I to say how many knees Saint Filbert was having?"

"Quite so. And, for contrast, here is the eyebrow of Saint Sillán. He had only one. But this is not unheard of among the Irish. Gived by the president of Ireland as a farewell tribute to the Reichsambassador. Here you can see letters of intercession to Saint Lipstrob the Indifferent. From his shrine in Antwerp."

"¿Have you shown him Saint Andrew's cross yet?" Doktor Rotgütt had arrived, bearing my brandy. Frau Rotgütt shook her head.

"Is a very fine specimen, Manuel—I'm sorry, I am having only German brandy, I hope it will suffice—and you can even make out the dried blood where the nails went in."

"Fascinating," I said, concealing my disappointment at the libation. "¿Who would imagine all of this beneath a beach in the arse end of nowhere?"

"And there is much, much more to show you. Come this way. ¿Are you a connoisseur of fine art? We have Titians, Rembrandts—"

"I have no time for it, I'm afraid. In my opinion, Franco was the world's finest artist. And Spain was his canvas."

"Indeed. No matter. But 'arse end of nowhere,' as you put it, is not quite right. You know, I am sure, your Fascist history. How Franco surreptitiously gifted the south of Fuerteventura to the Führer as thanks for Germany's help in the Civil War. During the Second World War Two, German submarines patrolling the Atlantic would pull in here to refuel while their crews enjoyed the pleasures of the local villages and all the recreation they could provide. This is why you see so many pot-bellied blonde Guanches in the bars and cafes around town. What's more, Fuerteventura is in a strategicly advantageous position in several ways. Just as NATO uses Gran Canaria today as an aircraft carrier to launch its air strikes in Africa, so Fuerteventura once provided a Nazi way-station en route to Uruguay, Argentina, Brazil, Bolivia, Chile, Peru. As the war wound down and the preferred outcome faded from view, many of our comrades began to do likewise, moving their wealth abroad. Not just to Swiss bank accounts but also to Spain and then, from Spain to the Canaries, especially Fuerteventura, for transfer to their refuges in the New World ... to keep the flame burning. Alas, as you can see," he stretched out his arms as if to embrace the plunder, "Many did not make it. Or, they made it and went into hiding, never to recover their goods." His shoulders slumped gently as he sighed the sigh of eternal dejection. "Still, we wait. Faithfully. For our comrades."

"You may be waiting for some time yet."

"This is true." He perked up. "In any case, we are having plenty to occupy us. Please, step this way, Manuel, and you will see." He motioned for me to follow them both through to an adjoining space of similar dimensions, which held a host of comparable diversity and wealth, only this time palpating, living, and agitated, the heat and stench stealing away my breath.

"I apologise for the smell. And the noise," the Doktor shouted above the racket of a squawking, roaring, squealing mass of mammals, birds, marsupials. "Normally we play music through the tannoy system to drown out this bombardment. ¿What would you like? ¿The Rolling Stones? ¿The Beatles? I have an extensive collection of vinyl."

"To be honest, I have always preferred a good speech. Music is not my thing and I am not knowing much about it."

"Oh, I am entirely in agreement, although marching bands are my favourite. This record collection, in fact, is the only anomaly you will find here, not plunder but an inheritance, bequeathed to me by Lord Haw-Haw himself, the original Reichsdeejay."

I frowned.

"You are having the fun with me, Herr Doktor. ¿Wasn't Lord Haw-Haw hanged by the British after the war? ¿How could he have collected music from the sixties and seventies?" He chuckled.

"Officially, he was executed, Ja. But the British are a most pragmatic people. They had a use for a man like him. Bear in mind that he had previously been an informer for the British against the IRA and had once served as a British soldier. After facial reconstruction and fingerprint removal, he was infiltrated into Eastern Germany to work as what I think they call today a 'cultural influencer', broadcasting on national radio to denounce Western pop and rock music in the knowledge that doing so would only make it more attractive to the country's rebellious youth. Look. These record covers still have the wildly inaccurate summaries pinned to them that he used for his broadcasts. They were designed to increase the masses' suspicion of the East German state media."

I picked up *Pet Sounds*.

"I think perhaps this would be appropriate."

"Hah. Very good. The Beach Boys. A well-known racist Irish pop group. There was a lot of them around back then, you know." Frau Rotgütt tapped me on the shoulder, intent on changing the subject, drawing us away from the vinyl. She led me towards her menagerie.

"This collection was to be the living foundation of our new Eden. Aardvarks, alligators, and alpacas to your left," she waved an arm summarily, "anteaters and armadillos to your right." Doktor Rotgütt quickly caught up.

"¿Did you know, Manuel, that in the U.S. state of Arizona, you are not allowed to use armadillos as paperweights?" I shook my head. "Is true. They wield a surprising amount of political clout there for some reason."

"Don't mind him," said Frau Rotgütt, a little impatiently. "For some reason, he is obsessed with all the obscure and bizarre laws of the American states. They exemplify the country's decadence and depravity ... or something."

"Correct. And I make no apology," the Doktor insisted. "Every country has a criminal justice system, but I think we can all agree that the American version is the most criminal of all. Their laws are a palimpsest of decline. I have filled several notebooks with examples of their moronic legislation. I will show them to you later, Manuel. You would not believe the idiocy of that people. Proof of their empire's vacuity written into its legislation like tattoos on a chameleon."

"And now written down by you for posterity," Frau Rotgütt continued, her incomprehension manifest. "No use to man nor beast." The Doktor was happily oblivious to her objection, however, having already moved on to the next item in the tour.

"We have temperate, tropical, and arctic climates down here, Manuel, as well as hydroponic and desalination plants for freshwater creatures and herbivores in the floors below. Their ambience is somewhat fresher and cooler ... but also damper."

"The measurements gived in the Bible for Noah's Ark are a severe underestimate, we have found," Frau Rotgütt said sardonically.

"Ja. Or else there was remarkably rapid evolution and speciation after the Flood," added the Doktor, "with the result that there are now far more species than in Noah's time."

"Is probly a good thing then that so many species are dying out," I observed.

"Ha ha. Ja. ¡Bring on the climate change! Of course, our intention here was never to save the wildlife for its own sake but for the future Reich, wherever it might eventually be established. And for us, personally, well, our interests was more scientific. But either way, as you can imagine, animal husbandry is a full-time task. You have to keep them fucking and reproducing in order to maintain the stock, and then you must—"

Suddenly, from my right, came a series of thundering stomps, like a charging rhino, vibrating through my bones, accompanied by a screeching yowl, a scream of maniacal madness. I turned to locate the source of the noise and what should I see but a huge adult baboon, jaws agape, leaping through the air in my direction, arms and legs outstretched. Instinctively, I recoiled and shielded my face, with no time to react except to make a small prayer. Then, just as I thought my number was up, I heard a dull thump mere inches from my head, my best feature, and ... complete silence. I opened my eyes and there he was, unconscious on the floor of his cage, having knocked himself out on its reinforced plexiglass wall. The twat.

"I am so sorry Manuel," said the Doktor. "They can be on top of you in an instant and wearing your face before you have had a chance to introduce yourself."

"They have escaped from their cages more than once," continued Frau Rotgütt. "The Doktor has had to shoot them a few times to slow them down, but it only seems to make them more cantankerous."

"This one obviously liked the look of you," smiled the Doktor as the baboon groggily revived and retreated to the far corner of his cell, lip curling, face flatted by the impact.

"Fucking baboons," said Frau Rotgütt. "They are sent by God to torment us."

The Doktor laughed. "On this occasion, my dear, I think we are looking only at a case of mistaken identity. Manuel here is such a hairy chap himself. Look."

A long, skinny, pink stork protruded like an exotic plant from between the baboon's legs. I hope never to see such a sign of affection again. Frau Rotgütt bowed her head with resignation.

"We will never run out of baboons," she said.

Work: There are two types of men who need never to work: the landlord and the landlord's son. Were they to work, it would be at the expense of some poor unemployed pleb who could probly do with the money. To pay his rent. To the landlord. The market has a logic of its own.

X

Xanadu, Saint (1123–1134): Survived on a daily diet of a sliver of wood from the True Cross and a handful of the Virgin's tears yet still lived to be 11.

Xenophobia: "So, I understand that the practice of animal husbandry ensures that your stock always remains full. ¿But don't some animals eat others?"

"Oh yes," said the Doktor. "We are obliged to produce a surplus for precisely this purpose. But the science is not so precise. You always end up with leftovers, which you must dispose of one way or another. Hence—"

"Hence your market stall in Lajares. I understand now. But you mentioned before having a more scientific goal. ¿What goal?"

"That will all become clear in the next room. First, you must wear these."

He proffered a pair of heavy-duty industrial gloves, the kind that a welder or smelter might use, extending up to the elbow. "And don't make any sudden moves."

Suitably warned and adorned, I allowed the Doktor the pleasure of surprising me, a surprise I was not having to feign, since I had not expected to be confronted with kennels. Row upon row of iron-bar cubicles, three storeys in height, the occupants a wild, crazed host of bardinos. Rabid bardinos. Drooling, snarling, barking, straining to reach me, eyes yellow and bulging with deranged, mindless rage. Frau Rotgütt taked my begloved hand in hers.

"We will move very slowly through this room, Manuel. We want no unnecessary excitement."

"Don't worry," said the Doktor. "You are perfectly safe. The doors to these kennels can only be opened electronicly, from outside the room. Besides, these animals, their bark is worse than their bite."

"Actually, *Schatzi, I think* that is not correct in this case."

"Ach, no. You are right. Their bite is terrifyingly dangerous, whereas their bark is comparatively crap. Hmm. My bad. Perhaps we should go through to the next room so that we can explain our project to you without all this ... distraction."

Is true that my mind was distracted, but by my search for Lobo and Reina, not because a hundred rabid dogs were grinding their frothing, frenzied muzzles against the bars in an effort to bite my balls off. ¿Would my darlings still have recognized me in such a crazed state? Possibly not. But seeing them might perhaps have brought me the comfort of knowing that they was still alive.

Frau Rotgütt calmly led me past the kennels and out the other side of the room, closing the door firmly behind us, a reinforced window allowing us to look back where we had been, at the tempest we had left behind. I struggled for a while to make sense of what I had seen, my confusion only compounded by now finding myself in an operating theatre.

"You see, Herr Estímulo," the Doktor was already expostulating, "throughout the Nazi period of rule, the Führer was insisting that Germany would be the home of the New Man, the new *Fascist* Man, to ensure the Reich's thousand-year reign. Fearless in battle, incapable of confusion by the intellectual sophistries of Jews and Marxists, and impatient with abstract philosophy, compromise, and prevarication. A true Man of Action. I was one of the chosen few, the team gived the honour of pursuing the Führer's dream. And we made great strides very quickly when we realized that the rabies virus, if it could be modified, would provide the ideal vehicle to transform the Wehrmacht, the German people, and ultimately the world."

He was idly lifting a scalpel from a row of surgical instruments sitting on a counter; I say "surgical instruments," but they could just as easily have been for torture: bonesaws, needles, hammers, drillbits.

"Sadly, as you know, the Reich was cheated of its destiny. The outrageous Soviet barbarians, deploying our own Hegel against us, prevented a qualitative change in Mankind by their overwhelming quantitative power, throwing millions upon millions of bodies into the fray, the meatgrinder of Eastern Europe. They were like ants. Red ants. Insects. Inferior and simple in form and breeding but triumphant by sheer force of number." He paused, said nothing, and half-turned. I waited for him to conclude this thought. Then, all of a sudden, he threw the scalpel to the floor, doubled over, and curled his fists into balls of anger.

"¡We were not gived enough time, Manuel! ¡If only we'd had more time!"

I offered no response. I think his outburst surprised even himself. It required a capacity for unrestrained explosiveness he had shown no previous sign of having had. He remained there, knees bent, shaking with rage, for what felt like an hour. I thought it best not to comment and display my confusion. Eventually, he pulled himself up straight in an attempt to regain some composure.

"I am sorry, Herr Estímulo. It still rankles. Defeat, I mean. You understand." A twist of brilliantined hairs, bonded together like fasces, had come unstuck and fell across his eyeline. He flicked it back with a toss of his head. "I am only regretting what might have been. We failed the Führer in his mission. If only the war had lasted another ten, fifteen years, we might have ... we might have ..."

Frau Rotgütt interceded.

"There was a change of plan, Manuel. When it became clear that we were losing the war, the Doktor was sent here to prepare the programme of re-entrenchment. Here, we conducted our surgeries on our glorious leaders—those who would carry the struggle forward—removing their fingerprints, replacing their teeth, changing their noses, hairline—"

"—The first thing Rudolf Hess asked for was a giant penis, but when we explained that it was not possible ..." The Doktor mimed with his hand an airplane taking to the sky.

"A rat-line smuggled our comrades out of Germany, through Switzerland, through Spain, whence they was transported by submarine to here, their wealth accompanying them or sent separately to be forwarded when convenient."

"Naturally, we were having a few accidents on the operating table," the Doktor said, shrugging. "Some of the treasures are now having nowhere to go, so we keep them here."

"Still, the struggle continues. And we remain here, Manuel, because during our research, we made a remarkable discovery. You see, we found that we could modify the rabies virus to slow down ageing. Normally, each time a cell reproduces, its lifespan decreases; there are only so many times a cell can split because of the telomeres on the end of its chromosomes, which get shorter every time, and when the telomeres disappear, the cell dies. We were able to produce a version of the new virus that retarded the speed at which cells reproduced, meaning that the telomeres—and life—could last longer. Much longer."

"If only we had been able to infect the Führer. He would still be alive today." The Doktor and Frau Rotgütt shared a wink, the meaning of which eluded me.

"Ja. Only after the war years was I able to perfect the technique ... Well ..." he pursed his lips ruefully, "Not 'perfect.' I am flattering myself a little."

"Ach, *Schätzi*," said Frau Rotgütt, laying a comforting hand on the Doktor's shoulder.

"But consider the *hundts*, Manuel, for example. Each one of those infected dogs will live as long as the average man. We have managed to extend their lifespan by seven times. Imagine if we could do that to a human. Imagine six centuries of life. Enough time to fuck every woman in Madrid."

"Should you want to," I said.

"Should *they* want to," said Frau Rotgütt, casting a sly eye sideways to her husband.

"Sí. Is true," I conceded. "Time does not always mean social progress but, sadly, sometimes it does."

X-Men, The: Some people say that the X-Men is a metaphor for homosexualism and the gay rights, with the Mutants standing in for the perverts, and the normal human beings standing in for the normal human beings. I am not one of the people saying this. I have never met a homosexual with super powers, although one time I met a lady lesbian who could do extraordinary things with a blowpipe.

X Rays: A Protestant invention intended to steal God's thunder by enabling puny Man to see everything. Especially pernicious is its use in the medicine, where doctors use it to identify illnesses bestowed by God (holy tumours, epilepsy, and cetera) that could lead to important manifestations of religiosity, such as speaking with tongues, visions, weirdy dreams, precognition, and so on.

Xylobone: A wooden trombone peculiar to Galicia, where it rains all the time and consequently all the metal instruments go rusty. The sound is dreadful. Like the trombone, this instrument should not be played by ladies in case it gives men ideas. Or wood.

Y

Yachts: In the same way that all business deals are sealed on the golf course, so yachts are where all the bodies are buried. Some bodies are having no choice about being buried (e.g., Osama bin Laden), some opt for self-burial (e.g., Robert Maxwell), and some are exploded to pieces (e.g., Earl Mountbatten). Famous yacht owners include Errol Flynn, Roman Abramovich, Earl Mountbatten (again), and Duran Duran. Straight away, I hear you ask, "¿Manuel, are *all* yacht owners paedophiles?" "No," I reply. "That is just a well-founded rumour." Some yacht owners use their yachts instead to smuggle hashish, and other yacht owners simply rent their yachts out to paedophiles. Similarly, not all paedophiles own yachts. Some of them can only afford a pleasure cruiser or a barge. It doesn't matter, so long as it can reach international waters to dispose of the children's bodies. However, once you realize that all yacht owners *are* paedophiles, everything begins to make sense, and all the Hollywood allusions to paedophilia become clear in, for example, *The Bourne Identity, The Little Mermaid, Finding Nemo, Bednobs and Broomsticks*, and *Privates of the Caribbean*. Indeed, oceanographers have expressed concern that the Marianas Trench is rapidly filling up with the bodies of fucked children and that this will lead to the disappearance of many low-lying coastal cities as a result of the rise in water levels currently being blamed on climate change. This is why many billionaires are spaffing their cash on escaping to Mars or on off-shore turbine farms to blow the water away from the land. Other paedophiles just say we need to find a bigger trench.

Yoga: A Satanic practice based on ancient Hindus' attempts to suck themselves off or to spend the afternoon sniffing women's farts. Saint Paul reminds us that apparently pleasant experiences such as the attainment of

Nirvana and autofellation may well be portals to evil. "Satan himself masquerades as an angel of light." Despite what the Yogis are teaching us, we should always remember that we are *not* at one with God and the universe; rather, we are cut off from him, separated by a vast chasm of sin that only Jesus can cross, and Jesus doesn't cross it by doing the downward dog.

You: won't believe what happened next. Through the other side of the operating theatre, I was taken aback to find not so much a recovery suite as a recovery mansion. The Doktor sensed my surprise but was quick to disabuse me of my presumption.

"We are rarely having time to rest," he said even as he casually indicated a four-poster bed with silk sheets in a room adorned with looted Bruegels. "These were mostly used by our guests. For our everyday needs, we generally make do with the ground-floor residence.

A peacock nonchalantly passed us in the hallway.

"¿An escapee?" I ventured. The Doktor gave a quick shake of the head. "One of Frau Rotgütt's frivolities. ¿What is life without frivolities?"

Normalmente, I would have fumingly explained that a life *with* such *tonterias* is an insult to Our Lady, a shameful self-indulgence deserving of painful retribution involving needles. But on this occasion, I said nothing because I was a guest.

After reviewing a series of suites, each more luxurious than the last, as well as a fully equipped Michelin-star-level kitchen ("We are not having the chef to come with it, sadly, but Frau Rotgütt can whip up a raclette you would kill for"), I was brought into the Rotgütts' lair, the nerve centre of their operations. Walnut bookcases reaching to the ceiling extended around three of the walls, filled to overflowing with thick, lavishly bound hardback volumes. What a waste of space.

"¿Another brandy, Manuel?" said the Doktor, requesting my glass. "I am sure that there is something better than German down here. We keep the *echt* item for our special visitors. From the cellars of Richelieu himself." He motioned to the armchair in front of me. "Please sit."

The chairs and sofa encamped in a circle around a low oak coffee table had a Swiss chalet air, with fur throws and plump cushions liberally distributed over their surfaces. Pouffes and beanbags between them and a log-burning stove in the corner added to this effect, bizarre so far below ground.

"The chimney must take some cleaning," I quipped.

"Ach, we rarely need to use it," the Doktor said over his shoulder, pouring my brandy while standing before a bottle-laden secretaire. "Is so warm down here that we have little need of heating. The chimney is more for show."

"*Entendido*. The stove contributes to the ambiance. Is very cozy."

"Well," said Frau Rotgütt, "When you are living somewhere as long as we are, you do your best to make it homely." She was sitting on the sofa across from me, awaiting her husband, who leaned across the table to pass my glass. "I do hope you enjoy this one, Manuel. I think you will find it rather special."

"Salud," I said. "And thank you."

"Good health," the Doktor said. He paused briefly as the pair of them shared a knowing look before both erupted in hysterical laughter. *Muy* disconcerting.

"I am so sorry Manuel," said the Doktor when they had finished. "We Germans are not normally big on the irony. I say to you 'Good health' when of course this place is dedicated to not-so-good health."

"¿In what way?" I quickly sniffed the brandy for any signs of doctoring. Doktoring. Instead, a hot wave of ethanol suffused my sinuses, a sherry-scented fireball behind my eyes.

"When Frau Rotgütt said 'living somewhere as long as we are,' I thought the *pfennig* might drop. The dogs, as you know, live seven times as long as they should. As long as the normal human lifespan. Although we have not perfected the process yet in humans, we have had made much progress in that direction."

"¿How old would you say I am?" asked Frau Rotgütt, pushing her face toward me so that I could see all its crags and crevices, the grooves and lines in her neck, with unnecessary, unnerving clarity. "Be honest. You will not hurt my feelings, I assure you."

"Frau Rotgütt. I would not presume ..."

"No, I insist. You recall that the Doktor talked of failing the Führer."

"This is true."

"So, let us imagine he was a researcher when the Führer escape—I mean died. Died. If he was, say, thirty at the end of the war, he would have to be over a hundred now. ¿Wouldn't you say?"

I glanced at the Doktor.

"A very well-preserved hundred-plus," I conceded.

"Aw, shucks. You are just being kind. Is the natural Spanish way." The Doktor may have been blushing. I could not tell. The brandy had added a glow to the room.

"And perhaps assume that, as with most traditional heterosexual cis-normative white-supremacist couples, the male partner is the older of the two ..." Frau Rotgütt was doing the work for me.

"¿Then you are ninety, perhaps?" I was still hesitant to make so brazen a guess.

"¡¿What?! ¡*Ninety!* ¡How dare you!" She rocked back in her chair in angry disbelief. Quickly, I backtracked.

"I mean, you don't look it. You don't look a day over seventy."

I could see that the Doktor was almost folded over with glee.

"¡Nobody has ever said ninety before! ¡Seventy-five was the oldest anyone has ever said!"

"¡I'm so sorry, Frau Rotgütt! *So* sorry. Of course, I was not going by your appearance but by a process of inference. I was following your lead."

The Doktor reached over to place a comforting arm around his wife.

"¿You don't know women at all, Manuel, do you?"

"It has never been a priority, I confess."

Frau Rotgütt was still breathing heavily with indignation but, soothed by her spouse's ministrations, eventually managed a response.

"I am one hundred and thirty-two," she said. "You were nowhere fucking near."

"Please don't take offence, Frau Rotgütt. I am a mere amateur at such games. I don't know how they are played."

"Clearly not." She was still annoyed. "¿What would you have had guessed for him? ¿Two hundred?"

"Now, Dearest," the Doktor said, trying to calm her, but the die was cast. Frau Rotgütt had turned her back to me in what I at first thought was a huff. In fact, to my even greater chagrin, she was disrobing. First, her blue gingham apron. Then, her smock. Then, a pleated black cotton underskirt. Then, her thick, baggy, flesh-coloured tights. Then, her spanx. And finally, her adult diaper. The horror. The horror. Because it was at that point that she bent over and turned her face around to look at me, a vision from some nightmarish geriatric porno. With a bony, arthritic forefinger, she directed my gaze toward her cratered, scarred, pitted, dimpled, dented arse. But this was not an "arse" as you or I would normally imagine or define it. For one thing, there was no obvious cleavage. Just a round, swollen, lumpy, pale, fatty mass of flesh.

"¿Does this look like the arse of a ninety-year-old, Estímulo?" she growled. It was a rhetorical question, which I would have done well to have realized. Instead, I answered.

"I am not having the experience to judge, if I am honest."

"Show him, Klaus. Show him," she instructed the Doktor, who looked at me pitifully before breathing "Very well," dropping his trousers, and bending over to show me his own prize pumpkin.

"I am a hundred and thirty-five," he said, by way of explanation for his even more pock-marked überbuttock, scrawnier than his wife's but with the wounds denser and the terrain more undulating.

"We are not hypocrites, Herr Estímulo," he said, still bent over as he spoke, which was entirely unnecessary, in my opinion. Rubbing my nose in their arses, as it were. "Yes, we have experimented on others with different strains of the virus, but if the patients did not die, we also tried it on ourselves."

"There must be twenty different strains coursing through our blood," said Frau Rotgütt. I was trying to meet her gaze rather than stare at the globe of marbled, putty-like flesh she had presented to me. "Twenty bites on the arse from rabid bardinos. ¿Do you have any idea how much a single bite hurts?"

Again, she was being rhetorical, but I shook my head anyway.

"Imagine it times twenty."

I was at least having enough sense to avoid pointing out that since I could not conceive how much a single bite hurt, multiplying that by twenty was meaningless.

They both pulled up their unnecessaries.

"¿But why did you not use syringes and Petri dishes like normal researchers?"

"Because you build up a resistance that way," explained the Doktor. "We did not want resistance. We wanted the disease itself in its modified form."

"We could not avoid acquiring *some* resistance, of course," said Frau Rotgütt, "so perhaps we will not live as long as those who receive the perfected, finalized virus. But if that is the price that must be paid for completing our task, then so be it."

"Your task?" I should not have asked. It was a cue for the Doktor to pontificate. He raised his chin as if speechifying to history.

"As the war came to a close, our research was making great progress, but I was not a young man. In fact, I was close to retirement, having reached the apogee of my field and received the highest scientific awards from the Reich for my work. The Führer himself telled me in 1939 that I was a shoo-in for the National Order of Art and Science award, but the war intervened and the awards were stopped."

"He was an honorary recipient," Frau Rotgütt inserted. "Whatever the history books say, *we* know." She kissed his sagging cheek with her cadaverous lips.

"Our activities were integral to the war effort. And to the postwar effort too. And is fair to say, I think, that we are the only ones still carrying forward the Führer's vision."

I was all at sea.

"¿The Führer's vision? I don't follow."

They looked at me as if I was an imbecile. I suddenly understood how Candelaría would have felt if she hadn't been an imbecile. The Doktor pointed to the kennels.

"The dogs. The New Man. The perfect warrior. ¿Who do you think has been seeding the island with rabid bardinos, Manuel? ¿Did you think we keep them here for a hobby? This is the Führer's work."

"¿What? Wait. ¿What?"

"We have modified the virus so that it does not kill but instead *extends* the lifespan—not yet seven times in humans, but we are getting there. You spoke of Petri dishes. This island is the perfect Petri dish for our tests. Water on all sides, which hydrophobes find insurpassable, so none of the subjects can ever leave, ideal for monitoring. We ship out the batches of bardinos with different strains and track their effects on the gambies they produce through their biting."

"We personally will never be the Führer's ideal man and woman, we have come to accept that. Never will we enjoy the blind unquestioning obedience, the unremitting aggressiveness, the complete absence of empathy and compassion, or the devotion beyond reason that you display to the Generalísimo."

"Now you are flattering *me*," I said. "At least you do not have the delirium experienced by the experiment's subjects." They looked at one another quizzicly.

"I think you have misunderstood," said the Doktor. "It is the *descanso* that we do not have. The 'delirium' to which you refer: we have that permanently. That is the aim. That is the plan. But our delirium, while constant, is, like yours, refined, sharp, hard, impenetrable, like a diamond. This is what has enabled our research to advance so fast. The absence of any pathetic *descanso*."

"And now you can see the results of our work across the island," Frau Rotgütt said. "You personally have seen the pinnacle of our achievements."

"¿Pinnacle?"

"The owners of the microlite you used to reach our home. Don't say you weren't impressed."

"¿Those monsters I saw butchering gambies?"

"¿Monsters?" The Doktor's eyebrows lowered. "No. Not at all. They are the first of the Führer's super soldiers. You see, our research has reached the point where we can increase not just age and rage but also stature, musculature, bulk, power. Through manipulation of the virus we have been able to modify the human genome to make men stronger, more vicious, more obedient. Like the bardinos themselves. Human hunting dogs. 'Butcher' is something of a dysphemism, don't you think?"

"Perhaps, if I knew what a dysphemism was. All I saw was two blood-soaked crazies slaughtering like maniacs. Hardly the pinnacle of anything."

"They are not slaughtering. They are harvesting our research materials. Of course, they are still refining their techniques, but it cannot be denied that our work has shown remarkable progress." Frau Rotgütt joined in.

"They are capable of fighting without rest for months on end and will live ... who knows how long. Imagine that. A permanent warrior force let loose across the world."

"¿Let loose how? I had to fly over a forest of cactus to get here. ¿Do you possess a *fleet* of microlites?"

A voice from behind me provided the answer.

"That was to be the next stage of the tour." It was a voice I recognized instantly, but before I could turn to face its source, I was startled by the flight of several small projectiles past my face, over my shoulder. I dodged, reflexes still sharp, despite the brandy. The projectiles landed on the table in front of me like yarrow sticks. Read them and weep. Three fingers. Candelaría's fingers. It was the Beast.

"I believe you've been looking for these," he said. And then, "Stay where you are. There's a bullet in the chamber and a bead on your skull."

I looked across at the Rotgütts, both of them still, their eyes fixed on the Beast.

"What the Doktor was about to tell you is that the door behind you provides access to the old submarine bays used by the German Navy during the war to drop off and pick up Nazi dignitaries during their escape to the Americas. They transport their bardinos using the same method—a smaller sub but enough space for a dozen crates and two ... researchers—resurfacing up the coast where their land transport awaits. A little inconvenient but easier than crawling through cacti."

He skirted the room, keeping me in his sights. A shuffling sound behind me alerted me to the presence of a second unwelcome guest. I immediately knew who. His MI6 storker, fan, and rescuer, Seymour Stiveley, had come along for the ride. Armed.

"Joseph, what a surprise," I said. "Although the greater surprise is you, Herr Doktor." He shrugged.

"¿What can I say, Manuel? You must be familiar with Operation Paperclip. For many years, we rescued our comrades from the Soviets, and the Americans taked their pick. Is no different to your beloved Generalísimo. He too had no choice but to cozy up to the Allies once it was clear the war was lost. ¿Where do you think Lord Haw-Haw underwent his facial reconstruction?"

"Don't pretend you wouldn't have worked with America yourself, Estímulo," the Beast said. "Your track record speaks for itself."

This couldn't be denied.

"Touché, Mr. Chambers … I must say, you are a sight for sore eyes. Oh. I'm sorry. Is a poor word choice."

"¿What? ¿This?" He fingered the patch over the socket I had excavated in order to show his one eyeball to the other. "I think it lends me an air of adventure."

"You look like Millán-Astray himself," I said. The compliment was not appreciated.

"But with more fingers, I think. At least, I did have before I gave you those."

Candelaría's fingers lay scattered on the table.

"I am so sorry about your sister, by the way. She was brave until the very end. And gave her life for a good cause: keeping you busy while the blaze was set at your home."

"¿May I?" Upon his affirmation, I leaned forward to retrieve the fingers. They were hard and dense, like teak.

"I don't know if you have considered availing of the good Doktor's services," I said, stalling for time while surreptitiously scanning the room and considering my options—death or escape—"Although he has yet to perfect regeneration of the skin or organ tissue. I have seen the evidence of his expertise with my own eyes. For me personally, the sacrifice isn't worth it. For you, perhaps …"

I calculated that I would have to get past Stiveley behind me to reach the submarine bay, with its unfamiliar layout and possible dead end, or past Frau Rotgütt to the operating theatre, where I could arm myself with medical instruments and at least put up a defence. I am not as young or as agile as I once was, but I fancied my chances against a wizened one-hundred-and-thirty-two-year-old woman, her older spouse, and a gunman with one eye and three fingers. The gay British archaeologist behind me had already proved his mettle when he rescued Chambers the first time. He was the one to avoid.

"You would have needed skin grafts if you had been caught in the fire we set," Chambers said. "Particularly if *all* the phosphorous grenades had gone off."

"¿That was you?" The Beast shook his head and nodded in the direction of the Rotgütts.

"You were kind enough to give the Doktor a tour," Stiveley explained. "He realized you had a fortress set up and had to be prevented from retreating to it."

I turned my head to gain a better look at him, size him up.

"And the phosphorous burns would have needed hospital treatment. ¿Was that the plan? ¿Track me down to the hospital? Very smart. The way the world is burning, I'd say we all need to be salamanders. Grow back skin, limbs ... fingers." I turned back to Chambers. "You wouldn't need to use both hands to hold your Beretta, for one thing."

"Well, indeed," said Chambers. "But our interest in the Doktor's work lies more in its potential to produce citizens who don't require feeding in a time of rationing. Citizens who bite without feeding, who can be put to work without dissent, deliver pizzas without being tempted to scoff the lot."

"Pizzas they cannot afford to buy but which they have no desire to eat," Stiveley added.

"Your elaboration is meaningless to me," I said. "I have never eaten pizza and cannot understand the desire to eat one."

"Perhaps you missed your vocation," Chambers joked. "An avenue you will never now explore. How sad. But you won't be alone. Climate change will mean civil war, chaos, unrest, unless a firm hand takes the country by the throat and starves it, apportions resources sensibly—by force," he jiggled the Beretta. "The kind of government you would approve of, I'm sure."

It was now or never. They were distracted by their own exposition.

"Then you truly don't know me at—"

Midsentence, I launched Candelaría's fingers into Chambers's face. He automaticly recoiled but got off a shot that whizzed past me and into the sofa. By positioning himself directly behind me, Stiveley had foolishly put me and Chambers in the same line of fire. I taked advantage of this by leaping straight at Chambers and diving between his legs, simultaenously obscuring me from Stiveley and reducing my size as a target. The other side of him, I scuttled toward the operating theatre. Doktor Rotgütt was fixed to the spot, this turn of events offering new opportunities that he was still processing. Frau Rotgütt, by contrast, was having none of it. She divined my intentions and moved to cut me off. Thankfully, she was fatally weighed down by age and the need to put her diaper back on. I was too fast, clambering over a Louis Quatorze day bed, using it as a springboard to evade her lunging claws. I forward-rolled into the theatre and seized a bonesaw from the counter. As Frau Rotgütt entered in pursuit, I ducked beneath her clutches, swerved, and nipped behind her, scrambling onto her back and wrapping my legs around her ample torso, trapping her arms, before bringing the saw to her neck. I had no idea whether blood would flow if I cut through the skin, but I was gambling that Chambers wouldn't take the risk.

"Stop where you are," I said, as Stiveley and Chambers entered the theatre. They raised their weapons, but I offered them almost no target other than my shins and feet.

"¿Or what?" Stiveley said, with his British froideur, angling for a better shot.

"Or the old lady gets it," I said, in case he was simple.

"¿You mean the rabid racist Nazi old lady gets it?"

He had a point. And it was a point he pushed home by fluting a precise, single hole into the middle of her forehead, the echo of the round deafening in the confined space and more painful than the impact of the bullet itself. For me, anyway. For Frau Rotgütt, the jury was out. She continued to stand, no blood spurting from the wound, as if it had already congealed. Slowly, however, I could sense that she was beginning to give, like a meringue, crispy on the outside, squidgy on the in. I could feel the squidge yield and the erect Frau Rotgütt tremble, a gnarled Nazi Twin Tower, before collapsing. Gingerly, she managed to turn her head, in search for the Doktor, finding him at the edge of the room, out of harm's way, further recalibrating his options. Seeing his wife waver, rather than rush to comfort her, he taked a step back, out of the room. Frau Rotgütt moaned weakly at his retreat. She attempted to reach out to him, it seemed, but my legs were still wrapped around her arms. As I dismounted, realizing I needed new cover, I released my hold and she was able to lift her arm to complete her gesture toward her husband. A Nazi salute.

And with that, she fell to the floor, a blob of Third Reich blancmange never to be resurrected, exposing me to the ire and fire of my foes. I still had the bonesaw, but Chambers had few bones of interest left for me to saw, and the prospect of me doing so no longer held any fear for him, having previously endured my worst.

I don't want to say that I turned and fled, since this would imply some degree of cowardice on my part at a moment when I was being offered the opportunity to die a glorious Fascist death, that of a warrior on the battlefield in close proximity to his enemy, seeing the whites, yellows, and reds of their eyes, my face to the Sun—or where I imagined the Sun to be—a song in my heart, and the image of the Generalísimo's face imprinted on my mind. However, having seen the ignominious and farcical death of Frau Rotgütt and the stupidity of her devotion to the very end to her Führer, a devotion that did *not*, let us remember, forbid her cooperation with the Masonic, Illuminati, capitalistic CIA and the homosexually inclined British Intelligence, I clearly understood that my death at this moment and under these circumstances would only be a source of future mockery, one that I would never live down, like those ISIS fighters who die at the hands of the women of Rojava, spending their eternity in Heaven being laughed at by seventy-two virgins.

It was this insight into the ignoble and risible ending that I risked if I hung around that compelled me to withdraw, the better to die at a moment of my own choosing, with dignity and honour, and which thrust me manfully in a backward direction through the exit of the operating theatre and into the kennels where the Rotgütts' rabid offspring awaited. Fully aware that it was not beyond my craven pursuers to shoot a man in the back, I zig-zagged at full pelt through the room, elusive both to bullet and slimy imperialist hands but also aware at each spring, each leap in a contrary direction, that it might be my last as a Man of Action. Much as every career in politics must end in failure, so too must every trajectory of human activity advance ultimately toward a final act that will prove its undoing, be it stepping on a mine in a foreing field, lowering one's guard against a duplicitous woman, or groping a nurse while still attached to an intravenous drip. My error lay in imagining that the cause of my demise would be the insufficient randomness of my path, enabling Stiveley to predict my movement and get off a shot. Had I but turned to check my adversaries, however, I would have seen that they were not at all in hot pursuit. They were merely watching, somewhat bemused, and possibly impatient, as I jigged and jogged and spurted and leaped and jaunted and bobbed and weaved my way through the kennels. It was only when I reached the far end that I finally looked over my shoulder and realised that, instead of giving chase, they had shut the kennel door behind me and had initiated the sequence to unlock the cages, liberating the Doktor's rabid canine army so that they might continue my persecution.

I slammed the door to the kennels behind me just in time and reinforced it with a nearby crate of galagos, which I clambered onto to peer through the spyhole and survey the chaos separating me from my foes. Sure enough, gnashing, thrashing hounds of hell were already storking and strutting around the room in a maelstrom of frothing maws, wild bulging eyes, and powerful muscular bodies that could outlive the average man without the need for sustenance. I was safe. Without Frau Rotgütt's voice to activate the main door to the Ark, and with the churning

Charybdis of bardinos covering my rear, my enemies had no way of reaching me through either entrance. I had made good my escape.

Across the kennels, at the opposite spyhole, one eye. The eye looked down at the dogs, then across at me. The skin around the eye wrinkled, as if the Beast was smiling. ¡Hah! Smiling with disappointment. Acknowledging my victory and untouchability. This is why American civilization will ultimately fail: its willingness to accept defeat gracefully.

The eye withdrew, to be replaced by a hand with one finger. To this day, I am unsure of its significance. ¿How many fingers did he intend to present? ¿Was he waving goodbye? ¿Was he, in the absence of thumbs, giving me a thumbs up, a comradely concession that he had met his equal on the battlefield? I will never know. I only know that it was the last I will ever see of him. And he knew it too. Victory was mine.

Z

Zeron, Saint (TBA–34 BC): The time-traveling saint from the future who discovered much to his disappointment that time machines are good only for one trip. He had been expecting to get back home in time for the Apocalypse and *Bargain Hunt* but instead found himself participating in a regional gladiatorial show when the pre-match sacrificial goat suffered an ACL tear during the warm-up.

Zeugma: "In protest at a wage freeze, rioting workers at Spain's largest lentil processing plant broke windows and wind inside the company's Head Office, say police." ¿Which police? ¡Not the Grammar Police!

Zidane, The Imperious: The second-best football player in the world ever, behind the Wizard Cronaldo. Although Zidane played for France, he was Algerian, which historicly belonged to Spain, making him, like Cronaldo, technicly Spanish. The only blots on his copybook are that headbutt in the World Cup final and that being Muslim thing.

Zombies: There is no such thing as zombies. There are, however, gambies, constantly increasing in number beyond the bulwarks of my Ark, carrying the world onwards to its ineluctable, terminal, entropic state of pure chaos. Only in here, my shelter against disorder, can civilization endure as it should; I have become the new Noah, the new Adam, giving names afresh to the animals and bringing meaning to their existence. Of course, like Adam, I have had to learn animal husbandry on the hoof, excuse the pum, and mistakes have had been made; I should have waited until the anteaters had had a chance to reproduce before cooking them, so that I would have something to eat the ants other than the vacuum cleaner, and although idiot environmentalists would have us believe that Nature is a carefully balanced ecosystem, there is no place in it for baboons, who escaped their cages within days of coming under new management and have plagued me ever since. My fashioning of tools and weapons owe much to having read my father's *Manual del Cadete*; ¿who knew knot tying and whittling would come in so handy all those years down the road and could be used on baboons as well as Catalans? Makes sense, I suppose.

Other animals are finding their meaning in providing me with clothes, footwear, and sexual release. Some of them function as handy sports equipment. (I have become an adept at pelota, better no doubt than any Basque, making both bat and ball from one of the beavers, a most versatile creature which can also no longer tell people how I used it for sexual release.)

Is almost a full-time job to care for God's creation—full time, at least, for one man, which is as God originally intended it—with no time left over, no *descanso*, for idle speculation, fantasy, philosophy, or other such infantile pursuits that occupy the empty hours of urban sophisticates. The world would have been spared the mewlings of Borges, Saramango, Beckett, Joyce James, and other exponents of the "modern sensibility" if they had been brought up on a farm. ¿Indeed, who now needs their works when there is this "book" of mine, which casts its harsh and revealing light on the self-indulgence and narcissism of the Intelligentsia, demonstrating their irrelevance and unnecessarinyness?

Indeed, is fair to say that, as an accurate and precise mirror of the world in which I live and the story of how I got here, this text could be considered the perfect work, rendering all other books redundant, the work that Adam might have written in Eden or which Noah might have written in his Ark had he remembered to pack pencils, for what is this work but my very own memory palace, a world entire unto itself, a narrative that both describes the place in which I live and a chronology of how I got here. What is more, it performs the function of an encyclopaedia, telling the reader everything they might need to know about this world, one that is complete, self-contained, self-sufficient, and autarkic; almost, dare I say, an ideal Fascist nation-state. And thus, as a reflection and description of that world, my text, too, can be considered complete and perfect. Perhaps, one day, and I say this in all humility, Fascist schoolchildren of the future will be taught to memorise my story just as I have done, in the same way that Muslims teach their offspring to memorise the Koran. ¡¿Wouldn't that be something?!

You might think it would make more sense for me to write down my magnificent work rather than recite it faultlessly from memory, as Homer once did his *Odyssey* and *Aeneid*, but as I have already made plain, I am having no time for writing when I must service all the animals that God has seen fit to create. Moreover, as another dead Greek, Plato, pointed out, writing is the enemy of memory. It renders memory irrelevant. ¿Who needs to consult their memory even to remember the date when they can check the newspaper? Providing that you can remember how to read, you don't need to remember anything else. ¡But there's the rub! Remembering how to read, an overrated skill in itself gived the preponderance of trash published these days, is one of the first things to go when dementia kicks in. By reciting purely from memory, I not only obviate the need for the lesser skill, reading, but also stave off the Alzheimer's that claimed the minds of my grandmother and my father, both of whom, let us not forget, continued to serve long, proud, distinguished careers within the Franco regime regardless of their infirmities, dying in situ. Sadly, I was not to be blessed with such an opportunity, the conspiracy of Western Masonic nations ultimately proving too strong for the Generalísimo's social experiment. And yet, in me, the Generalísimo still triumphs, albeit it a small way. Is me alone who now enjoys the paradise to which Franco aspired and which he struggled to impose on the Spanish people—a self-sustaining Ark, with no need of the outside world, capable of enduring for an eternity, withstanding all external attempts to undermine it. I am both humbled and proud that it has fallen to me to continue the True Fascist legacy, perpetuating the worldview of our leader with the determination and single-mindedness of a dedicated Falangist.

One man does not a nation-state make, you might say, in petulant protest, and be surprised when I agree with you. Perhaps, in due course, when the Sun has done its work and the *descanso* no longer gives relief from delirium, the gambies' brains completely fried, I may venture forth in order to recruit and train them as a workforce. Unquestioning, long-lived, but disposable, requiring minimal sustenance or rest. I realize now what Sartre meant when he said that hell is other people; other people are unruly, disobedient, require feeding, care, surveillance, and disciplining if you are to get anything out of them. Gambies, by contrast, need only the basics. They would be the perfect Fascist population. If there is hope, it must lie in the gambies.

I no longer hear the voice of my beloved sister, Candelaría, but I know that she waits for me, either in the outside world or in the next life. In any case, her presence in this, my new Eden, would almost certainly have sullied its purity, polluted the piety. Not because she is a woman or because she is now devoting all her time to feeding birds, worms, and bacteria, but because she is simply an imperfect human being. Indeed, is fair to say that the presence of *any* other human in here but myself, the last remaining True Fascist, would serve only to dilute its perfection. An Eden without women offers a second chance to mankind. And thus, ever conscious of my responsibility, I take up my burden with renewed vigour, with conviction and confidence in the ultimate triumph of the Falangist vision, and I begin again the recitation of my tale, secure in the knowledge that doing so simultaenously preserves, embodies, and enacts our Holy Falangist Dream.

And so we begin again …

A

Aardvark: The aardvark is a four-foot marsupian indigent in Africa ...

THE END

Also by Jay Spencer Green:

Breakfast at Cannibal Joe's

Joseph Chambers is a CIA operative working in Dublin. Assigned to an agency-fronted publishing house, his problems include, but are not limited to, errant MI6 agents, insane profit-making schemes, a Spanish Falangist brothelkeeper, and a tenacious tapeworm named Steve. He is an utterly reprehensible character, fond of submerging his head in a sink-full of whiskey and fantasising about brutally murdering irritating teenagers. He is, in other words, the perfect guide to this bizarre and repulsive journey into Dublin's gutters.

Jay Spencer Green presents a twisted and exaggerated, but wholly recognisable vision of Dublin. A place of suicide bombings, mass canine culling in the Phoenix Park, "cheap Moore Street socks (35 euros for 6 pairs)," online divorce, and enough red tape and bureaucracy to drive a man to murder. A place where "cat's cheese salad" and a dubious pork/human hybrid meat share the menu. It is a Dublin of no redemption.

Ivy Feckett is Looking for Love: A Birmingham Romance

The "nerds-against-the-patriarchy" romcom guaranteed to tickle your inner geek! When brainiac dweebs and smooth-talking power players meet up, there's no telling what can happen. In the case of Ivy Feckett, what happens is a nonstop romp of wry, quirky fun.

Bookish Ivy's cluelessness is as endearing as it is comical, from the first peek into her random sexual fantasies to the moment she realizes that her boss, the rich, handsome Ned Hartfield, is a serial manipulator with "wealth-induced Asperger's." Her search for love may not go as smoothly as her search for geocaches, but its route through awkward hookups, clumsy intrigue, and fake evangelicals is both hilarious and touching.

Fowl Play

Ladies' man Josiah Joshua Jordan King is a rising star for the Trafford Titans in the new and wildly popular sport of Chicker. But he's also a professional hitman and union buster on behalf of the league's management. With the European Championship final against Barcelona looming, he gets wind of a filthy commie plot to scupper the whole shebang. Can he lead his team to victory while neutralizing the Reds, or will his dreams of international glory be thwarted by a faceless conspiracy that threatens civilization itself?

A mutant cross-breed of *Rollerball*, *The Wicker Man* and *Chicken Run*, *Fowl Play* is satirist Jay Spencer Green at his weirdest and most outrageous, a laugh-out-loud dark comedy in which the headless chickens are not confined to the farmyard.

Available in paperback and eBook formats from all good bookstores

https://jayspencergreen.com/
https://www.instagram.com/jayspencergreen/
https://www.facebook.com/jay.spencer.green/